Black Bird

Book Ten in Detectives Daniels and Remalla
J. T. Bishop

Eudoran Press

To my fellow authorpreneurs and friends...there is no more supportive community whose talents and gifts bring joy to so many.

I am blessed and thrilled to be one of you.

Other Books by J. T. Bishop

Previously...

(careful–spoilers ahead)

DETECTIVES DANIELS AND REMALLA deepen their investigation into the secretive black bird society. A society whose sinister secrets and alarming reach are connected to the murders and branding of three men—Rex Beelson, Donald Morgans, and now Reginald Durning, a prominent attorney and former prosecutor. When Durning's murder is witnessed by Jerry Lee Caruso, a hotel employee who escapes the killer and disappears, Daniels and Rem go on the hunt to find him before the killer does.

Believing the killer to be a woman with the alias of Rhonda Champlin, an elusive assassin working for the black birds, Daniels and Remalla investigate Durning's murder and the law firm he worked for, Crenshaw, Ingram and Willoughby, or CIW. After CIW's partners provide minimal help, they learn from Durning's assistant that he had a client named Dirk that no one at CIW wants to discuss. Their search for answers becomes even more complicated when an FBI investigation linking Rem and Daniels' captain, Frank Lozano, to crimes allegedly committed by Reginald Durning, results in Lozano's suspension.

Elsa Crow is appointed captain in Lozano's place, but her oversight of Daniels and Remalla's cases results in conflict when her opinions clash with the detectives'. Despite her doubts about the existence of the black birds, Daniels and Rem continue to work with Lexie Logan, an investigative journalist, without the support of Crow.

Meanwhile, Detective Luca Manetti becomes suspicious of his partner, Detective Frank Monk, when he discovers that the name of a murdered cult member, Vera Canmore, was not mentioned in a file where Monk claims to have found her. Manetti also finds drawings by Margaret Redstone, a violent criminal in a psychiatric facility, in Monk's desk. Unbeknownst to Manetti, Rem, and Daniels, Monk is a prominent member of the black bird society, and the assassin Rhonda's lover.

Rem, Daniels, and Lexie Logan continue to dig into the contents of a mysterious box left behind by Marvin Ackerman, a disgruntled former member of the black birds. They find themselves caught in the crosshairs, though, when Rem's cousin Cain remains aligned with the black birds, and someone new appears on their doorstep—Erin Gerard. Erin's revelation that she is Daniels' half-sister creates tension between Rem and Daniels when she offers to use her connection to Cain to help bring down the black birds.

When Lexie reveals she's located an encrypted list of the society's members' names that Ackerman hid, Daniels takes a risk and gives the file to computer-savvy Erin, hoping she can decrypt it, but Rem disapproves.

The case becomes even more complex when Sammy Caruso, the corrupt, mobster-related politician and Jerry Lee's grandfather, contacts Daniels and Rem, and insists they find his grandson alive—or else.

Hoping that decrypting the drive will lead to the black birds' downfall and Jerry Lee's safe return, Daniels and Rem are caught off guard when Daniels' pregnant wife, Marjorie, is hospitalized after a car accident, which results in a miscarriage. A witness to the accident implicates Erin.

When Rem reluctantly tells his partner about his sister's potential involvement, the rift between them grows deeper. After an emotional confrontation with Daniels, Rem races to Cain's, who is ready to talk about his involvement with the black birds, but finds Cain mortally wounded. Before dying in Rem's arms, Cain identifies the man known as Tex, the black bird member who tried to kill Rem and Daniels in the town of Elmwood, as his killer.

Daniels and Rem make amends when they discover Marjorie's accident was planned, along with Cain's involvement and murder. Erin decrypts the list and, after proving her innocence, provides them with the members' names. The list reveals familiar players, including Barbara Ingram from CIW; Elsa Crow's father, Chogan Crow; and Winnie, the elusive cigarette-smoker who is Margaret Redstone's accomplice and the man Mikey witnessed shooting Vera Canmore; Rhonda, the assassin; Victor D'Mato, the deceased cult leader; and Dirk, the mysterious client of Reginald Durning. The detectives believe they finally have some solid leads to follow.

While Lexie Logan researches the remaining unfamiliar names, and Mikey attempts to jog her memory to identify Winnie, Rem and Daniels search for Jerry Lee and the perpetrators behind Marjorie's attack and Cain's murder. The murder scene of Arnold Bertrand, a former employer and friend of Jerry Lee, reveals evidence that Bertrand had been harboring Jerry Lee before Jerry Lee escaped yet again.

Although determined to discover Tex's true identity and locate Rhonda before she finds and kills Jerry Lee, Rem and Daniels are sidetracked once more when they learn Cain and Bertrand were both shot with the same type of gun as one in Rem's closet. When Rem's gun turns up missing and Daniels' medical debt is unexpectedly paid, they visit Jerry Lee's mother and learn the reward offered to find Jerry Lee matches the amount of Daniels' paid debt.

She also provides information that leads the detectives to a meeting with Tex and the mysterious Dirk, who reveals himself to be Damien Rook, a real estate tycoon with an ugly grudge against the detectives. He threatens to frame them for the murders of Cain and Bertrand if they don't agree to kill Jerry Lee Caruso and become Rook's assassins.

Shocked by Rook's vendetta against them, Rem and Daniels conclude their only way to survive, protect the ones they love, and stop Rook and his society...is to become black bird members themselves...

Cast of Characters

(in alphabetical order by first name)

Detective Aaron Remalla - a detective based in San Diego

Arnold Bertrand - former employer and friend of Jerry Lee Caruso

Ben Crenshaw, Barbara Ingram, and Charles Willoughby - partners in the law firm of Crenshaw, Ingram, and Willoughby (CIW)

Cain Carson - Remalla's cousin

Chogan Crow - city council president and Elsa Crow's father

Damien Rook - founder of Rook Enterprises, which owns Pinnacle Properties

Delaina Desmond - Ben Crenshaw's personal assistant

Donald Morgans - murder victim branded with a star

Elsa Crow - police captain promoted from the Special Crimes unit and daughter of Chogan Crow

Erin Gerard - Daniels' half-sister and friend of Cain Carson

Ezra Grimm - attorney for Montes Pharmaceuticals and Ruben Montes' cousin.

Captain Frank Lozano - the head of the squad

Detective Frank Monk - Manetti's partner

Detective Gordon Daniels - Remalla's long-term partner and friend

Hans Morrow - a name from the list of black bird members

Jennifer Chambers - Aaron Remalla's deceased girlfriend

Jerry Lee Caruso - son to Patricia Caruso and grandson to Sammy Caruso

Lena - shaman and grandmother to Kyle, Mikey's co-worker

Lexie Logan - investigative journalist

Lonny - Lexie Logan's neighbor

Detective Luca Manetti - a detective in the same precinct as Remalla and Daniels

Margaret Redstone - Mikey's psychopathic sister and a former high-ranking member of Victor D'Mato's cult

Marjorie Daniels - Daniels' wife

Martin Bailey - a name from the list of black bird members

Marvin Ackerman - former Pinnacle Properties accountant and black bird member

Mason Redstone - medium, paranormal PI, and former Texas Ranger. Brother to Margaret and Mikey.

Mikey Redstone - works at SCOPE with her brother Mason; is Rem's girlfriend

Nathan Briars - a former cult member and friend of Vera and Mikey

Patricia Caruso - Jerry Lee's mother and Sammy Caruso's daughter

Raymond Daniels - Detective Gordon Daniels' father

Reginald Durning - defense attorney for Crenshaw, Ingram and Willoughby

Rex Beelson - murder victim branded with a star

'Rhonda Champlin' - an assassin

Rita Vittorio - a name from the list of black bird members

Chief Ronald Patterson - chief of police and Captain Lozano's superior

Sammy Caruso - a powerful politician from Chicago with mob connections

Tommy - nickname given to Tex's partner, who helped Tex try to kill Rem and Daniels in Elmwood

Tyson Croft (aka Tex) - a member of the black bird society who attempted to kill Rem and Daniels in Elmwood

Vera Canmore - a former cult member and close friend of Mikey

Victor D'Mato - cult leader

Chapter One

MARTIN BAILEY DROVE DOWN the dark alley. A soft rain fell, and his wipers made a high-pitched squeak as they slid over his windshield. Squinting through the wet windows, he drove beneath a dim light fixture that, along with his headlights, cast eerie shadows. Nervous and looking for his destination, he slowed down. The rain picked up in intensity, and he cursed, wishing he were back on his couch with his cat Butters, drinking a beer and watching an old movie.

The moment he'd gotten the call, he'd dreaded every moment of this assignment. He'd done this twice before, but never in the rain, and never at this time of night. The first time he'd done it, he'd simply stopped in the alley beside a heavy metal door, and a man the size of a prizefighter had come out. Martin had popped the trunk, and the man had grabbed the box in the back, shut the trunk, and Marty had driven off.

The second time, Marty stopped at the door, but no one showed. After waiting several minutes, he'd received a text telling him to bring the box inside. He'd reluctantly left the car, collected the box, and had gone to the door. He'd knocked, but no one had answered. Uncertain, he'd opened the creaky door and stuck his head in. Not seeing anyone, he'd stepped inside.

Not sure what to do, he'd waited, and an awful smell made his hair rise. He held his nose and debated leaving the box when a man's deep voice pierced the quiet.

"Bring it here."

Trembling, Marty cautiously walked down a hall and turned a corner. A room came into view that he could only describe as right out of a horror movie. Lighted candles stood around the room at various heights, strange symbols covered the walls, and a chalk circle marked the floor. The horrid smell had almost made him gag.

The voice spoke again. "Put the box in the circle."

Marty couldn't see anyone. He couldn't even identify the source of the voice. His heart hammering, he'd stepped farther into the room and approached the circle. Staring at it and the strange symbols on the walls, he realized that whatever this place was used for, it wasn't good. Aware that he was about to step inside the circle, he jumped back. Intuitively, he knew not to step past the chalk. He lowered the box, set it on the ground, and shoved it into the circle.

He heard a crackle, and goosebumps ran over his skin. "Leave," said the male voice.

Marty wasted no time. He turned, ran out of the building, jumped in his car, and squealed away.

Now, three months later, he was back, and the memory of that last visit made him tremble again. He prayed that this time around, the prizefighter would be back, and Marty wouldn't have to return to that room, and the awful smell.

Slowing more, he looked for the metal door. He passed another light fixture, and just beyond that, he spied where he'd stopped the previous two times. Saying a prayer, he pulled up and stopped. He waited, watching the door, hoping it would open, but it didn't. Groaning, he spoke to himself. "Take it easy, Marty. It's just a room. No big deal."

He thought of the box in his trunk and wondered what sort of delivery would warrant this level of secrecy. Whatever was in it had to be important, but to whom and why was a mystery.

Several minutes passed, and Marty expected the text, but it never came. He debated whether to keep waiting or to bring the box inside when he saw headlights in his rearview mirror. The light fractured into irregular shapes on the wet glass as Marty watched the car stop behind him.

Expecting all he'd have to do was pop the trunk and let whoever was in the car take the box, Marty breathed a sigh of relief, thrilled he wouldn't have to leave his vehicle. His phone buzzed with a text notification, and he picked it up and read it.

Bring the box to me.

Marty lowered his phone with a curse. "Figures I'm the one who has to get wet." He popped the trunk and opened his door. Stepping out into the rain, he pulled his hood over his head and grabbed the box from his trunk.

The car behind him idled, and the passenger door opened. A man wearing a dark raincoat with the hood pulled up got out. Holding the small box, Marty closed his trunk. He stepped to the side, expecting to hand the box over to the man, when the man stopped and slid his hands into his pockets.

Getting closer, Marty recognized him. "Croft? Who'd you piss off to have to come out in this crappy weather?"

Croft half-smiled. "I could ask you the same."

Marty grunted. "I'm just a messenger boy. You know that. I don't carry the clout you do." He paused. "Unless you're no longer Mr. Sidekick." He snickered. "Don't tell me. Did you finally tell the bossman the truth?"

Croft didn't move. "What truth is that?"

The rain fell harder, and Marty pulled his hood higher over his head. "You know what I mean. The rumors are circulating."

"What rumors?"

Marty wiped the rain from his face. "It's a mess out here. Can we get this over with? Pop the trunk or take the box. I want to go home."

Croft's expression didn't change. "What rumors, Marty?"

Rain splattered against the box. "Seriously?"

"Seriously."

Marty scoffed. "I think you've gone as bonkers as he has. What's up with all this delivering strange boxes in the middle of the night crap?" He tapped the box. "What's in this thing?"

"Nothing that concerns you."

Marty squinted. "It concerns me when I have to deliver it to some crazy room with candles, circles, and weird symbols. What the hell is going on, Croft? This is more than I signed up for. I'm all for the group support, and the nice paycheck, but this is getting strange."

"I'm sorry to hear that, Marty."

Marty pointed. "And I'm not the only one thinking it, either."

"Really? Who else is questioning their membership?"

Marty detected a clip in Croft's voice. "Hey, man. Don't take it personally. It's just that when you see and hear things, you have to wonder."

"Wonder what?"

"Just who exactly I'm working for." A clap of thunder and a flash of lightning made Marty grip the box tighter. The cardboard, softened by the rain, bent under his grasp. "You better take this box. It's getting soaked."

Croft remained still.

"C'mon, man. Don't just stand there." Marty shivered. "I'm freezing."

Croft's eyes narrowed. "I'm sorry, Marty."

"It's okay. Just take this already." He lifted the box.

Croft pulled his hand from his pocket. He was holding a gun. "As you say, it's not personal. But the boss does not abide disloyalty."

Marty widened his eyes in shock. "What the hell is this?"

"The group must remain cohesive, and those who stir the pot, well, they have to go."

Marty stared at the gun. "You want me out? Just because of a few rumors?"

"Rumors are just the beginning. If they aren't controlled, then it leads to more disloyalty."

Marty couldn't believe what he was hearing. "Are you listening to yourself? You're as bad as he is. He's crazy, and you know it. Why aren't you questioning it, too?"

"I'm not the one who makes the rules. He is. And he pays the bills."

Scared, Marty raised his free hand. "You want me out? That's fine with me. I'm out. I'll drive off and you never have to talk to me again."

"You've seen too much." Croft glanced at the box. "You know too much." He glared. "And you talk too much."

Marty spoke fast. "I don't know shit. And who would believe me, anyway?"

Croft blinked, and Marty thought of his cat, whose eyes gleamed the same way when he was about to pounce. "And if there's dissension in the ranks," said Croft, "someone needs to be an example."

Marty's mind whirled. How was he going to get out of this? "An example? Of what?"

"Of what happens when you question your superior and spread lies."

Marty gaped at Croft. "I won't say another word. I swear it."

"Put the box down, Marty."

It hit Marty that the box was secondary. Croft was there to kill him. Another crack of thunder jolted him into action. Panicking, he swiveled, dropped the box, and ran. The first thing he saw was the metal door. Thinking at warp speed, he imagined getting behind it and locking it. It could be the only thing that might save him. He raced toward it when a cold, sharp sting sliced into his back. Crying out, his legs gave way, and he crumpled into a puddle on the ground. His hood slid down, and rain pelted his head and face, but he crawled toward the door. He reached for it, grabbed the handle, and felt a measure of hope when it opened. But before he could get inside, another shot rang out. He fell forward, his face hit the wet pavement, and his last thought was of Butters, who was waiting for him to come home.

· · · · ● · ● · · · ·

Holding the gun, Croft walked past the taillights of Marty's car. He approached and squatted in a puddle next to Marty's body and checked his pulse. Feeling nothing, Croft stood and tucked his gun back into his pocket.

The driver's side door of his car opened, and the driver got out. He easily towered over Croft and had arm muscles the size of basketballs. He wore a black knit cap, jeans, a sweatshirt, boots, and gloves, but no protection from the rain.

Croft slid his gun into his pocket. "Russell. Put the body in the trunk of his car." Thunder rumbled, and there was another flash of lightning.

Russell closed his door and approached Marty's body. Croft returned to the other side of their car to retrieve the box and stopped short when he saw the box had opened and its contents were strewn across the pavement. The tape must have loosened in the rain. Cursing, he raced to pick up what had spilled from the box, and hoped it wasn't damaged and could still be used. Rook would not be happy to know it had been exposed to the elements.

Squatting and picking up the contents, he heard Russell yell from behind him.

"Croft."

Hearing the big man's tone, Croft swiveled. Rain blew into his face, but it didn't prevent him from seeing swirling lights at the far end of the alley. He froze. It was a police car, and two cars parked in a dark alley on a night like this would likely draw the officers' attention. "Get back in the car." He turned and raced to grab whatever he could from the ground and throw it into the box.

Russell hesitated. "But the body."

"Leave it." He thought fast. "Leave the bag, too. In the front seat." Croft stood with the box. "Let's get out of here. Now." He slid into the passenger seat, grabbed a bag from the back seat and handed it to Russell, who ran through the rain and tossed it into the front of Marty's car. Russell raced back and jumped into the driver's seat next to Croft. He slammed the vehicle into reverse, and looking behind him, shot backward out of the alley.

Chapter Two

REM SAT ON HIS couch and yawned. His eyes watering and his legs propped up on his coffee table, he studied his laptop screen, which displayed another search result on the name he was studying. Chester, his and Mikey's female cat, who had once belonged to Mikey's sister Margaret, was curled up against his hip. His head throbbing and his eyes blurring, he blinked several times and reached for the thermos of coffee beside him.

"How long have you been up?"

Mikey's voice startled him, and he almost dropped his thermos.

Dressed in her usual snug black jeans and T-shirt, with a diamond stud sparkling in her nostril, she came into the room. "Sorry. Didn't mean to scare you."

"It's okay." Rem took a swig of coffee and closed the thermos. "I'm just tired."

She sat beside him and brushed back her long brown hair with highlighted purple tips. "Honey, you need to sleep. You've been up early every morning this week."

Rem pinched the bridge of his nose. "The only time I can do this is before I go to work. It's too risky to do it at my desk."

Mikey glanced at the laptop screen. "Any luck?"

Rem groaned at his lack of progress. "Not much." He sighed. "It's harder than you'd think. All we have are names." He thought of the current name on the black bird member list he was researching–Rita Vittorio. "Do you know how many Rita Vittorios there are in the San Diego area? And what's worse is she might not be local. Do you know how many Rita Vittorios are in L.A.? And we can't just limit it to L.A.. She could be anywhere in this state."

Mikey tucked a strand of his hair that had fallen into his face behind his ear. "Rita Vittorio isn't *that* common of a name. How many can there be?"

"Apparently, there are more Italians in California than I expected." He rested his head back on the couch. "Daniels and I have narrowed it down, though. If you take out the obits and anyone over eighty and under twenty, and no criminal record, which are all assumptions we had to make, that leaves us with eight possibles."

"That's not too bad."

"And that's just one name." He picked up the piece of paper beside him and glanced at it. "Want to take a guess how many possible Curtis Styles there are, or Natalia Ferndales?" He grunted and dropped his head back again. "At this rate, Daniels and I are going to be black bird members for months, if not years."

"You think you two can pull off being assassins for that long?"

He smirked at her. "I'm good at a lot of things, babe, but that's stretching it."

She propped her elbow on the back of the couch. "Maybe you two should consider dropping your membership."

He rolled his head back and forth. "Can't do that. The only way to stop these people is to get them to trust us."

"But that means killing Jerry Lee."

Rem shrugged. "That requires finding him first, which appears to be impossible. Where the hell did this kid go? Russia?"

"Maybe that's a good thing. It means you don't have to kill him."

"If we don't, they'll frame us for the murders of Cain and Bertrand. They've got my dad's gun, remember?"

"You think they'd actually go that far?"

Rem recalled Damien Rook's anger with him and Daniels. "In a heartbeat. Rook is itching to put us in our place. He hates us."

"But why?"

Rem sighed and yawned again. "That's one more mystery to solve."

Mikey took his hand. "I'm worried about you."

Rem squeezed her fingers. "I know. But try not to. Daniels and I will figure this out."

"I'm not just talking about the black birds."

He met her gaze. "What's on your mind?"

She propped her chin on her palm. "Honey, you've been going nonstop since Cain died. His funeral was three days ago, and you showed more emotion when we went furniture shopping last month. I know Daniels noticed it, too. You're not sleeping well, and now you're diving into this list, so you can take down Damien Rook, a man who wants to destroy you and Daniels, and who expects you to kill for him."

"Sounds like a typical month."

"I'm not kidding."

A memory flashed of Cain lying on the floor with an ugly wound in his chest, and his blood pooling beneath him. Rem looked away. "I'm fine."

"I don't think you are."

Recalling Cain asking for forgiveness, Rem closed the laptop. "It's just my way, Mikey. I need to distract myself, and working is the best way to do that. And it's not like I have a choice. I'd prefer not to have to kill Jerry Lee. I suspect Daniels feels the same."

Mikey ran her thumb over the back of Rem's hand. "You're blaming yourself, aren't you? For Cain's death? I heard what Mabel said to you after the funeral."

Rem gripped Mikey's hand. "She lost her brother, and she's devastated. She has a right to be angry."

"Not at you. You didn't do anything wrong."

"He died in my arms. Of course, she blames me. She needs a target for her grief."

"And I admire your compassion, but it's not fair. He was your cousin. You're grieving too."

"I can handle it."

"You always say that, but I can sense you're not yourself." Mikey squeezed his fingers. "I don't mean to bring up another tough subject, but you blamed yourself for Jennie, too."

Rem almost corrected her choice of past tense. He still carried the weight of his first love's loss. "Honey, I get why you're worried. I know it's taken years for me to come to terms with Jennie's death, and now this." He paused. "I can't deny I wish I'd handled Cain and his situation differently. Maybe if I had..."

"You tried, Rem. He didn't want your help. What else were you supposed to do? Throw handcuffs on him and toss him behind bars?"

Rem ran his free hand over his face. "Maybe I should have."

Mikey slumped. "See. That's what I'm talking about. You're carrying a ton of guilt. I think more than you realize."

"Hey." He rolled his head to face her.

She scooted lower on the couch and laid her head on the cushions next to his. "What?"

"Don't worry about me. I want you to worry about you. Rook is crazy enough to come after you to get to me. He did it with Marjorie. And if he somehow finds out you're trying to retrieve your memories, and if this cigarette smoker we believe is Winnie is involved the way we think he is, that puts you in danger. Have you thought about what I said about staying with Mason?"

"You're changing the subject."

"I know, but I don't want to talk about Cain. I want to talk about you."

Her face softened. "Aaron—"

He smiled softly. "Michaela—" They rarely used their first names with each other unless the subject turned serious. "Trust me. I'm okay."

"No, you're not. But I understand if you need time. Just take it easy, all right? If you push yourself too hard, this wall you're building will come crashing down, and I don't want to be the one who takes the brunt when it does."

He stared into her lovely warm eyes, and his heart thumped for a different reason. "That's not going to happen because there is no wall. Maybe just a short chain-link fence. Easily scalable." He let go of her hand and trailed a finger down her cheek. "Promise."

"Says the man who's good at lying."

"I wouldn't lie to you."

"You're going to lie to Rook when you tell him you've killed Jerry Lee."

"That's different."

Mikey groaned. "What am I going to do with you?"

He grinned. "A few things come to mind." He reached around her waist and pulled her closer. Chester, looking annoyed, jumped off the couch.

She moaned when he leaned in and kissed her neck. "You're changing the subject."

He ran his lips up to her cheek. "I know." His skin warmed when she ran her hands up his arms, but he groaned when she pushed him back.

"Tempted as I am," she said, her cheeks flushing, "we're not done with this conversation, Romeo." She held his gaze. "But hold that thought."

He fought the need to pull her back into his arms. "Don't make me wait long, or I'll be forced to ravish you."

"Promise?"

He chuckled and sat up. "Okay. Let's get back to you then. Did you talk to Mason about staying with him?"

"Do you see Marjorie going anywhere?"

"If Daniels could pack her and J.P. up and send them to South America until this mess blows over, he would, but she's not budging."

"And neither am I." She took his hand again. "We're in this together, remember?"

Hating her being at risk, he sighed. As much as he loved her bravery and stubbornness, it also drove him nuts. "Just be super careful, okay? Watch your surroundings and keep this whole memory retrieval thing to yourself. Remind Lena too."

"She knows. She won't say anything." Mikey studied their entwined fingers. "But I need to update you on something."

Imagining the worst, he straightened. "What? Did something happen?"

She shook her head. "No. Nothing bad. But I've made some progress with my meditations with Lena." Mikey hesitated. "Remember when I told you that instead of trying to figure out who Vera's killer is, Lena suggested I try to contact Vera instead?"

Rem had a vague memory of Mikey telling him that, but with all that had recently happened, he hadn't been keeping up with any new developments. "I do. Has it helped?"

Mikey held his gaze. "I saw her."

Rem frowned. "You mean in your meditations?"

"No. I saw her spirit. In Daniels' house. The day after Marjorie's accident."

Rem wasn't sure he understood. "You mean, like Mason sees spirits?"

"Yes."

"And you're just now telling me?"

"There's been a lot going on, Rem. And there's not much to tell. She didn't say anything. She just floated there and disappeared when you and Daniels came home."

"Have you seen her since?"

Mikey resumed her stare at their hands. "Not in spirit form." She looked up. "She showed up in a dream last night. And she spoke to me."

That had Rem's full attention. "What did she say?"

"She said she's been watching me."

"That's comforting. I think."

"I told her if she appears in the middle of the night, standing over the bed, I'm going to freak out."

"I hope you conveyed I feel the same."

Mikey smiled. "I think she knows."

"Good. What else?"

"I asked her about Margaret's friend. The man we think is Winnie. She just stood there in silence. I asked again, and she told me I already know him."

That caught Rem by surprise. "Who the hell is he?"

Mikey huffed. "I have no idea. I know a lot of people. I asked for a hint, though." She squeezed Rem's fingers again. "She said Margaret knows him, too."

Rem's stomach clenched at the thought of Margaret, Mikey's psychotic sister, currently residing in a psychiatric facility because she'd been deemed unfit to stand trial. "We know your sister knows him. That's nothing new."

"I think Vera was suggesting I ask her."

Understanding the implications, Rem stiffened. "Oh, hell no. That's not going to happen."

"Rem, listen—"

Rem set his laptop on the coffee table and stood. "If you think for one second you're going to go talk to your sister, then you need to change your mind. Right now."

"I've been thinking about it. What can it hurt? I'll take Mason with me. We're her family, for God's sake. We should visit her."

"That's not what you said before Vera came into the picture."

"Vera said to talk to her. That must mean something. If Margaret tells us who Winnie is, that will change everything. You and Daniels might not have to go down this road with Rook. It could solve a lot of problems."

"And create a lot more." He ran his hand through his long hair. "You can't trust your sister, Mikey."

"This isn't about Margaret. This is about Vera. I owe her."

"Now who's feeling guilty?"

"Then you know exactly how I feel. If this might help, I have to do it."

"I completely disagree. And something tells me Mason might feel the same."

"Mason will come around. It's you I need to convince."

Rem didn't like where this was headed. "Have you already talked to him about this?"

"No. I just had the dream last night."

"But you have talked to him? About Vera?"

"Of course. He gave me plenty of tips and pointers to help Vera come through and to prepare me in case she did. His advice has been instrumental."

Rem put his hands on his hips. "I wish you'd felt comfortable coming to me."

Mikey stood. "I do, but you lost Cain, and then this thing with Rook happened. I didn't want to give you one more thing to deal with. But I'm telling you now." She took his hand again. "And I want your support."

"To go see Margaret?" He shook his head. "I can't give you that. It's too dangerous. Even with Mason there. Your sister knows how to manipulate a total stranger. She'll make mincemeat of both of you and only make this situation worse."

"As you like to say, I can handle it."

Rem straightened. "If you can call me on my bullshit, I can call you on yours."

Mikey paused. "I want to do this."

"And I *don't* want you to do this."

They stared at each other until Mikey broke the silence. "I'm a big girl. I can make my own decisions."

"I'm well aware. I'm used to it. I know I can't stop you from seeing her, but I can't give you my blessing. And I'll argue with you every step of the way."

Mikey's brow furrowed. "Why are you so damn stubborn?"

"I could ask you the same."

They stared again, and Rem softened his voice. "I'm only trying to protect you."

"I want the same for you. Vera, too. That's why it's important for me to do this."

Frustrated, Rem looked away.

"There's another reason to talk to her. Don't forget who else is on that list." She pointed at the paper on the couch. "Victor D'Mato. If he talked to Margaret about the black birds—"

Unexpected anger bubbled up. "Absolutely not," yelled Rem. "Leave him out of this."

Mikey's eyes widened, and she leaned back.

Rem reined it in. "Sorry." He held up his hand. "I'm sorry. I didn't mean to yell. It's just the mention of his name, and you getting deeper into this...and remembering what happened with Margaret." He groaned. "It makes me a little crazy."

Mikey studied him. "I'm sorry, too. I know what Victor did to both of us, and I didn't mean to upset you."

Memories flared of his past with Victor and Allison Albright, the two people responsible for his abduction. "I can only take so much, Mikey."

She stepped closer. "I know it's scary, but remember, Margaret's in an institution, and Victor and Allison are dead. They can't hurt either of us anymore."

Rem recalled Allison's smug smirk when she'd used her pregnancy against him. She'd lied about carrying his child in order to prevent him from testifying against her at trial. It made his stomach turn at how close she'd come to succeeding.

Mikey put her hand on Rem's wrist. "I'll talk to Mason first, and I promise I won't do anything without telling you. Okay?"

He looked back. "Telling me? Or asking me?"

"What is the point of asking when I already know your answer?"

Rem recalled his argument with Daniels when his partner had revealed he'd given Ackerman's encrypted file to his sister Erin without talking to Rem first. "You sound like Daniels."

"That's because I know you. You're never going to agree to this."

"You're damn right."

"But I'm going to try anyway."

"Mikey, you know your sister, and her weird infatuation with me. I—" His phone rang, and he cursed at the interruption. He picked it up and saw Daniels' name on the display. "Hold on." He answered. "Hey. You're up early too?"

"Glad you're awake," said Daniels. "Crow called. We've got a body."

Rem dropped his jaw. "You're kidding? And she gave it to us? Don't we have enough on our plate?"

"I expressed my displeasure, but she didn't care. We're up next, and since, in her words, we're not getting anywhere with Jerry Lee and Reginald Durning, we might as well take this."

Rem ran his hand over his head. "Son-of-a..." He eyed Mikey with a grunt. "I don't know why I'm surprised. Send me the address. I'll take a quick shower and head that way."

"You're gonna love it. The body was found near an abandoned building, where that new development is going in."

Rem cursed. "How do we always end up over there?"

"Cheer up. Maybe this has some connection to Rook. We'll take him and his empire down and be home before dinner."

"And I might have broccoli and peas for breakfast."

"Stranger things have happened. I'll text you the info. See you soon."

"Yeah," said Rem. "See ya." He hung up. "I've got to go."

"A new case?" asked Mikey.

"Crow's feeling generous today." He pointed. "But we are not done with this conversation."

"Rem, I just think that—"

Rem waved his hand. "Nope. Not right now. You want to talk to Mason? Talk away. We'll discuss it tonight. Okay?"

Mikey squinted. "Does that mean you're considering it?"

Rem's phone beeped with a text message. It was from Daniels, sending him the address of the crime scene. "No. What I'm considering is how to change your mind."

Mikey crossed her arms. "And I'll be thinking about how to change yours."

"Good luck with that." He leaned in and gave her a quick kiss. "You know I love you."

"You know I love you, too."

"And I still plan on ravishing you later."

"You better."

Despite their disagreement, he winked at her and headed to the shower.

Chapter Three

DANIELS PULLED UP IN the alley and parked behind a police cruiser with flashing lights. A coroner's wagon was pulled up beyond a second cruiser, and police tape was strung across the alley. Not seeing Rem's car, he sat and waited. He figured the body wasn't going anywhere. Thinking of Marjorie, he debated calling her. This was her first day back at work since the accident and miscarriage. She'd taken some time off, and he'd wanted her to wait another week, but she'd insisted it was time to return. Sitting in the house and dwelling on their loss wasn't good for her, she'd told him, and she needed to get back to work.

The cast on her arm and the fading bruise on her cheek were the only visible signs of her injuries, but Daniels knew the grief from losing their child had taken the shine from her eyes and the smile from her face. J.P. was the only thing that could bring her smile out, and it was sticking around a little longer every day, but he still heard her tears when she showered and when she thought he slept. And when he heard them, he'd pull her close and hold her until the tears subsided. He understood she would recover with time but hated her suffering.

That morning, she'd left when he'd left, and his gut still churned. It was her first time driving since the accident, and it scared him to death that someone could come after her again. He'd wanted to follow her to work, but she'd refused, determined to get back on the horse and not let her fears get the best of her. Marjorie was not the type of woman to cower, and Daniels loved that about her, but he also loathed her vulnerability. He'd do anything to protect her and J.P., and if someone went after either of them again, he didn't know what he'd do. He'd probably end up in prison with no help from Rook.

He studied his phone and willed it to ring. He'd asked Marjorie to contact him the moment she got to work. Not wanting to hover, he told himself a million times she was fine, but until she called, he would worry.

Deciding he'd waited long enough, he started to dial her number when a text came through from her, telling him she was safe in her office with no incidents on the way in, and that she would text him before she left for the day.

Saying a small prayer of thanks, he texted her back, told her he loved her, and would call her during her lunch hour. He didn't care that he was hovering. She'd just have to get used to it until he felt calmer.

A rap on the window made him jump, and he lowered his phone and saw his partner waving at him through the glass. He put his phone away and opened the door. "Morning."

"Morning," said Rem. "You been here long?"

"Just a few minutes. I was texting Marjorie."

Rem raised his brow. "How is she? She stick to the plan and go into work?"

"She did, and you're lucky I didn't have a heart attack and leave Rook and his buddies all to you."

"I appreciate that. I could use the help." He walked toward the crime scene tape. "Any word from her? She get in okay?"

Daniels could see Rem was as worried as he'd been. "She's fine. She got there with no problems."

Rem visibly relaxed. "Good."

Daniels got a good look at his partner. "How are you? You get any sleep?"

Rem swiped his slightly damp long hair back with his fingers. "Enough to keep moving and breathing and not leave Rook and his buddies all to you."

"That's great, but how about getting enough so you can think straight and not drink a gallon of coffee just to keep your eyes open?"

Rem looked him over. "Look who's talking."

Daniels smoothed his normally gelled blond hair back and looked down at his rumpled clothes. He imagined his eyes reflected his own lack of sleep. "I was worried about Marjorie. What's your excuse?"

Approaching the scene, they flashed their badges to an officer and ducked beneath the tape. "Life," said Rem. He didn't offer more.

Daniels suspected Cain was on his partner's mind, but that was expected. Rem would carry the weight of his cousin's loss for a while, and all Daniels could do was be there for him. Rem was good at keeping his grief to himself, though. Daniels had learned that the hard way with Jennie.

They approached a yellow sheet covering an inert form on the damp cement just outside a metal door. Thunderstorms had rolled through in the early morning hours, and small puddles remained on the ground around the scene. Daniels glanced up at the building. It looked to be about five stories, with grimy windows running up the side of it. Colorful graffiti covered the walls on both sides of the alley. Other than a parked car near the body and the official vehicles at the scene, the alley was quiet. Forensic techs took pictures of the area and the car, and an evidence marker sat on the pavement on the other side of the alley.

Rem squatted next to the body as an officer approached. Daniels was glad to see it was Jim Parsons, a reliable officer with a good head on his shoulders. Rem and Daniels knew him well. "Hey, Parsons," said Daniels. "What's the story?"

"Hey, Daniels. Rem." He eyed Daniels. "How's Mrs. Daniels doing?"

"Great," said Daniels. "She's better every day. Thanks for asking."

"Glad to hear it." Parsons lifted a small notebook as Rem lifted the covering over the body. "Our vic here took a shot to the back and to the head, the head one being fatal."

Rem eyed the body of a Caucasian man lying face down on the ground. His head and hair were bloody, and blood pooled beneath the man's face. "That's a safe deduction." Rem pulled the covering higher to get a look at the lower body of the victim. "Any ID?"

"His wallet was still on him, with cash in it, so not a robbery." He pointed to the vehicle. "And that's his car. License says his name is Martin Bailey. Age thirty-eight."

Daniels stilled, and Rem's eyes narrowed. "Martin Bailey?" asked Rem. He shot a look at Daniels.

"Yeah," said Parsons, looking between the two of them. "You two know him?"

Daniels recalled the list of black bird members' names. Martin Bailey was on it. "No, but we've heard the name."

Rem lowered the covering and stood.

Parsons nodded. "Looks like Mr. Bailey pulled up into the alley. His clothes are wet, so it was raining when he died or after. He tried to make it to the door but was killed before he could get there. A patrol doing their nightly rounds saw Bailey's car and a second car. The second one left the scene before the patrol arrived and found Bailey. Ibrahim says he's been dead two to three hours, so not long."

"What's behind the door?" asked Rem.

"An empty hall leading to an empty room. It may have been a restaurant in the past. This building is scheduled to be demolished soon. Forensics hasn't been in there yet, but they'll check it out."

"Got any gloves?" asked Daniels. "And shoe coverings?"

Parsons lowered his notepad. "Sure." He glanced behind him. "Hey, Butler. Get me two pairs of gloves and shoe covers."

Butler nodded and headed to a patrol car.

"There's more," said Parsons.

"I can hardly wait," added Rem.

"In his car. There's a bag." Parsons stepped toward the vehicle that belonged to Bailey. On the opposite side, a technician was dusting the driver's side door for prints.

Daniels and Rem walked closer. "Anything in it?" asked Daniels.

Butler ran over with the gloves and shoe covers and handed them to Rem and Daniels. "Thanks," said Rem.

Parsons wrinkled his nose. "It's a weird doll."

Daniels approached the vehicle and looked inside. A plastic bag was on the front seat.

"We left it in the bag so you guys could see it. We got pictures, though, so you can take it out."

Daniels put on his gloves, along with Rem, and grabbed the bag. He opened it and frowned. "What the—?" He pulled out the doll and put the bag back in the front seat.

Rem stared at it, too. "What the hell is that?"

It was a handmade doll with fat arms and legs, but a narrow waist and a round head. The fabric was rough and appeared to be burlap, and it was stuffed with something soft. Black plastic buttons sewn on the head formed the eyes, and a circular piece of black felt served as its mouth, glued into place. Daniels poked at a small slit in the fabric on the chest of the doll. "Looks like cotton balls inside." He turned it over and saw a crude seam running up the back, tied with black thread, and another piece of round felt, this one red, glued on the back of the head.

Rem leaned closer. "Is that supposed to be his head wound?"

"I don't know," said Daniels, "but that's what it looks like."

"That is creepy as hell," said Rem.

"Thought you'd like to see it before we bag it and the plastic bag," said Parsons.

Wondering what the doll meant, and how Martin Bailey was connected to the black birds, Daniels put the doll back in the bag and put it on the front seat. "Maybe we'll get lucky and find some fibers or DNA on it."

Rem shivered. "I'd just as soon never see it again. It's got a vibe."

"You think that's strange?" asked Parsons. "Check this out." He walked away from the car and approached the yellow evidence marker on the wet ground on the other side of the alley.

Daniels and Rem followed, and Parsons pointed to an object on the cement. "Look at that."

Daniels squatted next to it. "Is that a bone?"

Rem leaned close and paled. "Did Ibrahim see this?"

"Sure did. Says it's a proximal phalanx." He pointed to the lower part of one of his fingers. "This part."

"So it's human?" asked Rem, straightening.

"It is," said Parsons. "Doc says he can tell you more, like if it's male or female and how old it is, after he gets it to the lab. Hopefully, he can pull some DNA from it."

"Well, Bailey's got all his digits, so it's not his." Daniels looked around. "What the hell happened here last night?"

Rem shook his head. "I don't know, but I feel a sudden urge to sage this place."

"Sage?" asked Parsons.

Daniels stood. "Nothing you need to worry about." He eyed Rem. "What do you think?"

Rem widened his eyes. "What do I think? We've got a bizarre doll and a human bone next to a dead body."

"Not your average murder," said Daniels, thinking of Rook. Was he somehow mixed up in this?

"Definitely not." Rem's gaze traveled back to the body of Bailey, which was being zipped into a body bag. "Bailey obviously met someone here. And like Parsons said, it didn't go well, and he headed for that door to save himself, but didn't make it."

Daniels glanced back at the building. "You want to see what's behind that door?"

"I sure as hell do." Rem stepped away. "I think."

They stopped in the alley until Bailey's body was carted away, and put on their shoe covers. "You ready?" asked Daniels, approaching the door.

"Has Parsons officially freaked me out?" asked Rem, glancing at the officer.

Parsons shrugged. "Don't blame the messenger."

Daniels pulled the door open. "Age before beauty."

Rem smirked and walked inside.

Daniels followed him, and they entered a dark hallway with minimal light. The door banged shut behind them, and Rem jumped.

"Don't worry," said Daniels. "I'll save you."

Rem made a face. "It's the last guy out that needs saving, and that's not going to be me."

Daniels headed down the hall. "We'll see about that." He followed the murky corridor until it opened up into a bigger room with high ceilings. The only light came from two small dirty windows across from them. The walls were brick, and the floor was cement. A faint odor made Daniels cringe.

"What is that smell?" asked Rem.

"I don't know." Daniels looked around. "But it's not pleasant."

"Smells like my Aunt Marta's three-day-old oxtail and crawdad soup."

Daniels fought the urge to gag. "I'm not even going to ask."

"Probably a good idea." Rem went to another door across the room and pushed it open. "Looks like a kitchen. Maybe this was a restaurant at one point." He let the door swing shut, then stopped and stared at something near his foot. "Someone has been here." He squatted and pointed at a candle on the ground. Wax had dribbled down the side and hardened, and the wick was black. "Somebody's been burning candles."

Daniels studied the floor. "Do you see this?" He pointed at the faint outline of a circle.

Rem walked over and squinted at the floor. "You can barely see it in this light."

"Looks like someone tried to erase it." Daniels squatted beside the line and touched it. "I'm guessing they drew it with chalk."

"Hey," Rem stepped inside the circle. "Check that out."

Daniels joined him and saw what Rem referred to. A small dark stain on the cement. They both squatted beside it. "Is that blood?" asked Rem.

Daniels barely touched the stain, but his gloved finger came back with a speck of red. He smelled it. "I'd say that's a good guess."

Rem rested his hands on his knees. "What the hell have we stumbled onto? This has all the markings of some sort of occult practice or ceremony."

"Could be kids doing stupid stuff. You saw the graffiti out there."

"With Martin Bailey lying dead in the alley? And a creepy doll and human bone nearby?" Rem stood. "This is more than just kids."

Daniels straightened. "And Bailey just became a victim of it."

"The question is, did he stumble onto something he shouldn't have? Or was he part of it?"

"Bailey is on the list. He's a black bird. So does that mean that all of this has to do with the black birds?"

Rem sighed. "If it does, Rook may have gone down a deeper hole than we thought."

"Or some of his members have." Daniels eyed the blood stain. "I was kidding this morning when I said this may have something to do with Rook."

"Every time we step into this neighborhood, it always leads to him."

"Then we need to thank Crow for assigning this case to us. It may be exactly what we need."

"Because of Bailey?"

"We found a name on the list. We dig deeper into Bailey, we might find more members, and Crow won't be the wiser."

"It's a hell of a lot better than searching the internet, trying to get lucky." Rem paused. "Let's hope Martin Bailey's secrets can lead us to some answers before we have to...you know."

Daniels thought of Jerry Lee Caruso. "Pay our membership dues? Yeah. I know."

Rem looked around. "Maybe Forensics can find something of interest." He shivered again. "Let's get out of here. This place, and the smell, are giving me the heebie-jeebies."

"Right behind you, partner."

Walking faster than usual, they turned and headed out of the room.

Chapter Four

Detective Luca Manetti sat at his desk and stared at the open file in front of him, but his mind wandered. His partner, Detective Frank Monk, had taken the morning off for an appointment, and Manetti was taking the time to review their current case.

He glanced toward the captain's office and saw Elsa Crow behind the desk, talking on the phone. Captain Lozano remained suspended, pending an FBI and internal investigation into whether he'd taken bribes along with Reginald Durning, when they'd worked together as a prosecutor and detective. Manetti didn't believe for a second that Lozano was guilty of anything, but until it was proven, there was little anyone could do.

Daniels and Rem's desks were vacant, and Manetti guessed they were on a fresh case. They'd made little progress solving Durning's murder or finding the witness to that murder, Jerry Lee Caruso. And, like Manetti and Monk, who'd been assigned to Cain Carson's case, Daniels and Rem had not gotten far with who'd killed Arnold Bertrand.

Once it had been determined that the same .38 Special had killed both Bertrand and Cain, Monk and Manetti had worked with Rem and Daniels to find the perpetrator. Bertrand had been harboring Jerry Lee and had been murdered for his trouble, but the motive behind Cain's murder was less clear. All Rem had told Monk and Manetti was that Cain had named Tex as the man who'd shot him. According to Rem and Daniels, Tex had been one of the men who'd attempted to kill them while transporting Rhonda Champlin back to San Diego through the small town of Elmwood. Rhonda had turned out not to be a witness, though, but a killer working with Tex.

Why Tex and Rhonda had been after Daniels and Rem remained unclear. If Cain was telling the truth, Tex hated Rem enough to return and kill his cousin, but Manetti didn't know why. And he couldn't help but think that Daniels and Rem weren't telling everything they knew. Why would the man who'd killed Cain also kill Bertrand? What was the connection? And if Tex hadn't killed Bertrand, he'd certainly given the gun he'd used on Cain to Bertrand's killer, which meant there was a connection between the two. Groaning, Manetti rubbed his face. The more he thought about it, the more it gave him a headache. Something was missing, but he couldn't figure out what it was. And Daniels and Rem weren't sharing.

He wondered if their reluctance had to do with Monk. It was no secret the relationship between Monk, and Rem and Daniels, had deteriorated after Monk had accused Rem's girlfriend Mikey of the murder of Vera Canmore. Mikey had eventually been exonerated, but the grudge between the detectives remained. And it didn't escape Manetti that Rem was a logical suspect in Cain's death. The relationship between the cousins had been strained. Cain's neighbor had overheard an argument between them, and Rem had been found with Cain at the time of his death, covered in his cousin's blood.

None of that was enough to arrest him, though, and Manetti knew Rem would not murder his cousin. But Monk was the wildcard. If he'd gone after Mikey, he could go after Rem. To his credit, though, he'd remained levelheaded and almost at ease with the whole thing, which surprised Manetti. But he wasn't going to rock the boat. Until they found more evidence or the gun that killed Cain and Bertrand, there wasn't much more they could do.

Manetti sighed, drank some of his ginger tea, and flipped through the file containing crime scene photos from Cain's apartment. He'd been through it already, but as Lozano had told him, when you weren't making progress, go back over what you knew, cover your bases again, and be thorough. You never knew what could jump out at you the second, third, or fourth time around. That hadn't worked so far with Vera Canmore's murder, which remained unsolved. But he hoped it might work with Cain's.

He grimaced at the photo of Cain's living room. The floor was covered in blood, with medical waste discarded by the EMTs strewn about the scene. For obvious reasons, Rem had not looked at the photos, and Manetti hadn't offered. Daniels hadn't looked either, but only because Manetti realized Daniels was still reeling from his wife's accident and subsequent miscarriage. It had broken Manetti's heart when he'd heard. His own wife, Annabelle, was due in two and a half months, and he'd anticipated the day their children, being close in age, might play together.

With Daniels and Rem both going through tough times, Manetti had given them space, but as time passed, he knew Elsa Crow would expect results. Despite their grief, Manetti was going to have to push a little harder. Whatever Daniels and Rem were keeping to themselves would have to come out into the open, whether or not they trusted Frank Monk. Manetti just had to figure out how to get them to come clean.

He flipped through more photos, looking at pictures of Cain's kitchen and bedroom. The techs had photographed what was on Cain's desk and inside his desk drawers. Most of it was mundane stuff–papers, pens, work stuff, a laptop, and pictures of his family. His laptop hadn't provided much information, nor had Cain's phone, other than several calls from Rem and a few angry text exchanges. Rem believed Cain had used a burner phone, but it hadn't been found in Cain's apartment. When Manetti asked why Cain would have a burner, Rem would only say he believed Cain didn't always hang with the right people, but wouldn't elaborate about who those people were. Manetti wondered why the killer would take the burner phone unless it could link him to the crime. If this mysterious Tex took it, that meant Cain knew Tex. Had they been working together?

The questions swirled in his mind, and he rubbed his eyes. He looked up when the squad doors opened, and Daniels and Rem entered. "Hey, guys," said Manetti. "Busy morning?"

Rem headed for the coffee machine. "You could say that."

Daniels slid off his jacket. "We caught another murder. Over on the south side."

Manetti swiveled in his chair. "Like you didn't have enough to do?"

"Tell us about it." Rem poured coffee into a mug. "How's your morning going?" He glanced at Monk's desk. "Where's your friendly partner?"

"He had an appointment," said Manetti. "He'll be in later."

Rem returned the coffeepot to the machine. "At least one thing's going right today."

Manetti closed the folder. "Cut him some slack, Rem. He's been doing better."

Daniels sat at his desk. "We'll see how long it lasts."

"I'm not getting my hopes up." Rem added sugar and cream to his mug.

Manetti decided not to push it. "How's Marjorie, Daniels?"

"She's okay," said Daniels. "Went back to work today."

"That's great. Glad to hear it." Manetti thought of Annabelle again. "If you guys need anything..."

Daniels smiled. "Thanks, Manetti. But we're good. That vegan hamburger casserole you two brought over fed us for a week."

"Didn't feed me," said Rem.

"That's because you wouldn't eat it," said Daniels.

"I prefer real hamburger with dairy-loaded cheese, plus french fries with lots of salt." Rem sipped his coffee, closed his eyes, and sighed with appreciation.

"Your loss," said Daniels. "It was delicious." He glanced at Manetti. "Annabelle's a great cook."

"Yeah, she is," said Manetti. "I'm lucky."

"How's she feeling?" asked Daniels.

Manetti nodded. "Good. Fine."

Daniels' face softened. "It's okay to talk about her pregnancy, Manetti. You don't have to worry about me."

Manetti relaxed. He'd been doing his darndest not to mention Annabelle and the upcoming arrival of their child. "Is it that obvious?"

"I appreciate you trying to spare my feelings, but you have a lot to be excited about, and you can talk about it. It's fine." Daniels leaned back in his chair. "Not talking about makes it even worse."

"Okay," said Manetti. "I hear you. Annabelle is fine, but cranky. She's not sleeping well and is uncomfortable most of the time. I tell her she's beautiful, and she smirks at me."

Daniels smiled. "Comes with the territory. The last trimester is tough. Lots of massages worked for me."

"What about Marjorie?" asked Rem, sitting at his desk.

"Ha, ha," said Daniels. "I made sure Marjorie got some too."

Manetti smiled. "Massages. I'll try that. Thanks for the tip."

"You got it." Daniels sat up. "What are you working on while Monk's out?"

Manetti glanced at Rem. "Cain's case."

Rem's face fell, and he set his coffee down. "Anything new?"

Manetti shook his head. "No. I've been going through the crime scene photos again just to be sure I didn't miss anything." He tapped the folder. "But I'm not having much luck."

"I can't help you there, Manetti," said Rem.

"I don't expect you to."

"I haven't seen them," said Daniels. He held out his hand. "Let me take a look."

Manetti straightened. "You sure?"

"I should have looked at them sooner. Maybe I'll see something you don't." He stood and walked over to Manetti's desk.

Rem stayed where he was, sipping his coffee, and not saying a word.

Daniels took the file and opened it. He frowned and studied the pictures. After studying the first two, he looked at Rem. "You are definitely not looking at these."

Rem leaned over his desk. "I already had a front-row seat."

Daniels flipped through more photos. "You're right, Manetti. There's not much here."

Manetti rested an elbow on his desk. "If we could figure out the connection between Tex and Bertrand, it might help. I mean, if Tex went after Cain because of you, Rem, what connection does that have to Bertrand, who was killed protecting your witness, Jerry Lee?"

Rem rested his forehead on his palm. "It's complicated, Manetti."

Manetti debated whether now was the right time to push. "Do you know something I don't?"

Rem looked over at him.

"Are you not telling me everything Cain was into?" asked Manetti.

Rem glowered. "Are you calling me a liar, Manetti?"

Daniels lowered the folder. Manetti shook his head. "I'm not calling you any—"

Rem raised his voice. "Cain died because he was an idiot, okay? And I...I..." He gripped a pen from his desk, opened his top drawer, tossed the pen in, and slammed the drawer shut. "And I should have known better."

"What should you have known?" asked Manetti, surprised by Rem's outburst.

Rem's glower deepened. "Just leave it alone." He went back to sipping his coffee and staring off into space.

Daniels studied Rem. "You okay, partner?"

Rem clenched his jaw, and after a pause, he sighed. "Sorry, Manetti. I didn't mean to jump down your throat." He took another deep breath.

"Understood," said Manetti. "I can understand why. There are a lot of questions without answers."

Rem nodded and stared off again. "Yeah."

Daniels stared at Rem for another second before returning to the photos. "I think you just need food, partner." He turned to the next picture. "Have you had any break—" Daniels froze and, looking closer at the picture, his jaw fell open.

Manetti swiveled to face Daniels. "You find something?"

Daniels pulled out the photo he was staring at and closed the folder.

"What is it?" asked Rem, perking up.

"Rem. Look at this." He set the folder down and put the photo on top of it. Manetti leaned over and saw a picture of Cain's desk with one of the bottom drawers open.

Rem came over and looked at the photo. His face paled, and he gaped at it.

"What?" Manetti looked again. Inside Cain's drawer were a couple of notebooks. On top of them was a small brown child's doll that had buttons as eyes and a black piece of felt as a mouth. Another red, round piece of felt was glued to its front, and a black feather poked out of the fabric over its chest. Monk had discounted it as a toy made by one of Cain's many cousins, and Manetti hadn't thought much more about it. Manetti pointed at the doll. "That?"

Daniels pointed at it, too. "We just left a crime scene where this same type of doll was left behind, we assume by the killer."

Shocked, Manetti stared at the doll in the photo and then at Rem and Daniels. "So your new case is attached to Cain's, which is attached to Bertrand's?"

Rem and Daniels, both stunned into silence, regarded each other.

Manetti smacked his palm on his desk. "What the hell is going on here?"

Chapter Five

STUNNED BY THE APPEARANCE of the doll in Cain's desk drawer, Rem didn't know what to say. Daniels appeared just as stumped.

Manetti was more vocal. "I know you two know something."

Daniels closed his eyes and opened them. He shared a gaze with Rem that communicated the risks and rewards of revealing everything to Manetti, and they silently came to the same conclusion.

Daniels tucked the photo back into the folder. "You hungry, Manetti?"

"Hungry?" asked Manetti. "You two want to eat? Now?"

Rem glanced into the captain's office. Crow was on the phone. "Daniels is right. I need to eat. You should eat something too."

"But I had breakfast."

"I'll buy you a muffin," said Rem.

"I don't eat muffins," said Manetti. "You know that."

"Then you can buy me one." Rem went to his desk, took a big gulp of his coffee, and set the mug down.

Daniels nudged Manetti's arm. "Let's go."

Manetti flicked his gaze between the two of them. "I guess I could get some more tea." He eyed Crow in her office. "What about Crow?"

"She can get her own food," said Rem, heading to the doors.

Manetti stood and followed Rem and Daniels out of the squad room and down to the cafeteria. Rem got more coffee, a chocolate muffin, and an egg and cheese biscuit. Daniels got some juice and a banana, and Manetti bought some hot tea and an apple.

Once Rem doctored his coffee and joined them at the small table in the cafeteria, he sat and stared at Daniels, wondering how to start this conversation.

Daniels unpeeled his banana and didn't seem to know what to say either.

Manetti dunked his tea bag in his tea and was the first to speak. "You two got me down here. Are you going to tell me what's going on, or are we going to watch each other eat?"

Rem scooted closer to the table. "We need to set some ground rules first."

"What ground rules?" asked Manetti.

"First," said Daniels, "what we're about to tell you stays between us."

"That means no talking to Monk, and no talking to Crow," added Rem.

Manetti's eyes widened. "But he's my partner. And she's my captain."

Rem picked up his biscuit. "Then enjoy your apple, Manetti." He bit into his food.

Daniels cracked his juice, opened it, and took a drink. "You see the basketball game last night?" He set his juice down.

Manetti pursed his lips. "Fine. I hear you. This is just between you and me unless someone's life is in danger. Then I reserve the right to do what I have to do."

Rem glanced at Daniels, who nodded. "We can live with that," said Rem.

"Second," said Daniels. "Full disclosure. What we're about to tell you will put you at risk. It's why we've said nothing up to this point. The more anyone knows, the more dangerous it becomes. Are you okay with that? And it's okay if you're not. Remember, you're about to be a dad."

Manetti paused. "Hell. That's ominous."

"You need to know what you're getting into," said Rem. "If we had a choice, we'd keep you out of this, but that's getting harder to do."

Manetti leaned in. "Obviously, whatever it is means you two are at risk, too."

"You better believe it," said Daniels. "Marjorie and Cain weren't accidents."

Manetti stilled. "They were targeted because of you two?"

"They were," said Daniels. "And you could be too, especially if we bring you in on this. That's why we can't tell anyone."

Manetti took the tea bag out of his tea and set it on a napkin. "I understand. I'm aware of the risks. Like you two, I'm a cop. That means catching the bad guys and risking my life in the process. I signed up for it."

"I'm not sure you signed up for this," said Rem.

"Does this mean taking down someone big?" asked Manetti. "Someone who's hurting people besides you two?"

Daniels set his banana down. "Yes. Someone big."

"With lots of connections," added Rem.

Manetti studied his apple. "I've never been a fan of the big guy beating up the little guy. It's why I took this job." He set his elbows on the table. "Tell me what you know."

Rem took a second and started with Elmwood. He and Daniels took turns telling Manetti how it began with Tex and Tommy coming after them. They'd both sported the same black bird tattoo and were working with Rhonda, the supposed witness they were transporting. They mentioned Lexie Logan's involvement, and how she connected Rhonda to other crimes, including the Star Killer, who branded his victims with stars.

Manetti asked clarifying questions but mostly remained silent until they got to Vera Canmore's murder investigation and Daniels and Rem's suspicions that they'd stumbled upon a secret society whose members were tattooed with the image of a black bird. Manetti was dubious but became more so when he heard that Daniels and Rem had suspected Monk as a potential black bird member.

"Are you serious?" asked Manetti. "Monk? That's ridiculous."

"You and Monk found Vera's body through an anonymous tip," said Daniels. "That wasn't coincidental. And then Monk went off on some crusade to prove that Mikey was a murderer."

"None of that means he's a member of this society," said Manetti. "I haven't seen a tattoo."

"That doesn't mean he doesn't have one." Rem shifted to face Manetti. "You have to see this from our point of view. Monk was pushing hard to arrest Mikey. If he'd been successful, that would have put me in a vulnerable position. Add to that, he got Judge Gunderson to sign that search warrant for my house."

"What do either of those things have to do with this black bird group?"

"If Mikey had been arrested for murder, the society could have used that to get Rem to work for them," said Daniels. "That's their MO. They did it to Beelson, Morgans and Durning."

"How can you be sure of that?" asked Manetti. "Maybe Rhonda's a legitimate sociopath who works for herself."

"Because of Ackerman's box," said Rem.

Manetti furrowed his brow. "What's an Ackerman's box?"

Rem finished his biscuit while Daniels explained Marvin Ackerman, his connection to the society, and the box he gave to Rem and Daniels before blowing himself up.

Manetti sat up. "Nobody else knows about this box?"

"Nobody other than Lexie Logan," said Rem. "And Mikey and Marjorie."

"And Erin," said Daniels.

"Who's Erin?" asked Manetti.

"My half-sister," said Daniels. "My dad had an affair, but that's a different story."

Manetti froze in mid-sip of his tea. "I didn't expect to hear that."

"Believe me," said Daniels. "Neither did I."

"We're trying to keep her out of this," said Rem. "But aren't doing very well."

Daniels groaned. "Tell me about it."

"Why not just tell Lozano or Crow about this box?" asked Manetti.

"The box holds the clues to the black birds." Rem picked at his muffin with his fork. "The problem is, we don't know the players in this game. If we'd told Lozano or Crow, they'd have had to report it. If the wrong person learns we've got the box, it could get us killed."

"They came after Lexie Logan," said Daniels. "They took the box, beat her up and threatened her. If she hadn't made a copy of the contents, we'd have nothing right now."

Manetti scrunched his face. "Wait a minute." He huffed and ran his hands over his face. "Are you telling me that cops are black bird members? That's why you suspected Monk?"

"It's way bigger than that." Rem took a bite of his muffin and sipped some coffee.

"How much bigger?" asked Manetti. "And how do you know?"

Daniels wiped his fingers on a napkin. "After going through Ackerman's information, we learned he created a file of members, which he'd hidden. Lexie studied Ackerman's notes and did some digging..."

"Literally," said Rem.

"...and she found the file."

Manetti widened his eyes. "You have the list of members?"

Rem nodded. "We do."

Manetti looked around, leaned in, and spoke softly. "Isn't that all you need? Why not go public?"

"It's not that simple," added Rem.

"A name on a piece of paper isn't enough," said Daniels. "We need to determine who these people are, how they're involved, and get them to talk."

"All while ensuring no one in the society knows we have this list. If they were to find out..." Rem stabbed another piece of muffin with his fork. "...they'd come after it." He ate the bite.

Manetti stared off as if trying to assimilate the information. He shook his head. "Where do Cain and Marjorie fit into all of this? Why go after them?"

Daniels paused as a uniformed officer passed the table. "Cain was a member of the black birds."

"They recruited him, likely to get to me." Losing interest in the muffin, Rem set his fork down.

Manetti pointed. "I remember. He had a tattoo. It was on the autopsy report."

"They used Cain to get Marjorie out of our house," said Daniels. "Rhonda followed and caused the accident."

"And Tex killed Cain to keep him from talking," added Rem.

Manetti narrowed his eyes. "All that to get to you two? But why?"

Rem glanced at Daniels. "We suspect the main reason was to drive a wedge between us."

"But also to hurt us," replied Daniels. "Whoever runs the black birds holds a grudge, and they're making it very clear they don't like us."

"Which is why we're reluctant to bring anyone else into this mess," said Rem. "There's no telling how far these people will go."

"Or how far up the ladder these members have climbed." Daniels hesitated. "Judge Gunderson was on the list."

Manetti dropped his jaw.

"So are Beelson, Morgans, and Durning, but we suspect they were listed as victims, not members." Rem wiped his mouth with a napkin.

Daniels tossed his banana peel into a nearby trashcan. "Barbara Ingram, a partner at the law firm CIW, where Durning worked, is also on the list."

"And so is Victor D'Mato, the cult leader who came after me," replied Rem.

Daniels took a drink of his juice. "The good news is Monk wasn't named, and neither was Chief Patterson."

Manetti's cheeks darkened. "Patterson? You suspected the chief of police?"

Rem lowered his voice. "He's friends with Chogan Crow, city council president...Elsa Crow's father." He waited for that nugget to hit Manetti.

Manetti cursed, which he rarely did. "Elsa Crow's father is a member?"

"He is," said Daniels. "Elsa wasn't listed, but we can't be certain how much she tells her dad."

"Which is why we have to be careful what we say," said Rem.

Manetti gripped his mug of tea. "So Crow knows nothing about this?"

"When she became captain, we told her about our suspicions regarding the society," said Daniels, "but only because Lozano knew about it, and she'd read his notes. But she discounted it. Told us we were over-blowing the whole thing."

"What we can't be sure of, though," added Rem, "is whether she's doing that to protect her father. We don't know how much to trust her. With Chogan Crow's influence, Patterson could have put Crow's daughter in Lozano's place to keep an eye on us."

Manetti rubbed his head as if trying to assimilate this information. "But how could they have anticipated Lozano's suspension?"

"Because Lozano's been targeted too," said Rem. "Durning was going to go to Lozano and tell him everything. They had to get Lozano out of the way. Plus, he believed us about the black birds. So, removing him was killing two birds with one stone."

Manetti fell back in his seat. "I don't believe this."

"After talking through it," said Daniels, "I have a hard time believing it myself."

Rem wished they were on their way to Bolivia. "You can see now what we've been dealing with."

Manetti tapped on the table. "So, Bertrand was killed by whom? Rhonda? Because she was looking for Jerry Lee, who witnessed her killing Durning?"

"Yes," said Daniels.

"And Tex murdered Cain to keep him from talking to Rem?" asked Manetti. "Then Tex gives the same gun to Rhonda to kill Bertrand?" He squinted. "Why do that?"

Rem didn't say a word. Daniels looked over and raised his brow. Rem realized the implications of telling Manetti that Rem's father's gun, which had been in Rem's closet, had been used to murder Bertrand and Cain. And Damien Rook was using that to blackmail Rem and Daniels into killing Jerry Lee. Asking their friend to keep that level of confidence was risky. "Who knows, Manetti?" asked Rem. "I'm sure we'll find out soon enough."

His face taut, Daniels nodded. "They have a motive for everything."

Manetti raised his hand. "And what's with the dolls? Have you guys seen them before?"

"That's a new wrinkle," said Rem. He tossed his rumpled napkin on the table. "One we haven't seen before."

"Who's your vic from this morning?" asked Manetti.

"Name's Martin Bailey," said Daniels. "His name is on the list, so we assume he is, or was, a member. He'd been shot in the head."

"We found the doll in Bailey's car," said Rem. "With a red piece of felt on its head."

"And Cain's doll had a red piece of felt on its chest, which is where Cain was shot," said Daniels.

Manetti stared in surprise. "So someone's leaving dolls behind as some sort of threat or warning?"

Daniels scratched his jaw. "We can't be sure when Bailey's was left, but Cain must've had his before he was murdered."

Rem flashed back on his cousin, bleeding to death in his arms. He squirmed in his seat. "You sure? Tex could have tossed it in Cain's drawer."

"Why not leave it out in the open?" asked Daniels. "Cain must have gotten it, had no idea what it was, and tossed it in his drawer."

Rem's skin prickled. "If I'd gotten that thing, I'd have thrown it away."

"Either way," said Manetti, "the dolls are obviously a message. Someone knew those men were going to die. The dolls mean something."

Rem thought of Damien Rook. Would he have some reason to create weird dolls to warn or threaten someone with murder? Or to leave them behind as a warning to others? He pressed his palms into his tired eyes. "I have no idea."

"Why now, though?" asked Daniels. "What about the other vics? Like Durning? Or Beelson? Or Morgans?"

"Bertrand didn't get one," added Rem. "Maybe Rhonda's not a fan of dolls."

"Bertrand's an exception," said Daniels. "He got killed for protecting Jerry. Not because of some black bird slight."

"How do you know the others didn't get one?" Manetti straightened. "Monk and I didn't think twice about the one in Cain's drawer. How do you know that didn't happen with Durning or the others?"

Rem considered that. There hadn't been a doll at any of the crime scenes, but that didn't mean they didn't receive one at home, especially if they'd been sent to the victim before the crime. "That's a great point, Manetti."

"We need to check that out," said Daniels.

"What do you want me to do in the meantime?" asked Manetti. "If I can't tell Monk any of this, how do I steer him away from the obvious questions?"

"Tell him whatever you want," said Rem. "We can suggest there's a bad guy behind all this. Just don't mention the black birds."

Manetti drank some tea and set his cup down. "You two still think Monk could be a member?"

"His name wasn't listed, so that's a good sign." Daniels recapped his juice.

"I'm glad to hear that," replied Manetti. "And for what it's worth, I don't think he is. I know he can be intense, but that doesn't make him evil."

Rem recalled almost coming to blows with Monk. "I hope you're right, but I still don't trust him." He thought of another name. "You know who else was on that list? Winnie."

Manetti's expression tightened. "Margaret Redstone's accomplice?"

"And the man who killed Vera Canmore," added Daniels. "The one Mikey saw at the grove, smoking a cigarette and wearing a mask."

"He's a member too?" Manetti's grip tightened around his cup.

Rem nodded. "He is. Along with Rhonda. She was listed too."

Manetti's tone sharpened. "I'd love to get that guy."

"Join the club," said Rem.

Daniels eyed his watch. "We should head upstairs before Crow comes calling."

"You okay, Manetti?" asked Rem. "We dropped a lot on you."

Manetti stared at his apple, which he hadn't touched. "I'm okay. I just wish I knew what to do next, or how to help you guys."

"We'll keep you up to date as we learn things," said Daniels, "but for now, all we can do is keep researching those names. And dig deeper into Martin Bailey. Hopefully, his death will lead us in the right direction."

Rem squeezed his temples. "God. Let's hope."

"You need help with that, let me know." Manetti stood. "I need to return to Cain's and get that doll."

Rem looked up. "His apartment is still a crime scene?"

Manetti tossed the tea bag and napkin in the trash. "I didn't want to release it just yet. I was worried we were missing something. The landlord's screaming, but he'll get over it."

"You've got good instincts," replied Daniels.

"Let's hope I'm just as good at lying," said Manetti. "It's never been my strong suit."

"You'll be fine," said Rem. "You just need practice."

Manetti dropped his apple into his jacket pocket. "How much practice have you two had?"

Daniels and Rem looked at each other, and Rem sighed. "More than enough, Manetti." He pushed back his empty coffee cup. "More than enough."

Manetti paused. "That's what I'm trying to avoid." He picked up his tea. "I'll see you guys later. And thanks for filling me in. I appreciate it."

"Don't thank us yet," said Daniels. "Let's get these guys and stay alive at the same time. Then you can thank us."

Manetti stared for a second, nodded, turned and left.

Chapter Six

FRANK MONK SAT AT the small dining table in the kitchen and watched Rhonda pace. It was his first time to see her since Bertrand's death and Jerry Lee's second escape. He took a long drag of his cigarette and tapped the ashes into a paper cup. "I don't know why you're still so upset."

She stopped pacing and faced him with a glare. "I got replaced. If this happened to you, how would you feel?"

He shrugged. "Pissed, of course. Nobody likes to be replaced. But I wouldn't dwell on it." He took another puff of his cigarette. "What you need to do is look for the diamonds in the coal. You look hard enough, you'll find one."

"Stop being so cryptic." She put her hands on her hips. "And don't act like you weren't a part of this decision."

He chuckled. "I wasn't. You know how it goes with him. He decides and discusses his decisions later."

"I thought you two were partners." She scoffed. "Obviously, that's what *you* think. Not him."

Monk bristled at the implication. "Listen, honey. The secret to Damien Rook is to let him get his rocks off by allowing him some leeway. Then, when he screws up, he always comes back to me to figure it out. This whole thing with him getting Daniels and Remalla to kill Jerry Lee? That's going to blow up in his face. And when he realizes that, I'll suggest he return to the reliable killer standing in the wings. You."

"He's not going to do that. He's lost faith in me." She tossed out a hand and raised her voice. "Because of this stupid Caruso kid." She paced again. "I can't believe he got away from me in that pawn shop."

"Shit happens, baby." Monk tapped more ashes into the cup. "But we can use this to our advantage. Let Rook get his jollies by dragging Daniels and Rem around by the balls. While he's doing that, it keeps him out of my hair and gives me time to stir dissension among the group."

She stopped pacing again and leaned against the kitchen counter. "I don't think you should underestimate him. Based on what you've told me, he's got allies that are way more formidable than you."

"And as soon as those allies realize he's nuttier than a bag of almonds, I'll make my move."

"He's a powerful man."

"Powerful men get overconfident, and he's zoomed past overconfidence and is settling comfortably into arrogance. Plus..." Monk shook his head. "There's something else going on with him." He thought back on his last meeting with Rook, when they'd argued about how best to handle Daniels and Remalla. Rook held a grudge against the detectives that Monk had yet to decipher, but since he had his own grudge, he'd gone along with Rook's decisions. Until the plan had changed and Rook had kept them alive. Monk didn't mind messing with the detectives' heads a little, but at some point, you had to make your move.

Rook had chosen to keep stringing them along by blackmailing them into becoming assassins. Rook's little buddy, Tyson Croft, who Daniels and Rem had nicknamed Tex, had become Rook's right-hand man, and, much to Monk's annoyance, Rook had used Croft to do his latest dirty work. Monk and Rhonda had worked together to arrange Marjorie's accident, but Croft had stolen Remalla's gun, arranged for Daniels' debt to be paid, and had killed Cain, all without consulting Monk.

Monk had come close to communicating his anger to Rook about Croft becoming Rook's go-to guy, but as he'd told Rhonda, sometimes it was better to let the action play out and then determine how to benefit from it.

Rhonda pulled out a chair and sat at the table. "You've mentioned that before. What's going on with him?"

Monk stubbed out his cigarette in the paper cup. "He's been playing with his own medicine."

Rhonda frowned. "Is this that drug thing you've mentioned before? That Rook's supposedly created?" She pulled a fresh cigarette from the pack. "I think he's touched in the head."

"He's touched all right. I think he's been sampling the goods."

"How do you know? The man controls major companies and influential people. What does he need a drug for?"

Monk picked up his lighter and flicked it on. "Men like him get bored. They need new projects. This one has been going on since my days in the cult." He held the lighter out and lit Rhonda's cigarette.

"That long?" She puffed on the cigarette and sat back. "What's the hold-up?"

"He's been working with someone he met through D'Mato." He recalled meeting D'Mato's terrifying friend, who'd been an enormous influence on D'Mato and the sole reason he'd started the cult. It was one of the few times Monk had felt insignificant. It was not a memory he relished.

"Victor D'Mato? That lunatic? From what I've heard, he was crazier than Rook."

"Crazy like a fox." Monk thought back on those days. "I learned a lot from him about how to control people. He and Rook thought they were going to live forever and take over the world. But D'Mato got cocky, and look where it got him." He held out his hand, and Rhonda handed him the lit cigarette. "Which is exactly where Rook's headed. It's just taking longer."

Rhonda studied him. "You mean the natives are restless?"

"Restless is a good word." Monk puffed the cigarette and blew out smoke. "And I plan to be there when it all falls apart."

"What about this supposed drug?"

Monk smirked. "If it's what Rook claims it is, then who knows?" He smiled. "You and I might become kingpins."

"I'm much better at murder. And I don't like drugs."

"Neither do I, but they serve a purpose." He leaned against the table. "So we sit back, let Rook play his games, and when his plans fail, his mind deteriorates, and his supporters scatter, we make our move."

She leaned in too. "What move is that?"

Monk laughed, leaned up, and kissed her. "Total annihilation, baby." He sat back and sighed. "Total annihilation."

· · • • • · • • · ·

Rem and Daniels watched Manetti leave, and Daniels turned back toward Rem. "You think we did the right thing?"

Rem hated to imagine what might happen if they hadn't. "I don't know. We went with our gut. When that stops working, we're in trouble." Planning to get a refill, Rem eyed the coffee machine. "I just hope he can keep it to himself. I'm worried he'll tell Monk."

"He said he wouldn't."

"He also said he didn't like to lie."

Daniels leaned back in his seat. "I guess we'll find out soon enough."

Rem stood to refill his coffee. "Be right back."

"Get me one too, will ya?" Daniels rubbed his eyes. "I could use it."

"Sure thing." Still thinking about Manetti, Rem headed to the register and purchased a cup of coffee for Daniels. He grabbed a fresh cup, filled it with coffee, refilled his cup, and doctored it. He brought both cups back to the table and gave the black coffee to Daniels.

"Thank you." Daniels stifled a yawn and took the coffee. "You think we should have told Manetti about Rook's plans for us?"

Rem sat at the table. "Hell no. It's going to be hard enough for him as it is. He can handle a secret society, but throw in that my gun was used to kill Bertrand and Cain? That may be more than he's ready for. For all we know, he could have arrested me."

"Manetti wouldn't do that."

"You sure?"

Daniels hesitated. "There's no point in arresting you until he finds the gun and can prove it belongs to you. He'd definitely question you, though, and Monk…"

"Monk would start shooting darts at me."

"And Crow would likely suspend you. Me too." He shook his head. "Maybe it is better we keep Rook to ourselves."

"At least until we figure out what happens next. If we get in a pickle, we can bring Manetti in."

Daniels smirked. "I'd say we're already *in* a pickle. How much worse can it get?"

"You really want me to answer that?" Rem sipped some coffee.

"No." He drank some coffee, too. "Speaking of pickles, we need to discuss a few things."

Rem could imagine what they might be. "Probably more than a few."

"Now that some time's passed, we need to contact Lexie. Find out what progress she's made with the list. Since Rook is unconcerned about the box and its contents, I think it's probably safe to communicate with her."

"Should be. Especially since he thinks we're under his thumb and wouldn't dare go against him."

"That's what I was thinking." He swirled the coffee in his cup. "You want to tell her about the gun?"

Rem blew on his coffee. "Let's decide that when we see her."

Daniels paused. "And Erin wants to help, too."

Rem tensed at the suggestion.

"Don't get upset. I haven't done anything yet. I know how pissed you got the last time I didn't talk to you."

"What does she want to do?"

"Help with the list."

Rem narrowed his eyes. "You sure about that? I thought you wanted to keep her out of this."

"I do, but she's determined and stubborn."

"Both Daniels traits with which I am familiar."

"I figure I can give her a couple of names. See what she comes up with."

Rem hesitated.

"She's good with computers, Rem. Better than us, at least. I figure it can't hurt."

"She gets caught, it can hurt plenty."

"Look how well she handled decrypting Ackerman's file." He leaned in. "She knows what's at stake, and I trust her. Don't you?"

Rem heard a laugh and eyed a smiling couple at a nearby table. He envied them. "For someone who was trying so hard to protect her, you've done quite a U-turn."

"Only because I think this is as low risk as it can get. All she has to do is check names and let me know what she finds. With Cain—" He stopped.

Rem shot him a guarded look. "...out of the picture?"

Daniels slumped. "Sorry. I didn't mean it to sound flippant. I only meant that her connection to Cain, which is what made it dangerous for her, is no longer an issue. The black birds shouldn't even have her on their radar."

"She's still your sister. That puts her on the radar. You heard what Rook said. She and Lexie are targets."

"Only to threaten us. As long as that list remains a secret, no one will suspect they're researching it."

Rem picked at the side of his coffee cup. Cain's last phone call to him, where Cain begged Rem for his help, echoed in his mind. "If you say so."

Daniels studied Rem with a gaze that told Rem his partner's mind was whirling. Daniels scooted closer to the table. "What's going on with you?"

Rem almost chuckled. "Seriously? After the last few weeks? What isn't going on with me?"

"I get all that. But you blew up at Manetti, and you haven't been yourself." Rem started to respond, but Daniels raised his hand. "I know what you're going to say. That you're fine. You're tired and have a lot on your mind. That Rook's blackmail is messing with your head, and there are a lot of unknowns in front of us. I understand. I feel the same. But I also know you're having a hard time with Cain's death."

Rem felt the uncomfortable constriction in his chest. "I don't know why everyone's worried about me. Mikey said the same thing this morning. I'm not the only person who lost someone, you know? You and Marjorie lost your child."

"We did, and it's heartbreaking and tragic, and yes, we're grieving, but Rem, you knew Cain his whole life. He idolized you growing up. I know you two were close before the estrangement, and dare I say it, but I suspect you thought of him as the little brother you never had."

Thinking of the past, Rem closed his eyes. "That was a long time ago." When Cain's face popped into his head, he opened his eyes and stared at his coffee cup.

"No, it wasn't. You two may have been mad at each other, but the bond was still there. And now the guilt is eating you up."

"It's only been a couple of weeks. I'll manage."

"It took you a long time to come to terms with losing Jennie. Maybe you should talk to someone."

The anger bubbled up. "I've dealt with enough shrinks to last me a lifetime. Cut me some slack, will you? I'm fine. I just need time." He cursed and lowered his voice. "And getting Rook off our backs wouldn't hurt either."

Daniels' stare intensified, and Rem realized he'd lost it again.

Daniels shifted in his chair. "You forget who you're talking to. I can deal with your anger. It doesn't faze me. But this whole 'I'm fine,' crap. I'm not buying it."

Rem didn't answer.

"I'll give you time if that's what you say you need. Let's handle Rook first, but at some point, you're going to have to deal with Cain and the mind games his death is causing. Because until you do, it's only going to get bigger and eventually, you'll blow."

Rem's stomach churned. "Well, if Rook gets his way and ultimately kills us, then I won't have to worry about it, will I?"

"That's not the healthiest way to look at it."

"But we can't rule it out, can we?"

"Rem—"

"I know what you're trying to say, Daniels." He met his friend's gaze. "I know my mind isn't right about Cain. I'm pissed, and I've got nowhere to direct it other than the people around me. I know that's not fair, but right now, the best way for me to deal with it is to focus on the job, okay?" He paused. "If we can bring down Rook and Tex, and the whole damn rest of the black birds, that will go a long way toward making me feel better." He recalled Cain asking him for his forgiveness. "Cain deserves justice, and I plan to get it for him."

Daniels softened his expression. "You and me both, partner. Just be careful not to let your anger impede that justice. We don't want to do any favors for a defense attorney."

Rem took a slow breath and settled himself. "I hear you." He blinked. "Can we talk about something else now?"

"What else would you like to talk about?"

"Where do you want to start with that crazy doll?"

"Let's dig into Martin Bailey and see what we can learn about him. Then we need to see if Beelson, Morgans, or Durning got a doll."

Rem sipped some coffee. "Maybe their families know something."

"We'll get in touch with Lexie, and I'll talk to Erin. We've got to get through that list."

"And we need to find Rita Vittorio. She was listed with Beelson, Morgans, and Durning, which means if she isn't dead already, she may be soon. She could be a wealth of information."

Daniels pointed. "And don't forget Barbara Ingram. We need to dig into her."

"That sounds like a job for Lexie. Maybe she can dig into Rook, too, if we tell her about him."

"What about Winnie? Any progress in that area?"

Thinking of his conversation with Mikey that morning, Rem moaned.

Daniels raised his brow. "I'm guessing that's a yes?"

"You could say that." Rem rubbed his face, wishing he could crawl into bed and stay there. "Mikey saw Vera at your house."

"Excuse me?"

"Not in a haunted way. Mikey's been trying to contact Vera with Lena and Mason's help. Apparently, it worked. Vera showed herself the day Marjorie came home from the hospital."

"Did Vera say anything?"

"No. She just stood there."

"That doesn't do us much good."

Rem made a snort. "Mikey had a dream last night, though. About Vera. She emphasized to Mikey that Margaret knows Winnie." Rem shook his head. "Now Mikey wants to go see her sister." He scoffed. "Can you believe that?"

Daniels picked up his coffee cup. "Is that such a bad idea?" He drank from the cup.

Rem gaped at his partner. "You too?"

"Margaret can identify Winnie. That's huge. I know she's psychotic, but somebody should ask her about it. And let's not forget D'Mato's role in all of this. Maybe she knows something about his connection to the black birds."

Rem couldn't believe what he was hearing. "Are you out of your flipping mind? There's no way I'm agreeing to Mikey visiting Margaret. Even if Mason goes with her, which Mikey suggested."

"What if Mason went on his own?"

"I'd consider that, but you know Mikey. This is about Vera, and she wants to be a part of it."

Daniels rested his forearms on the table. "I know it's scary, Rem, but Margaret can't hurt anyone anymore."

"Have you forgotten the last time we talked to her? I almost threw up, and we couldn't get out of there fast enough." He thought back to Margaret's capture. "And she almost killed me and Mikey in my own house."

"The circumstances were different. You were still reeling from Allison's attack and her pregnancy disclosure, and Margaret wasn't where she is now. She's heavily medicated, and certainly not the acid-tongued, aggressive, and vengeful woman from before."

Rem didn't believe that for a second. "Do you want to go visit her?"

Daniels squirmed. "Not particularly, no. But I would if I thought it would help."

"Then maybe it should be me who goes to see her."

Daniels' demeanor shifted. "Absolutely not. You're staying away from that woman."

Rem sat back with satisfaction. "Now you know how I feel about Mikey going. Margaret Redstone is never as helpless as everyone thinks she is. You should know that."

Daniels' shoulders fell. "Point taken."

"Thank you."

"But if Mikey goes, I can join her and Mason too, if that makes you feel better."

Rem couldn't understand why anyone thought seeing Margaret would help. "None of it makes me feel better. You know her. And you three visiting will only feed her. She'll try to use all of you to get to me, and you'll get nothing in return. I appreciate the offer, but no. I don't want anyone to go. Hopefully, I can steer Mikey away from this plan and have a stern talk with Vera about what she's telling my girlfriend."

"Good luck with that." Daniels finished his coffee and tossed his cup into the trash can. "We should head up. I'm surprised Crow hasn't called looking for us."

Rem thought of the burner phone Tex had given him and Daniels. "Speaking of calls, anything from our not so friendly foes?"

Daniels looked around and lowered his voice. "You mean Tex?" He patted his jacket. "The phone's in my pocket."

"You're carrying it with you now?"

"Where do you expect me to keep it? Don't worry. It's on vibrate. If someone calls, no one will know."

Rem looked around too, half expecting someone to be watching them, but saw no one suspicious. "I'm surprised they haven't been in touch, wondering about our progress with Jerry Lee. Rook doesn't strike me as a patient guy."

"Maybe they forgot."

"And maybe Crow will promote us." He thought of another concern. "You know who else has gone quiet? Sammy Caruso."

Daniels ran a hand through his hair with a huff. "What's one more problem to add to the plate?" He paused. "I guess the good news is he didn't threaten us. Just said he'd take matters into his own hands if we didn't find Jerry."

"Our deadline has long since passed, but you know he's not sitting on the sidelines. The question is, what's he been up to?"

"Well, whatever it is, until he shows himself again, we work on what we can." He sat up. "Which means dealing with Rook."

"And finding Jerry Lee."

"We really need to find out why Rook hates us so much. That would—" Daniels widened his eyes and put his hand over his pocket. "The phone. It's vibrating." He pulled out the burner. "Someone's calling."

Rem's heart thumped. "Guess we were right. They're getting anxious."

Daniels took a deep breath and blew out his cheeks. "Here goes nothing." He hit a button and answered. "Hello?"

Rem watched as Daniels listened and said little. After a few seconds, he responded. "It's not that easy. We haven't found him. We need more time." He went quiet again and set his jaw. "Threats aren't necessary. We realize what's at stake." He paused again and then spoke with an edge. "Yeah. I hear you." He hung up and slid the burner back into his pocket. "That was Tex." Daniels' cheeks turned red. "We've got forty-eight hours to kill Jerry, or they'll kill Lexie next."

Shocked, Rem imagined wrapping his fingers around Tex's throat.

Chapter Seven

JERRY LEE LAY CURLED on his side on the narrow cot, listening to the squeaking bedsprings from the floor above him. A woman giggled, a man groaned, the squeaks sped up, became more abrupt and then stopped. The quiet didn't last long, though. He heard footsteps climbing the stairs, more laughter, and what sounded like an argument between two women.

The noises from inside the house had become so familiar, Jerry barely heard them anymore. When he'd first arrived, he'd imagined calling his mom, hearing her joy that he was alive and her telling him to come home. But just as quickly, he'd remember what had happened to Arnie. Watching the video on the TV screen from the basement, he'd witnessed Arnie's shooting.

It had taken Jerry a few seconds to absorb the shock, but when the killer turned toward the basement door, and he'd recognized her as the woman who'd killed Mr. Durning, Jerry jumped into action. As he and Arnie had planned, he grabbed the duffel bag beneath the bed, sprinted over to and up the ladder against the wall, and climbed out of the small window at the top of the basement.

Not looking back, he'd done exactly as Arnie had told him. He'd put on the oversized jacket Arnie had provided, pulled up the hood, slid on a pair of sunglasses, and walked straight to the house about five miles away. He'd stayed off the streets and stuck to the alleys and done his best to avoid people. He'd cried most of the way, knowing that most likely Arnie was dead, and had died protecting Jerry.

Arnie had drilled into him that no matter what happened, Jerry was to keep walking and not stop until he got to the house. And when he got there, to knock and ask for Roseanna.

Jerry had done exactly as Arnie had instructed. When he'd arrived, though, the house had surprised him, considering the neighborhood it was in. It was big and ornate, like one of those Victorian homes Jerry had seen on his drives around the outskirts of Chicago, but those neighborhoods had been much nicer, with sprawling manicured lawns, statues, and fountains.

This house had none of that. The weeds were tall, the grass uncut, and cobwebs hung outside the windows, but Jerry didn't care. He did as Arnie said, wiped his eyes and nose with his sleeve, and knocked.

A woman with short spiky blonde hair and heavy makeup, wearing minimal clothing, had answered. She looked him over with curious eyes. "You're a young one. But cute." She smiled, rested her hand on the doorframe, and smacked her gum. "Who you looking for, handsome?"

"Roseanna."

Her smile fell, and she appraised him. "You in some kind of trouble?"

Jerry didn't know how to respond. "I'm just supposed to ask for Roseanna."

"What's your name?"

A Hispanic woman with long braided hair, wearing big silver earrings and a long flowy dress, emerged from the back. "I'll take it, Becca. You can go."

Becca hesitated. "You sure, Rosie?"

Rosie came to the door. "I wouldn't have said so if I weren't."

Becca smacked her gum. "Okay." With a last glance at Jerry, she walked away.

Rosie regarded him. "What's your name?"

His hands in his pockets, Jerry looked down. "Jerry Lee. Arnie sent me." He half expected her to turn him away and, for a moment, panicked when he wondered what he would do if she did.

She stepped back. "Come in."

Relief bloomed in his gut, and he stepped inside. "Thank you."

She closed the door behind him. "Arnie okay?"

Jerry looked at her as tears sprang to his eyes. She stared for a second, and he detected the slight tension in her body before she nodded. "Follow me."

She'd taken him to a back room beneath the stairs with a cot and a chest of drawers, but no windows. "You can stay in here." She pointed outside the door. "There's a bathroom in the hall, and grab any food you want from the kitchen. Just stay out of the girls' way." She perused him. "Or maybe I should tell them to stay away from you."

He tried to grasp what was going on and where he was. "What girls?"

She smiled. "You'll find out soon enough." She studied him. "You look like you could use some sleep."

"I haven't slept much."

"Get it while you can. Things get busy around here at night, but you'll get used to it. You need anything?"

He shook his head but still didn't understand. "I...I can't pay you."

Rosie paused. "Arnie took care of that. Don't worry about it. You can stay here as long as you like. I'll let the ladies know."

"But...but..." He stammered. "You don't know me...or do you?"

"No. I don't. But I know Arnie. He helped me out when I needed it, and he was a good friend and a regular customer of mine. I owe him. He told me you might stop by, and I told him if you did, I'd help."

Jerry thought of all the trouble he could cause if the killer found him here.

"Arnie just said you would need to stay hidden, and we can do that," she said. "No one needs to know your name. Just say your name is Lee. No one will care. You're not the first I've taken in, and you won't be the last."

Jerry thought about the reward that his mother had offered for his safe return. "Anyone around here watch the news?"

She laughed. "My girls? No."

Jerry Lee slumped with relief.

"But I'd suggest you stay out of sight on evenings and weekends. Those are our busy times. But even if you don't, most of our customers keep to themselves. They don't want to be seen any more than you do. They're far more interested in the ladies."

Jerry Lee was getting the picture of the kind of house Roseanna ran. It's what his grandfather would have called a house of ill repute. "Okay. I will. Thank you."

"You're welcome." She hesitated before leaving. "Arnie told me one thing about you."

"What's that?"

"He said to tell you that you can't stay here forever. At some point, you'll have to make a decision."

"What decision?"

She shrugged. "I don't know. I suppose that's up to you." She patted his arm. "Get some rest."

Rosie walked away, and Jerry had spent the next several days sleeping on the small cot, eating food from the kitchen, and listening to the sounds of the various customers being entertained by the women of the house. The ladies he'd met called him Lee but mainly ignored him and didn't ask questions.

The days weren't terrible, but the nights were awful. He'd replay in his mind what had happened to Arnie and blame himself. Then he'd imagine contacting his mother, but the thought of her getting hurt terrified him. Then he'd think of his grandfather and consider calling him. If anyone could keep Jerry safe, it would be him. But that decision came with a price, for both him and his mom, and Arnie had cautioned him about paying that price. So Jerry had held off.

But now, as the days rolled into nights and back into days again, Jerry recognized Arnie was right. He was going to have to make a choice. He couldn't live like this much longer.

Listening to the sounds of the bedsprings resuming their monotonous squeaking, he seriously considered his last option. Arnold and his grandfather had never trusted cops, but Jerry recalled the visit from the two detectives before Arnie had died. They'd seemed genuinely concerned about Jerry Lee's safety, even though Arnold had balked at involving them.

A sprinkle of hope building, he reached for his duffle bag, opened the pocket, and pulled out the card printed with the name and number of Detective Aaron Remalla. Lying back on the bed, he clutched the card, debating again what to do, before finally falling asleep.

· · · · ● · ● · · ·

Rem knocked on Lexie's apartment door.

Daniels looked up and down the walkway and caught the slats in the window shade next door lowering. Eyes stared back at him. He frowned at the person watching, and the slats closed.

"Who is it?" asked Lexie from behind the door.

"Holmes and Watson," answered Rem.

Lexie opened the door. Her brown hair brushed her shoulders, and she wore her typical jeans, T-shirt and sneakers. "More like Laurel and Hardy." She stepped back. "Come on in."

Daniels followed Rem inside. "Who's the neighbor on this side?" asked Daniels, pointing.

Lexie closed her door. "Lonny."

Daniels recalled meeting Lonny the last time he and Rem had visited. He'd definitely been interested in Lexie and curious about the two men visiting her. "Oh, that guy. I should have known."

"Why?" asked Lexie.

"He was watching us."

"That guy's weird," said Rem. "Why doesn't he just ask you out on a date and stop with all the cloak and dagger stuff?"

Lexie went into her small kitchen. "Who says he didn't?"

"Oh," said Rem, standing on the other side of the counter. "Now I feel sorry for him. Did you let him down easy?"

Lexie opened her fridge. "I told him the truth. My life has no room for a relationship right now." She leaned over. "Water, orange juice, iced tea, or..." She glanced at Rem. "Let me take a wild guess. Coffee."

"You got it," said Rem.

"I'll take orange juice," said Daniels.

Lexie grabbed a bottle of juice and a pitcher of tea and set them on the counter.

"If you told him no, then why does he keep watching you?" asked Daniels.

Lexie grabbed two glasses from a cabinet. "He wasn't watching me. He was watching you." She opened the juice and poured some into a glass. "I don't think he likes you guys." She handed the juice to Daniels. "Imagine that."

Rem grunted. "Tell him to get in line."

Lexie flicked her gaze at Rem and poured herself some tea. "Someone got out on the wrong side of the bed this morning."

Daniels held his juice. "He's grouchy today."

"I'll be much better after a fresh cup of coffee." Rem glanced back at Lexie's dining table, which was covered with papers, notebooks, and folders. Her open laptop sat among the mess. "Looks like you've been busy."

Lexie set her glass of tea down and grabbed the coffeepot. "I've barely slept since you gave me that list of names."

Rem grunted again. "You and me both."

Lexie went to the sink and added water to the pot. She eyed Rem with a somber expression. "I didn't get much of a chance to talk to you at Cain's funeral."

Daniels noted Rem's slight stiffening of the shoulders. "Sorry about that," said Rem. "Daniels and I were thinking it was better to keep our distance. In case you know…"

Lexie turned off the faucet. "They were watching. I get it." She poured the water into the machine.

Daniels didn't recall any conversation with Rem about keeping their distance from anyone. He knew his partner had just preferred to keep to himself.

"I wanted to say how sorry I am about your cousin." Lexie set the empty pot on the burner and grabbed a bag of coffee grounds from the counter. "What happened to him…was awful."

Rem eyed the countertop. "It was…and thank you."

"I met your Captain Lozano," said Lexie. "He's a nice man."

Rem made a snort. "Frank Lozano? Since when?"

Lexie smiled. "Nice to me, at least. He seems to be doing okay considering his suspension."

"He's hanging in there," said Daniels. "He took a few days after the funeral to go to his cabin up at Secret Lake with his wife. Try to take his mind off things."

"I don't blame him." Lexie added a filter to the machine. "Has there been any progress in finding out who murdered Cain?" She scooped grounds into the filter, closed the top of the machine, and flipped it on.

Rem shot a look at Daniels. They hadn't told her about what Cain had said to Rem. "No," said Daniels. "Nothing yet."

"But it obviously had to do with his connection to the black birds, and what happened to Marjorie?" She closed the bag of grounds and returned it to the pantry.

Rem gripped the edge of the counter.

"Yeah," said Daniels. "Something like that."

Lexie leaned against the counter and crossed her arms. "So spill it."

Rem straightened. "Spill what?"

Lexie furrowed her brow. "Why this visit? What's changed?"

The sound of the coffee percolating prevented the deafening silence, but not the added tension. Daniels debated how much to say. "We figured it's time to talk about the list." Daniels determined they would have to tell her everything but didn't see a good place to start.

"Plus, a few other things," replied Rem.

"What other things?" asked Lexie.

"I'm gonna need my coffee before we have that conversation."

Lexie studied Rem. "You look like you may need a shot of whiskey in it."

"That's damn tempting." Rem rubbed his neck.

"Why don't we sit at the table?" asked Daniels. "Get comfortable." He drank some juice and walked over to Lexie's cluttered workspace.

Rem walked over with him. "We haven't been comfortable since before that trip to Elmwood." He pulled out a chair and sat.

Daniels sat beside him, and Lexie, holding her glass of tea, came over and sat in front of her laptop. "Why stop by today? Did something happen?"

That one Daniels could answer. "We've got a new victim. Martin Bailey." He told her about the circumstances of Martin's death.

Lexie sat back in surprise. "A doll? Why do you think that's connected to the black birds?"

Rem told her about the doll found in Cain's desk. "That one had a black feather tucked into a slit on its chest. I doubt that's a coincidence."

Daniels thought of the doll in Bailey's truck. "You know, Bailey's doll had a slit in the front but no feather. I wonder if it fell out."

Rem pursed his lips. "That could be interesting. Especially if we find someone with a black feather floating around nearby."

Lexie leaned forward. "What is the point of the doll? And who's making it?"

"We called the Morgans and Durning families to see if they ever saw a doll," said Rem. "The detective in L.A. is handling Beelson's family. Morgans is a bust. No one can remember a creepy doll. Durning's wife can't remember one either, but we're still waiting to hear from Martha Cravitz, Durning's assistant, to see if she recalls anything."

"Our thought is it's a warning," said Daniels.

Lexie frowned. "So, if you get a doll, that means you're dead?" She paused. "But how does that explain Bailey? Why is it in his car? If he got it early, wouldn't it be in his apartment? Or tossed in his trash?"

"Bailey must have been last minute," added Rem. "There wasn't time to warn him."

"Then why bother with the doll?" asked Lexie.

"We haven't figured that out," said Daniels. "But there must be a reason."

"Maybe Bailey and the doll were a warning to others," added Rem. "A way to say don't do what Bailey did?"

"It's an effective strategy," added Daniels.

Lexie moved a notebook. "You think Rhonda could have done this?"

Daniels shook his head. "Don't think so. This isn't her style. She's more flashy."

"Plus, she likes to brand her victims," added Rem.

"Not always," said Lexie.

Daniels wondered what Lexie would think if he told her he and Rem were the supposed new hitmen who'd replaced Rhonda. He chose not to ask.

Lexie grabbed a blue notebook next to her and opened it. "Who is this Martin Bailey?" She wrote his name at the top of the first clean page. "What's his story?"

"We've learned he worked at the port of San Diego for US Customs and Border Patrol. He was in Operations Support." Rem moved some papers around and sighed. "You got any chips or something?"

Daniels grabbed a paper before it fell off the edge of the table. "Chips? We just had lunch."

"You know me," said Rem. "I think better on a full stomach."

"I'll get some." Lexie stood. "Keep talking." She walked into the kitchen.

Daniels shook his head at Rem's unrelenting appetite. "We're wondering if Bailey's connections could have served a purpose for the group."

"Since his name is on the list," said Rem, "and we assume everyone on that list provides some sort of function or benefit to the group."

"Maybe in exchange for something else," said Daniels. "Either money, or clout, or help of some kind."

Lexie grabbed a bag of potato chips from her pantry. She grabbed a container from the fridge, some napkins, and returned to the table. "Coffee's almost ready." She set the bag of chips on the table and opened the container. "French onion dip."

Rem's eyes brightened for the first time that day. "If Lonny doesn't marry you, then I will." He grabbed a chip and dunked it in the dip.

Daniels smirked. "If I had known it would improve your mood this fast, I would have had this delivered to your desk."

Rem munched on a chip. "I'll expect a delivery tomorrow."

Daniels rolled his eyes.

Lexie reached for a chip. "The question is, why is Bailey in that alley, and why is there a human bone nearby? Plus, what about that strange room with the circle and candle? And that blood? Is it human?"

"We're still waiting to hear from forensics," replied Daniels.

"I mean, this has all the earmarks of some sort of occult practice." She ate her chip. "You think Bailey stumbled onto some sort of ceremony?"

"He was running toward the building. Not away from it." Rem dunked another chip and ate it.

"He was meeting someone in the alley," said Daniels. "He must have realized he was in trouble but couldn't get away."

Lexie swallowed and tapped her jaw. "So, a black bird member who works for customs has a late-night meeting in the rain in the alley of an abandoned building." She squinted. "Where apparently there's been some sort of ceremony." She paused. "A patrol car sees two vehicles, but one gets away before the police arrive." Her eyes widened. "Could Bailey have been delivering the bone or bones?" She sat up. "Maybe for the ceremony?" She typed on her keyboard.

Daniels considered the possibility. "You think the bone, or possibly bones, came from Bailey?"

Lexie typed some more and read the screen. "A friend of mine did a story once on the black market. There's a demand for items used in certain darker practices that you can't get through legal channels over here." She narrowed her eyes at the screen. "Things like animal skins, potions, statues, fabrics, oils, incense..."

"You can get a lot of that stuff here," said Rem.

"Not all of it. Especially if you want it from a certain country." She grimaced. "How about blood, teeth, and bones?"

Rem blanched and stopped chewing. "Seriously?"

"That's pretty dark," said Daniels.

"Why else would that bone be there?" asked Lexie. She closed her laptop. "It sounds like Bailey got something through customs and was delivering it. But whoever met him wanted more than the bones."

"Maybe Bailey wanted a bigger payout," said Daniels, "and threatened to go to the cops."

"That would explain his death and the doll being a warning to others," said Rem. "Don't mess with the big guy."

Lexie stood. "Did you go to Bailey's place of business?" She headed into the kitchen.

"We did this morning," said Rem, resuming his eating. "Didn't learn much, though. And his family is back east. We talked to them, but that didn't help either."

Lexie grabbed a mug and filled it with coffee. "Cream and sugar, right?" she asked.

"And lots of it." Rem ate another chip.

Daniels reached for a chip, too. "How does this whole occult thing fit in with the black birds, though?" He popped the chip into his mouth. "It doesn't make sense."

Rem spoke through a mouthful. "Have you come across anything occult-related in your research of the list?"

Lexie returned with a mug of coffee and set it in front of Rem. "No. I haven't."

"What have you come up with?" asked Daniels.

Lexie sat again. "I wish I could tell you I hit the jackpot, but it's slow going."

"Tell us about it." Rem sipped his coffee and sighed. "It's good. Thanks."

"Any names pop out at you?" asked Daniels.

She dug through some papers and grabbed an open notebook. "A couple." She picked up a pen. "The first is Olivia Nightingale. I recognized the name and wondered if it was the same person."

"Who is she?" asked Daniels.

"I worked for *The Independent* for a while. You familiar with it?"

Daniels nodded. "Yeah. Smaller, local paper?"

"Yes. Olivia Nightingale was an editor while I worked there. She never liked me, and I despised her. She's the reason I left. I looked her up after I saw her name on the list, and guess what? She's since been promoted to editor-in-chief."

"Interesting." Rem dunked another chip in the dip. "You find anything that ties her to the black birds?"

Lexie tapped her pen on the notebook. "Just that *The Independent* has done a series of articles heavily in favor of that new development going in. One of them even featured an interview with Pinnacle Properties, which is overseeing the project. Considering Ackerman worked there, I find that pretty coincidental."

Daniels immediately thought of Rook, who owned Pinnacle, and looked at Rem. "That is coincidental," said Daniels.

Rem swallowed his bite. "So, if this is the right Olivia, she's using the paper to support the development."

"The question is, what is she getting in return?" asked Daniels. "Or is she just an ardent follower who believes in the cause?"

Rem sipped some coffee. "Who else you got pegged?" he asked Lexie.

"The other is Ezra Grimm." Lexie looked up. "You heard of him?"

Daniels didn't recognize the name. "No."

"Remember that big story about Montes Pharmaceuticals?" asked Lexie. "When they were accused of manufacturing and testing drugs on patients in rehab facilities without their consent? And some died? Ruben Montes, the wealthy philanthropist who left the family business, died not too long ago in Texas."

Daniels dropped his jaw. Mason Redstone, Mikey's brother, had gotten on Montes' bad side after Mason's experience in a rehab facility where the illegal drugs had been tested on fellow patients. His involvement had led to the arrest of Ruben's son, Rain, for murder. When Mason's father had later gone missing in Texas, Mason had immediately suspected Ruben's involvement. He and Mikey had luckily located their father, but not long after, Ruben had been found murdered.

"We've definitely heard of Ruben Montes," said Rem.

"What does Montes have to do with Ezra Grimm?" asked Daniels.

"Grimm is the Montes' cousin and the family attorney. His firm is currently defending the family name in the government's case against them. He's been pretty successful at delaying and putting off all the civil and criminal filings against the business. Ultimately, it's going to catch up to him, but for now, he's giving the government, and the families who are owed restitution for the death of their loved ones, fits. It could take years to get through it all."

Daniels tried to absorb that Ezra Grimm was Montes' cousin. "How would that benefit the black birds?"

Lexie shrugged. "I don't know, but word is Grimm is just as smart and diabolical as Montes and his family."

"Ruben's sister, Gloria, isn't too nice, either," added Rem. "The whole family is dangerous."

"And loaded," said Lexie. "With that kind of money, you could do some damage and put on a lot of pressure. Enough to scare people or influence them." She stared off. "I know you two think this mysterious Dirk on the list is a big player, but could Ezra Grimm be the ringleader?"

Daniels eyed Rem, who fiddled with a chip and didn't say a word. Daniels stared at his glass of juice.

Lexie abruptly sat up. "Okay. That's it. I thought I picked up on something between the two of you. What are you not telling me?"

Daniels cleared his throat. "There's been a few developments." He took a big swig of his drink and set the glass down.

Lexie closed her notebook. "What developments?"

Rem moved some more papers around. "It's a lot."

"When is it ever a little?" she asked. She sat back and crossed her arms. "Is this about Jerry Lee?"

"You could say that," said Daniels.

"Do you know something about Cain and Arnold Bertrand?"

"You could say that too," said Rem.

"Oh, for God's sake. Just tell me."

Daniels glanced at Rem. "You want to, or should I?" asked Daniels.

Rem fell back in his seat. "Hell. Okay. Here goes." He paused and cracked his knuckles. "Cain and Bertrand were killed with a gun from my closet, and Daniels had a hefty personal debt paid off anonymously. Turns out Damien Rook, along with his new sidekick Tex, are blackmailing me and Daniels into killing Jerry Lee Caruso. If we don't do what Rook wants, he's threatening us with prison."

Lexie dropped her jaw. "Are you joking with me?" She paused and scoffed. "Very funny, you two. Can we be serious now?"

Daniels intervened. "How's this for serious? If we don't kill Jerry Lee within forty-eight hours, they're going to kill you next."

Lexie's face went white.

Rem grabbed a chip, ate it, and wiped his fingers on a napkin. "You got anything sweet to eat? I could go for a cookie."

· · • • · • • · ·

Lexie sat in stunned silence. Staring at the detectives, she waited for them to laugh, but they stared back with flat faces. "You're not joking?"

"Not about the cookies," said Rem.

"Or the other thing," replied Daniels. "Damien Rook is the ringleader of the black birds. Not Ezra Grimm."

Lexie, trying to wrap her head around their revelation, stammered. "How...when...did all of this happen?"

Daniels filled her in about Rem's gun, his debt, meeting Tex and Rook, and Rook's plans to recruit them because of some ugly grudge. If they didn't comply, Tex would ensure the gun was found and that Daniels and Rem would be tied to the crimes. Adding to the pressure, Rook had threatened Lexie and Erin as well.

Trying to grasp it all, Lexie held her head. "Wow. I did not see this coming."

"Guess how surprised we were," added Rem.

Lexie rubbed her forehead, trying to think.

"You okay?" asked Daniels.

"Not really." As a reporter, Lexie prided herself on handling the unexpected, but this level of corruption surprised her. "Who else knows about this?"

"The three of us, Mikey and Marjorie," said Rem. "That's it."

Lexie widened her eyes. "Don't you think you should tell someone?"

"Like who?" asked Rem. "Crow? What's she going to do other than arrest us?"

"Her father is a member," added Daniels. "That makes it hard to trust her."

"We told Manetti about the society," said Rem, "but didn't mention Rook and the assassin thing. We figure that may be a bit much for him."

Lexie's mind raced. "Um, forgive me if I'm overreacting, but what the hell do you two plan to do? Jerry Lee is nowhere to be found, and that forty-eight hours won't last long."

"Don't worry," said Rem. "We don't think they'll actually kill you."

"It's a threat," replied Daniels. "Like the doll."

Lexie, perplexed, shook her head. "And Martin Bailey is dead, along with Cain and Bertrand."

Rem glanced at Daniels. "I think she's worried."

Daniels grabbed a chip and dunked it into the dip. "I don't blame her." He ate the chip. "That's good dip."

Lexie couldn't understand how calm they were. Recalling the two men who'd assaulted her and taken Ackerman's box, Lexie stood. "How can you be so cavalier about this? Rook is blackmailing you. He wants you to kill people." She raised her hands. "How do you know he won't expect *you* to kill me?"

Rem raised his brow. "I hadn't considered that."

Lexie bit back a curse. "You need to tell someone. If not Crow, then the FBI." She put her hands on her hips. "Before someone else gets hurt."

"Can't risk it," said Rem. "Rook would plant that gun, and the FBI could end up going after us like they did Lozano. Then where would we be?"

Daniels swallowed his bite. "Plus, someone on that list could be with the FBI." He licked his finger. "Too risky."

"So you're doing this alone?" asked Lexie. "That's crazy."

"We know it looks that way," Daniels swiped some crumbs off his shirt. "And we're not taking it lightly."

"As bad as it seems," said Rem, "there's actually an opportunity here. And we need to use it."

"What opportunity?"

Rem wiped his fingers on a napkin. "Rook wants us to work for him. We figured if we do, and play the part, we can get behind the scenes and find out the players in this society."

"But we have the list of members," said Lexie.

"Which makes this even more ideal," said Daniels. "Rook doesn't know about the list. When we suggested we'd gone through the contents of the box, he ridiculed us. It didn't bother him at all."

"Which means he has no idea the list exists." Rem sat up. "If we can get inside the organization, and put names to faces, and maybe even get them to trust us…"

"We can blow this wide open," said Daniels.

Lexie couldn't believe what she was hearing. "This is suicide. The only way to do any of that is to kill Jerry Lee. How do you plan to accomplish that?"

Rem tossed his napkin on the table. "Daniels and I have been talking. There are ways to fake Jerry's death and convince Rook we did it."

Lexie flapped her arms again. "But you can't find him."

"We have some ideas about that too," said Daniels. "But we have to be careful."

"We can't let Jerry Lee turn himself in," said Rem. "If he goes into custody, this becomes much harder, if not impossible."

"We've got to get to him first," said Daniels. "Before anyone else."

Trying not to think about being dead in the next forty-eight hours, Lexie paced. "How do you plan to do that?"

"After we leave here, we're meeting with Crow," said Daniels. "We have an idea on how to draw Jerry out."

Rem finished his coffee and set his cup down. "We want to use his mother, Patricia." He sat forward. "If Jerry thinks she is in trouble, he'll come running."

"What kind of trouble?" asked Lexie.

"We say she's sick," added Daniels. "And in the hospital."

Lexie sat again and thought about it. "I don't know. That means you're actually going to have to put her in the hospital. Will Patricia go for it?"

"She will if it means finding her son," said Rem.

Lexie tapped one of her notebooks. "Hospitals mean involving lots of people. If Jerry comes out in the open, he could be seen. Maybe turned in. And then you two are screwed."

"You got a better idea?" asked Rem.

Lexie considered another option. She grabbed one of her notebooks and flipped through it. She stopped and pointed to a name and number on the page. "Austin Rieckart. Head of the broadcast news division at a local affiliate. I can call and tell him I have the inside scoop on a big story."

"What story is that?" asked Daniels.

Lexie tapped her jaw. "What if Patricia Caruso had a break-in? The assailants threatened her, demanding to know where Jerry Lee was. They roughed her up, broke things, and then left when she couldn't tell them anything. They warned her not to go to the police, or they'd be back."

There was a brief pause before Rem spoke to Daniels. "Patricia would have to verify that with the news."

"She'd have to make a police report," said Daniels.

"She can make it to us. We can handle that."

"It's a false report."

Rem sighed, but then raised his brow. "Let's bring Crow in on it. We tell her this is the plan. She's been on our ass to find Jerry Lee, and this is a good way to do it."

"She may go for it as long as Patricia's on board." Daniels stared off. "And if Crow tells her father, he should be all for it if he knows Rook's plan to recruit us." He paused. "So the news channel airs the report, and we pray Jerry Lee sees it, or hears about it. He calls Patricia to check on her…"

"…only we're there when she answers." Rem sat back. "It's not bad."

"But what about Captain Crow?" asked Lexie. "She'll know Jerry called in."

"Only if we tell her," said Rem.

"All we need is to talk to Jerry and get him to turn himself over to us, and only us." Daniels' eyes gleamed with a look of hope. "We do that, and we might just survive this."

"And keep Lexie alive," said Rem. "An added bonus."

"It's a good idea, Lex," said Daniels, "and it just might work. Let's just pray Jerry's watching the news."

"In the meantime, go stay with your mom," replied Rem. "And keep the alarm turned on."

Lexie groaned at the thought of staying with her overbearing mother. "I think I dread that more than the death threat."

"If we really thought they'd follow through," said Daniels, "we'd tell you to get out of town."

"Which you can do if you want." Rem closed the bag of chips. "No hard feelings."

"If we get to hour forty with no results, we'll make sure you're safe," said Daniels. "Rem and I will risk our lives, but that's by choice. We're not going to risk yours."

Lexie appreciated the sentiment. "Like you said, it's by choice. And I'm not going anywhere."

"We'll see about that at hour forty," said Rem. "None of this is worth your life."

"When it comes to Damien Rook, something tells me nowhere I go is safe." Lexie stood. "So I might as well stick around." She grabbed Rem's coffee cup.

"Is that our cue to leave?" asked Rem.

"No. That's my cue to get you a second cup and get one for me. Only mine will have that shot of whiskey. Besides, I can't kick out the two guys who have to kill someone to protect me." She headed into the kitchen.

"We appreciate that," said Rem. "But I'm jealous of the whiskey shot."

"Me too," said Daniels.

Lexie opened the pantry and pulled out a bag of Oreos. She brought them to the table and set them on top of it. "This should make you feel better."

Rem's eyes rounded. "I can see why Lonny likes you."

"Enjoy 'em, sport," said Daniels. "If this plan doesn't work, you may never eat them again." His cell phone rang. He pulled it out and answered. "Detective Daniels." He listened and glanced at Rem. "Hi, Martha. Thanks for calling me back."

Lexie poured two glasses of milk while Daniels talked on the phone. She brought them to the table.

Rem spoke softly. "That's Martha Cravitz. Durning's assistant."

Lexie nodded, returned to the kitchen, got her coffee and Rem's, and returned to the table.

"You're sure?" Daniels' eyes widened. "When was this?"

"Sounds promising." Rem took his coffee from Lexie and bit into a cookie. "Thanks."

Listening, Lexie sipped from her mug and grabbed a cookie.

"That's great, Martha. That's a huge help. If you remember anything else, please call me." Daniels said his goodbyes and hung up. "Guess what?" He tucked his phone back into his pocket.

"Martha's having a secret affair with Rook," replied Rem.

"She knows all the secrets of the black birds, and she's ready to come clean." Lexie pulled the Oreo apart and ate the insides first.

Daniels stared at them flatly. "Reginald Durning got a weird doll, with buttons for eyes, a black feather on its chest, and a black star on its leg, two weeks before he died."

Rem stopped chewing. "Oh, shit."

Chapter Eight

FINALLY HOME AFTER A long day, Rem sat back on his couch with a groan and laid his head back on the cushions. Mikey had texted, telling him she had stopped for food and would be there soon. Trying not to think, he did the opposite. After his and Daniels' meeting with Lexie, they'd returned to the station, only to learn that Crow had postponed their meeting until the following morning and had left for the day. Frustrated, he and Daniels had debated what to do. Waiting meant losing a news cycle, but going ahead meant jeopardizing their jobs if they didn't clear their plans through Crow first. After talking it over, they decided that one news cycle might be all they'd need, and if Jerry didn't initially get in touch, they'd call Tex and ask for an extension. It was all they could do. In the meantime, Lexie had agreed to stay with her mom until they knew more.

Trying to relax, Rem wondered how Rhonda managed the stress of being an assassin and decided he wasn't suited for it.

Hearing the key in the lock, Rem opened his eyes as Mikey walked in. Carrying a takeout bag, she shut the door and tossed her keys onto the front table.

Rem sat up. "There you are."

She raised the bag. "I stopped at the Italian place on the corner. Got us some lasagna."

Rem's belly rumbled. He stood and walked over to her. "Now I know why I fell in love with you." He gave her a kiss.

She smiled at him. "You fell in love with me because of my intelligence, beauty, and charm."

"That too." He took the bag from her. "I'll get some wine."

"I'll get some plates and silverware."

A few minutes later, after a sip of wine and a bite of lasagna, Rem was feeling better. While they ate, he updated Mikey about his day, and she updated him about hers, and Chester let them know vocally that she was hungry.

After feeding the cat, Mikey sat again. "I talked to Mason."

Rem guessed she was referring to her intention to see Margaret. "What did he say?"

"He was as enthusiastic as you are."

Relieved, Rem sipped some wine.

"I'm still not giving up."

Rem set his glass down. "Believe me. I'm aware." He stabbed some lasagna with his fork. "I'm just not sure why you're so convinced your sister is actually going to help. If anything, she'll mislead you and stir up trouble."

"I know, but I can't ignore Vera's advice. I have to try."

Rem swallowed. "Why does that someone have to be you? Vera didn't tell you to visit Margaret. All she said was, 'Margaret knows.'"

"Well, how else are we going to learn what Margaret knows until someone talks to her?"

He shrugged. "Maybe Mason can go on his own?"

She poked at her food with her fork. "I'm not asking him to do what I should do."

"Exactly." Rem set his fork down. "You've decided that you're the only one who can do this."

She wiped her mouth with her napkin. "Vera's death is on me."

He shifted to face her. "No, it's not. Vera's fate was sealed, no matter what you did or didn't do. Stop blaming yourself."

She knitted her brow. "You should take your own advice."

Understanding, Rem grunted. "It's not the same."

She scoffed. "How is it not the same? You feel responsible for Cain, and you're pretending to be an assassin to find the people who killed him."

"They've done a lot worse than killing Cain."

"So has Margaret."

Rem sighed. "Mikey..." He dropped his napkin on the table. "I understand why you think that, but we don't have a choice. These people could kill me, Daniels, you, Marjorie—"

"And the man who killed Vera is part of that group. He's just as important as—"

"I don't want you to do it," yelled Rem. "I want you to stay as far away from Margaret as possible. I don't care what she has to say." Mikey's eyes flared, and he cursed himself for losing it again. "I'm sorry. I didn't mean to yell."

She sat back. "I'm not some docile girlfriend who asks her boyfriend for permission to do anything."

Rem shoved his plate back. "We're not talking about painting the house, Mikey."

She went quiet and stared at her hands. "How many times have I waited here, worried sick about you? How many times have you risked your life, knowing that you were doing it because you knew it had to be done?"

"That's my job. It's not yours."

"It's not just about the job. It's about doing what's right."

"And if I thought there was a smidgeon of a chance that your sister might actually help, I'd go with you, but you know—"

"Please. Stop telling me what I know."

"Your sister is manipulative and cruel. What are you going to do when she expects something in return? What will you do when she asks about me?"

Her eyes rounded. "I can handle my sister."

"And when she shuts up because you don't comply, what then? Are you going to give her what she wants?"

Mikey stiffened. "I wouldn't do that. And you have no idea what could happen—"

"She tried to kill you, me, and Daniels, and you have the nerve to insinuate that I don't know what might happen?"

She stood and picked up her plate. "Stop talking to me like I'm a child."

"Then stop being so naïve."

Mikey put her plate into the sink. "I'm doing what I think is best." She rested her hands on the edge of the counter and stared out the kitchen window.

"For both of us." She looked back at him. "It's what you tell me you do every day, including this whole assassin thing. And yet, I'm supposed to accept that, whether I like it or not."

Rem stood too. "Do you think that if Daniels and I had been offered a different choice, that we wouldn't have taken it? They have my gun, Mikey. Would you prefer I go to prison?"

"I get it, but I sure as hell don't have to like it. Don't you see that's exactly what I'm asking of you?"

"You're not risking incarceration if you don't visit Margaret."

She put her hand on her hip. "Maybe not prison, but this isn't just about Vera. It's about you too. The man who killed Vera is involved in this secret organization. Don't tell me the stakes aren't as high as yours."

"And all of you have suffered enough." Rem picked up his plate and brought it to the sink. "I've already lost Cain, and Daniels lost his baby, and almost Marjorie. Don't ask me to be okay with risking you too."

"I can't just sit on the sidelines when there is a genuine opportunity to learn something that might help." Her voice softened. "Don't you think I want to protect you the way you want to protect me?"

"I don't want you to protect me." All his fears fired at once. "I've already lost one girlfriend. You think I want to lose another?" Wishing she could understand, he turned away, flipped on the faucet, and, even though they had a dishwasher, started scrubbing the plates with a sponge.

Mikey didn't respond, and after a pause, she came up beside him and watched him clean the dishes. "I know this is hard."

Rem kept scrubbing.

"I'm not trying to scare you."

Trying not to make comparisons between Jennie and Mikey, Rem rinsed the plates.

She put her hand on his arm. "We're going to have to deal with this."

He stopped scrubbing. "Do we have to deal with it right now?"

Mikey hesitated. "No. I guess not."

"Can we just see how tomorrow goes with Crow and Jerry Lee? If it works out, you may not even have to see Margaret."

"Now who's being naïve?"

With the events of the day catching up with him, Rem's patience was wearing thin. He finished cleaning the last plate. "Just promise me you won't go see her without telling me first, okay?" He set the plate in the drainer, shut the faucet off and leaned against the edge of the sink.

"I wouldn't do that."

"Good." Fatigued, he turned. "Can we talk about something else?"

"Like what?"

He thought about the closet upstairs. "I know I've put off finishing the closet with Jennie's things. I just want you to know I haven't forgotten."

"It's fine, Rem. You've had other things on your mind. We'll get to the closet, eventually."

"I just wanted you to know that I'm not avoiding it."

"I never thought that."

"Okay." Weary and rubbing his tight shoulders, he headed out of the kitchen. "Then I'm going to jump in the shower."

"Rem, listen—"

He turned back. "I get it, Mikey. You want to go, and I don't want you to. I understand your motivations, and I know you want my blessing, but I can't give it."

Her face fell, and dejected, he turned and left the kitchen.

· · • • • • • • · ·

"So if Durning, Cain, and this Martin Bailey all got dolls, are we assuming Beelson and Morgans did too?" asked Crow. Her stick-straight black hair hung to her jawline and was parted on the side. Her long-sleeved navy blouse was buttoned to her neck, and she wore a navy blazer, and a simple gold necklace with a teardrop-shaped gold pendant.

"That would be a logical assumption," said Daniels, sitting in Crow's office. He was grateful Crow had been available to meet early. If she was supportive of his and Rem's plan, they'd need all the time they could get to enact it.

Rem sat beside him and, after pulling in two more chairs, Manetti and Monk sat on the other side of Rem. "We're guessing Beelson and Morgans must have tossed theirs," said Rem. "Martha Cravitz said she opened the box with the doll and showed it to Durning. He thought it was some sort of joke and told her to throw it out, which she did. She didn't remember the doll until we asked her about it."

Crow chewed on the end of her pen. "So the Star Killer has some connection to your cousin, Cain, and Martin Bailey?"

"Whoever sent the dolls may not have been the killer," said Manetti.

"But the sender knew the recipients were on the hit list," said Monk. "Which suggests two people are involved. Maybe the sender is directing the killer."

Elsa Crow shot a look at Rem and Daniels. "You two initially thought your former witness, Rhonda, was the Star Killer. You still think that?"

"We still think Rhonda did the Star killings, and she's certainly capable of killing someone without branding them," said Rem. "We suspect she killed Bertrand. But she didn't kill Cain, and I doubt she killed Bailey."

"Cain told Rem before he died that Tex shot him," said Daniels. "Our guess is Tex killed Bailey too."

"So, according to your theory, Rhonda and this so-called Tex are working together?" asked Monk.

"So-called?" asked Rem.

"You're the only two who have seen him," said Monk. "And you don't even know his real name."

Rem shifted toward Monk. "My cousin told me Tex shot him. Are you calling us both liars?"

"I'm simply stating the facts," replied Monk. "No one else can verify anything about this Tex, or what Cain said to you."

"Rem wouldn't lie," added Manetti. "If he says Cain told him Tex is responsible, then he is."

"I'd feel more comfortable if we had more than just these two," Monk waved his hand at Daniels and Rem, "claiming this Tex is involved." He spoke to Crow. "Wouldn't you?"

Daniels sat up straight. "Listen, Monk. Why don't you take your comfort level and shove it up your—"

"That's enough," said Crow. "Just cool your jets, Daniels." She swiped back a piece of her hair. "No one's accusing you or Rem of anything."

"Doesn't sound like it," said Rem.

Crow stared at a pile of papers on her desk and moved a folder to another pile. "This connection between your cases is baffling. Who is sending these dolls and why? And why didn't Bertrand get one?"

"Bertrand was protecting Jerry Lee," said Rem. "He was never part of whatever Beelson, Morgans, Durning, and now Cain and Bailey were involved in."

"You think Cain and Bailey knew something about what happened to the other three?" asked Crow. "And that got them killed?"

Daniels glanced at Manetti, almost hearing his mind race, and wondered what Manetti would say. While it was clear the black birds were the connection, Elsa Crow had made it clear she thought that the secret society theory was ludicrous. But whether she'd decided that based on her father's involvement was unknown.

"Rem said Cain was caught up in something," replied Manetti. "But he wouldn't tell Rem what."

"He was about to," said Rem, "but whoever these people are, they got to him first."

"And Martin Bailey may have been a last-minute decision," added Daniels. "He pissed someone off and got killed for it."

"But now we have a finger bone found at the scene and the smelly room with the circle and candle in it." Rem grimaced. "None of that makes sense, either."

"Sounds like kids having some sort of party in an abandoned building," said Monk. "It may have nothing to do with Bailey at all."

"I might agree with you, Monk, which would be a first," said Rem, "but when you add the weird voodoo doll into the equation, we can't dismiss any of it."

Crow leaned back in her chair, and Daniels thought of Lozano. He wished his captain were there. "Anything on the building itself?" asked Crow.

"It was bought by Pinnacle Properties six months ago," said Daniels. "It's scheduled to be demolished next month to make way for the new development. Prints were found inside and on the door, but so far none of them point to anyone sinister. We're still checking."

"Where are we on forensics?" asked Crow.

"The bone came from the finger of an older woman of European descent," said Rem. "The bone itself is old, so this woman didn't die recently."

"And the blood in the circle is goat's blood," said Daniels. "Not human."

"They've got the doll I took from Cain's desk," said Manetti. "So far, they've found nothing on it other than what was in the drawer."

"Same with the Bailey doll," said Daniels. "No hair or fibers. Not even Bailey's."

"And no black feather either," said Rem. "The Cain and Durning dolls had black feathers tucked into a slit in the doll's chests, which suggests the feather in Bailey's doll may have fallen out."

Monk lowered his voice and spoke into his hand. "Be on the lookout for a black feather."

"C'mon, Monk," said Manetti.

"I'm just pointing out the obvious," said Monk. "That's not much of a lead."

"It's better than nothing, which is all you've contributed, Monk." Rem bounced his knee with agitation.

Monk's face tightened. "Maybe when you tell us what really happened when you found Cain and he supposedly died in your arms, I can be of more help."

Daniels stood at the same time as Rem. He grabbed Rem's arm as Rem took a step toward Monk, who also stood. Manetti jumped up and got between Rem and Monk.

"You son-of-a-bitch," snarled Rem.

Monk snarled back. "Just callin' it as I see it."

Manetti turned toward his partner. "Ease up, Monk."

Crow smacked her hand on her desk. "That is enough," she yelled.

Daniels thought so, too. "Then tell him to back off and have a little respect for his colleagues," he said. Still holding Rem's arm to keep him from lunging at Monk, he glared at Monk. "Especially ones he works with."

Rem and Monk continued to glower at each other.

Crow sat up. "Monk. Stop being an asshole. Manetti, get your partner out of here. Keep working on that doll and dig into Cain's background. Talk to his family again, too. Push a little harder and see what falls out." She eyed Rem and Daniels. "And you two. Have a seat."

Manetti pulled Monk toward the door. Monk reluctantly went with him. "Does pushing a little harder include Detective Remalla, Captain?" asked Monk. "I have some questions for him."

"If you need to question him again, then do it," said Crow. "Just ask nicely or don't expect much cooperation."

Surprised she hadn't thrown Rem under the bus, Daniels glared at Monk. "Think you can handle that, Monk?"

Monk directed his gaze at Daniels. "I can handle a lot more than you and your partner can imagine."

Rem raised his voice. "I'm imagining you getting out of this office a lot faster."

Manetti opened the door and pulled on his partner. "C'mon, Monk. You've caused enough trouble for today."

With a last glare, Monk followed Manetti out, and Manetti closed the door behind them.

"God, I hate that guy," said Rem.

"Oh, I don't know," said Daniels with annoyance. He stared out the glass as Manetti and Monk returned to their desks. "With a lot of spit and polish and a year-long training in manners, he might be bearable."

"What about the asshole attitude?" asked Rem.

Daniels faced Rem. "I think that's a lost cause."

Crow huffed. "So is working with all this testosterone." She stretched her neck. "You two sit."

Rem and Daniels returned to their seats but didn't say anything.

Crow studied them. "Where are you on Durning's murder?"

Daniels picked a piece of lint off his pants. "Same place we are with Morgans."

She pursed her lips. "What about Jerry Lee? Any progress?"

Rem glanced at Daniels, and Daniels' heart rate ticked up. "Nothing," said Daniels.

"What about his grandfather, Sammy? Any interference from him?" Crow had since learned that Jerry Lee was Sammy Caruso's grandson.

"None so far." Rem knocked on his armrest. "Knock on wood."

Crow leaned back and crossed her arms. "You think Jerry contacted him and Sammy picked him up? And that's why you can't find him?"

Daniels shook his head. "No. Because if Sammy had Jerry, he'd tell Patricia, Jerry's mom. He wouldn't leave her behind. She'd want to be with her son."

"Could she be lying?" asked Crow. "To protect Jerry?"

"Possible but doubtful," said Rem. "She doesn't want her father involved, with good reason. He brings a whole unknown element to the table she'd just as soon not deal with."

"Minds can change when your son's life is at risk," said Crow.

"And if Sammy had Jerry, she'd be with him," said Daniels. "She wouldn't leave Jerry alone with his grandfather."

Crow pushed up in her seat. She set her elbows on the desk. "You two still following this secret society theory?"

Daniels didn't answer, and Rem poked at a hole in the knee of his jeans.

She narrowed her eyes. "You are, aren't you?"

"We can't rule it out," said Daniels.

"You got evidence to prove it?" asked Crow.

Daniels thought of the list of names and the contents of Ackerman's box and wondered what Crow was searching for. The truth? Or proof of her father's involvement? Was she protecting him? Or legitimately curious about the black bird theory?

"Nothing concrete yet," said Rem.

Crow hesitated as if gauging their honesty. "Well, until you do, I can't do much to help, and you know my thoughts about it. Until you can provide someone or something to back up your theory, it's just a theory." She regarded Rem. "And like it or not, Remalla. Monk is right. We've got no evidence other than you two that this man, Tex, even exists."

"He exists, Captain," said Daniels.

"He killed Cain," said Rem, his voice taut. "And he'll pay for what he did."

"Just like Rhonda," added Daniels, thinking of Marjorie.

"Just make sure the two of you don't do something stupid. I don't need vigilantes. This department has enough struggles as it is, and two cops finding justice on their own time is a stain not easily removed, so keep your noses clean. You got it?"

Daniels thought of his paid debt and Rem's stolen gun. "We got it."

"Monk's a pain in the ass, but so are you guys." Crow leaned back and swiveled in her seat. "I know Lozano put up with a lot from you, but don't expect the same from me."

"Perish the thought," said Rem.

"Anything else you want to enlighten me with?" she asked.

Daniels straightened. It was now or never. "Actually, yes." He paused. "Rem and I had an idea about how to bring Jerry in."

"What's that?"

Rem sat up. "We thought we might use Patricia."

"For what?"

Daniels dove in. "We want to put out a news story that Patricia was attacked by two men who broke into her house and demanded to know Jerry's location. They roughed her up and threatened her not to tell anyone, or they'd be back."

Crow knitted her brow. "Is any of this true?"

"No," said Rem. "But we spoke to Lexie Logan..."

"The reporter?"

"Yes," said Rem. "She said she could contact a news station and let them know the scoop she had on Patricia's attack. If Patricia verified the report and the station broadcasted the story, and if Jerry Lee saw it, he'd call and—"

Crow's face clenched. "Absolutely not."

Her reaction surprised Daniels. "Why not? We want to find Jerry. This is the way to do it."

"What's wrong with it?" asked Rem.

"You want to lie to the news and get Patricia Caruso to back up that lie? Do you know how stupid we would look if the lie were discovered?"

"Who said it would be discovered?" asked Rem.

"And what happens when a pesky reporter wants an update about who broke in and threatened Patricia Caruso? And when Sammy Caruso finds out someone accosted his daughter, what do you think he's going to do? Nothing?"

"If it means finding Jerry Lee, then we can deal with Sammy Caruso, and any pesky reporters," said Daniels.

"Apparently not," said Crow. "Since you're still involving Lexie Logan when I told you to leave her out of this investigation."

"She offered to help," said Rem, his voice rising. "That's it."

"And what happens if Jerry Lee isn't watching the news, and this doesn't work? Or, God forbid, he's already dead. What happens then with this charade?"

Daniels did his best to keep his temper under control. "I think you're overreacting."

Crow scoffed. "And I think you two are under-reacting. You can't do something like this without considering all the implications."

"All the implications you've considered can be handled." Rem bounced his knee again. "Or is your worry more about this coming back on you and making you look bad?"

"If we worried about failure all the time," said Daniels, "we'd never solve a case."

Crow rocked in her seat, but her eyes were like lasers. "Thank you for the advice, detective. I'll take it under consideration."

Daniels bit back a curse. "This is a good idea."

"It will work," added Rem. "Once Jerry hears about his mom, he'll—"

"He'll what?" Crow leaned over her desk. "Call his mother? Want to see her? Don't you think whoever is looking for him will think the same? If that's Rhonda, she'll see the news report too. And she'll be lying in wait for Jerry, just like you two."

"We'll be ready for that," said Daniels. "We might even kill two birds with one stone and catch Rhonda."

Crow made a sarcastic snort. "Rhonda, if she is who you say she is, has been playing you two from the start. You don't think she'll expect that?"

Rem stopped bouncing his knee and gripped the edge of the desk. "Why are you fighting us on this? Don't you want us to find Jerry Lee?"

"Of course I do," she said. "But not like this." She fell back into her seat. "Find a better way." Her jaw tightened. "And leave Lexie Logan out of it."

Daniels sat in stunned silence. "We're just trying to do our jobs."

"And I'm trying to do mine." Crow pulled her chair closer to the desk. "And after that stupid suggestion, I have half a mind to pull you from this investigation."

Rem dropped his jaw. "What for?"

"Because if you're willing to make a false report, lie to a news station and get Patricia to lie too, I have to wonder how far you're willing to go."

Daniels couldn't understand her logic. "Police officers can lie to suspects to get confessions, but we can't do this?"

"Don't compare the two," she said. "You know it's not the same."

Rem stood. "You're making a mistake."

She interlaced her fingers. "By keeping you two on this case? Let's hope not. But you suggest something like that again, and I may change my mind." She pulled a folder off a pile and opened it. "Do better, detectives."

Seeing her study the contents of the folder as if she'd dismissed them, Daniels gritted his teeth.

Rem gaped at her. "If Jerry Lee doesn't survive this, I'm going to say the same to you."

She looked up. "If you do your jobs, then you won't have to."

Daniels raised his hands. "That's what we're trying to do."

"We're done here." Crow returned her attention to her folder. "You two can go."

Flummoxed, Daniels stood for a second in shock, before Rem, shaking his head, walked to the door. Daniels followed, and they left the office.

"Can you believe that?" asked Rem. "Unbelievable."

Frustrated, Daniels walked to his desk. "I don't even know what to say."

Monk, sitting at his desk, looked over. "Trouble in paradise, boys?"

Rem glared at Monk and spoke to Daniels. "Care for a protein bar? My treat."

Daniels glared at Monk, too. "Love one."

Rem headed for the door, and Daniels joined him in the hall outside the squad room. Two officers walked by, and Daniels bobbed his head toward the bathrooms.

Getting the message, Rem walked down the hall and entered the men's restroom. Daniels went in and locked the door behind him.

Rem paced. "Now what do we do?"

Daniels tried to think. "We should never have told her."

"Why didn't she go for it? This is a chance to find Jerry."

"It's a good sign she's not working for the society, or else she'd have been all over it."

"Or, the society isn't making it easy on us."

"Why wouldn't they want it easy? We can't kill him if we can't find him." Daniels leaned against the counter. "Damn it."

Rem stopped pacing. "We could do it without her approval."

"And get pulled from the investigation, or worse, suspended? You want to risk that right now?" He squeezed his temples. "Although she had a point. Rhonda would see the broadcast, and Sammy Caruso would certainly hear about it."

"According to Rook, Rhonda's been pulled off the assignment."

"You really think that would stop her?" asked Daniels. "What better way to get back in the boss' good graces than by killing Jerry before we do?"

Rem groaned. "And make us look like idiots."

His head hurting, Daniels made a mental note to take some aspirin when he got back to his desk. "So much for infiltrating the black birds. At this rate, you and I will be lucky if we end up cellmates."

Rem resumed his pacing and put his hand on his head. "Let's think. There's got to be a way out of this."

"Before or after Lexie, or Erin, or whoever else, winds up dead?"

Rem dropped his hand. "Hey, where's Mr. Positivity?"

"He's in Bolivia, having a margarita, which is where we should be right now."

Rem ran his fingers through his hair. "Okay. Okay. It's not looking good at the moment."

"You think?" Daniels turned, faced the mirror, and studied his reflection. "What the hell are we going to do, Rem?" He let out a long breath. "Maybe Lexie's right. We should go to the FBI."

"You want to take that risk?"

"We have the box and the list of names. It might be enough."

"And unless someone comes forward to testify against Rook, or Tex, or Rhonda, none of it is enough to bring down Rook or his organization. You know that."

"Then we leave it to the FBI. Let them deal with figuring it out."

"And what about my gun and your paid debt? You think the FBI will deal with that? And what about Rook's grudge? We still don't know what that's about. If he's determined, or hell, has an FBI contact on that list, we're screwed."

Daniels realized Rem was right. Talking to the FBI was too great a risk. He turned away from the mirror. "Then what do you want to do?" He looked at his watch. "We have thirty hours left. Should we call Lexie? Tell her to get out of town?"

Rem looked away. "We told her we'd warn her when we got to the twenty-hour mark, so we still have ten hours."

Daniels snorted. "Why isn't your Mr. Positivity with mine in Bolivia?"

After a long pause and a pensive look, Rem leaned a hip against the bathroom counter. He crossed his arms and spoke softly. "After D'Mato took me, and when I was in the rat-infested room, sitting in the pitch dark, listening to the squeaks..." He paused again and took a breath. "...I thought I was going to die."

Daniels instantly went back to the time of Rem's abduction and recalled that horrible small room where D'Mato's cult had held Rem captive. He faced Rem but didn't respond.

Rem cleared his throat. "The only thing that saved me was my telling myself over and over that there was hope. That you would come."

Daniels remembered the shock of seeing Allison Albright straddling Rem and holding the knife to his neck. "And I did."

Rem nodded. "And you did." He laughed softly. "I wish it had been a little sooner..."

Daniels half-smiled. "Better late than never."

"Yeah. Better than dead, at least." He gripped his neck and took another breath. "We just have to have faith, Daniels. No matter how bad it looks, something will turn. It has to."

Daniels dropped his head. "Let's hope that Remalla luck kicks in."

Rem turned and leaned against the counter next to Daniels. "Let's hope." They stood quietly until Rem's phone interrupted the silence.

Rem groaned, pulled out his cell, and eyed the display with a frown. "Who is this?" He answered the phone. "Detective Remalla. This better be good."

Listening, he widened his eyes and knocked his elbow into Daniels' arm. "Jerry Lee Caruso?"

Daniels straightened, uncertain he'd heard right.

"Take it easy," said Rem. "It's okay. I'm glad you called." He listened. "Yes, Jerry. We can help you. You did the right thing." He held his chest and met Daniels' gaze. "Listen to me, Jerry. We can bring you in, but I need you to do exactly as I say."

Closing his eyes, Daniels gave thanks for Remalla's luck.

Chapter Nine

Tyson Croft walked down the narrow pathway overgrown with vines, roots and weeds, heading toward the small, dilapidated guest house at the rear of Damien Rook's property. Rook had a sprawling estate on twenty acres of prime real estate, most of which was well-maintained, but back here, at the far corner of the property, away from prying eyes, Rook had let nature take its course.

When Croft had once asked about the declining section, Rook had bluntly told him to mind his own business. Croft hadn't bothered to ask again until he'd been asked to deliver a package to the small guest house. Surprised someone was staying in the run-down home, Croft had questioned Rook about the guest and why they weren't residing in the main house. Rook had offered him another blunt response—to do his job and stop asking questions.

He'd delivered the package and had been genuinely creeped out by the state of the small house. Enormous trees and their large branches swayed over the walkway and the home itself, creating a shadowy world where little grew in the shade. The windows of the house were dirty and covered with spiderwebs. Weeds sprang up from the rotting slats of wood on the porch, and a mouse ran across the walkway as Croft approached the front door.

Having no interest in whoever was staying there, he placed the small box at the entry, knocked and left. He remembered someone had hung a strange twig-entwined wind chime above the front door, but had wrapped the chimes in fabric, silencing them. The odd creation reminded Croft of the creepy hanging twig structures from the movie *The Blair Witch Project*. And worse, when he'd knocked, he'd heard something from inside, like a low moan or chant.

Not wanting to stick around, he'd left the package, run from the house and breathed a sigh of relief when he'd made it back to the main house.

Now Rook had given him another item to deliver. Croft had almost balked at the errand, but stopped himself. If he wanted to stay in Rook's good graces, and stay one step ahead of Monk, he'd have to do as Rook asked. There was too much at stake to risk his quick climb up the ladder. It had taken some time to reach Monk's level, but now that he was here, Croft wasn't going to relinquish it.

Holding the plastic bag Rook had given him to deliver, Croft headed down the same narrow walkway as the manicured lawn gave way to the overgrown path. Looking back and seeing he was far enough away from the main house, he let his curiosity get the best of him and peeked inside the bag.

Inside was another doll, similar to the one he'd been told to leave with Martin Bailey. Recalling that night, Croft cursed his stupidity. When Rook had heard about how close Croft and Russell had come to getting caught, the spilled bones, and leaving Bailey's body outside the building, Croft had expected a quick demotion. Rook had expressed his outrage at losing the use of the property, the damaging of the bones, and the sloppiness of the execution, but after enduring the verbal assault, Croft had remained in his position. He suspected the reason was that Rook needed him.

Monk could do only so much as a working detective. While his position offered plenty of advantages, it also limited his movements and availability. As a former detective, Croft was accessible to Rook whenever Rook wanted, and Croft's knowledge of and experience with Detectives Daniels and Remalla made him a valuable asset. Plus, he was good with a gun and had no problems using it.

Croft realized he had stiff competition with Monk and his killer girlfriend, Rhonda. But Croft wasn't stupid. He hadn't gotten to where he was without smart planning and stealth. He'd done a good job working with Rhonda in the town of Elmwood. Unfortunately, his friend who'd joined him, who Daniels and Remalla had called Tommy, hadn't made it. That had pissed Croft off. It was one of the main reasons he'd rejoined Rook after paying off his debt with his work in Elmwood. He wanted payback. Plus, the money was good.

And now that he was helping Rook blackmail Remalla and Daniels, he was having even more fun. He didn't know what was driving Rook to destroy those two, but he understood it. They needed to be put in their place. And when Rook tired of his games, Croft would happily kill the detectives, provided Monk didn't get in the way. Monk wanted to kill them as much as Croft did, but Croft was happy to wait until Rook was ready. Monk was less patient, and Croft could sense Monk's frustration.

If Croft played his cards right, after dealing with the detectives, he'd take care of Monk and Rhonda, and when the time was right, handle Rook. It was no secret his boss had shown signs of instability. It was one reason Martin Bailey was dead. Bailey had seen the signs and discussed his observations with other members. Once Rook learned that, Croft knew Bailey had signed his own death warrant.

Croft had no intention of going that route. Rook was a powerful man with powerful enemies and allies. If Croft showed allegiance, and played the game, he'd earn the respect of the other members, and hopefully Rook's trust. The more he knew, the better. And right now, he planned to stay as close to Rook as he could, because Rook had something cooking on the sidelines. Croft didn't know all the details, but just by listening to Rook talk, it was big.

He didn't know what the weird packages, strange dolls, or odd house guest at the back of the property had to do with it, but he planned to find out. If the opportunity presented itself, he could step in if Rook couldn't, and judging by some of Rook's bizarre actions, that opportunity might soon arrive. Croft recognized Monk had sensed the same thing, so it was more important than ever that Croft stick close, pay attention, and prove himself.

Nearing the guest house, he tucked the bizarre doll back into the bag, guessing by its presence that someone else was about to get a deadly delivery. He wondered who and hoped it wasn't him.

Considering the plans for Daniels and Remalla, though, he doubted it. Rook required his help, especially now that the detectives were expected to kill Jerry Lee Caruso. Croft doubted they'd actually do it. They were too strait-laced. So he bided his time, waiting for them to fail, and waiting to see what Rook would do when they did.

Would he want Croft to deliver Remalla's gun and reveal Daniels' paid debt to the authorities? Or would he want Croft to go after the reporter, Lexie Logan, or Daniels' sister, Erin Gerard? The choices were many, and Croft would be happy with any of them.

It had been forty-eight hours since he'd contacted and threatened the detectives. He'd expected a phone call from them, either begging to be let off the hook, or asking for more time. Surprised it hadn't come, he'd waited, relishing the anticipation of their expected failure. Now that the deadline had passed, it was time to call them back and let them know Lexie Logan was next on his list. He expected they'd try to hide her, but with Rook's contacts, she'd eventually be found. Croft even wondered if she'd bother to hide. She was determined enough to stay put and dare him to kill her.

Nearing the run-down house, he slowed his steps and approached with caution.

The wind blowing through the trees gave it an even spookier feel. Storm clouds gathered in the distance, and he heard a rumble of thunder. Hoping to get back before it rained, he walked up to the door, put the bag on the front step, and bumped his head on the ugly chimes with the twisted twigs. Chills ran through him, and he stepped back, rubbing his head. He banged his knuckles on the door and froze when he heard an eerie laugh from inside. Chills blossomed over his skin, and he turned and fled down the walkway.

Getting past the decrepit section, he slowed and breathed a sigh of relief, feeling better after putting some distance between him, the eerie house, and crazy laughter. Recalling the sound, more chills ran through him, and he rubbed his arms.

He jumped when the phone he used to contact the detectives rang. Surprised, he quickly pulled it out. Apparently, they were ready to admit defeat.

Eager to revel in their weakness, he answered. "Your forty-eight hours are up. I assume Lexie Logan has been warned?"

Remalla responded. "Lexie is safe and sound."

Croft raised the side of his lip. "If you think hiding her will help—"

"There's no need for her to hide, Texie boy. Because it's done."

Croft gripped the phone. "Done?"

"Yes. Rook's assignment. It's done."

Croft stopped on the path back to the house. "You're serious?"

"You didn't give us much choice."

"Where? When? I haven't heard anything."

"And you're not going to. We're not stupid. You think we want Sammy Caruso on our ass?"

Croft stood in quiet shock.

"Cat got your tongue?"

Croft found his voice. "We'll want proof."

"We figured, and we can provide it. Where and when?"

Croft thought fast and gave them an address and time to meet.

"I want my weapon back," said Rem. "That's the deal."

"The deal is whatever Rook says it is. Plus, I'm not convinced you actually completed your assignment, and until I am, you get nothing."

"It's done, Tex. We made sure of it. Just make sure Rook knows."

Croft didn't know what to think. Had he underestimated the detectives?

"And Daniels and I want to talk about the future."

Croft frowned. "What future?"

"We'll discuss it at the meet. And don't be late." The phone went dead when Remalla hung up.

Chapter Ten

SITTING AT HIS DESK in the squad room, and watching the clock, Rem bounced his knee.

"Relax," said Daniels. "This is going to work."

Rem picked up his thermos of coffee but was too anxious to drink it. "Looks like Mr. Positivity has returned from Bolivia."

"Now that our plan is coming together, I'm feeling better."

Rem eyed the clock again. "What time should we leave?"

"Two minutes sooner than the last time you asked." Daniels picked up a pen and made a note in his notebook. "Why are you so nervous? You're usually a rock in these situations."

Rem sat up and spoke softly. The squad room was quiet. Manetti and Monk weren't at their desks, and Crow was in a meeting. Other detectives worked quietly around them. "When have we ever been in this situation?"

Daniels stopped writing. "Point taken."

Rem thought back over their last twenty-four hours. After talking to Jerry Lee, he and Daniels had driven to the address Jerry had provided to pick him up. After running the address through the computer, they'd learned that Bertrand had sent Jerry to a house of prostitution. The woman who'd answered the door, named Roseanna, had taken one look at them, pegged them as cops, and become instinctively wary. They'd assured her they weren't there to bust or harass anyone, but to pick up Jerry Lee. After a second, she'd widened the door, and told them to come in. Rem had seen a couple of scantily clad women quickly disappear and another one staring down at them from the second floor, smacking her gum.

Roseanna had looked up at the woman and told her to find Lola and bring her down.

The woman had nodded, popped a bubble, and disappeared.

Roseanne showed them into the living room and told them to wait. A few minutes later, Jerry Lee, carrying a backpack, entered the room. He looked just like a scared twenty-year-old kid who wanted nothing more than to go home. Remalla felt for him. The kid had been through a lot, and it wasn't over yet. Roseanna had left, and Jerry had immediately asked about seeing his mom. They'd sat him down and talked to him about what needed to happen next.

To his credit, Jerry handled it well. Even the part where they'd told him they were going to fake his death in order to save his life. He'd cried a little, especially when they'd told him what had happened to Bertrand, but by the end of the talk, Rem believed Jerry had come to trust them. That part was crucial. Without it, the plan would not work.

Getting up to leave, Rem had seen Roseanna speaking to a woman in the hall by the stairs. The woman was tall and thin, wore heavy makeup and had her long brown hair teased up as high as it would go. She took one look at him and Daniels as they approached, shook her head at Roseanna, and ran up the stairs.

Roseanna watched her leave with a look of frustration.

Jerry walked up to Roseanna and hugged her. "Thank you, Rosie. For everything."

She hugged him back. "Looks like you made your decision."

He pulled back with a sniff. "I did. I think it's the right one."

She patted his shoulder. "They gonna do the right thing by you?"

Jerry nodded. "I think so."

Rosie narrowed her eyes at Daniels and Rem. "You better."

"He's in good hands, Roseanna," said Daniels. "We'll make sure he's safe."

Her gaze flicked between the two of them, and she spoke to Jerry. "Jerry, grab a cookie on your way out. There's some in the kitchen."

"Cookie?" asked Jerry.

Rem got the hint. "Get one for me, too."

Jerry shrugged and walked into the kitchen.

Roseanna returned her attention to Rem and Daniels. "If he's going with you two, I assume you can be trusted?"

Daniels glanced at Rem. "We can." Daniels paused. "But I get the feeling you're not asking about Jerry."

"One of my girls. Lola. The one who just ran upstairs. She had an altercation about six months ago with a customer."

"What kind of altercation?" asked Rem.

"The rough kind. Beat her up. Almost strangled her. When I realized what was going on, I got in there and stopped it. Kicked him out. He was drunk, and probably high. I took her to the hospital and, thankfully, she was okay. It took some persuading to get her to let me call the cops. She finally agreed, and I called. They sent over two young patrol officers, who took one look at the place, and it was obvious what they were thinking. Lola saw them and changed her mind. I haven't been able to change it back since."

Rem eyed the upstairs and glimpsed Lola staring down at them from around the corner. She ducked back when she caught Rem's gaze. "What would you like us to do?"

"Talk to her. See if she'll come out of her shell. I know more happened than she's letting on. You two seem a hell of a lot more competent and understanding than the other two officers."

Well aware of their dwindling amount of time, Rem sighed. "Unfortunately, we've got to help Jerry, and we're on a tight schedule."

Roseanna's eyes flashed. "Lola's a good girl. She didn't deserve what happened to her. Just because she's a—"

Daniels raised his hand. "That's not what we mean. If it were any other time, we'd be happy to talk to her."

"Well, if not now, when?"

Rem shrugged at Daniels. Their next forty-eight hours were going to be busy ones. "How about this?" asked Daniels. "After we take care of Jerry Lee, we'll be back. And if we can't, we'll send someone else just as capable as us."

"In the meantime, talk to Lola," said Rem. "Encourage her. Tell her she can trust us, or whoever we send."

Daniels pulled out his card. "Here's my card. Call if you need to."

Roseanne took his card, reached into her pocket and pulled out one of her own. "And here's mine. You call me when you get some time."

"We will," said Rem. "And tell Lola she's got nothing to worry about. All we want to do is talk. Whatever happens after is up to her."

Roseanna nodded. "I will." She swiveled toward the kitchen. "Come on back, Lee."

Jerry reappeared with a plastic bag of cookies, gave Roseanna another hug, and joined Rem and Daniels as they left the house.

· · • • • • • · · ·

The next twenty-four hours were a whirlwind of activity as Rem and Daniels set up their false murder. Jerry Lee handled it like a pro, and when they were ready, Rem had called Tex, telling him the deed was done, and they wanted to meet. Rem had delighted in hearing the shock in Tex's voice. The man had not expected that they'd actually go through with it. But now came the tricky part. Proving Jerry was dead and finding an avenue into the organization.

Checking his watch again, Rem looked up when Manetti entered the squad room and headed to his desk. "Hey, guys," he said.

"Manetti," said Rem. "You leave Monk behind?"

Daniels dropped his pen into a penholder. "Perfectly understandable if you did."

"He's on the phone." Manetti sat at his desk. "You guys have been scarce since yesterday." He looked around the room and lowered his voice. "Any progress in your investigation?"

Rem did his best not to react. "Some."

Daniels picked up his bottle of green juice. "Nothing major." He took a sip.

Glancing around the squad room, Manetti rolled his chair closer to their desks. "I've been thinking."

Rem leaned closer. "I keep telling you, that never leads to anything good."

Manetti kept his voice down. "I want to help. You mentioned that list. Why don't you give me a few names? Let me do some digging."

Daniels furrowed his brow. "You sure about that?"

"It means getting in deeper," said Rem. "You couldn't tell anyone, especially Monk."

"I get it," said Manetti. "I can do it on my time, like you guys."

"What do you think?" Rem asked Daniels.

Daniels rubbed his jaw. "I gave Erin a couple of names. I don't see why we can't give Manetti a few."

Thinking, Rem tapped his finger on his desk. "We're trying to focus on the males first. We're looking for the man we call Tex."

"We think he's a former cop," said Daniels, "but we can't be sure."

Manetti nodded. "I can do that."

"I'll call you tonight with some names," said Rem. "Just be careful. I'd keep Annabelle out of it if you can, but that's up to you."

"You learn anything, you tell us. Don't do anything on your own," said Daniels. "Okay?"

"I got it," said Manetti. "Glad I can help."

Rem thought of Lola. "Actually, there's something else you can help with." He eyed Daniels. "Lola."

Daniels raised his brow. "That's a good idea."

"Who's Lola?" asked Manetti.

Without mentioning Jerry Lee, Rem explained meeting Roseanna and their discussion about Lola. "Daniels and I aren't going to make it over there today, and maybe not tomorrow, either. You think you could swing by and talk to her?"

"I can call Roseanna and let her know you're coming," said Daniels.

"And you can't bring Monk," said Rem. "This lady is skittish enough as it is. Monk and his attitude won't fly with Lola, and especially Roseanna."

Manetti pursed his lips. "Sure. I can go. But if you want to keep Monk out of it, I'll have to go Saturday."

"That would be great, Manetti. Thank you," said Rem. "She may not choose to come forward, but you're the perfect person to talk to her."

Daniels pulled a card out of his wallet and picked up his phone. "I'll call Roseanna now. Tell her to expect you." He dialed and put the phone to his ear.

"Okay." After a pause, Manetti regarded Rem. "Can I ask you something personal?"

"Shoot," said Rem.

"Have you ever had any doubts about bringing Mikey into this? I want to tell Annie, but it scares me. But I don't want to lie to her."

Rem thought back on his argument with Mikey. "Every day, Manetti. Every day. But she and I made an agreement. I don't like it, but it's the deal. Same with Marjorie and Daniels. We've learned the hard way that keeping secrets always backfires. But in the end, it's up to you. You don't tell Annie about all the bad stuff you encounter each day. This shouldn't be any different unless she comes out and asks you directly."

Manetti fiddled with the edge of a notebook on Rem's desk. "If she does that, I can't lie to her."

"Then I think you have your decision. Just make sure she knows the stakes involved."

"I will."

Daniels hung up. "Roseanna knows you're coming, and she says thank you."

"No problem." Manetti started to roll back to his desk.

"Hey," said Rem, thinking about Mikey. "Now I have a question for you."

Manetti rolled back. "I thought you said thinking was a bad idea."

Rem chuckled. "I never learn."

"That's the truth," added Daniels.

"Shoot," said Manetti.

Rem almost reconsidered but pushed forward. "When you and Monk went to see Margaret Redstone, what happened?"

Manetti widened his eyes, and Daniels stopped what he was doing and listened.

"You mean, when we were investigating Mikey?" asked Manetti.

Rem swiveled in his chair. "Is there another time?"

"No," said Manetti. "I'm just surprised you want to know. You weren't very thrilled when you heard about it."

"With good reason. She's unstable at best." He paused when Manetti continued to stare, as if expecting to hear more. "And Mikey wants to see her sister. I think you can imagine what I think about that."

Manetti interlaced his fingers. "I can." He took a second. "It...uh...went well, I guess. Although I didn't like being there. All I could think about was when we arrested her at your place, and how crazy she...well, you know."

"Yes. I know." Rem's heart pounded with the memory. "Did she talk to you and Monk?"

"She did, and she drew pictures. With crayons."

Rem frowned.

"Pictures? With crayons?" asked Daniels. "I find that hard to believe."

"The nurse said she'd stabbed someone with a pencil, so crayons were safer." Manetti shivered. "I still didn't get too close."

"You mean you were *with* her?" asked Rem. "With nothing between you and her? Was she handcuffed?"

"No. She was in a wheelchair. Apparently on heavy medication. She was docile but coherent. She spoke, but didn't say much. The nurse told us she was harmless before leaving us with her."

Rem sat up in shock. "He *left* the two of you with her?"

"I didn't like it either. But the nurse seemed unconcerned. And he was right. She didn't do anything. Just drew her pictures while we talked."

"But she could have done something if she'd wanted?" asked Rem.

"I don't know what," said Manetti. "She couldn't escape. There was nowhere for her to go."

Rem tried to comprehend how Margaret Redstone was in a facility unrestrained and free to talk to anyone as if they were visiting for Sunday brunch.

"What did you talk about?" asked Daniels.

Manetti hesitated. "Monk asked a lot of questions about Mikey and Vera, and their time in the cult."

Rem's heart thumped harder at the memory of Monk accusing Mikey of murder.

"We knew there was a man involved who was their friend," said Manetti. "We asked about him."

Rem guessed that was Nathan Briars, the other friend who was present when Vera was shot.

"How was she handling the questioning?" asked Daniels.

Manetti shrugged. "Okay. She offered short answers and just kept drawing. She gave me a picture. Monk too."

Rem dropped his jaw. "She drew you a picture?"

Manetti scrunched his face. "It was awful. It was these red circles among all these black scrawls. She called it *Bloody Tears in Hell*. I didn't want it, but was too scared to tell her no. Before they wheeled her out, she told me to—" Manetti stilled.

"She told you to what?" asked Daniels.

He eyed Rem. "She told me to give the picture to you."

A chill ran up Rem's spine. "She said that?"

Manetti clenched his fingers. "I threw the picture away. I figured you wouldn't want it."

"Good deduction, Manetti." Rem turned toward his desk and leaned over it. There was no way Mikey was going to visit her sister if he had anything to say about it.

"What about Monk's picture?" asked Daniels.

"He kept it."

"Figures," said Daniels. "Did Margaret answer your questions in a good way? Was the visit worth it?"

Rem waited to hear the answer.

"It was actually," said Manetti. "I didn't think it would be, but Monk insisted. Said we had to try. Margaret spoke in riddles at the beginning. When we asked about the cult and Vera and Mikey, she said there were a lot of secrets. Monk kept talking calmly to her, though, and she ended up giving us Nathan Briars' name."

Daniels scooted closer with his chair. "So she was competent enough to remember the past? And understand and answer your questions reliably?"

Manetti nodded. "She was."

With a sigh, Rem rested his forehead in his palm. "Great."

"Maybe she was just having a good day," added Manetti.

"It's okay," said Daniels. "It's helpful to know."

Rem didn't think helpful was the right word. Horrifying was more appropriate. And it annoyed him that instead of doing hard time, which is what she deserved, Margaret was being rolled around in a wheelchair, seeing visitors, and drawing pretty pictures.

"Anything else?" asked Manetti.

Rem sat back with a groan. "I think that about covers it. And I appreciate you getting rid of the picture."

"Yeah." Manetti picked at a seam in his pants before looking up. "I'm sorry if our visit upset you, Rem. That wasn't the intent."

"I know it wasn't *your* intention," said Rem. "But Monk's a different story."

"In his defense," replied Manetti, "he was following his instincts, and they weren't wrong."

Rem swiveled his chair back toward Manetti. "His intention was to put Mikey in jail for a crime she didn't commit."

"I know it looked bad, but we were doing our jobs."

Rem didn't have the energy to debate with Manetti about his partner's supposed instincts or intentions.

"Nobody's arguing with you, Manetti," said Daniels. "Rem and I just see things a little differently."

That familiar anger reared up, and Rem scoffed. "Next time Annabelle's accused of murder, and me and Daniels are leading the investigation? And we talk to the psychopath who stalked and almost killed you to get evidence against her, you let me know how you feel."

Manetti paled and didn't say a word.

"Rem," said Daniels softly. "Be nice."

Rem deflated and realized he'd barked at Manetti for all the wrong reasons. "Sorry. This whole discussion is making me grumpy. I don't mean to take it out on you, Manetti. I usually reserve my snappy comebacks for Daniels."

"Don't I know it," replied Daniels. "And remember. You opened this can of worms, partner."

"Yeah. I know. Serves me right." Rem groaned out a heavy breath. "We appreciate you, Manetti, even though it doesn't always look like it."

"It's okay," said Manetti, looking relieved. "We all have our moments. You two have been through a lot. You're allowed a few snappy comebacks." He rolled his chair back to his desk. "I'll let you know how it goes with Lola."

"And we'll call you with those names," said Daniels. He checked his watch. "You ready to go, partner? We've got to be at that thing."

Rem forgot about Margaret, stood, and grabbed his jacket. "Ready when you are."

"Be safe out there," said Manetti. "Don't do anything stupid."

"That's the plan," said Daniels.

"Let's hope we can stick to it," said Rem, following Daniels out of the squad room.

Chapter Eleven

DANIELS REARRANGED THE NAPKIN holder and the condiments sitting on the table.

"You keep doing that," said Rem, "and the server is going to take it personally."

Daniels stopped fiddling. "Guess I'm more nervous than I thought."

Sitting beside Daniels, Rem shifted in his seat. "Glad I'm not the only one." He checked his watch. "Where is he?"

"We got here early, remember? He's not due for another five minutes."

Rem looked around. "I feel like everyone's watching us."

Daniels looked around, too. They were sitting in a back booth of a dive bar where Tex had picked to meet. It had the look and feel of a place untouched by time, and not in a good way. The floors were dirty, the tabletop was sticky, the seats of the booth had holes in them, and the uneven table tipped back and forth when they leaned on it. There were a few older patrons at the bar, and a table of four men, who all wore trucker hats and overalls, sat at the front, drinking beers. "This place? I bet Charles Manson could walk in here, and no one would notice."

"It's got Tex written all over it."

"It's a little upscale for him."

Rem chuckled.

Needing a distraction, Daniels asked the question he'd had on his mind since leaving the station. "Since we've got a few minutes, did Manetti's answers about Margaret help?"

Rem, who'd had trouble sitting still, finally did. "Was it that obvious?"

"Why else would you ask? I take it you and Mikey still aren't seeing eye-to-eye?"

"Hell, no. If anything, we're getting further and further apart."

Daniels picked up the salt shaker. "I'm sorry to hear that." He moved the salt shaker around the table.

Rem narrowed his eyes. "Just admit it. You think I'm being a hardass, don't you?"

"Not at all. I understand your ambivalence. I'm sure Mikey does too."

"But?"

Daniels hesitated, unsure how to word it. "But I also see Mikey's point, and based on what Manetti said, Margaret is capable of cooperating."

"That scares me even more. That means that despite whatever medication she's on, she's lucid. Which tells me her mind is a lot clearer than she's letting on. She's just milking the insanity act to prevent a trial, going to prison, and doing serious time."

"Or the medication keeps her just lucid enough to keep the crazies at bay and allows her to talk without going berserk."

Rem huffed. "I don't believe this. You think Mikey should go see her?"

Daniels turned to face his partner. "I'm saying there has to be a happy medium here."

"There's nothing happy about any of this."

"Margaret's a witness, Rem. She saw things in Victor's cult. She knows the man who killed Vera. She may even know Damien Rook. If you had no history with her, you'd talk to her in a heartbeat."

"But I do have a history with her," said Rem, his voice raising. "So do you. And so does Mikey."

"I am not discounting that. But somebody needs to speak to her."

"I'm fine with that, but it doesn't have to be Mikey, even if Mikey disagrees."

Daniels understood Rem's concerns, but also Mikey's. "What does Mason say?"

"He's as against it as I am, but he'll cave eventually. He won't let her go on her own."

"Would she go on her own?"

"She would if she saw no other way."

"What if we sent Mel and Garcia?" he asked, referring to two other detectives in the squad.

"I thought of that, but Margaret won't tell them anything. She wields her madness well. The only people she'll talk to are the ones she can mess with."

"She helped Monk and Manetti."

"And she gave Manetti a freaky drawing and told him to give it to me. Can you imagine what she'd tell Mikey? Or you if you went?"

Daniels could easily imagine. "I know. But if Mikey's intent on going to see her sister, then someone has to go with her. Whether it's Mason or me, or even Manetti."

Rem snorted. "Manetti would love that."

"It's not a terrible option. He's already seen Margaret once, and she cooperated. He can watch out for Mikey and get her out of there if needed."

Rem tossed out his hand. "And that's another thing. Margaret's gettin' wheeled around that facility with her crayons and no restraints. According to Manetti, she could chat with Mikey unsupervised. That's unacceptable. What kind of facility are they running there? Club Med?"

Daniels made circles with the salt shaker. "Then call the facility and tell them Margaret either needs to be restrained or there needs to be a barrier between her and Mikey."

Rem waited while a server walked by. "It helps, but Margaret can do as much damage with her words as she can with her hands. That's what scares me most."

Daniels recalled Margaret's insane ramblings against Rem and Mikey when she'd been arrested. It had taken him a while to forget it. "Believe me, I'm familiar, but we can't let this woman dictate this investigation."

"Says who?"

"She has information, and we'd be remiss if we—"

Rem's gaze traveled behind Daniels, and he made a whistling sound with his lips. "Heads up. Tex is here."

Daniels gripped the salt shaker.

"Put that back," said Rem, pointing at the shaker. "Unless you plan to throw it at him."

"Tempting." Telling himself to relax, Daniels put the salt shaker away and swiveled to face Tex.

· · · ● ● · ● ● · · ·

Seeing the detectives in a back booth, Croft approached them, took off his leather jacket, and slid into the seat across from them. "Afternoon, Detectives." He sat his jacket beside him.

"Unfortunately, I can't say it's a pleasure," said Remalla.

Daniels looked around. "Lovely place you've brought us to."

"Don't tell me. You're a regular?" asked Remalla.

Croft caught the edge in their voices. "Where'd you expect to meet? The Ritz?" He eyed the bar and didn't see anyone of interest or concern. "You two order anything?"

"Yeah. The Surf and Turf. We hear it's delicious," said Remalla.

"And two Piña Coladas," added Daniels. "With the little umbrellas."

Croft smirked. "Has the server even been to the table?"

"Not yet," said Rem. "We figure somebody will stop by eventually."

"Probably for the best," said Croft, "since we've got business to conduct." He pulled a small device out of his pocket and turned it on. "Before we get started, put your phones on the table and turn them off." He held out the device. "Wave this over yourselves, and over and under the table."

"I sense a lack of trust," said Remalla, pulling out his phone.

"Shocking." Daniels pulled out the burner cell and his phone, turned them off, and set them on the table. Remalla did the same with his phone and took the device and waved it over his head and upper body. He handed it to Daniels, who did the same, plus waved it around the table. The device remained silent. Daniels handed it back to Croft. "Satisfied? No bugs in the hot sauce."

"Assuming that thing actually works," said Remalla.

"It works." Croft turned off the device and put it back in his pocket. He set his elbows on the table. "Where's your proof?"

Daniels glanced toward the entry. "Rook isn't joining us?"

Croft chuckled. "Hell no. He wouldn't be caught dead in this place. He trusts me to decide."

"Decide what?" asked Remalla.

"Whether you two are blowing smoke up my ass or you actually completed the assignment." He leaned in. "I'm guessing the former."

The detectives glanced at each other. "You be the judge," said Daniels. "Proof's in the envelope. Beside the napkin holder."

Croft noticed the white envelope wedged between the holder and the condiment tray. He reached for it and pulled it out. After a pause, he opened it. Inside were several photos of the body of Jerry Lee Caruso. He was lying on his back on a plastic sheet. His eyes were open and glazed, and his skin had a bluish pallor. There was a garish bullet wound in his head. Spattered blood dotted the surrounding sheet, and there was a pool of blood beneath Jerry's head. Another photo was from a distance, showing a full body shot, and a third was another close up with a newspaper next to Jerry's head, showing the previous day's date.

Croft studied the photos closely to determine the validity of the shots. It was definitely Jerry Lee, and the wound appeared real. He returned the photos to the envelope. "Where's the remains?"

"At the bottom of Secret Lake," replied Daniels.

"It's north of here," said Remalla. "Our former captain has a cabin out there."

"Why there?"

"It's quiet and secluded. We brought Jerry to the cabin," said Remalla. "Told him we'd hide him there. We told him the plastic was for some repainting. He bought it long enough for us to do what you asked."

"Then we rolled him up in the plastic," said Daniels, "and brought him out onto our captain's boat last night. We weighed down the body and dropped him into the lake."

Croft studied the detectives to determine whether they were lying. "Pretty convenient. There's no way to prove he's dead."

"That's what the pictures are for. What would you have preferred?" asked Remalla. "Kill him in broad daylight? Leave the body to be found? Have the press talk to his grieving mother, and then Sammy Caruso, who'd want revenge for his grandson's murder?"

"This way, he's still missing," said Daniels. "Everyone still thinks he's alive, and we can keep looking for him." He paused and smiled. "Except we'll never find him."

Croft narrowed his eyes. "You could have called me. I'd have come out and verified."

Remalla gave a sarcastic chuckle. "You think we've got time to wait for you? While Jerry's body lies on the floor of our captain's cabin? We're busy. And you didn't say how to do it. You just told us to do it, and we did."

Croft hesitated, debating what to do. "How'd you find Jerry?"

"He came to us," said Daniels. "We had a plan to draw him out, but before we could enact it, Jerry called. We picked him up and brought him out to the cabin."

Croft looked between them, still uncertain. "Who shot him?"

The detectives glanced at each other, and Croft looked for any signs of hesitation.

Remalla looked back. "We both did."

Croft frowned. "You both shot him?"

"Whoever pulled the trigger doesn't matter," said Daniels. "Because we're in this together. If one of us goes down, the other goes with him."

Croft kept up his stare. "Well, aren't you two a *Little House on the Prairie* episode?"

"It's called partnership," said Remalla. "I believe you're familiar with it?"

Croft thought of the man the detectives had referred to as Tommy and glared. "I was until—"

"I killed him," said Daniels. "In self-defense, and you know that."

Croft held Daniels' gaze and, for the first time, wondered if these two actually were the killers they were making themselves out to be. Had he missed the signs? He tucked the envelope into his inside jacket pocket. "I'll talk to Rook." He started to slide out of the booth.

"Whoa there, Tex," said Remalla. "We're not done here."

"We did what you asked," said Daniels. "Where's his gun?" He tipped his head at Remalla.

Croft remained in the booth. "The deal was for you to take care of Jerry Lee, and we wouldn't reveal the gun or the debt. And we won't. Rook's not done with you two yet. He made that pretty clear."

"Not done?" asked Rem. "If he thinks we're his little errand boys, he's dead wrong."

"We don't take orders from him," added Daniels.

Croft chuckled. "It appears you just did." He leaned closer. "And now we have you for the murder of Jerry Lee."

"The hell you do," said Remalla. "Our faces aren't in those photos. There's no evidence linking us to the crime at the cabin or boat."

"And the only fingerprints on those pictures are yours," said Daniels with a flat stare. "We aren't stupid."

Croft cursed. "You two choose to bump heads with Rook, and you'll realize just how stupid you are."

"Then maybe there's a better way," said Daniels. "One that benefits both of us."

"What do you mean?"

Remalla shrugged. "Rook wants our help? Then he needs to show a little leniency. Threatening us only creates a lot of friction."

"Nobody wants friction," replied Daniels. "He can get what he wants by bringing us in."

Croft almost laughed but remained still and kept his cool. "Bringing you in? To his organization?"

"Where else?" asked Remalla. "It's what he wants anyway. To make us evil? Right?" He raised the side of his lip. "Well, he made a big assumption about us."

"And we all know what assuming does," said Daniels. "We're not as nice as we look." He shot a look at Rem. "Or at least as I look."

Not expecting this turn of events, Croft gaped at them.

"I think we got his attention," said Remalla.

"Seems so," added Daniels.

Croft sat back in the booth. "He'll never go for it."

Remalla glowered at him. "Rook hates us. That's obvious. He came right out and said he wanted us to kill for him. And we did."

"We've proven ourselves," said Daniels. "But it made us think."

"There are obvious benefits to working with a man like Rook," replied Remalla. "We've seen them. And if Rook is going to threaten us to do his dirty work, we'd rather do it without all the muss and fuss."

"Plus, the monetary aspect is attractive too," added Daniels.

Croft sputtered. "Money? You want to get paid?"

"Why not?" asked Remalla. "You don't work for free, do you?"

Croft sneered. "Why would he pay you when he's got your gun and can use it against you?"

"Because I think there's one thing Rook wants more than to threaten us into working for him," said Remalla.

"What's that?" asked Croft, curious.

"He wants to turn us," said Remalla. "He wants us to become the very thing he is. Cold and ruthless."

"Something tells me if you go back to him with our offer," said Daniels, "he'll be eager to bring us on board."

"And see just how far we're willing to go," replied Remalla.

Croft wondered if that was true. "Or he could tell you to do what you're told or prepare to go to prison."

"And we'll tell him no," said Remalla. "He got what he wanted. Jerry Lee is dead. But no more freebies. He wants us, he has to bring us in."

"And if we go to prison, so be it," said Daniels. "We're willing to take the risk." He tilted his head. "But something tells me your boss is far more interested in us being killers instead of prisoners."

"Prison is boring," said Rem. "And I'm guessing Rook hates being bored."

Croft wondered again how he'd misread these two so badly.

A server approached the table. He wore ripped jeans, had long stringy hair, gauges in his earlobes, and a food-stained apron wrapped around his waist. "Sorry. Didn't see you guys. I was on a smoke break. Can I get you something to drink?"

Croft eyed the server and then the detectives. "I'll bring it to Rook. Wait for my call."

"With bells on." Remalla smiled.

"Don't keep us waiting long," said Daniels. "We get crabby when we wait, especially him." He shot a thumb at Rem. "So the sooner, the better."

While the server stared at his dirty nails, Croft slid out of the booth, put his leather jacket on, and stopped before leaving. "Get these two jokers a couple of Piña Coladas ...with umbrellas."

"Pina what?" asked the server.

Croft turned and left.

· · • • • • • • · ·

Daniels watched Tex leave and blew out a relieved breath.

"Just a couple of waters," said Rem to the server. He squinted his eyes at the server's nametag. "Crusty?"

The server looked at his tag, which was smeared with what looked like jam or chocolate. "It's Rusty. Two waters coming up." He walked away.

"Although I could use a serious shot of alcohol," added Rem.

Daniels slid out of the booth and slid into the seat across from Rem. "What do you think?"

Rem moved into the center of his booth. "I think he bought it." He shook out his hands. "Although my heart was beating so hard, I thought I was going to break a rib."

"I hear you. I was afraid he could hear mine thumping."

"The bigger question is, will Rook buy it?" said Rem. "He's the one we have to convince."

Daniels replayed the conversation with Tex in his head. "You think Tex would even bring it to Rook if he didn't think it was viable?"

"Hard to say." Rem massaged his shoulders. "Tex is a yes man. He won't risk making the wrong decision."

His adrenaline surge abating, Daniels sat back. "So, now we wait. That'll be fun."

"A blast." Rem rubbed his stomach. "You hungry?"

"You're not serious. You want to eat here?"

"After that exchange, I could eat anywhere."

Daniels rolled his eyes. "Why don't we—"

Rusty returned with a tray, which he sat on the table beside them. Daniels saw two waters and two shot glasses with clear liquid in them. Rusty grabbed the water and set the cups in front of Daniels and Rem. "Two waters..." He turned and grabbed the two shot glasses. "And two grappas."

Daniels frowned. "We didn't order these."

Rusty picked up the tray. "They're compliments of the gentleman." He pointed to the other side of the bar. "And it's the good stuff. Kenny, the owner, keeps it in the back."

Daniels leaned to look at their benefactor, and Rem turned in his seat. Back in the corner sat a distinguished older man wearing a silky, brown-collared shirt and a well-cut navy jacket. His slicked-back salt and pepper hair gave him the look of a luxury car salesman, and there were big rings on his fingers. A man and a woman dressed in suits sat on either side of him.

Recognizing the trio, Daniels' adrenaline surge returned.

Rem sucked in a breath. "I don't believe this." He shot a wide-eyed look at Daniels. "It's Sammy Caruso."

Chapter Twelve

SHOCKED TO SEE CARUSO sitting in the bar, Rem stared as the man and woman from Caruso's table stood and walked toward them. Rem recognized them as Tina and Tito, Caruso's bodyguards, whom they'd met outside the office building where CIW was located the day he and Daniels had first met Caruso.

Daniels spoke quietly. "How much you think he saw?"

"Guess we're about to find out."

Tina and Tito approached their table. "Detectives," said Tina. "Nice to see you again."

"Can you spare a few minutes with Mr. Caruso?" asked Tito. "He'd like to speak with you."

"Do we have a choice?" asked Daniels.

"You do," said Tina. "But every choice has consequences."

"Your boss is violating bail by being in this state," said Rem. "Are there consequences for that?"

"Mr. Caruso is well aware of his legal requirements." Tito didn't offer more.

Daniels arched his brow at Rem. "Guess we should say 'hello.'"

Rem slid out of his booth. "Can't hurt to be neighborly."

"Mr. Caruso appreciates your time," said Tina.

Daniels stood too.

"And please," Tito gestured at the table, "bring your drinks."

Rem figured it wouldn't look good if they left the grappa behind. He picked up his shot glass, and Daniels picked up his. They walked over to Caruso's table.

Caruso, who'd been studying his phone, put it down when they approached. He had his own shot glass in front of him. "Join me, Detectives."

Reluctantly, Rem took one seat beside Caruso, and Daniels took the other. Tito and Tina sat at an adjacent table and watched the door.

Rem settled into his seat. "What can we do for you, Mr. Caruso?"

His eyes as sharp as shards of glass, Caruso crossed his arms. "I think you're confused, Detective. The better question is what are you doing for me?"

Daniels set his shot of grappa on the table. "You mean about Jerry Lee?"

Caruso set his jaw. "I'm not asking about Elvis." He eyed Rem, and a vein in his neck bulged. "Where is my grandson?"

Rem debated what to say. He and Daniels hadn't discussed what they'd tell Sammy Caruso if he showed. "He's safe."

Caruso raised his brow as if surprised by the answer. "You know where he is?"

Daniels squirmed in his seat. "All we can tell you, sir, is that he's okay."

"All you can tell me?" asked Caruso in the same threatening tone. "What the hell does that mean?"

"It means that until we can be sure he'll stay safe, we can't tell you anything more," replied Daniels.

Caruso squinted at both of them. "Does this have something to do with your friend that you met in this dump? Who just left?"

Rem gripped his shot glass. "We can't tell you that either."

Caruso's expression hardened. "Who the hell do you two idiots think you're talking to?" He leaned in and lowered his voice, although the menacing tone remained. "If you know where my grandson is, tell me, or I'll get it out of you the hard way."

Rem tried to relax his bunched shoulders but failed. "Threatening us won't work. At this point, it's becoming routine. We're not doing this to piss you off. We're doing this for Jerry."

"He's the priority," said Daniels.

"What are you suggesting?" asked Caruso, raising his voice. "That I can't protect my grandson?"

Daniels kept his voice even. "You taking him out of the state is not what Jerry or his mother wants, and it doesn't solve the bigger problem."

Caruso pointed. "You leave my daughter out of this." The silver ring on his finger reflected the fluorescent overhead light.

"We can't do that," said Rem. "We have to protect both of them."

Caruso slammed his palm on the table, and Rem jumped. "Listen, you two. I gave you forty-eight hours a long time ago to figure this out. You said you were close. Now you're telling me you know Jerry's safe, but can't tell me anything?"

"We're working on something even bigger than Jerry," said Rem.

Caruso glared. "Nothing is bigger than Jerry Lee."

"We're aware of that," added Daniels. "But if you want your grandson safe long-term, let us finish what we've started. This is about more than just finding the killer Jerry witnessed in the act. It goes way deeper."

"There are big players involved," said Rem. "And we have to be careful. Jerry's life is not the only one at stake."

Caruso paused, studied them, and leaned back with a sneer. "You're suggesting you two are at risk?"

"If our plan fails, then yes," said Rem. "Definitely."

"And what happens to Jerry Lee if you fail?" asked Caruso. "If you two can't save him, who can?"

Rem wasn't sure how to answer. They hadn't thought that far ahead.

Daniels studied his shot glass. "If something happens to us, then talk to your daughter. She'll know what to do."

The lines between Caruso's brows deepened. "Then I'll talk to her now."

"I wouldn't." Rem prepared for another outburst. "She won't talk to you."

"And who told her to do that?" yelled Caruso.

"That's her decision. Not ours," said Daniels. "You think we could stop her if she wanted to bring you in?"

"We just need time," said Rem.

"I gave you time," Caruso squinted with one eye and pointed with a meaty finger. "I even gave you extra. And I told you what would happen if you didn't deliver."

"You getting involved in this is a bad idea," said Daniels. "Let Rem and me play this out. We're closer now, and may have found a way in. If our plan works, we might take down an entire organization, including Reginald Durning's killer and the person who hired that killer. If we can do that, Jerry Lee may not even have to testify."

"Testify?" yelled Caruso. "Who said anything about testifying? There's no need to testify if this killer is dead."

One trucker at the front table glanced back at them.

Fed up with Caruso's attitude, Rem's own anger flared, but he kept his voice down. "You get involved, and you could start a war with this organization, which puts me, Daniels, Jerry, and your daughter at risk. So stop bullying us. We're not a couple of street cops. You want us to save your grandkid? Then let us do our jobs."

"Go home, Mr. Caruso," said Daniels. "When this is over, and Jerry's safe, you'll know it."

"And if you're dead?" asked Caruso.

"Then you'll know that, too," answered Rem.

His face furrowed. "I don't take directions from two lousy detectives."

"Then consider it friendly advice," said Rem.

"How do I know I can trust you?" asked Caruso, his gaze piercing. He'd lowered his voice but didn't sound any less threatening. "How do I know you two aren't working for this organization, and that Jerry Lee isn't already dead?"

Rem hesitated, and Daniels sighed. "I guess you're going to have to go on faith," replied Daniels.

Rem waited as a server approached the table, and Caruso waved her away with a sneer. "Something tells me you've already checked us out. If you'd found something suspicious, we'd probably already be out of the picture, right?"

Caruso eyed them both with the look you'd expect from a mob boss who didn't like what he was hearing. "You two want more time?" He cursed. "Fine. I'll give it to you." He pointed with two meaty fingers, and his voice tightened. "But if I discover you're lying to me, you're going to meet some friends of mine who won't be as nice as me." His cold eyes glittered. "And if Jerry Lee dies, I'll deal with you personally."

Rem glared back. "We've got enough pressure right now. You adding to it doesn't help your grandson, or us."

Daniels leaned his forearms on the table. "We could make one phone call. And your bail would be revoked. You're not the only one who can make threats."

Caruso paused and gave an ominous chuckle. "You two clowns think you can scare me? Or that I can't get to you from jail?"

"At least it would stop these unexpected visits," added Rem. "They're a little jarring."

"And time-consuming," added Daniels.

Caruso looked between them with a flat yet terrifying expression, and Rem half-wondered if he would tell Tina or Tito to shoot both him and Daniels while Crusty watched in horror from behind the bar. After a pause, Caruso's face relaxed, but his eyes still flared. "I can respect men who stand up for themselves, especially to me. I rarely see it."

Rem let go of a held breath.

"And you're right," said Caruso, his voice maintaining that intimidating tone. "I had you both checked out, and you came out clean, but that doesn't mean you're not good at keeping secrets." He paused. "My trust with you two only goes so far without results, which I expect to see. And soon."

"We're doing our best," said Daniels. "I can promise you that."

Caruso twisted a ring around a big finger. "You bring Jerry Lee home safe and sound, and you and I got no beef. But if you fail..."

"Yeah. We know. A visit from your friends. But you won't have to worry about that," said Rem. "Because if we fail, we'll probably already be dead."

"And if you aren't, you soon will be. Got it?" Caruso didn't wait for a response and raised his shot glass. "To a healthy Jerry Lee. And two healthy detectives."

"We're on duty," said Daniels.

Caruso's gaze hardened. "Never refuse a toast of grappa with an Italian."

Ready to end this conversation, Rem raised his shot glass. "I'll drink to that."

After a pause, Daniels raised his drink too. "Same."

They all downed their drinks. Rem gasped when the strong alcohol blazed a path down his throat. It was his first shot of grappa, and likely his last.

Daniels sucked air between his teeth and lost the color in his cheeks.

Caruso laughed and returned his glass to the table with barely a grimace. "Grappa will put meat on your bones."

"And nails in my lungs." Rem clutched his chest as his whole body flared with heat.

Caruso offered a dismissive wave. "We're done here, but don't think I'm far away. I'll be expecting to hear of Jerry Lee's safe return soon or expect another visit."

Rem put his shot glass down and, regaining his composure, stood along with Daniels. "Don't take it personally," said Daniels. "But I hope we never see you again."

Caruso's hard stare returned. "That, detectives, is entirely up to you."

Eager to leave, Rem hastily followed Daniels out of the bar.

Chapter Thirteen

SITTING AT HIS DINING table, Daniels stifled a yawn and scrolled through the information on the page he was researching on his laptop. Once he arrived home, Marjorie had warmed up some dinner for him while he spent time with J.P. After playing with his son and eating dinner, Daniels had resumed his internet search while Marjorie took J.P. upstairs to put him to bed. Daniels flipped through the names on the list to determine which to give to Manetti and continued researching his current name—Archie Nesbitt. So far, he'd found several Archie Nesbitts but none that fit the expected job description of a member of a secret society.

Frustrated and tired, he flipped to a new page, realizing that any of the Archie Nesbitts he was checking could be a member, and a job description might have nothing to do with it. He blinked, rubbed his eyes, and felt hands on his shoulders.

"Hey," said Marjorie from behind him. She kneaded his shoulders. "How's it going?"

He groaned as she dug her thumbs into his tight muscles. "Slow."

"Why don't you take a break? Rest your eyes."

Daniels closed his laptop and groaned again when Marjorie found a knot in his neck. "J.P. asleep?"

"Went down like a brownie in front of Rem. He was tuckered."

Daniels chuckled. Feeling better, he took his wife's hand and pulled her over. She still wore the cast on her wrist, which was due to come off the following week. "And how are you?"

She sat in the chair beside him. "I'm okay."

Getting a closer look at her, he noticed her red-rimmed eyes. "How was work?"

She shrugged and studied her fingers. "Work was work."

Sensing something was up, he squeezed her hand and stood. "Come here."

Looking up, she frowned. "Come where?"

He gently pulled her arm, and she stood. "Let's take a few minutes and act like a normal couple." He guided her into the living room and told her to sit. She did as he requested, and he went to the kitchen and poured them each a glass of white wine. He brought it back to the living room and handed one to her.

"What's this for?" she asked.

He sat beside her. "We're going to relax and talk." He touched his glass to hers. "To my beautiful wife."

She smiled softly. "And my handsome husband."

They both took a sip, but seeing her stare off, he took her glass and set both his and hers on the coffee table. He shifted to face her. "Spill it."

"Spill what?"

"I'm going to ask you again. How was your day? Only this time, tell me the truth."

After a pause, tears filled her eyes.

"Hey, what's the matter?" He reached for a tissue from the box on the side table. "Did something happen?"

She shook her head. "It's stupid."

He handed her the tissue. "Tell me."

Marjorie took the tissue and dabbed her eyes. "I was at lunch today. In the cafeteria. There was a new teacher who joined us, and she announced she was pregnant."

Daniels' heart fell.

Marjorie sniffed. "I held it together until I got back to my office, and then I bawled for an hour, and I've been weepy ever since."

Daniels took her hand. "It's okay. You're allowed to be sad. You've suffered emotionally, physically and mentally. Cut yourself some slack."

"I just..." her breath caught. "...I thought I was better."

"Honey, you are better, but you're grieving. That takes time to process. Go easy on yourself."

She sniffed again. "I hate feeling sad."

"Come here." He pulled her close, and she rested her head in the hollow of his neck. "You're the strongest woman I know, but you don't have to be strong around me."

"But you're already dealing with so much. You don't need more to handle."

Surprised to hear her say that, he frowned. "Hey. I always have time for you."

"You and Rem are trying to infiltrate an ominous society. I can see that it's taking its toll on you. And after today, it's only going to get worse." She fiddled with a button on his shirt. "And I worry about you."

Daniels had told her about his and Rem's meeting with Tex and Sammy Caruso. He knew she'd be concerned but had sworn to tell her the truth. Hearing the fear in her voice, it was obvious grief wasn't the only thing on her mind. "I know I've been preoccupied."

"It's not just that. I know what you have to do, but I can't help but wonder..."

Daniels rubbed her shoulder. "Wonder what?"

She hesitated. "If something happens...what will I do?" She paused. "I think about Rem and how he survived losing Jennie. I know he's strong, but when I think about losing you, I realize how strong he really is. I don't know if I could survive if...if..." She looked up at him.

Daniels' chest tightened, and he recalled how he'd felt when he'd heard Marjorie had been in a car accident. "I understand that. When I'd learned you were hurt, it was the worst feeling in the world."

She snuggled closer. "When you almost died, I told myself I'd survive. It was the only way to keep going. But now that you're okay, and we're here, I'm not so sure I could."

He closed his eyes and held her.

She rested her forehead against his jaw. "What are we going to do?"

He hated that she had to deal with this. "We've talked about this before, and my offer still stands."

She stayed quiet for a second. "You mean leaving the force?"

"Yeah."

Marjorie placed her hand on his chest. "If I thought it would help, I'd say yes."

"What do you mean?"

She sat up and rested her elbow on the back of the couch. "You think leaving your job will stop these people? They hold a grudge against you and Rem, and I don't think you having a nine to five is going to convince them to back off."

"We could move."

"Move where? Bolivia?"

"It's an option."

"What about Rem?"

He shifted and put his own elbow on the back of the couch. "Rem and I have discussed this. We've both agreed that if one of us wants out, the other will be hundred percent supportive. We can't do this job without it. The same goes for you and me."

"It's not the same. If you want out, of course I support you. But I can't ask you to do it for me. The same way you wouldn't ask me to leave my job if you wanted me to. At some point, regret sets in."

"When it comes to the safety of my family..."

She wiped her nose with the tissue. "I don't question your love for us, or your determination to keep us safe. We've been down that road, and it almost ended us."

He didn't enjoy recalling when Marjorie and he had separated. "I want to do what's right." He ran his fingers through a strand of her blond hair. "You and J.P. come first."

"You're part of this equation, too." She paused. "Be honest with me. Do you want to leave the force? If J.P. and I were safe, would you resign?"

Daniels didn't have to think hard, because he knew he wouldn't.

"Hesitation," said Marjorie, "means no."

"If you were safe, I wouldn't leave. I love what I do. Despite the hours and the so-so pay, I do something that has meaning. I work with my best friend. I'm never bored, and I help people."

"And that's why I can't ask you to leave."

"Honey, you just told me you're scared something might happen to me." He raised his hand. "And after what happened to you..."

Sighing, she rested her head in her palm. "How many times have we had this conversation?"

"A lot, but it's always worth revisiting, especially after recent events."

She poked at a pillow on the couch. "And I was having a hard day, but that doesn't mean we need to uproot ourselves and move away."

"I'd do it if that's what you want."

"I know you would, but that's not the answer."

"Then what is?"

"If I knew that, then we would have done it by now. But one thing's for sure. Until this society is dealt with, we'll never feel safe."

Tired, he leaned back against the couch and eyed the ceiling. "Well, if we're not moving, and I'm staying at my job, perhaps we need to have the hard conversation." He glanced over at her. "What to do if the worst happens?"

"We've already made arrangements in case something happens to both of us."

He thought back to when he'd had his near-fatal head injury. "I'm not talking about that. I mean, what if it's just one of us?"

She stilled, and her forehead furrowed. "I hate to think about that."

"Me too, but after what's happened to both of us, we should have discussed it sooner."

After a pause, Marjorie sat up. "This requires a gulp of wine." She reached for her glass.

"Agreed." Daniels reached for his glass.

They both swallowed a significant portion of their drinks before returning their glasses to the coffee table.

"Obviously," said Marjorie, her tone somber. "J.P.'s well-being comes first."

"Definitely." Daniels rubbed his pant leg and tried to think seriously about what he would do if he lost Marjorie. "I'd take time off work and evaluate my options. I'd make sure J.P. spent a lot of time with family, especially your mom and sister."

She nodded. "I'd do the same."

"I'd want him to stay around his friends and stick to his routine as much as possible, so I don't think we'd move. I think I'd get counseling for both of us."

"I agree. Routine would be important for him, as would the counseling."

Daniels thought of Rem. "And being around Rem would be important. It goes without saying he would be the father figure I'd want J.P. to have."

Marjorie's eyes watered again. "Of course. Rem would be a major part of J.P.'s life. I'd feel the same about my sister and Mikey, too. They'd both be important people to J.P."

"I'd make sure of it." Thinking about losing Marjorie made his own emotions rise. "Sounds like J.P.'s in good hands."

"He is." She dabbed her eyes again. "I, however, would be a mess."

"So would I, but we'd have great support systems."

"We would." She rested her hand on his wrist. "And when you're ready, I want you to find love again, provided she's a good stepparent to J. P. And..." She poked at the couch cushion. "...she's really ugly."

He chuckled and stroked her cheek. "I feel the same. I want you to be happy too." It was hard to think of Marjorie moving on, but he knew, as it had been for Rem, it was imperative. "So we'd survive, although we'd never be the same."

A tear escaped and trickled down her cheek. "Never."

Imagining his life without her, Daniels' voice tightened. "Other people somehow manage. Rem did, and he's still kickin' and eating his Taco del Fuegos, although it took time."

"But we were there to help him through it, just like he would be for us."

"He would, in a heartbeat."

"So that decides it, then."

"Decides what?"

"Rem can't die, or we're both screwed."

Amused, Daniels raised the side of his lip. "I'll let him know."

"You better." Marjorie slid her fingers into Daniels' hand and squeezed it. She held his gaze, and her watery eyes glistened in the lamplight. "Strangely, this conversation helped."

Daniels gripped her fingers. "It did." Talking about the worst took away some of the fear. "But you better not die."

"You better not either." She shifted closer and leaned into him.

He wrapped his arms around her. "So we stick with the plan. We both keep doing what we're doing? And stay alive?"

Marjorie wrapped her arms around him. "We just keep taking one step, and the next, and then the next..."

"And we'll reevaluate as we go." He smelled her flowery-scented hair. "And reserve the right to change our minds."

She tucked her forehead into his neck. "And no matter what happens, just know that I love you, and always will."

Feeling her warm breath against his skin, he relaxed against the cushions. "I love you too, Marjorie Daniels. Until J.P.'s great grandkids are old and gray." She tightened her grip on him, and he stroked the back of her head, wondering how he'd gotten so lucky to find a woman like her. "You feel better?"

She nodded against him. "I do."

Her breath tickled his neck, and his mind and body responded. He ran his hands down her back. "You want to fool around?"

She laughed, and the sound made his skin tingle. She brought her hand up, trailed it up his neck into his hair, and kissed his skin above his collarbone. "I'd love to."

Her touch made his heart race, and he wanted her as much as he had when he'd first met her. His breathing picking up, he trailed his hand to her jaw, where he tilted her head back and teased her lips with his own.

She moaned, slanted her mouth over his...and the doorbell rang.

· · • • • • • · · ·

Rem ran down the dark street, breathing fast, terror making his voice stick in his throat. Daring to look behind him, he saw the giant black bird chasing him. He picked up his pace, raced down the road and into a field, looking for any cover he could find. The bird swooped down and pecked at his head. Rem screeched and ran faster, desperate to find help. Seeing an alley, he turned into it and ran straight into Sammy Caruso.

The impact caused him to lose his balance, and he hit the ground hard, just as the bird swooped again, aiming its claws at Rem. A loud boom rocked the air, and Rem jumped at the noise. He turned to see Caruso holding and aiming a shotgun at the bird. Unharmed, the bird flew off, and Caruso turned the gun at Rem and sneered. "Now it's your turn."

Rem scooted backwards and raised his hand. "No, don't."

Caruso pulled the trigger, and the gun boomed again.

Rem came awake with a gasp. Clutching his chest, he blinked and pushed up on his couch, relieved he was in his living room, and not lying dead in an alley.

Trying to catch his breath, he swung his legs to the floor and held his head.

"Hey," said Mikey, coming into the room. "You okay?"

Rem looked up. "Yeah. I fell asleep on the couch. Had a bad dream."

She came over and sat beside him. "How bad?"

"Pretty bad." He took a cleansing breath. "But it's not the first, and it won't be the last."

"You want to talk about it?"

He straightened. "Not really."

"Did what happened today trigger it?"

"That would be a logical assumption."

She rubbed his arm. "How about some food? You must be starving."

His stomach rumbled. "I could eat."

"I can warm up the chicken casserole we made the other night."

He stood. "I'll get it. I need the distraction." He headed into the kitchen.

Mikey followed. "Speaking of dreams, I had another one last night. About Vera."

Rem groaned and opened the fridge. "I thought we agreed to a forty-eight-hour reprieve of discussing Margaret."

"Vera seems to have other plans."

"Good for Vera." He pulled out the casserole dish. "Did she say anything new?" He set the dish on the counter.

"She said the same thing. 'She knows.'"

"Great. It would help if Vera could tell you directly. Any chance you asked her?" He grabbed two plates from the cabinet.

"She's not that cooperative." Mikey rested her hip against the counter. "But I did ask her who should go with me."

That got Rem's attention. "What did she say?"

"She said I'd know when the time came."

Rem set the plates beside the dish. "Vera's just a wealth of information."

"That also suggests I'll know the right time to go."

He opened the silverware drawer. "Did you tell her you're getting a little pushback from me?"

"She understands, but she wants me to see my sister, hon, so I need to do this."

He grabbed two forks and shut the drawer. "You don't have to do anything."

"Yes, I do."

"No, you don't."

She crossed her arms. "I have to."

Frustrated, he set the forks on the plates. "We said we'd take a couple of days to sit with it. So let's sit with it."

"It won't change my mind."

"It won't change mine either." He grabbed the forks and used them to dish some casserole onto a plate.

She studied him. "Mason said he'd go with me if I insisted."

Rem's stomach clenched. "Of course he did."

"If he can agree to it, why can't you?"

"He's not agreeing to it, Mikey. You're forcing his hand. Just like you're trying to force mine."

"Why don't you come with us?"

Rem dropped his jaw and made a snort. "Are you out of your mind? You and me? Going to see your sister? That's like dangling a frightened deer in front of a starving tiger. Your sister would pounce faster than the tiger, and you know it."

She hesitated. "I admit. It's not great."

"Then why can't you admit that this whole plan is not great?"

"Because Vera said—"

He dropped the forks onto the plate. "Why is it always about what Vera said? What about what I say? Does that carry any weight?"

"Of course it does. If it didn't, I wouldn't bother to ask."

"And I've told you what I think. I'm not going for it. But that doesn't seem to concern you." He fought to stay calm.

Her jaw clenched. "I can sit and listen about your visit with Tex and Caruso and then wait to see if you get accepted into a society that is responsible for your cousin's murder? And pray you don't get murdered too? And you can't support me on this?"

He grabbed the forks again and added casserole to the second plate. "Damn it, Mikey. It's not the same, and you know it. And it's not fair."

"Why isn't it fair? I want to know who killed Vera, and you want to know who killed Cain."

Rem's head started to pound. After his lousy nightmare, all he could imagine was the bird chasing Mikey. "We're going in circles. I don't know what else you want me to say."

"And I don't know what you want me to say."

Tired of arguing, Rem finished doling out the casserole. "Can't we have one night where we discuss something else?" He picked up one plate and put it in the microwave. He set the timer and hit Start.

Her face tense, Mikey faced him. "What if I was a detective or a private investigator like Mason? Would you stop me then?"

His frustration bubbled over. "I don't care if you're Dick Tracy or Nancy Drew. I don't want you to go," he yelled. "Your sister will use me and your desperation to find Vera's killer against you. You're not equipped to deal with her, Mikey. Neither is Mason. Why can't you see that?"

Mikey's face turned red. "You have no idea what I am *equipped* to deal with."

"Yes, I do."

"Just like you were equipped to deal with Allison?"

He froze. "Where the hell did that come from?"

"Allison Albright was a killer and psychotic, but you went to see her."

"How can you possibly compare the two?" he yelled. "She was threatening me."

"How can I not compare them?" she yelled back. "You did what you had to do."

"And Allison Albright did exactly what your sister would do. She messed with my head. Told me she was having my baby when she wasn't. I left the force because of it. And you wonder why I don't want you to see Margaret?"

"Margaret doesn't hold the amount of power you think she does. Maybe it's time to stop reliving the past."

Rem gaped at her. "And maybe it's time you remember the damage she's done to you, to me, to Daniels, and plenty of others whose names we'll never know." He lowered his voice. "I can't, and I won't, forget that." He paused. "If you go see your sister, then you are just as psychotic as she is."

Mikey's cheeks flared a deeper red. "Well, I guess I know where I stand."

Rem swore under his breath. "I love you, but I'm not changing my mind. Stay away from your sister."

Mikey gritted her teeth and pushed off the counter. "That food is all yours. I've lost my appetite."

He cursed. "Mikey—"

She stomped out of the kitchen.

· · • • • • • • · ·

Kissing his wife, Daniels barely registered the sound of his doorbell until it rang again.

Marjorie pulled back with a sigh, and Daniels' cursed. "If that's Rem, I'm going to kill him."

Marjorie smoothed her hair. "You can't. He has to live, remember?"

"We reserved the right to reevaluate." He stood when the doorbell rang again. "I'm coming." Annoyed by the interruption, he walked to the door and looked through the peephole. Seeing his sister Erin, his annoyance quickly turned to concern, and he opened the door. "Erin?" He looked around. "Everything okay?"

His sister, carrying a large bag over her shoulder, walked inside. "Yes. But I need to talk to you."

He closed the door. "Ever hear of a phone?"

She rolled her eyes. "So you can tell me to stay out of it, stay home, and stay safe?"

Marjorie walked over. "That Daniels' gene runs deep. Hi, Erin. Can I get you something to drink?"

"No, because she's leaving," said Daniels. "You shouldn't be here."

"I'd love a soda," said Erin.

Marjorie hid a smile. "I've got diet. Will that work?"

"Perfect. Thanks, Marjorie."

"Since when do we have diet soda?" asked Daniels.

"Since Rem brought it over," said Marjorie, heading into the kitchen. "Said he didn't want it and wondered if we would since we're so healthy."

Daniels grunted. "Another reason to reevaluate our decision."

Erin pulled the bag off her shoulder. "What decision?"

"Long story," said Daniels. "And why are you here again?"

"I want to show you something." She walked to the dining table, pulled a laptop out of her bag, and tossed the bag onto the floor.

Still annoyed, but curious, Daniels walked over. "What is it?"

She set the laptop on his dining table and opened it. "When you gave me those names to research, and what to look for, I came up with something." She sat at the table.

Daniels pulled a chair over. "I'm afraid to ask." He sat beside her.

Her laptop screen brightened with a password prompt. She typed one in and clicked the touchpad. "Believe me. You need this. Without it, you and Rem will search for years."

Daniels watched her open a screen, which was blank except for one prompt. It asked for a name. "What is this?"

"I created a program that does everything you asked me to do, but way faster."

Daniels scooted closer. "You've got my attention."

She typed in the name Hans Morrow, which was one of the names Daniels had given her, along with two others. She hit enter, and the cursor turned into a swirling circle. Several seconds passed, and the screen changed to one with a list of Hans Morrows.

He leaned closer. "What is this?"

"The criteria you gave me? I fed it into the program. I could give you a lot of tech speak, but I don't want to overwhelm that non-technical brain of yours."

He frowned at her.

Marjorie placed a glass of soda in front of Erin. "She's not wrong, honey."

Daniels frowned at her, too. "I'm not that bad."

"You're not great either. I suspect Rem's even worse." Erin picked up her glass and took a drink. "Thanks, Marjorie."

"You got it." Marjorie pulled a chair closer and sat on the other side of Erin. "What does this do?"

"Well," said Erin, "we're looking for people this society may have recruited, so that likely means prominent people. So, like you said, Gordon, people in high places who could benefit the society."

Daniels followed that much. "Okay."

"So I asked the program to look for a certain age range of people who live in California, with a minimum net worth, and who work in certain professions, like doctors, attorneys, judges, former and current police officers, military, FBI, CIA, business owners, and politicians. You get the gist."

Daniels eyed the screen. "I do."

"And I also included anyone with a criminal record, since we know Victor D'Mato doesn't fit any of the above."

"You can do that?" asked Marjorie.

"I can," said Erin.

Daniels raised his brow. "What exactly do you access to retrieve this information?"

She smirked at him. "As a police officer, it's best you don't know."

Daniels hesitated. "Erin..."

"It's fine, Gordon," said Erin. "Stop worrying. No one is going to know."

Daniels didn't like where this was going. "You're accessing people's private information. If you get caught—"

"Honey," said Marjorie. "Be quiet. Let her talk."

"And I won't get caught," said Erin. "I know what I'm doing. Unless you'd rather take the next six months to research the next two names on the list."

Daniels couldn't argue with that. "I see your point."

Marjorie pointed at the screen. "So who are these Hans Morrows?"

"The results," said Erin, "in order of the highest number of matches. So, your top result is your best candidate." She eyed the screen. "The first Hans is sixty-two, lives outside L.A., has a net worth of twenty mil, give or take, and is a prominent psychiatrist."

Daniels looked closer and saw the headline of a news story. "Is this referencing newspaper articles?"

"Yes," said Erin. She clicked on the first article. "Anything noteworthy in the press will be included."

"That's incredible," said Marjorie.

Daniels scanned the article. "He worked with the military? On mind control experiments?"

Erin nodded. "He did, and when his experiments with soldiers were exposed, they were shut down, and Dr. Morrow disappeared until five years ago, when he reemerged and has since rebuilt his reputation as a prominent doctor in behavioral conditioning."

Daniels sat back. "That would make him a valuable asset to Rook and his society."

"It would," said Erin. "And if you click here..." She moved the cursor to a link and clicked it. "You get his photo."

An image appeared of a distinguished gray-haired man with a weathered face wearing an expensive suit.

"Honey," said Marjorie. "This is amazing."

Daniels couldn't deny this was exactly what they needed, even though he didn't want to imagine the number of laws Erin might be breaking. "Who else has access to this program?"

"Just me," said Erin. "But I can give it to you, Rem, and whoever you want to have it." She ran her finger over the touchpad and opened another screen. "I also created a spreadsheet where you can transfer all of your results, so your information is in one place. That means Rem could update this from home, and you can see his results, and he can see yours. All in real time."

"Much more efficient," added Marjorie.

Daniels glanced at the sheet and saw the names he'd given Erin already listed, with their results, plus three additional names. He frowned. "Where did those names come from? I only gave you the initial three."

She hesitated. "I got them from the list."

"I thought Lexie, Rem and I had the only copies."

She shrugged. "I may have kept a copy after I decrypted the file."

Daniels stared at her. "You kept a copy? For yourself? Where is it?"

She sighed. "I use it as a bookmark. Currently, it's between the pages of *Pride and Prejudice*."

Daniels widened his eyes. "Are you kidding? Erin, do you know how much trouble you could be in if it's found? Why didn't you tell me you kept a copy?"

"Because I knew you'd freak out. And no one will find it. It's hiding in plain sight."

"You shouldn't have it."

"Why not? I can search way faster than you and Rem. Probably Lexie, too. I've done six names in the time you take to do one. I can't promise the results mean they're in the society, but I can be sure they're suitable candidates, and ones worth pursuing." She sat back. "Besides, after what happened to Cain, I feel partially responsible. I want to help bring these people to justice."

Thinking of Mikey's involvement and how much Rem disliked it, Daniels decided to go easier on his partner. "The more you get involved, the more dangerous it is."

"How is this dangerous, Gordon?" asked Marjorie. "She's only doing research. How will anyone know? As long as the list is a secret, it shouldn't be an issue."

"Besides, you didn't even hear the best part," said Erin with a grin. "One of the names I researched? He's a former detective. From Santa Barbara."

Daniels sat up.

"Didn't you say you were looking for a former police officer?" asked Erin.

"We did. We think he might be Tex." He looked at the spreadsheet. "Who is he?"

She tapped the screen with a fingertip. "His name's Tyson Croft. He worked for the Santa Barbara Police Department for twelve years, four of them as a detective, until he was suspended for unlawful use of force, when he almost beat a man to death for stealing a lighter. It never went to trial, and he later resigned."

Daniels' heart hammered with anticipation. "Let me see his face."

Erin clicked the link, and Daniels cursed when Tex's face appeared on the screen. "That's him. That's Tex." He couldn't believe it.

Marjorie smiled. "I'd say that's a convincing reason to use Erin's program."

Daniels studied the photo and reconsidered his options. "You say Rem can get access to this? And Lexie?"

"What about Manetti?" asked Marjorie. "He wants to help, too."

"Yes, they can," said Erin. "The spreadsheet, too. I can get them all on a video call and set them up."

"And none of this will come back to haunt us?" asked Daniels. "It can't be traced back to you?"

"As long as whoever uses it can be trusted, yes," said Erin. "I'll make sure of it." She smiled with satisfaction. "And once we're done, I can erase the whole thing. Like it never existed."

His mind racing with the implications of using Erin's program, Daniels eyed Tex's photo and knew what he had to do. "Let me call Rem." He reached for his phone when the burner phone rang. He'd left it sitting on the table next to his laptop.

He froze, wondering if this was the call they were waiting for. "You two. Don't say a word." He reached for the phone.

Marjorie paled. "Is that him?"

Daniels nodded and put his finger on his lips. Marjorie and Erin went quiet, and he answered. "I'm here. Did you bring our proposal to Rook?"

Tex's voice traveled over the line. "No hello?"

"I think we've gone well past pleasantries."

Tex chuckled. "I suppose we have."

"Well?" asked Daniels. "Are Rem and I going to prison?"

There was a moment of silence. "Even worse, Detective. You've been invited."

Daniels gripped the phone. "Invited where?"

"To Rook's seventy-fifth birthday party. Tomorrow evening at Rook's estate. No gifts required, and leave your guns at home."

Daniels eyed Marjorie and Erin, who were staring back with uncertainty. "Any dress code?"

"Do your best to look decent if you want to influence Rook. Especially your partner. Impressions matter."

"Where and when?"

"I'll text you the details. And don't be late. Rook values promptness."

Daniels spoke calmly so Tex wouldn't pick up on his nervousness. "Then I'll take this as a positive sign."

Tex paused. "Ah, Detective. If you knew what you were getting yourself into, you might reconsider prison."

Daniels' stomach churned.

"See you and your partner tomorrow." Tex hung up.

Daniels lowered the phone and disconnected the call.

"Well?" asked Marjorie.

Daniels put the burner down and picked up his own phone. "One sec." He hit the button to call Rem, who answered on the second ring.

"Hey," said Rem. "I hope your evening is going better than mine."

"Judging by the sound of your voice, I'm going to say it is."

Rem breathed heavily into the phone. "I'll fill you in later. What's up?"

"Two things. Erin created a reliable computer program to research the names on our list in seconds. One of her results identified Tex as Tyson Croft, a former detective from Santa Barbara. Croft just called, and we've been invited to Damien Rook's birthday party tomorrow night."

"Is this a prank call?" Daniels flinched when Rem banged the phone on something hard. His partner came back on the line. "Hello? If this is Daniels, what's Marjorie's middle name?"

Daniels rolled his eyes. "Dana."

"It is? I didn't know that."

"She's named after her grandmother." Daniels shook his head at Marjorie. "Can we get back to Tex?"

"How can you be sure he's Tyson Croft?"

"Because Erin's program hacked God knows what to find him, so using it could get us arrested."

"So, what else is new?"

"And Rook has a dress code, so no holes in your jeans for the party."

"I'll see what I can do, but no promises. Does he have anything against stains?"

"The better the impression, the better, partner, because tomorrow," he made a quiet plea to the gods and hoped they were ready, "...I think we're going to meet the black birds."

Chapter Fourteen

STUDYING HIS PHONE, CROFT leaned against the wall outside Rook's home office. The door was closed, and angry voices traveled from the other side of it. A housekeeper vacuumed in the hallway, and other staff walked through the house, prepping for the big party. None of them paid any attention to the obvious argument, but Croft did. While he didn't catch every word, he caught enough to know that Monk wasn't happy about Daniels and Remalla's invitation.

Monk had arrived at lunchtime, and other than a glare, had ignored Croft and headed into Rook's office. He'd shut the door, and the argument had begun soon after.

Croft listened with interest, wondering how Rook would handle the interruption. Monk barging in without even a warning told Croft the sway the detective had with Rook. No one else would dare do that, including Croft. Rook also didn't like to be questioned about his decisions. Monk's rashness could do exactly as Croft hoped—create a wedge between the two, or it could do the opposite and solidify their relationship. Rook appreciated powerful risk-takers who weren't afraid of him, as long as he respected them and they agreed with him on most points. This altercation between the two would be telling.

Croft had to admit that Rook's about-face with Daniels and Remalla had surprised him, too, although he knew the man had an ulterior motive. He always did. If he was inviting the detectives into the circle, or at least pretending to, he had an ace up his sleeve. Or maybe he planned to use them to do his dirty work until he tired of them. Croft could only wait and see.

The office door opened, and Monk stormed out. "You're making a mistake," he said to Rook, who Croft could see was sitting at his desk. "Those two are playing you."

Rook appeared calm and unfazed. "You let me worry about that." He shot a look at Croft. "See Detective Monk out, Croft. He needs to get back to work."

Judging by the look on Monk's face, Croft half expected Monk to pull his weapon and shoot Rook in the head.

"I can see myself out." Monk grabbed the door handle. "But don't ever say you weren't warned." He shut the office door before Rook could respond.

Croft waved his hand toward the front of the house. "Right this way."

Monk smirked at him. "And you're just as deluded as he is." He headed down the hall, and Croft followed.

"He knows what he's doing," said Croft.

"He's losing it, and you know it. He's reckless."

Croft couldn't deny that but wasn't going to admit it. "I'm monitoring things, and he trusts me."

Monk kept walking. "The only person he trusts is the person in that guest house."

That surprised Croft. "You know about that?"

Monk stopped in the front foyer. "I've been here a lot longer than you, and I know a lot more than you realize." He took a step closer and sharpened his tone. "And if you have some fantasy that you're going to push me out by kissing Rook's wrinkled ass, you're going to find out the hard way that I'm not going anywhere."

Determined to assert his dominance, Croft didn't move. "You sure about that? I'm the one who's here, learning everything I can. It won't be long before I know more about this organization than you do."

Monk glared. "Be very careful what you wish for, Croft. You don't want to make me an enemy."

Croft suspected Monk already considered him a threat. "I'll do whatever Rook asks of me."

"Judging by his recent decision-making, you'd better think long and hard about continuing that, or he's going to take you down with the ship."

"So you can stand by and pick up all the pieces?"

Monk grinned. "I'm very good at taking care of myself."

"So am I."

"Then we'll see who's the last man standing, because it isn't going to be both of us."

Croft didn't break his gaze with Monk, and something uncomfortable fluttered inside him. "Who's in the guest house?"

Monk's grin widened. "Pray you never find out." He turned and walked to the door. "Have fun at the party."

Croft stared as Monk left. The flutter of discomfort grew, and his mind spun with the possible next steps. It was obvious Monk would not be an easy foe to bring down. He knew too much, and he'd clearly made an impression on Rook. Thinking of his options, Croft closed the door and returned down the hall.

· · · ● · ● · · ·

Walking toward his car, Monk pulled out his phone, hit a button, and put the phone to his ear.

Rhonda picked up. "How'd it go?"

"He's moving forward. He believes he can turn them."

"He's a fool."

"Maybe. Maybe not. But at least I told him what I thought. He'll do what he wants." He got to his car and got in. "But that could benefit us." He shut the door.

"How so?"

"The crazier he gets, the more likely he is to fail. And he could end up losing control. Bringing those two in will rouse concern among the members. They're already questioning the dolls and ceremonies. This could be our opening."

"It will bring Daniels and Remalla closer, too. If they learn too much, it could lead straight to us."

"They're going to be dead long before that happens. If Rook can't do it, I will."

He heard her moan. "Now you're turning me on." She paused. "I assume you'll need my help?"

"Always. But not with Daniels and Remalla. Not yet. First, we have another issue." He eyed the driveway as a large caterer's truck pulled up and parked. "We're going to have to do something about this Tyson Croft."

"Love to, baby. I have the star whenever you're ready."

The sexy sound of her voice made his body heat. "I love it when you talk dirty." Already imagining Croft's death, Monk started his car and drove away.

······ ● ● ·····

Rem pulled up behind a row of cars that led to the valet in the driveway of Damien Rook's gated estate. "You ready?" he asked Daniels.

Daniels eyed the walkway that led to the house. "Are you?"

Rem studied the three-story mansion encircled by a vivid green landscaped lawn and round, thick shrubs. A stone walkway led to a wide stone porch with four tall white columns that spanned the first and second floors. Paved steps led up to an immense wooden and intricately carved door. "I don't know if ready is the right word. Maybe cautiously prepared." He inched his car closer to the valet stand.

One valet ran up and opened the door. Rem got out and handed him his key fob and pertinent info to collect his car later. The valet got behind the wheel, and Rem followed Daniels onto the walkway. "How we doing on time?" asked Rem. "Are we prompt enough?"

"It's a little after seven," said Daniels. "So prompt enough without looking too eager."

Rem smoothed his white-collared shirt and pulled on the sleeves of his black leather jacket. "At least he can't accuse me of not following the dress code."

Daniels looked him over. "Did Mikey help you dress?"

He sighed. "No, she didn't. I didn't see her when I got home. She worked late today. She's still mad at me."

"Don't worry," said Daniels. "You two will figure it out. You're just both headstrong and obstinate."

Rem hoped Daniels was right. He'd been disappointed not to have seen Mikey before going to the party. After their argument, they'd said little to each other. Marjorie had called not long after Rem had spoken to Daniels, and she'd invited Mikey to have dinner with her and Erin while Rem and Daniels were at the party, so at least Rem knew where Mikey was. He hoped her spending time with the girls might help her talk through her frustrations, since Rem's opinions seemed to only make things worse.

Daniels adjusted his navy blazer over his yellow shirt. "I'll admit. We both clean up nice."

"Let's hope Rook is just as impressed."

"You got those faces memorized?"

Rem almost laughed. "Clear as mud."

"Me too. Let's hope once we meet people, it'll be easier."

"Let's hope."

After talking with Daniels the previous evening, Erin had arranged a quick video call with Rem, Lexie, and Manetti. Lexie had whooped out loud when she'd heard about Erin's program. Manetti had seemed more dubious but was willing to try it.

After giving access to everyone, Erin had added all the names on the list to the spreadsheet and assigned the ones to be researched. It didn't take long to realize, though, that Erin and Lexie could work much faster than Rem, Daniels and Manetti. By lunchtime, Erin and Lexie had gone through the entire list and had populated the spreadsheet with all the likely candidates who were potential members of the society. After Rem and Daniels got home, they'd gone through as many photos as possible, trying to memorize the faces. If they saw them at the party, they could confirm who was a member. By the time they'd gone through all the pictures, Rem could barely see straight.

They approached the impressive doors, where other partygoers mingled on the porch. Rem studied them, but no one looked familiar. More arriving guests walked up the steps behind them, and Rem fought the urge to turn and stare.

"Just act natural," said Daniels. "And don't gawk at people, especially Croft, when you see him."

"Gawking's not the issue," said Rem. "I'm worried I'll call him by his name, and not Tex."

Daniels frowned. "Try not to do that."

The doors opened before they could knock. A man dressed in a black and white suit welcomed them inside and guided them to a front table. "All phones must be turned in. You can collect them before you leave."

A woman, also dressed in a black-and-white uniform, sat behind the table. She offered them a ticket when they handed over their phones. Next to the table were a man and a woman, each holding the same wand-like device Rem and Daniels had been scanned with when they'd met Rook. As the guests left the table, they were inspected with the wands. "Talk about being cautiously prepared," said Daniels, taking his ticket from the woman.

"Rook doesn't take chances." Rem put his ticket in his pocket. He stepped to the side and held out his hands as the woman waved the device over him. Daniels did the same as other partygoers arrived and turned in their phones. Those already at the party gathered and chatted in a large sunken living room with white couches and a long glass coffee table. Most of the color came from elaborate oil paintings on the walls. Rem saw others walking past an immense kitchen and out into a backyard. "Care to look around?" asked Rem.

"Love to," said Daniels.

They passed a wide staircase with an iron railing that led to the second floor. Beyond that was the enormous kitchen where staff worked to prepare drinks and food. The nearby dining area had a table loaded with trays of fruit, cheese, crackers, dips, and caviar. A server walked by with a tray of champagne and offered each of them a glass. Sipping champagne, they passed a smaller den with more paintings and a big TV, where other guests mingled, before stepping into the backyard. Standing on the back porch, Rem saw a tall, billowy white tent set up over several round tables with white chairs. Elaborate place settings for dinner were arranged on the tables. A band on a stage near the tent played soft jazz music, and two couples danced on a dance floor set up on the lawn in front of the band.

"Not bad," said Rem. "If you like this kind of opulence." Cobblestones and lawn chairs encircled a long lap pool with a bubbling fountain and a hot tub.

Near the pool was an outdoor kitchen, where more servers worked, and a tennis court was at the back of the property, behind the pool.

"It is a little gauche," said Daniels.

Rem raised his brow at his partner. "Gauche? How hoity-toity of you."

Daniels' face fell. "Please don't say hoity-toity."

"Then don't say gauche."

Daniels looked around. "Any sign of Rook?"

"I'm sure the birthday boy will make a grand entrance after most of his guests have arrived."

"I'm sure. What about Cr—" He made a face. "Sorry. Tex."

"And I'm worried about me."

"We're going to be fine. We just need to relax. Drink your champagne."

Rem took a sip. "We'd better be careful with the booze. The last thing we need is to get drunk."

"Then take small sips." Daniels stepped down the patio steps and out onto the lawn. Rem followed, watching the guests.

"See anyone familiar?" asked Rem.

Daniels studied the crowd. He started to shake his head but stopped. "Over there." He raised his champagne glass. "That's Chogan Crow."

Rem spotted Elsa Crow's father speaking to another guest. "So it is. Interesting." He looked around. "I hope Elsa isn't here."

Daniels gripped his glass. "I hope not. That would require some explaining."

Rem checked out the other guests. "I don't see her." He paused. "Although her father could easily tell his daughter we were here."

"He's a black bird. If he thinks we're potential members, he won't say a word."

"Assuming Elsa's not a member."

"She's not on the list."

"We're assuming the list is accurate."

"That is not helpful right now."

"We have to assume the worst, don't you think?"

"Not at the moment, we don't. Let's just survive this party."

"Okay." Rem sipped his champagne. "I'll think the worst later." He scanned the crowd, which was rapidly growing larger, and saw two more people he recognized. "Look. Over by the pool. It's Barbara Ingram and Ben Crenshaw."

Daniels glanced over. "Makes sense. Rook is a big client of theirs."

"A client who got Reginald Durning killed. Plus, if Barb Ingram's a member. It makes me wonder about Crenshaw."

"Can you see him taking orders from Rook?"

"Rook is their client."

"Who pays their law firm for its services. That's different. The egos on Rook and Crenshaw are too big to play well together in some secret club."

"I can believe that." Rem continued to scan the crowd. "See anyone who matches the possible Rita Vittorio photos?" Rita Vittorio remained high on their list to find.

"Not yet," said Daniels. His eyes narrowed, and he nudged Rem. "Over there. Older man in the fancy red and black suit with the red tie."

Rem found the man Daniels was pointing out. He was talking to an older, stately woman with silver-white shoulder-length hair, wearing a long sparkly dress. The man's face was familiar, and Rem kept a flat expression when he recognized him. "Is that Hans Morrow? The psychiatrist?"

"That's him. Number one on our list of results for Dr. Morrow. Erin's a genius."

"The next black bird member identified. I wish I had my phone."

"Just commit it to memory."

"My memory is full."

Daniels raised a brow. "When's the last time you had a Taco del Fuego?"

Rem thought back. "One week ago. Last Friday, to be exact. At seven thirty. Nope. Make that eight thirty. I'm overdue for another."

"I think your memory is just fine, sport."

"Food is one thing. Photos of secret society members are another."

They watched the crowd as more people arrived and worked their way around the lawn. Rem thought he recognized one woman as Natalia Ferndale. She was a judge or possibly a lobbyist. He couldn't recall.

Daniels pointed out a man he thought might be Marcus Corvus, a tech entrepreneur and wealthy owner of a surveillance and security company.

The crowd grew, and Rem found it harder to keep track of everyone. "Maybe we should mingle? Get a better look at people?"

"Probably a good idea." Daniels set his empty champagne glass on a tray, along with Rem.

Another server stopped and offered them fresh glasses, and they each took one again. "Maybe we ought to hit the cheese and crackers too," said Rem, "if we're going to keep drinking."

Daniels nodded, and they headed inside to grab a plate and some food.

"Detectives," said a male voice from behind him.

Rem turned to see Judge Thomas Gunderson approach with a young, attractive redhead likely half his age on his arm. "Judge Gunderson."

"I didn't expect to see you two here," said the judge. "How do you know Damien Rook?"

Rem gave thanks they'd prepared themselves for the question.

Daniels picked up a plate. "We met Rook during our investigation of the missing protestors who were against Rook's new development going in."

"He was at Pinnacle Properties," said Rem, "when we interviewed a few people there."

"You must have made an impression," said Gunderson.

Daniels glanced at Rem. "It wouldn't be the first time," said Daniels.

"We tend to be memorable," said Rem.

Gunderson made a meek attempt at a smile.

"It was nice of Rook to invite us." Rem waved his hand toward the kitchen. "He has quite the home."

"He does," said Gunderson. "And quite the circle of friends."

"We've noticed," said Daniels. "We've seen some powerful people."

"It must be slightly intimidating," said Gunderson. "Especially if you're not used to this type of crowd."

Rem caught Gunderson's hard-to-miss slight. "We're holding our own. Daniels and I are more comfortable than you'd think." He picked up a piece of cheese and popped it in his mouth.

Never bothering to introduce his date, Gunderson eyed Rem. "I heard your girlfriend was cleared of those murder charges. I'm sure you're relieved."

Rem stiffened and clutched his champagne glass. "I'm relieved an overzealous detective, who served me a rather convenient search warrant at my home, learned the hard way that he was wrong all along."

The wrinkles around Gunderson's eyes creased deeper.

"Thankfully," said Daniels, "Mikey was cleared. It was curious, though, how she was targeted."

"Targeted?" Gunderson shifted his attention to Daniels. "From what I heard, there was substantial reason to suspect her," he looked back at Rem, "and search your home."

Rem held Gunderson's gaze. "You heard wrong."

"You should reevaluate your sources, Judge," said Daniels. "Sometimes they're not as reliable as you think."

Gunderson's gaze flicked back to Daniels, and he didn't respond.

"Can I get you some cheese, Judge?" asked Rem. He perused the table of food. "They even have the stinky kind. That seems right up your alley."

The judge's eyes glimmered, and he put his hand behind his date's back. "I think I'll head outside." He guided his date to the door. "And talk to some of those powerful people."

"You do that," said Daniels, with a flat stare. "We'll be around, though. In case you get bored." He ate a cracker.

The judge didn't respond and walked away with his date.

Rem stared through the window as the judge stepped down the patio steps.

"What do you think of that?" asked Daniels, also staring.

"I'd like to stuff that search warrant he signed right down his throat."

"He deliberately brought up Mikey. Just to piss you off." He glanced at Rem. "Why? To test us? Or is he just annoyed Rook invited us?"

"I don't know," said Rem. He lowered his voice. "But when we bust this little society, he's gonna be my first stop."

Daniels handed him a plate. "Here. Eat some cheese and stop staring daggers at the judge. We might be bird brothers soon."

Rem grabbed a pair of tongs and added various cubes of cheese to his plate. "He comes at me again, and I'm going to shove these tongs right up his—"

"Nice to see you, detectives. Glad you could join us."

Rem straightened and saw Tyson Croft approach. "This party just keeps getting better and better."

"Glad you're getting some food," said Croft. "And getting to know some guests."

"It's quite the party," said Daniels. "Rook didn't spare any expense."

Rem kept repeating Tex in his head to be sure not to say Croft. "Where is the guest of honor?"

"On his way," said Croft.

"I thought he valued promptness," said Daniels.

"He does," said Croft, "with his guests." He reached around Daniels and picked up a grape. "Don't eat too much, fellas. The dinner buffet is coming up." He smiled and ate the grape. "And that's just the beginning." He grabbed a flute of champagne from a passing server. "Enjoy yourselves." He sipped the drink and walked away.

Rem watched Croft stop on the patio and greet some guests. "Doesn't he think we'd figure out his name at this party? All we'd have to do is talk to people."

"You're assuming these people know who he is," said Daniels. He glanced back. "I'm going to get some caviar."

Rem watched Daniels scoop caviar onto his plate. "Since when do you eat caviar?"

Daniels shrugged. "When in Rome..."

Rem added more cheese and some crackers to his plate. "Rook should have ordered tacos and beer. Then he'd have a party worth remembering."

Daniels spread caviar onto a toast point. "The night's still young."

They ate and wandered back out onto the patio, continuing to survey the crowd and talk to various guests. The band switched over to big band music, and more couples danced. Rem talked to various partygoers, none of whom looked like any of the photos he and Daniels had studied, but they had to engage and join the party. There was no way of knowing whether they were being watched.

Not long after speaking with Tiffany, a young woman with bleached blonde hair, wearing a skintight leopard dress, who proclaimed herself to be a social media fashion influencer in high demand with all the major fashion studios, Rem heard a murmur through the crowd and then a cheer.

Daniels, who'd been talking to a guest who claimed to host a popular podcast, turned. "Looks like the guest of honor has arrived."

Damien Rook stepped out onto the patio. Dressed in a tailored black suit with his salt and pepper hair slicked back, he held a champagne glass in the air. The band stopped playing, and the guests quieted.

"Welcome, everyone," he said. "I hope you're having a good time." He put his arm around the woman who stood beside him. She was much younger and wore a striking blue dress that emphasized her curves. Her long blonde hair traveled down her back, and she smiled up at Rook.

"Happy Birthday, Rook!" someone yelled from the crowd.

"You don't look a day over seventy-four," yelled someone else.

The guests laughed, and Rook chuckled. "Thank you all for coming. You're all my closest friends." The crowd laughed again. "Everybody eat and drink. The party is just getting started."

The crowd cheered, and a staff member appeared beside Rook. "Dinner is served," he said over the crowd. "Please help yourself at the buffet." He gestured toward the pool.

Rem glanced over and saw an enormous table with platters of food set up near the outdoor kitchen. Guests wandered toward the table and picked up plates.

"I guess that's our cue," said Daniels.

"Yay," said Tiffany. "I think I see Gianni Versace." She took off toward a well-dressed older man with spiky white hair wearing lots of jewelry.

Daniels' face fell. "You think we should tell her?"

"She'll find out soon enough." Rem looked back toward Rook, who was talking to partygoers, but focused on the woman at his side. "Does the woman with Rook look familiar to you?"

Daniels looked in that direction. The woman grabbed a glass of champagne from a server's tray and took a significant gulp. "She does."

Rem studied her and widened his eyes. "Is that Delaina Desmond?"

Daniels knitted his brow. "Ben Crenshaw's assistant?"

The woman took another hefty gulp of her drink while Rook spoke to a woman in a gold-striped dress with hair as big as the platter of beef on the buffet.

"It is," said Daniels. "What the hell is she doing with Rook?"

"It appears they're a couple," Rem watched as Delaina took another drink of champagne. "She has to be forty years younger than him."

"Look at him, though. As you said, he's like the guy in the beer ad. If I didn't know his age, I'd peg him in his sixties."

"The most interesting man alive," added Rem. "He's definitely doing something right. Or he's got a skilled plastic surgeon."

Delaina finished her champagne and picked up another glass from a passing server. "Judging by the way she's drinking," said Daniels, "all is not well in paradise."

Rem felt sorry for her. "That woman could have any man she wanted."

"Maybe that's who she wants."

"Doesn't look that way to me."

"Or, she's quickly realizing she's a toy on his arm, and not much more," said Daniels. "He hasn't spoken one word to her."

Rem had another thought. "Or Crenshaw planted her as one of his moles."

Daniels stepped past a woman talking to a tall, stately man with silver hair. "You think he'd go that far?"

"He tried it with Durning, remember? He sent Delaina after him to get information. It's possible he's doing the same with Rook."

"That would make Crenshaw one sneaky bastard."

"And Delaina one dangerous, or manipulated, woman."

Daniels finished his champagne. "She's not stupid."

"That all depends," said Rem, finishing his champagne, "on what Crenshaw, or Rook, told her."

Daniels set his empty glass on a nearby tray. "We'll have to keep an eye on her."

"Definitely." Rem set his empty glass down. "Let's eat."

They headed toward the buffet and stood in line for food. Rem could see prime rib, chicken, and fish, plus pasta, vegetables, and salad options. On its own table, toward the end of the pool, was an enormous five-tiered chocolate cake with a large candle on top. Hungry, he grabbed a plate when Daniels smacked his arm.

"Hey. Look who's joined the party."

Rem turned to see another man standing and talking to Rook. His mind whirled through the photos in his brain, and it didn't take long to make a match. "That's Ezra Grimm."

"Ruben Montes' cousin and the Montes' family attorney." Daniels picked up a plate. "So much for promptness. He showed up after Rook made his little speech."

"Rook doesn't seem to mind." Grimm had dark hair, a well-trimmed beard and sparkling white teeth. He wore a silk red shirt, white pants, and a tan jacket. "He looks straight out of *Miami Vice*."

Rook appeared to introduce Delaina to Grimm, who took her hand and kissed the back of it. "I hope Delaina knows what the hell she's getting herself into," said Rem.

Daniels nudged Rem. "I wonder if Crenshaw is thinking the same." He nodded toward the tents, and Rem looked to see Ben Crenshaw, holding a plate of food, watching Rook and Grimm with an intense expression.

"He's just as curious as we are."

"I doubt it's for the same reason." Daniels stepped up to the buffet.

They worked their way down the buffet table and, their plates full, headed toward the tents, where they sat at an empty table. A server came by and offered them wine with their meal. Rem got a glass of red and Daniels white, and hungry, Rem dug into his prime rib, while Daniels ate his fish.

A couple approached the table. "Mind if we join you?" asked the woman.

Rem recognized the older, stately lady in the sparkly dress who'd been speaking with Hans Morrow earlier. She held a plate of food, and Hans walked up beside her, also holding a plate.

"Please do," said Daniels, with a glance at Rem.

The woman sat beside Daniels and Hans sat on the other side of her. "Thank you," she said. She set her plate down and put the napkin in her lap. "I don't believe we've met."

Daniels wiped his fingers. "No. We haven't. I'm Gordon Daniels, and this is my partner, Aaron Remalla."

Rem set his fork down. "Nice to meet you."

"Partners?" she asked.

"We're detectives," said Rem.

"Oh, yes," she said. "Damien said he'd invited some detectives." She glanced at Hans. "Right, Hans?"

Cutting his meat, Hans barely acknowledged them. "Something like that." He put a bite in his mouth and chewed.

"You must know Damien well," said Daniels. "We just recently met him."

Hans offered a grunt.

"Oh, my yes," said the woman. "I'm his half-sister." She offered her hand. "My name's Rita Vittorio."

Chapter Fifteen

DANIELS DID HIS BEST not to react, took Rita's hand and shook it. He did not look at Rem. "Pleasure to meet you, Rita."

Rem leaned over Daniels and offered his hand. "Pleasure, Rita."

They shook, and Rem sat back, offering a quick knowing glance at Daniels.

Noting the potential photos of various Rita Vittorios Erin's program had acquired as possibles were all wrong, Daniels started asking questions. "We didn't know Damien had a sister."

He and Rem ate while having a casual conversation with Rita and receiving only the occasional grunt from Hans. They learned she was a retired attorney who used to work for Damien until they had a falling out. Estranged for a couple of years, Rita and Rook had only recently made amends, and Damien had invited her to the party. Daniels was struggling to understand how she'd ended up on the black bird list because Rita did not strike him as someone who would join a secret society nor the type of member Rook would want, unless he'd expected his family to join. Since Ackerman had listed her name along with Belson, Morgans, and Durning's, he wondered if she'd become a potential target because of the estrangement. But why would Rook want to kill his sister? It was another mystery to solve.

Another couple joined the table, and the group engaged in conversation while Daniels kept an eye on Rook, who'd made his way through the buffet and was now eating with Delaina at a table at the front of the tent. He was sitting with Grimm, Chogan Crow and his date, and Barbara Igram and Ben Crenshaw. Judging by Delaina's drink, she'd moved on to something stronger than champagne. Rook was drinking too, and the table occasionally broke into raucous laughter.

The band played a disco song, and more couples strode out onto the dance floor. Glancing at his watch, Daniels saw they'd been there for almost three hours and wondered at what point the reason they'd been invited would become clear.

Rita asked them about their detective work, and he and Rem spent the next several minutes discussing various cases and the unique situations they'd found themselves in. The servers continued to fill their wineglasses, and Daniels found himself enjoying Rita's company, although Hans's social skills were deplorable.

Not long after Rem told the story about arresting a naked man in a local park, the band changed songs as the birthday cake was rolled into the tent close to Rook. The candle on top was lit, the band played happy birthday, and they all sang to Rook, who beamed with a smile. Delaina took another hefty gulp of whatever she was drinking as Rook blew out the candle, thanked everyone for coming again, and, since the night was still young, told them to keep dancing, eating and drinking.

Needing to use the facilities, Daniels put his napkin on the table. "Anyone know where the little boy's room is?"

"It's just past the kitchen," said Rita. "Down the hall. On your right."

"Thank you." Daniels glanced at Rem. "Be right back."

"Don't get lost." Rem leaned toward Rita and narrowed an eye. "Do you believe in shapeshifters?"

Making a mental note to tell Rem to stop drinking, Daniels headed toward the house. He jogged up the patio, entered the back door, and passed the kitchen buzzing with activity. The bathroom was exactly where Rita had said it was, and after using it, he washed his hands, wishing he could text Marjorie to tell her everything was okay. He left the restroom and stopped short in the hall when he almost bumped into Barbara Ingram.

She regarded him with the same contempt she had when he and Rem had interviewed her, Crenshaw, and their partner, Charles Willoughby, at CIW. "What are you doing here?" she asked bluntly.

Daniels glanced at the bathroom door and shot out his thumb. "Nature called. The room's free if you need it."

She gave him a frosty look. "Why are you at Damien Rook's party?"

"Um...Rem and I were invited?"

"And you said yes?"

Daniels paused. "Are these the questions you'd ask a witness on the stand? Because I assumed you'd do a lot better."

She scowled. "You and your partner don't belong here."

Daniels couldn't imagine why she disliked him and Rem so much. "Why is that?"

"These people could eat you for lunch. And they will."

"Right now, they seem to be doing just fine with the prime rib and birthday cake."

She put her hand on her hip. "Have you even come close to solving Reginald Durning's murder? Or are you too busy going to millionaires' birthday parties?"

"Actually, this is the first." He wondered what she would say if he told her they knew who killed Reginald, and that's why they were at the party. But as a society member, Barbara likely already knew that. Was she trying to scare him and Rem away? "And no. We haven't solved Durning's murder. Yet."

He held her gaze, but she wasn't intimidated. "If you know what's best for you, get out of here," she said. "And take your idiot partner with you."

"And why should I do that?"

She jutted out her chin. "I don't know what your plan is, Detective, but Rook is playing you. As much as I'd love to see your downfall, this isn't the way to do it."

"What downfall? And why would you love to see it? Why do you hate me and my partner so much? You don't even know us."

The glimmer in her eyes intensified. "I know all I need to know. You're reckless, impulsive, and malicious. What you have done to..." She stopped.

He waited, wishing he could read her mind.

She huffed and tucked her small purse under her arm. "What happened to your wife and your partner's cousin is only the beginning, Detective."

Daniels scowled back at her. "How do you know about that?"

After a pause, she reached for the bathroom doorknob. "On second thought, maybe you and your partner are exactly where you need to be. Excuse me." She entered the bathroom and closed the door in his face.

Unnerved by her statement, Daniels shook his head and headed down the hall. He stopped at the kitchen when a line of servers, all carrying trays of drinks, walked past him. Waiting, he looked across the sunken living room and saw Rook and another man talking in an office. Based on their animated movements, the conversation was heated.

"Can I help you with something, sir?" said a male server from the kitchen.

Keeping an eye on Rook, Daniels stepped up to the counter. "Do you have any water?"

"Of course." The man grabbed a glass and filled it with ice. "Although I make a mean Old Fashioned."

"Tempting. But I'd better stick to water."

The server followed Daniels' gaze. "That Mr. Rook is always working. Even during his own party."

Daniels glanced at the man. "The curse of the workaholic."

The server nodded. "Especially Mr. Rook. I think he's in there more than any other room in the house." He added water to the glass from a pitcher on the counter.

Wondering what he might learn from the staff member, Daniels stepped closer. "How long have you worked here?"

He handed Daniels the glass of water. "Going on five years."

"Thank you." Daniels took a sip. "My name is Gordon." He offered his hand.

"Bernie," said the server, shaking Daniels' hand.

"I bet you've seen a few things, Bernie."

The server pursed his lips, glanced toward the office and back at Daniels. "That's the curse and blessing of the household help. After a while, we become invisible."

Daniels watched the man talking to Rook in the office stomp out. Rook followed, closed the door behind him, and returned to the party. Eyeing Bernie, Daniels acted drunk, which wasn't that hard. He chuckled and leaned in. "Any good stories?"

Bernie smiled. "I'm supposed to *act* invisible, too."

"That's no fun." He put his finger to his lips. "Promise. I won't tell."

Bernie hesitated but lowered his voice. "I've seen and heard arguments. And all kinds of people come and go. Some scared, some not scared, until they leave." He paused and leaned in. "I even heard chanting once."

Daniels frowned. "Chanting?"

"I walked by a room upstairs. Mr. Rook was talking to someone in there, and there were candles. And I even saw some bones."

Daniels thought of the finger bone found in the alley where Bailey had been murdered. "Bones? Why would Mr. Rook have bones?"

Bernie shrugged. "There are things that go on here that I don't ask about."

"You seen anything else?"

Another server walked by and bumped into Bernie, which seemed to remind him of where he was. "I shouldn't say anything."

Daniels looked around. "Don't stop now. You're on a roll."

"How do I know you're not a secret reporter?"

Daniels scoffed. "I doubt that would get past Mr. Rook. Besides, I almost flunked out of English class."

Bernie studied him and leaned in again. "There was one time another staff member went into Rook's office without his okay, and well..."

Daniels waited. "Well, what?" he whispered.

Bernie paused as a guest walked by. "Word is, they got curious. Too curious. Rook found out and..." He spoke even lower. "I heard they ended up at the guest house."

That was a new term. "What's the guest house?"

"I don't know, but I don't ever want to go there."

"What happens at the guest house?"

Bernie widened his eyes. "Don't know, but nobody saw that staff member again." He glanced towards the office. "All I know for sure is Rook is very particular about his office, and no one goes in there without him." He stopped when another server walked behind him. "The gossip is all his secrets are in there. And after I saw those bones, I don't want to know what those secrets are."

"Secrets, huh?" asked Daniels. "Interesting."

"Bernie," said a loud female voice from behind Daniels.

Bernie quickly pulled back.

Daniels swiveled to see Barbara behind him.

"Hello, Miss Ingram," said Bernie, picking up the tray from the counter behind him.

"You two seemed to be in deep conversation." Barbara narrowed her eyes at Daniels and Bernie.

"We were." Seeing Bernie's worry, Daniels gestured at him. "Bernie was telling me how to make a mean Old Fashioned. Apparently, he's a pro."

Bernie smiled. "I can still make you one."

"Nah," said Daniels with a wave. "I better slow down, but thanks."

"I should get back to the party." Bernie balanced the tray on his hand and left the kitchen.

"I should too," said Daniels. "Go find that partner of mine before he does something he shouldn't." He grinned at Barbara.

"You should have done that a long time ago." She aimed another steely gaze at him and stomped away.

· · · • · • • · ·

Rem finished his drink and laughed at a joke Rita told. The other couple at the table had gone to the dance floor, and Rem took a bite of his cake, which he'd just been served. Feeling oddly relaxed considering the situation they were in, he stabbed another piece of cake with his fork. "So, tell me, Rita. Why were you estranged from Damien?" He ate the bite.

Rita's demeanor shifted, along with Hans'. "That's a long story." She fiddled with her napkin, and after a pause, Hans stood and offered his hand to Rita. "Let's dance."

Her tension obvious, Rita eyed his hand and took it. "Of course."

Rem studied Morrow and wondered why he'd suddenly come to life, since he'd barely spoken during dinner, and had said little to Rita.

"Be right back," said Rita, following Hans onto the dance floor.

"Have fun," said Rem. He watched them dance, and debated how to get Morrow away from her, because he suspected Rita would be a wealth of knowledge about Rook, provided she could talk freely.

"Hey, handsome. Fancy seeing you here."

Rem turned to see Delaina Desmond sit beside him. "Delaina?" He glanced back at Rook's table. Rook, who'd left briefly, had returned and was in deep conversation with Ezra Grimm. "What are you doing here?"

She leaned in and spoke in a whisper. "I could ask you the same question." Slightly slurring her words, she looked him over. "Although I'm not sad about it. You're a sight for sore eyes."

Uncomfortable with her perusal, Rem scooted back in his seat. "You're drunk. Maybe you should go back and sit with your boyfriend."

Her face fell, and she shot a look at Rook. "What for?" She returned her attention to Rem. "I think I'd rather stay here." She smiled seductively and put her hand on Rem's knee. "Where's your partner?"

"In the john, but he'll be back in a minute." He moved her hand off his knee.

"Good. I like him too. You two are quite a pair." Her hand returned to his knee. "But at least you're not married."

He put his hand over hers to keep it from sliding farther up his leg. "I'm taken too, Delaina. Sorry."

She pouted. "Lots of guys say that. But they don't mean it." She leaned closer, and Rem could smell her perfume and the liquor on her breath.

"I'm one of the few who do." He risked another glance at Rook and was dismayed to see Rook staring at them. Rem cursed to himself. "You really should go back to your table, Delaina. Damien isn't happy."

Delaina glanced at Rook and smiled. "Good. Now he knows how it feels."

Rem moved her hand to the table. "Why are you with him if he makes you miserable?" Rem figured if he was in this situation, he ought to try to get some information. "He doesn't strike me as your type."

Her expression turned dark. "I do what I have to do to get what I want." She lowered her voice. "I know things, Detective. As Crenshaw loves to tell me, knowledge is power."

"Not if it costs you your soul."

She stared into his eyes, and he wondered what she was thinking when she abruptly stood and grabbed his hand. "Dance with me."

"I don't think that's a—"

She yanked on him and would have fallen if he hadn't stood and caught her. She laughed, grabbed his arm, and yanked him toward the other dancing couples. "C'mon, handsome. It's a party. Let's have some fun."

Groaning, he followed her out onto the floor. He caught another look at Rook, whose eyes were shooting icy shards at Rem. "This is really not a good idea."

Delaina moved closer. "Let him watch. He needs to know how to treat a lady."

Rem groaned again when the song ended and the band began to play *Moon River*, the absolute worst song for this moment. Delaina put her arm around his waist, wrapped her fingers around his other hand, and rested her forehead on his shoulder.

"This is nice," she said, swaying against him.

Rem looked for Daniels, praying his partner could get him out of this situation. "Rook is going to kill me."

She giggled and moved her lips closer to his neck. "Yes. He is. But not because of this."

Curious, Rem slowly danced with her. "What does that mean?"

She sighed, and her breath warmed his skin. "You'll find out soon enough."

He eyed the crowd for Daniels. "What do you know, Delaina?"

She didn't answer.

"Is Crenshaw using you to get to Rook?" He felt the slight tension in her body. "You don't have to do what he says. There are other jobs."

She let go of his hand and put her hand on his chest. "You don't know what I've been through."

"It doesn't matter what you've been through. What matters is where you are and what you choose to do next."

"Easy for you to say."

"It's not easy for me to say. I've been through the wringer. I've been at the bottom where I couldn't see my hand in front of my face, but I found a way out."

She looked up at him. "You have people who love you."

For the first time, he saw the desperation in her eyes. "If you need help, you can tell me."

She held his gaze, and the same dull expression returned. "Why? So you can turn on me? I know you and your partner are here to get in Damien's good graces. You're just like the rest of them."

"Not everything is as it seems." He understood the risk of telling her that, but his gut couldn't let this woman walk off without giving her some hope. "There's always a way out, Delaina." She slid her hand up his chest to his shoulder. "And you don't have to use me to get attention. You need help, all you have to do is ask."

Her body tensed again, and her eyes shimmered. Continuing to dance, she rested her head back against his shoulder. "I can't do that."

"You can do whatever you choose. Don't let anyone tell you otherwise."

She rocked against him, and he wondered if he'd gotten through to her when he felt a hand on his shoulder. He turned and came face to face with Damien Rook.

· · · • • · • · · ·

Daniels walked back through the crowd, thinking about his conversations with Bernie and Barbara Ingram. Barbara had known about Marjorie and Cain, which told him she was high on the society's ladder, and likely close to Rook. And since she seemed to hate him and Rem just as much as Rook, he guessed Rook had confided in her. That trust made her dangerous, but it almost appeared as if she'd tried to warn Daniels. That made little sense, but she was obviously aware of Rook's plans. Daniels half-wondered if he and Rem should push a little harder with Barb Ingram. Would she stand by Rook? Or would what little empathy she had left reveal itself? It was hard to know.

He returned to the table, but no one was there. Glancing at the crowded dance floor, he saw Rita dancing with Hans. He searched for Rem when a man approached. "Hello, Detective."

Daniels recognized Ezra Grimm. "Have we met?"

He offered his hand and a charming grin. "Ezra Grimm."

Daniels shook his hand. "Gordon Daniels."

Grimm sat at the table. "Damien told me about you."

Not seeing Rem, Daniels sat with Grimm. "He didn't tell me about you."

The grin returned. "I'm sure he didn't."

Staying relaxed, Daniels crossed one leg over the other. "Are you enjoying the party?"

"It's hard not to enjoy one of Damien's parties. He knows how to entertain...and who to invite."

Daniels picked up on the subtle communication. "You trying to tell me something?"

Grimm sat back and rested his ankle on his knee. "What's your interest in Damien Rook?"

"I could ask you the same."

Grimm tipped his head. "You know who I am?"

"I know about your connection to Ruben Montes and Montes Pharmaceuticals."

"You've done your homework. But so have I."

Daniels guessed that was why Grimm wanted to talk to him. He debated how much to say. He didn't want Grimm to suspect Daniels knew he was part of Rook's society. "How long have you and Damien known each other?"

Grimm watched a pretty woman in a revealing dress walk by. "A few years. How long have you known him?"

Daniels shrugged. "A few months."

"And yet you're invited to his birthday party?"

"I guess he took a liking to us."

"You and your partner must be effective detectives."

"We get the job done."

Grim smoothed his pants. "What sort of jobs do you get done?"

Daniels got the impression this was some sort of interview. Had Rook sent Grimm over? He eyed Rook's table but didn't see him or Delaina. "Detective ones."

Grimm made a slight nod, dropped his foot and leaned in. "Have you ever killed anyone?"

Daniels fought not to grimace. Grimm gave off an unpleasant vibe. "I assume you mean in the line of duty?"

"What else is there?" he chuckled.

Daniels tapped his finger against the tabletop. Was Grimm referring to Jerry Lee Caruso? "Somehow, Mr. Grimm, I think you already know the answer to that."

"Perhaps." Grimm sat back. "You intrigue me, Detective. Your partner too."

"In what way?"

He pushed the plate of half-eaten cake that was in front of him away. "You don't strike me as a man who would want anything to do with the people at this party, and yet..." he waved his hand. "...here you are."

"Here I am," said Daniels, waving his hand too. "Sometimes the space between what we think we know, and the truth, is awfully wide."

Grimm bounced his finger at Daniels. "Ahh. Now you're being cryptic."

"I could say the same about you."

Grimm surveyed the guests at the party before resuming his stare at Daniels. "It's becoming clearer now why they chose you and your partner. I assume your partner is just as mysterious as you?"

Daniels didn't think he'd ever been called mysterious. "Ten times worse. And who are 'they?'"

Grimm smiled again. "You make it through tonight, and you just might find out."

Daniels wondered again what was supposed to happen that night. "It seems to be going okay so far." He checked his watch. "In fact. It's getting late, and I need to find my partner." He stood. "Nice meeting you."

"Same." Grimm stood. "And I look forward to meeting Detective Remalla." He glanced toward the dance floor. "It appears he and Damien are engaged in an interesting conversation."

Daniels scanned the crowd of couples and widened his eyes when he saw Rem, who appeared to be dancing with Delaina, talking to Rook.

"Your night could end sooner that you think," said Grimm with another grin. "Have a nice evening, Detective." He walked away.

Unsure what to think, Daniels left the table but bumped into Rita, who was returning with Hans. "Are you leaving?" asked Rita.

Daniels pointed. "Just need to check in with Rem. Be back in a second." He started to leave when Rita took his arm, and he stopped again.

"Hans and I are heading out," she said. "We're going to make the rounds and say our goodbyes."

Daniels was disappointed they wouldn't be able to talk with Rita without Hans present. "I'm sorry to hear it. I hope we get a chance to meet again."

"C'mon, Rita," said Hans with a glare at Daniels. "It's late. Let's go find Damien." He took her arm, and when he attempted to pull her away, Rita stumbled and fell right into Daniels.

Daniels grabbed her, preventing her from falling to the ground. "Are you okay?" he asked, helping her up.

"Clumsy me," she said with a groan and holding her head. "I'm so sorry. I think I've had a bit too much champagne." She took Daniels' hand as she found her balance. "Thank you."

Daniels felt her press something into his palm. He kept a straight face and wrapped his fingers around it. "You're welcome." She straightened and stepped away. "You have a nice night," he said. "It was a pleasure to meet you, Rita." He eyed Hans. "Wish I could say the same about you, Hans."

Hans offered him a flat stare and guided Rita away.

Daniels looked at what she'd given him. It was a torn piece of a cocktail napkin with a phone number on it. It seemed Rita wanted to talk without Hans around as well. Hopeful about this new lead, he slid the napkin into his jacket pocket and went to find Rem.

· · • • • • • • · ·

Rem felt Delaina grip his shoulder and said the first thing that came to mind. "Happy birthday," he said to Rook. "Nice party."

Rook glared at Delaina. "Go back to the table. You're embarrassing yourself."

"Hey," said Rem. "I'm not that bad of a dancer."

Delaina snorted. "I'm fine. And I want to dance." She snuggled closer to Rem. "And you won't ask me."

Rem's insides clenched. This woman was way more dangerous than any secret society. "Delaina," he said. "Maybe we should go sit."

"I like this song," she said into his shoulder.

Rook's eyes flared. "You're embarrassing *me*. Go back to the table or I'll have you removed."

Rem tried to think about how to get out of this situation, but he'd had too much to drink. "I'll take her back."

"You'll do no such thing," said Rook with acrimony. "I want you to stay away from her."

Rem stood firm when Rook got in his face. "In my defense, she came to me." Caught between Rook and Delaina, he struggled with whose side to take. "Why don't you ask her to dance?"

"I didn't ask your opinion," said Rook. "Let her go."

"No," said Delaina. "I'm staying."

Rem tried to push Delaina back. "Delaina, listen to me. This isn't the way to do this." She looked up at him and then at Rook with indecision. *Moon River* ended, and the band started a new, more upbeat song. "But thanks for the dance," said Rem.

Rook took Delaina's elbow. "Come with me."

"Go easy, Rook," said Rem, not liking how rough Rook was with her. "She needs help, not judgment."

Rook's face hardened. "Don't you tell me what she needs," he said under his breath. "You're the last person I'd ever take advice from."

Rem could see their conversation was attracting attention from the other guests. "I'm not intending to step on your toes."

"Then back off, Detective."

Rem's anger bubbled up. "You invited me to this little shindig, and when I get asked to dance by a lovely lady who is clearly neglected, I'm going to say yes."

The icy shards returned to Rook's eyes, and Delaina smiled.

"Maybe if you paid more attention to her, she wouldn't need to come find me." Rem cursed inwardly at himself for letting Rook get to him. He braced, waiting for Rook to call security and have him thrown out.

Rook held his ominous stare. "I was told by...Tex, that you'd surprised him," said Rook. "I wondered if he was right. That's why you and your partner are at this party."

Rem's heart skipped a beat. "How are we doing so far?"

"You're doing great," said Delaina with a giggle.

Rook scowled at her and then at Rem. "Stay away from her."

"If you would pay her some attention, it wouldn't be an issue. Can't you see she's bored?"

Delaina eyed a server who walked by. "I need a drink."

Rook pulled her closer. "You've had enough. You'll go upstairs and sleep it off."

Delaina pouted and sighed at Rem. "See what I'm dealing with?"

"Cyrus," yelled Rook.

A tall, burly man who'd been standing on the sidelines, who Rem assumed was a guest, stepped up to Rook. "Yes, sir?"

"Escort Delaina up to her room. And make sure she gets no more alcohol."

Delaina dropped her jaw. "What? I don't want to go upstairs."

"You'll go, or you'll sleep in the guest house tonight." He pulled her against him. "I'm sure you'd be welcome."

Her face paled, and she stopped struggling.

"I thought that might change your mind." Rook pushed her toward Cyrus. "Go with Cyrus. And behave yourself."

Delaina took Cyrus' elbow. "Fine."

Seeing her deflate, Rem wondered who was in the guest house that could shift Delaina's demeanor so quickly.

"Thanks for the dance, handsome." She smiled at Rem and walked off with Cyrus.

"Hey," said Rem.

She looked back.

"Remember what I said...about choices."

Delaina stared for a second before Cyrus guided her off the dance floor, and Daniels stepped onto it, heading toward Rem.

"There you are," said Rem, seeing his partner.

"What are you doing? I left you alone for five minutes." Daniels glanced at Rook and spoke to Rem. "Why were you dancing with Delaina?"

"Because you have two left feet," said Rem.

Daniels frowned and spoke to Rook. "Happy birthday. Sorry about whatever he did." He gestured at Rem.

Rook looked between the two of them. Now that Delaina was gone, the guests had lost interest and went back to their dancing and socializing.

"Rook and I were just having a friendly conversation," said Rem. "And I'm waiting to see if we get kicked out."

"As I'm sure you're aware, Mr. Rook." Daniels waved his hand at Rem. "My partner is good at stirring up trouble, but he's harmless. Most of the time." Daniels leaned closer to Rook. "I hope your reasoning behind inviting us hasn't changed. We made it pretty clear to Tex what we wanted."

Rook's glare remained. "I don't like you two."

"That seems to be going around," replied Rem.

Ignoring the dancing couples, Daniels kept his attention on Rook. "What does liking someone have to do with business?"

"And money," added Rem. He waited to see if Rook's anger with him would ruin their plans or reinforce them.

"I think you'll find," said Daniels, "that we are capable employees."

Rook's eyes flashed. "Employees? Is that what you want?"

"What else is there?" asked Rem. He moved toward the edge of the dance floor as it became more crowded.

Rook gave a crooked smile. "You really want to know?"

"We really want to know," replied Daniels. "As much as Rem and I hate to admit it, we admire you."

Rem appreciated Daniels' ability to stroke Rook's ego, and it worked.

"Fine." Rook pulled on the cuff of his shirtsleeve. "Meet Tex at the back stairs in one hour. And you'll learn exactly what it means to work for me." He turned and walked into the crowd.

Chapter Sixteen

DANIELS WAITED WITH REM at the back stairs of the home, which were down the hall from the restroom, near to the kitchen. The hall led to another area of the house, but the doors were closed, and all they could access was the staircase. It was quieter back there, but the party was still in full swing as the band ramped up its dance tunes and the alcohol flowed.

Rem checked his watch and spoke softly. "It's been an hour. I hope Rook didn't change his mind."

"After that little episode with Delaina, it's a miracle we made it this far."

"What was I supposed to do? She practically forced me to dance with her."

Daniels offered Rem a flat stare. "She's way stronger than she looks." He pointed. "And you've got lipstick on your collar."

"I do?" Rem touched his collar. "Great. Another stain."

Daniels looked around but didn't see Tex. "Well, if we got ditched, at least we have Rita's number," he whispered. "She may be the key to the information we're looking for." He patted his pocket, where he'd placed the napkin with her number on it.

"Unless she's setting us up."

"I don't get that vibe from her, but we can't discount it. We'll have to be careful."

"I just want to get through this party. If Tex doesn't show, what do you want to do?"

Daniels rubbed his forehead. "I want to go home. We can try again with Tex later."

Rem checked his watch again. "We're so close, though. If Rook doesn't let us in tonight, he may never do it."

"We'll find another way. We've gotten this far, haven't we? And those we've met tonight are a gold mine of info. The people on the list are taking shape, which is a lot more than what we had twenty-four hours ago." He moved as a server walked by, opened the door to a closet, and pulled out a pile of cloth napkins. Daniels waited for him to walk away. "And Rook won't ignore us for long. We're still on his radar. At some point, he'll be back with another assignment."

"That's what I'm afraid of. I'm only good for one fake death a year."

"Let's hope it doesn't come to that." Daniels went still when he heard footsteps. "Heads up."

Rem turned as legs appeared on the stairs and Tex came into view. "Glad to see you two are prompt."

"As you said, Rook appreciates it," said Daniels.

"Are we doing this or not?" asked Rem. "It's getting late."

"He gets cranky without his beauty sleep," said Daniels.

Tex took the last few stairs to their level. "You two sure you're up for this? Once this begins, there's no going back."

"Once what begins?" asked Rem. "Is Rook going to knight us or something?"

"All we want is to join whatever group you've put together," added Daniels. "Although if I can opt out of the tattoo, I'd prefer it."

"He's not a fan of needles," said Rem. "Neither am I, for that matter."

Tex regarded them with a hard to read expression. "Nobody joins Rook's tribe without proving themselves first."

"Didn't we already do that?" asked Rem. He lowered his voice. "With Caruso?"

"Caruso got you to the door," said Tex, "but that's it. Now you've got to walk through it, and that's a different story."

"We're not killing anyone else, if that's what you're thinking," said Daniels. "Not without serious compensation."

Tex studied them. "That will come later, if that's what Rook wants."

Rem glanced down the hall. "Something tells me a few people at this party could be targets."

"You're not wrong," said Tex, "but murder is a buzzkill for a birthday cele-bration."

"So is this conversation," replied Daniels. "Are we doing this, or not?"

Tex eyed Rem.

"I'm ready when you are," said Rem.

"Right this way, Detectives." He turned and started back up the stairs.

Daniels and Rem followed.

Tex looked behind him. "Your cousin followed me up these same stairs, Remalla. I never would have guessed you'd do the same. Let's hope this works out better for you two than it did for him." He smiled and continued climbing.

His disgust rising, Daniels reached out and put his hand on Rem's wrist, knowing his partner was using all his strength not to attack Tex from behind and throw him over the railing.

Rem took a quiet breath but didn't say a word. They walked to the third floor, and Tex opened a door. They entered a narrow, dark hall. Daniels eyed the various closed doors and wondered what happened up here. He could hear the muffled sounds of the party below, but nothing from the floor itself. Did the staff stay up here?

Tex guided them down the hall. He put his hand on the knob of the last door. "Before we go in, one last check." He faced Rem and gestured with his fingers. "Arms up."

Rem rolled his eyes. "You've got to be kidding." He raised his arms.

Tex patted him down and even checked his pockets. When he finished, he turned to Daniels. "You next."

Raising his arms, Daniels thought about Rita's note. He made eye contact with Rem as Tex pulled the ripped cocktail napkin out of Daniels' jacket pocket.

"What's this?" asked Tex.

"None of your business." Daniels took the napkin and stuffed it in his pocket.

Rem glared. "Are you serious? Did you get that woman's number?" He jabbed his finger at Daniels. "I'm tired of keeping your secrets from Marjorie. You said you'd behave tonight."

Daniels shrugged. "She was cute. Plus, it's just her number. Who said I would use it?" He grinned.

Rem cursed. "Can you believe him?" he asked Tex.

Tex raised the side of his lip. "You two continue to surprise me." He eyed the closed door, and his serious demeanor returned. "Last chance to back out."

Relieved Tex had ignored the number, Daniels took steady breaths to slow his racing heart.

"Just open it," said Rem, with an edge to his voice.

After a pause, Tex did.

They entered a dark room brightened only by lighted candles. Three other people stood in the room—two men and one woman. They were quiet and didn't acknowledge Tex's entrance. A painting of a large black bird was on the opposite wall, and a white circle was drawn on the wood floor. Daniels got a whiff of sweet-smelling incense, but beneath it was a faint odor of decay. He instantly recalled the strange room in the abandoned building near where Martin Bailey had been murdered.

Rem grimaced. "Did something die in here?"

"Stand outside the circle," said Tex gruffly. "And be quiet."

They did as Croft asked. Daniels stood next to one of the men, and Rem stood on the other side of Daniels. The woman stood on the other side of Rem. Daniels tried to think if he'd seen the strangers at the party but couldn't recall.

"Stay here," said Tex. "And wait. No talking, no matter what you see and hear, and don't step inside the circle. If you try to leave, you won't survive the next forty-eight hours." He turned and left the room. Daniels heard the lock turn.

They stood in silence. Daniels studied the others but still didn't recognize them. Up in the corner of the murky room, he saw a camera and wondered if Rook was watching to see who followed orders. Rem remained quiet, but Daniels could imagine his mind was whirling as much as Daniels' was.

Several minutes passed with no activity, and Daniels wondered how long the other three had been waiting before he and Rem had arrived. Thankfully, the odor of decay faded, but the smell of the incense intensified. His eyesight blurred briefly, and he blinked. The room tilted slightly, and he leaned to compensate. The man across from him seemed to wobble a bit too. The woman raised her hand to her head as if she were dizzy, and Rem blinked several times and shook his head.

The room felt hot, and Daniels almost took his jacket off when the door opened. He tensed his muscles to keep himself from swaying when Damien Rook walked in. He carried a covered tray and set it on a small table in the corner. A brief gust of fresh air wafted in, and Daniels took a deep breath, and almost groaned when the door closed.

Rook stood outside the circle. His gaze traveled to each of them, but he studied Rem and Daniels intently. His eyes held a glazed look, and he'd taken off his jacket. Daniels was envious.

After several seconds, Rook spoke. "You are all here for a reason. You serve a purpose. And that purpose is to serve the whole. There is no you anymore. There is only us." He walked around them. "Joining has three requirements. None of which is negotiable. And since you've made it this far, you will be expected to abide by them." He stopped behind Rem. "Any attempt to break the rules will be met with certain death."

Rem glanced over at Daniels as Rook continued walking. "Anything that happens in here is secret. After you leave this room, nothing that occurs will be discussed again. Not to spouses, loved ones," he stopped behind Daniels, "or best friends."

A trickle of sweat ran down Daniels' back, and the room blurred again.

"There are no exceptions." Rook kept walking. "And I reserve the right to oust you at any time, at my discretion. But as long as you continue to serve your purpose, that should not be a concern."

More sweat trickled down Daniels' neck, and he hoped he wouldn't pass out. He didn't know why the room was so hot. Looking at his partner, he could see the flush in Rem's cheeks. All of them were hot, and Daniels swayed again when the room went out of focus.

"We work together as a group," said Rook, walking. "And we serve the Raven." He gestured toward the wall art.

Daniels perked up. Like the guest house, that was another new term.

"The Raven is all of us and none of us. She understands everything and nothing, and if you're confused, good. That's exactly where you need to be. True understanding will come later. After you've passed the first test."

The first test? wondered Daniels. Wasn't killing Caruso enough?

"The Raven honors three traits above all others. Follow them, and your membership will be long and rewarding. Ignore them at your own peril."

Daniels caught Rem sway and then straighten. Rook needed to get through this before they all collapsed from whatever was affecting them.

"They are loyalty," said Rook, "commitment and action."

Daniels wished he could have a glass of water.

"Your loyalty must be unwavering," continued Rook. "To me, to others, and to the Raven. Without it, we have nothing. Commitment is your dedication to the cause. That needs no explanation, and action...well, action is proof of your commitment. Action brings results. Action demands sacrifice but also honor."

Daniels forced himself to breathe normally. His throat stuck when he swallowed, and sweat ran down the side of his face.

Rook stopped beside the tray. "Your first test is to prove you can follow all three." He pulled the cover off the tray. From his angle, Daniels couldn't see what was on it. Rook picked up the tray and carried it inside the circle. He set it on the floor.

Daniels blinked, and the tray came into focus. There were six glasses half filled with liquid, and beside them was what appeared to be a pill bottle, but with no label. Rook picked it up and turned it over. Six pills fell onto the tray.

Rem shook his head again and blinked. So did the woman beside him.

"You will each step into the circle," said Rook. "Pick a glass and swallow a pill."

Alarmed, Daniels looked at Rem, who looked back with an expression of *what do we do now?*

Rook resumed his walk around the group. "This is the first step in purging your shadow side, which will empower you, the group, and the Raven. You cannot eliminate what you cannot face. Doing this will demonstrate your loyalty, commitment, and action."

Daniels could see the others glancing at each other, appearing just as un-certain.

"And to prove that we all follow the same rules," said Rook. "I will go first." He returned to the center, leaned down, picked up a glass and a pill, and downed the pill with the liquid. He finished the liquid in the glass and returned it to the tray. After a pause, he stepped to the edge of the circle. "Who is next?"

Nobody moved.

"There is a time limit," said Rook. "Effective action requires no hesitation."

The woman stepped forward and into the circle. Her bangs were wet with sweat. She stooped, took a glass and a pill, and swallowed the pill. She re-turned the glass to the tray and stepped back.

Another brief wave of dizziness hit Daniels as the man beside him stepped forward and did the same. Rem closed his eyes, and Daniels wondered what he was thinking. With everything he'd encountered with D'Mato's cult, he had to be seriously considering running out of the room.

The second man stepped back.

"Very good," said Rook. "Who's next?"

The third man stepped forward. Watching him take the pill and drink from the glass, Daniels prayed the liquid was water. His throat was so dry, it felt like he'd been walking through the desert for hours.

After the third man returned to the edge of the circle, Daniels debated his next move when Rem stepped forward. Daniels' heart thumped when Rem picked up the second to last pill and glass and swallowed the pill.

Knowing what he had to do, Daniels waited for Rem to return to his place. Rook glanced at him and, after a slight hesitation, and praying they got out of this without losing their badges or worse, Daniels stepped forward. He took the last glass and pill and popped the pill into his mouth. Thinking of Marjorie and J.P., he swallowed the pill, and drank all the liquid, giving thanks it was water.

And for a moment, as he set the empty glass on the tray, he thought he heard a woman cackle.

Chapter Seventeen

REM WINCED WHEN A slice of pain shot through his neck. He moved and gasped when his whole body protested. Opening his eyes, he tried to make sense of where he was, and it shocked him when he realized he was lying in a bathtub. His head was angled at an uncomfortable slant on the porcelain, and one of his legs was hanging over the edge. Blinking to clear the haze from his eyes, he gaped at himself. His shirt was covered in dirt, one sleeve was ripped, and he was missing buttons. His pants weren't much better. He had one shoe on, but his other foot was bare, and he didn't see his jacket.

His head pounded, and he groaned when he tried to move. Looking around, he wondered how long he'd been there. It took him a second to recognize he was in his upstairs bathroom. Somehow, he'd wandered up here and had either fallen or crawled into the tub, and had what? Passed out? Gone to sleep?

He tried to recall how he'd made it home, but his mind was blank. He raised his stiff arm with a curse and dug his fingers into his temples with a grimace. He desperately needed aspirin and a shower. And he needed to talk to Daniels.

Thinking of his partner, he sat up with another wince. Where was Daniels? Was he okay? His mind traveled back to the party. Rook had invited him and Daniels to that room. They'd stood in a circle, and it had been hot. Hot enough to make Rem dizzy. Rook had spouted off about requirements, and a raven, and Rem had taken a pill, and then...nothing. It was blank after that.

He shifted in the tub, his body protesting more when he heard a buzzing sound. It didn't compute at first, but when it continued to buzz, he realized it was a phone. He patted his pants pocket and gratefully felt his cell. It buzzed again, and Rem pulled it out. Relieved to see Daniels' name on the display, he answered. "'Lo?"

Daniels grumbled. "Good. You're alive."

Rem gripped his throbbing temples again. "I'm not too sure about that."

"This is the third time I've called. I was dreading having to move and come over there. Where'd you wake up?"

Rem rested his elbow on the edge of the tub. "I'm in the upstairs bathtub."

"Bathtub? How'd you get there?"

"I'm still trying to figure that out. Where are you?"

"Home. Marjorie woke me. I was face down in my front yard."

"You're kidding?"

"No. I have a vague recollection of walking up the stairs with her and Erin's help, and I fell into bed. I woke up a few minutes ago. I don't even know what time it is."

Rem looked around for a clock, since his watch was missing. "I have no idea."

"Hold on. I'll look." Daniels grunted. "Hell. It's a little after noon."

Rem couldn't believe it. "I've been sleeping in this tub all morning? What time did we leave the party?"

"Don't ask me. I can't remember a single thing after taking that pill. Can you?"

Rem tried again to remember. "Nothing. I don't even know how I got my cell phone back or how I got home." He paused. "I sure hope I didn't drive." He wondered where Mikey was. "Maybe Mikey can tell me something."

"I'm sure Marjorie isn't too thrilled about finding her husband doing a face-plant on the lawn. I can imagine what the neighbors are thinking."

"Maybe that's what Rook wants. To humiliate us. Make us look unstable?"

"I'm afraid to think about what may have happened. My clothes are ruined."

Rem poked at his torn sleeve. "Mine too. And my head is killing me."

"Same here. I need to take something before it gets worse. Can you get up?"

Rem attempted to sit straight. "I may just turn on the water and stay here. It would require less effort."

"Do yourself a favor and get out of the tub. Get some food, aspirin and a shower. I'll do the same. Maybe then we'll have some luck remembering what happened last night. You talk to Mikey, and I'll talk to Marjorie, and we'll reconvene to compare notes."

"You sure I can't just stay and soak in the tub?"

"When's the last time you used the bathroom?"

The question brought the pressure on Rem's bladder into sharp focus.

"I assume you don't want to do that in the tub, too?"

"Point taken." Rem shifted with some effort. "I'll call you when I'm coherent."

"Same."

They hung up, and Rem forced himself to his feet with another gasp. Everything hurt, and he wondered where Mikey was. Did she know he was up here? He stomped his foot when it tingled after not moving it for so long and stepped over the tub's edge and onto the floor. Getting his balance, he used the facilities, and went to the sink, where he washed his hands and splashed water on his face.

Looking at himself in the mirror, he couldn't believe how bad he looked. His eyes were bloodshot and his face puffy. His hair was disheveled, and his clothes were a mess. He straightened and stretched, trying to get the kinks out of his back. Feeling better, he left the bathroom and walked into the upstairs hall.

"Mikey? You home?"

He held onto the rail as he took the stairs slowly down to the first floor.

"Mikey?"

She didn't answer, and he didn't see her. Wondering if he'd pissed her off by coming home late, inebriated, or worse, he headed into their bedroom. She wasn't in there either. The shower beckoned though, and without hesitating, he flipped on the faucet, stripped out of his clothes, and as soon as it was hot enough, he stepped under the hot stream of water, letting it run over his face and body. Steam filled the shower, and after standing there long enough to feel his muscles unwind, he quickly washed his hair and body and got out.

Still wondering about Mikey, he pulled his phone from his discarded pants and called her, but it went to voicemail. He left her a message, asking her to call back, and hung up. He dried himself, brushed his teeth and put on some clean clothes, expecting to hear from her, but she didn't return his call.

Beginning to worry, he caught sight of an open drawer in the bureau on the other side of the bed. It was one of Mikey's drawers. He walked over to close it when he saw it was empty. Frowning, he shut it and saw the one below was partially open. He pulled it out and saw it was empty, too.

"What the hell?" he asked himself and took a closer look. He saw items of clothing tossed on the bed as if she'd gone through the closet. He went to the closet and flipped through the clothes on her side. It was significantly less full than it had been the day before, and some of her shoes were missing. And worse, he hadn't seen Chester, who was normally curled up on their bed.

Flummoxed, Rem returned to the bedroom and dialed her number again. It again went to voicemail. Rem did a better job of explaining how he'd woken up and hadn't seen her. He inquired about her missing clothes and asked her to call him asap.

After hanging up, he went into the kitchen, and that's when he saw it. An envelope. On the table, with Rem's name written on it in Mikey's handwriting.

His stomach tightened, and he wished he could remember what had happened the previous night. Had they fought? Had she left?

Praying it wasn't that bad, he went to the table and picked up the envelope, but his hand shook. He needed food, but he needed to know why Mikey wasn't there.

Nervous, he opened the flap and pulled out a folded piece of paper. Hoping she'd just gone to the store, he unfolded the paper and read it.

Rem,

I've done what you asked and left. I'll be back later to pick up the rest of my things. I'll stay with Mason, but don't call me. You made it very clear how you feel, and I won't be back. In fact, I no longer need your permission to do exactly what needs to be done. Stupid I didn't figure that out sooner.

I have Chester, so enjoy your time alone.

Mikey

Shocked and confused, Rem reread the note. He couldn't understand what she was talking about. He'd told her to leave? When? He lowered the paper and held his head, trying to think. His head pounded harder, and he had a flashback of standing on the stairs, yelling at Mikey. She yelled back, and he'd told her to get out, and he'd turned and stumbled up the stairs.

His stomach clenched again, and he fought the urge to throw up. What the hell had happened?

He grabbed his phone again, eager to call Daniels, when it rang. Seeing Daniels' name, he answered. "Hell. I think I did something really stupid."

"Rem?" asked Daniels, sounding breathless. "Is Mikey there?"

"No," said Rem, hearing the fear in his partner's voice. "I just found a note. She's left."

"I just found a note, too. From Marjorie."

Rem pulled out a dining chair and sat. "What? Did you kick Marj out too?"

"No. She's with Mikey. Mikey called her distraught this morning. You and I were still out of it. Mikey told her what she planned to do, and Marjorie went with her. She left Erin to watch J.P."

Rem gripped his head. "I don't understand anything right now. Marjorie went with Mikey? Where?"

There was a brief pause. "To see Margaret."

· · • • • · • • • · ·

Marjorie walked with Mikey down a sterile, beige hallway. They were following a staff member named Bennett, who was directing them to the visiting area in Margaret's psychiatric facility.

Passing a small table with two chairs, Marjorie took Mikey's arm. "One second, Bennett."

Mikey turned. "What's wrong?"

Bennett stopped. "Everything okay?"

"Bennett, would you mind giving us a few minutes?" asked Marjorie. "I need to talk to my friend." She guided Mikey to the table and chairs.

"No problem. I'll be just down the hall. Let me know when you're ready." Bennett walked away.

"What is it?" asked Mikey.

"Sit." Marjorie sat in one chair and Mikey sat in the other. "I know we've discussed this, but now that we're here, I want to be absolutely sure this is what you want."

Mikey stiffened. "Yes. This is what I want. It's what I've wanted since Vera first told me to do this."

Marjorie tried to think of a way to get through Mikey's defenses. Her friend had called her that morning, emotional and furious with Rem. She'd vented about their argument and spoke so fast, Marjorie could barely get a word in. All she could decipher was that Rem had stumbled home drunk around four a.m. and had immediately picked a fight. He'd said something about Mikey being wrong about Vera and Margaret, and she was stupid to consider it. He'd told her he was tired of arguing and that if she didn't like it, she could get out. And worse, he'd told her it was fine if she left, because then he wouldn't have to empty Jennie's closet. He'd be busy cleaning out Mikey's stuff when she ended up dead after visiting her sister.

Marjorie heard the hurt and pain in Mikey's voice but also recalled finding Gordon lying in the grass in the front yard. She and Erin had gotten him on his feet, but he wasn't himself. He was rambling about how he'd failed them. That he wasn't the husband or brother they deserved, and they should leave while they still could. No matter what she'd said to him, he couldn't be consoled, and he'd sobbed up the stairs until he'd collapsed in their bed and fallen asleep.

Clearly, whatever happened at the party had caused all of this, but Mikey didn't want to make any excuses for Rem and had decided that she would see Margaret. Right then. And would do it on her own.

Marjorie had tried to talk her out of it, but when that failed, she did the only thing she could think of—offered to go with her. Mikey had finally slowed down enough to agree and had picked up Marjorie soon after. Gordon was still out of it, so Marjorie had left him a note. She could imagine what he would think when he read it.

"Mikey," she said. "You're upset and angry. Maybe this isn't the best time to see your sister."

"There is no perfect time to see my sister. I shouldn't have waited this long. Rem said I was stupid to see Margaret, but what I was really stupid about was listening to *him*."

"Mikey, Rem and Gordon both weren't themselves last night. Maybe you should give Rem a chance to explain."

"He said what he said. He can't take it back now just because he's sober. Whatever happened at that party lowered his defenses, and he finally told me what he really thought."

"And what's that?"

Mikey tightened her jaw and crossed her arms. "That he still loves Jennie, and there isn't room for me in his life."

Marjorie gasped. "You think that's what he meant?"

Mikey's eyes watered. "It was pretty obvious. He even had lipstick on his collar."

"I'd ask about the lipstick before you jump to conclusions."

Mikey swiped her shimmering eyes with her fingers. "It doesn't matter anymore. He can have that closet and the woman who left that lipstick stain. I packed my bags and got out."

Surprised, Marjorie put her hand on her friend's arm. "You didn't tell me that."

"I can't stay there. Not after what happened. He's never spoken to me like that."

Marjorie squeezed Mikey's elbow. "All the more reason not to do this today. You're not thinking clearly. Don't you think Margaret will use that against you?"

Mikey sniffed and straightened. "I don't care. I'm tired of everyone telling me how dangerous Margaret is, as if I don't know that. I grew up with her. If anyone knows her best, it's me. I'm not some weak-minded fool, although Rem clearly thinks I am."

"He doesn't think that."

Mikey stood. "I'm going. You're welcome to stay here and wait if you're not comfortable."

Her rigid expression told Marjorie that Mikey would not be deterred. Marjorie stood too. "If you're going, I'm going. I don't want you to do this alone."

Mikey nodded. "Thank you."

"Just be careful, okay? I know what Margaret's done, and if it gets to be too much, and you want to leave, tell me."

Mikey wiped her wet cheeks and cleared her throat. "I'll be fine. Let's find Bennett and get this over with."

Nervous, Marjorie followed, and they found Bennett waiting down the hall. He guided them to a cheery room with a big window that had a TV, a brown couch, and assorted tables and chairs. A woman sat at one table reading a book, which appeared to be upside down, and a man with tousled white hair and long fingernails stared out the window and smiled. Marjorie wondered what he was looking at.

Bennett told them to take a seat on the couch and that he would bring Margaret in a few minutes. He left, and Marjorie waited with Mikey. The TV played an old black and white western at a low volume, and the man staring out the window mumbled something.

A nurse pushed a middle-aged, balding man in a wheelchair past them, and he yelled to turn off the TV because of the cancer-causing radiation. The nurse just smiled at Marjorie and Mikey, told them everything was fine, and continued to push him down the hall while he continued to yell about the dangers of electronics.

The longer they sat, the more Marjorie realized this was a mistake, and she should have told Mikey no. She started to object when a side door opened. Bennett appeared, pushing a woman with long, straight black hair and piercing blue eyes toward them. It was Margaret Redstone.

Chapter Eighteen

DANIELS SET THE PLATE of bacon and eggs in front of Rem, who bounced his foot while drinking from the cup of coffee Daniels had given him. "Are you going to be able to eat?" He set his own plate down and sat next to Rem.

Rem put his elbow on the table and held his head. "I can't stop thinking about Mikey. What the hell did I do last night to cause this?"

Daniels stared at his food and understood Rem's fears. Marjorie was with Margaret, too, and he didn't like it one bit. He and Rem had discussed what they could remember. Rem had a brief recollection of arguing with Mikey, and Daniels could remember sobbing while Erin and Marjorie helped him inside and up the stairs. They both remembered Rook saying how the pill would illuminate their shadow side but little else. Daniels had told Rem to come over for breakfast after Rem had found his car in his driveway and key fob on his entry table.

Daniels put his napkin in his lap. "I should apologize to you. I suggested it wouldn't be that bad if Mikey went to see her sister, but now that Marjorie's involved, I'm understanding how you feel. I should have stayed out of it."

"I know you meant well. Mikey too. But this has disaster written all over it." Rem picked up his fork but stared at his food. "I pushed Mikey right into Margaret's hands. Son-of-a-bitch."

"Don't blame yourself. We don't know everything yet."

Rem poked at his eggs. "I'm afraid of finding out everything. That pill did a number on us." He shut his eyes and groaned. "Margaret can sense weakness, and if she picks up on Mikey's sensitivity with me right now, she's going to use it." He opened his eyes and sighed. "God. What happened last night?"

Still trying to recover, Daniels had poured himself a big cup of coffee. "I wish I could offer some words of wisdom, partner, but I'm drawing a blank. I'm still not a hundred percent." He swallowed some coffee.

"I feel like I'm moving underwater. Everything is an effort."

"Me too. Let's eat. That might help." He scooped a bite of eggs with his fork.

Rem looked around. "Where's Erin and the little guy?"

"Backyard. Playing in the sandbox. So let's talk now because the second he sees you, he's going to want to play trains."

Rem stabbed some eggs with his fork. "What I wouldn't give to be a two-year-old right now."

"The diaper thing and excessive use of the word 'no' might make you reconsider."

"Dirty diapers vs. secret societies. Right now, I'm leaning toward the diapers."

"I'll remember that when J.P. needs his next change."

They ate a few bites of food, and feeling a little better, Daniels started the conversation. "Now that we've recovered a little, let's think of something other than Margaret. What else do you recall from the room we were in?"

Rem, who had more color in his face after eating some eggs, stared off. "It was stuffy and hot. I thought I was going to pass out."

"Plus, there was a strong smell of incense. Almost sickeningly sweet. And underneath it, a faint odor, like something had died."

"All I could think about was getting out of there. At first, I wasn't about to take that pill, but then I couldn't take it fast enough. I wanted out, and I could barely think straight."

A thought occurred to Daniels. "You think that was intentional? Maybe they piped in some sort of drug? Something that made us confused, disoriented, and less likely to object?"

"It's possible." Rem ate a piece of bacon. "And what was Rook spouting off about?" He scrunched his face. "Was it commitment?"

"Yes, plus action and loyalty. That I remember. The three pillars of..." he pointed when he recalled something. "The raven. Do you remember that? Rook kept talking about the raven."

"Vaguely. But who is the raven?"

Daniels scratched his jaw. "I don't know, but it sounded like a person. Is Rook working with someone else we haven't seen?"

"If he's working with this raven, and Rook's last name means crow, then I think we understand the tattoos."

"But what is the idea behind it all? What's their ultimate intent?"

"Control."

"But over what? These people are powerful enough as it is. They have control over their lives and businesses. What else is there?"

"Control over other people. Like us. You get enough influential people on your side, then you could effectively escape all persecution or justice. Your power would be almost unstoppable."

"That seems a little far-fetched. This isn't a Marvel movie. What do these people want to do? Take over the world?"

Rem pointed with his fork. "Rook's crazy enough to believe just that."

"I don't care who he controls or who he thinks he is, at some point, this whole '*I'm the King of the World*' crap is going to catch up to him."

"You just made two movie references. We were definitely drugged last night."

Daniels drank some coffee. "What do you think we took?"

"I'm afraid to find out, but whatever it was didn't do me any favors. I got angry."

"And I felt guilty." He studied Rem. "It makes sense if whatever it was brought out our dark sides."

"Are you saying I'm angry?"

Daniels raised his brow. "Is that a trick question? You're pissed about Cain, plus plenty of other past events."

"And you're carrying a lot of guilt about Marjorie and the baby. Erin, too."

Daniels slumped. "So, our vulnerabilities have been exposed. You think that's what Rook wanted?"

"It's valuable intel. But what concerns me more is what happened between the time we took the pill and the time we got home? Any recollection of that?"

Daniels did his best to remember. He frowned when he thought of something. "There is one thing."

Rem set his fork down. "What's that?"

"After a swallowed the pill, I thought I heard a woman laugh. Cackle might be a better word. Did you hear that?"

"Cackle? You mean like a witch does when she stirs her cauldron full of lizard tails and animal tongues?"

Daniels made a face. "You have an active imagination."

"I've seen way more movies than you have, and that's what they do. They don't laugh or chuckle. They cackle."

Daniels replayed the sound in his head. "Then that's exactly what it was."

Rem wiped his fingers with his napkin. "Then I'm officially creeped out."

"Maybe I just dreamed it." He paused. "But I don't think I did."

Rem ate another bite of eggs. "Were there any guests at the party who looked like cacklers?"

"What does a cackler look like?"

Rem offered a look of impatience.

"Right," said Daniels. "Someone who stirs a cauldron full of lizard tails and animal tongues."

"Exactly."

"What does a person who does that look like?"

Rem shrugged. "If you want the movie version, they're old, with long stringy hair, bad skin and crooked teeth, long gnarly fingernails and a wart on their nose."

Daniels pursed his lips. "I don't recall anyone at the party matching that description."

"Maybe they used their magic to disguise themselves."

"All right. Can we be serious now?"

"You're the one who brought up the cackle." Rem sipped his coffee.

"My mistake. Maybe I was dreaming." He stood to get more coffee. "Speaking of guests, you and Delaina were getting close."

Rem grunted. "She was drunk, and Rook was ignoring her. And she used me to make a point."

Daniels brought the coffeepot over and refilled Rem's mug and his. "You think she's the cackler?"

Rem chuckled. "No. But she is trouble. Rook wasn't happy that she and I were dancing." His brow furrowed. "In fact, Rook said something to her..." He stared off.

"What's that?" Daniels returned the pot to the machine and sat.

"He told her if she didn't behave, he'd make her stay in the guest house. That scared her."

Daniels recalled his conversation with Bernie. "I talked to a server in the kitchen. I asked about what he'd seen, and he confided that another staff member got nosy and went into Rook's office. His punishment was to go to the guest house. He hasn't been seen since."

Rem's face paled. "What is Rook involved in? I thought blackmail and murder were bad enough."

Daniels recalled the size of Rook's estate. "I wonder where the guest house is."

"It's a big property. Could be anywhere. But the bigger question is, who or what is there?"

Daniels thought about it. "Maybe it's our cackler."

Rem blanched. "That's comforting."

"Before we forget, we need to update that spreadsheet with all the names we learned last night."

Rem paused. "I remember Chogan Crow and Judge Gunderson. And Ezra Grimm. He's hard to forget."

"Grimm's delightful. I talked to him while you were wooing Delaina."

Rem rolled his eyes.

"He definitely knows who we are. I got the impression he was quizzing me, and if I didn't answer right, it might affect our membership."

"If Rook told the other members about us, I'm sure they're all wary of bringing us into the fold."

"Don't forget Tex, who we know is Tyson Croft. Plus Barbara Ingram, who's definitely not thrilled about us joining the fold. And you thought you recognized..." He tapped on the table, trying to recall the name.

"Natalia Ferndale," said Rem. "I think. I'll have to look at her picture again." He scrunched his face. "And did we see that Nightingale chick?"

"I thought I saw Marcus...somebody." He snapped his fingers. "And Hans Morrow and Rita Vittorio." As soon as he said Rita's name, he remembered the cocktail napkin with the phone number. "Hell. My jacket." He jumped up.

"What?" asked Rem. "Your jacket's not going anywhere. I don't even know where mine is."

Daniels ran into the front room and saw his rumpled, discarded jacket tossed over the couch. He didn't recall taking it off. "The phone number. Rita gave me a number. Remember?"

"And you're getting on me about Delaina? What would Marjorie think?"

Daniels grabbed the jacket and dug into the ripped pocket. "Rita wasn't hitting on me." He cursed when he didn't find the napkin.

"You sure about that? We were both looking pretty spiffy last night."

Daniels dug into the other pocket and breathed a sigh of relief when he found the napkin. "Here it is." He brought it to the dining table and handed it to Rem.

Rem studied it. "You think we should call? She could be setting us up to take a fall. She is Rook's sister."

"Half-sister. And for all she knows, we could be setting her up. We could work for Rook."

Rem set the paper down. "What was your impression of Rita?"

Daniels picked up his mug. "Morrow was sticking awfully close, and she mentioned that she and Rook had been estranged." He drank more coffee.

Rem rubbed his jaw. "You think Morrow was monitoring her? So she wouldn't talk to us?"

"Maybe." He eyed the napkin. "But there's only one way to be certain."

Rem fiddled with the napkin. "You sure about this?"

"Rem, we were drugged and have no memory of what happened after we took that pill. Despite that ceremony, something tells me Rook isn't going to welcome us into the black birds with open arms. If anyone is setting us up, it's him. And we have no idea what to expect next. Yes. We've learned some names, but nothing definitive. The only way we're going to crack this is to speak to someone on the inside." He pointed at the napkin. "And something tells me that person is Rita."

Rem hesitated and sighed. "Okay. I trust your gut." He pushed his plate back. "I just hope to God she's not the cackler."

Hoping the same, Daniels found his phone and dialed the number.

Chapter Nineteen

Mikey squirmed as Bennett wheeled her sister toward her and Marjorie. Her mouth suddenly dry, Mikey told herself again that she was doing the right thing. Margaret knew things, and Mikey needed to find out what they were, no matter what Rem or Mason said. Thinking of Rem again and their dreadful argument, she forced back her tears. Angry at herself for listening to him and not to herself when he didn't even love her, made her want to punch something. Just as strong, though, were her hurt feelings. What he'd said about Jennie had pierced her heart. Once Rem had gone upstairs after telling her he wanted to sleep alone, she'd sobbed while packing and, after writing the note, she'd left with Chester and gone to Mason's.

She'd told Mason little about the argument, only that she needed sleep and time alone. Tossing and turning though, she'd decided that morning to see Margaret. She'd called Marjorie, only intending to vent and not for her friend to join her, but now that the moment was here, Mikey gave thanks she wasn't alone.

As the wheelchair approached, Mikey tried to relax. She took a long, calming breath and focused. Margaret looked much the same as the last time Mikey had seen her, only subdued. Her black hair ran down her back, and her piercing gaze connected with Mikey's. Mikey caught the almost imperceptible shift in energy when her intuitive side kicked in, and she realized her sister understood exactly where she was and who she was talking to.

Bennett stopped the chair in front of the couch. He lifted a tray from the side near the armrest and raised it in front of Margaret. "You have visitors today, Margaret. Your sister and her friend. Isn't that nice?"

Margaret's gaze moved to Marjorie.

Bennett pulled something from a bag on the back of the wheelchair. "Here are some crayons and paper." He set three crayons — a red, green, and blue one — on the tray along with a loose-leaf piece of paper. "You can draw if you want." He looked at Mikey and Marjorie. "She's having a good day today. She's sedated but might be open to talking." He eyed Margaret. "I'll be nearby if you need anything, Margaret." He spoke to Mikey. "I'll be just down the hall." He set the brake on the wheelchair and stepped away.

Mikey stared at her sister, and Marjorie didn't say a word.

Margaret watched them both with almost no expression, but her eyes sparkled. She didn't touch the crayons.

Mikey interlaced her fingers. "Hi, Margaret," she said, trying to hide her nerves.

Margaret didn't even blink.

"How are you?" asked Mikey, feeling that was a stupid question. "I hope you don't mind a visit from me."

Margaret continued to stare.

Mikey wrung her hands. Realizing what she was doing, she laid them in her lap. "I won't stay long. I just need to ask you about that night. At the grove."

Margaret's eyes widened slightly.

"Who was the man with you? The one smoking the cigarette?"

Margaret's eyes flicked to Marjorie, and she picked up the red crayon. "How's Gordon, Marjorie?" she asked, drawing red lines across the paper.

Marjorie's face paled, but she answered. "He's Detective Daniels to you."

Mikey steered the conversation away from Marjorie. "We're not here to talk about Daniels or..." Mikey stopped short of saying Rem's name. "...we're here to discuss Vera."

Margaret continued to draw red streaks across the page. "Mason didn't want to come?"

"I didn't ask him," said Mikey. "I wanted to talk to you. He didn't."

"You've always been braver than him." Margaret put the red crayon down and picked up the blue one. "But not smarter."

Mikey ignored the slight. "What can you tell me about that night?"

Margaret continued to draw.

"Vera told me you know."

Margaret looked up. "Vera told you?"

"I've been talking to her."

Margaret curled the side of her lip. "How very Mason of you."

"It has nothing to do with Mason. I've been training myself. Vera was my friend. I want to know who shot her."

Margaret drew circles of blue. "You betrayed her."

Mikey braced herself. She'd expected Margaret's animosity. "I didn't betray her. I didn't know what was going to happen."

"She asked for your help," said Margaret softly. "You said no."

"Victor betrayed her, and so did you." Mikey did her best not to get angry. "I would have—"

In a sign of annoyance, Margaret clutched her crayon and drove it across the page. "You would have done nothing. You were too scared and weak. Just as you are now."

Mikey leaned back from the verbal attack. Marjorie reached over and took Mikey's hand. "She's not weak," said Marjorie. "She's one of the bravest people I know. And she's not the one sitting in a wheelchair in a psychiatric facility who gets sedated and pushed around by Bennett while drawing with her crayons."

Mikey squeezed Marjorie's fingers in an attempt to tell her to go slow.

Margaret's gaze settled on Marjorie. "Gordon made a wise choice." She aimed her sneer at Mikey. "Too bad Rem didn't." She leaned in. "Where is your handsome suitor, sweet sister? Didn't he want to protect you from the big, bad sociopath?" She paused and pouted. "Or is there trouble in paradise?"

The constriction in Mikey's chest grew tighter. "Leave him out of this."

Margaret emitted a harsh chuckle. "You're so stupid. You want something from me? Without giving anything in return?" She made a tsk-tsk sound with her tongue. "You know me better than that, sister."

Mikey had expected this but told herself she would try to reach whatever remained of her sister's soft side. It hit her then that there was no soft side left. Family was no more important to her than Bennett. "Wasn't there ever a time you loved me? Or Mason or Max?" asked Mikey.

"Love has always been your weakness." Margaret returned to her drawing. "Not mine."

Marjorie stood. "We should go, Mikey."

Margaret offered Marjorie a cruel smile. "So much like your husband. Trying to protect your friend." She stopped drawing. "When will you and Gordon realize you will both fail?"

"The best way to protect my friend is to get her as far away from you as possible." Marjorie tugged Mikey's hand. "Let's go."

Mikey didn't move, and Margaret put her crayon down. "Tell me about him," said Margaret.

Mikey understood what her sister wanted.

"Don't," said Marjorie.

Margaret drew more circles. "You want Vera's killer?"

Wrestling with herself over choosing Rem or Vera, Mikey debated what to do. Her argument with Rem flashed in her mind, but so did all the good times with him. In her heart, she couldn't betray him.

Margaret scoffed. "Protecting a man who loves someone else? Even you should know better than that." She held her crayon. "But then you've never been lucky in love, have you?"

"Stop it," said Marjorie. "Mikey. Don't listen to her." She tugged at Mikey's hand again. "Please. Let's go."

Rem's words echoed in Mikey's ears. *It would be easier if you left, so I don't have to empty Jennie's closet.* Jennie's closet. It had always belonged to Jennie. Never Mikey. Mikey swallowed, faced her sister, and straightened her shoulders. "What do you want to know?"

· · · • • · • • · ·

Wishing Mikey would answer her phone, Rem entered the small restaurant near Daniels' house. Daniels walked with him, holding his phone to his ear. "Damn it," he said, lowering it. "Marjorie's still not answering."

"What the hell are they talking about?" Rem hated to imagine it.

"Would it be too much to ask for world peace?" asked Daniels. He looked around. "There. In the back booth."

"World conquest would be more likely, at least for Margaret." Rem followed Daniels' gaze and saw Rita Vittorio. Her silver hair brushed her shoulders, and she wore a comfortable blue tracksuit. "Your gut still says this is okay?" Rem looked around but didn't see anyone watching.

Daniels looked around, too. "Based on how she sounded on the phone, yes."

"I hope you're right. Because if you're wrong..."

Daniels headed toward the back. "One more thing to feel guilty about. I'll add it to the list." He approached Rita. "Hello, Rita."

She smiled. "Thank you both for coming."

Rem slid into the booth next to Daniels. "I have to admit," said Rem. "This is unexpected."

She nodded. "I know it is. We don't know each other, and I'm asking you to trust me."

"And we're asking you to trust us," said Daniels. "It goes both ways."

The server appeared, and they all ordered drinks. "Knowing what I know," said Rita, "I'd find it hard to believe that either of you would ever side with Damien."

That piqued Rem's curiosity. "What do you know?"

"We'll get to that, but first I want to assure you I have nothing to do with Damien's group. I've been against it from the beginning. At first, I thought it was just his way of staying busy and entertaining himself. My brother is too smart for his own good and easily bored. Without new challenges, he gets depressed." She studied her hands. "But I never thought that...it would go this far."

"Is that what caused the estrangement?" asked Daniels.

She nodded. "When I learned what he was doing, I confronted him. Told him he was wrong, and he kicked me out. We didn't talk until recently, and I was surprised I was invited to the party."

"You think we're safe here?" Rem checked the restaurant again. "Is anyone watching you?"

"I was careful," said Rita. "And today is my volunteer day at the local animal shelter. Damien knows that I never miss it. If anyone stops by the apartment, they'll assume I'm at the shelter."

"Will he follow up?" asked Rem. "Call the shelter?"

"No," said Rita, shaking her head. "I doubt it. He lives in a bubble, comfortable enough to think that I would never betray him."

"Then why ask Morrow to stick close to you last night?" asked Daniels.

"That was about you two. Morrow has known Damien for years," said Rita, "and all of us are, or were, friends. When Damien invited me, he told me I'd have to come with Hans, and after I arrived and saw both of you, I understood."

Rem felt better about Rita but continued to monitor the diner. "Now that you've got us here, what can you tell us? And what's so urgent?" The server returned with their drinks. He gave Rita and Daniels an iced tea and Rem a coffee. Rem ordered a basket of french fries, and Rita and Daniels declined food.

Rita nibbled her bottom lip. "I don't know where to start."

"How about at the beginning?" asked Daniels.

She clutched her hands together. "Okay. As I mentioned, Damien has always been smart, but that came at a price. He was bullied as a child, so he kept to himself a lot. His father didn't abide weakness and was a taskmaster who pushed Damien endlessly to be the best at everything. He taught Damien that respect only comes from wealth and power. Despite his solitude or because of it, Damien became the top student in his class and was a self-made millionaire by the time he was thirty. Even though he struggled socially, everything seemed to come easily to him. Except he's been divorced three times."

"I hope Delaina isn't number four," said Rem.

"Unlikely," said Rita. "I think he's sworn off marriage."

"I think Delaina has more to do with Ben Crenshaw," said Daniels. "He's almost as slick as Rook."

"You're not wrong," said Rita. "Damien has been partnering up with some powerful, but not so kind, people."

"What started this whole thing?" asked Rem. "It seems like Rook had it all, other than a happy marriage."

"By the time Damien hit his mid-sixties, he was drifting," said Rita. "He'd accomplished everything he'd wanted to. He didn't feel challenged or excited and was debating leaving it all and joining an ashram in India until he met the cult leader, Victor D'Mato."

Rem stopped stirring his coffee.

She eyed Rem. "I believe you're familiar with him?"

"We are familiar, unfortunately," said Daniels.

Rita sat back. "D'Mato was a powerful man, but differently than Damien. D'Mato wasn't rich, but he was charismatic. He possessed a unique ability to manipulate people. Especially certain types."

Rem understood. "You mean those with abilities? Like mediums, people who can move things, or read the future?"

"And conduct electricity through their hands?" asked Daniels, glancing knowingly at Rem.

Rita widened her eyes. "You sound like you're familiar with the paranormal."

Daniels nodded. "We have some experience with it."

"Too much." Rem set his spoon down and took a sip of coffee. "Tell us about Rook's relationship with D'Mato."

Rita wrapped her fingers around her iced-tea glass. "D'Mato was fascinated by Rook, and vice versa. They talked about what they could do together through their combined efforts." She tightened her grip on the glass. "I thought it was a phase, but I was wrong. D'Mato had crazy ideas about life, and Damien bought into all of it. And then it got worse when D'Mato introduced Damien to someone he referred to as the raven."

Daniels sat up. "We heard that name last night. Rook mentioned the raven."

"And following this raven required three things," added Rem. "Loyalty, commitment and action."

She dropped her jaw. "You went through the initiation ceremony?"

"Is that what you call it?" asked Daniels.

"Damien told me a little about it before the estrangement. I told him he was turning into D'Mato, and creating a cult of his own. He tried to convince me that this would change the world, and wanted my support. I wouldn't give it to him."

"We did the ceremony to infiltrate Rook's organization," said Rem. "We want him to think we're Raven fans and eager to help."

"This is a dangerous game you're playing," said Rita, "in ways you have yet to understand."

"We know Rook holds a grudge against us," said Daniels. "He's blackmailing us into doing his bidding. Says he'll send us to jail if we don't comply. He's framing our captain, too."

"What?" asked Rita.

"The thing is," said Rem, "Rook doesn't want us in jail. Like everyone else, he wants to control us. So we're hoping to convince him that's what he's done."

"And while we do that, our plan is to learn more about the group and its members," said Daniels. "Which is why meeting you is so important."

"You're our first solid lead," replied Rem. "If we can find out the who and why behind this whole thing, and find others like you, we can prove our and our captain's innocence and end this whole society thing."

Her shoulders softened. "I knew when I saw you at the party that I had to connect with you. Something told me you couldn't possibly join Damien, and if Damien gets what he wants..." She held her head. "That's another reason I had to talk to you. I had to warn you."

"We know how dangerous this is," said Rem. "If Rook learns we're deceiving him, we'll end up in that jail cell..."

"Or dead," said Daniels. "He's already come after my wife," he tipped his head at Rem, "and his cousin."

They stopped talking when the server arrived with the basket of fries and three small plates. Forcing thoughts of Cain out of his head, Rem grabbed the salt and shook it over the fries. "Dig in, everybody." He put the salt down and grabbed the ketchup bottle.

"You don't understand," said Rita. "It's worse than you think."

Rem grabbed a plate and poured ketchup onto it. "How much worse can it get? Damien and D'Mato created their own evil mastermind using Damien's wealth and connections and D'Mato's charisma and this Raven person, whoever that is."

"And Rook's inviting his cronies to join, and if they don't, they're either blackmailed, threatened, or paid to come aboard." Daniels grabbed a fry.

Rita shook her head. "That's not what I mean." She picked up a fry and a plate. "Do you know who Barbara Ingram is?" She set the fry on her plate.

"Sadly, yes." Rem dunked a fry in ketchup and ate it. "She's Crenshaw's law partner and doesn't have many nice things to say about us."

Daniels chewed his french fry. "Damien is a client of Crenshaw, Ingram, and Willoughby. We think that's how Reginald Durning ended up dead."

"Durning was Rook's attorney, only he wouldn't do what Rook wanted and threatened to go to our captain. He ended up getting sent a creepy doll, a star branded into his leg, and a bullet in his heart." Rem dunked another fry in ketchup.

"A creepy doll?" asked Rita. Her face paled.

"We've learned that the last few victims of the black bird society all received these weird homemade dolls." Daniels reached for another fry. "We're trying to find the source, but aren't having much luck."

"Maybe this Raven has something to do with it," added Rem.

Rita hadn't touched her fry.

"You okay, Rita?" asked Daniels.

"You should know…" She looked over at him. "Barbara Ingram? She's Damien's daughter."

Rem stopped in mid-chew. "What?"

Daniels dropped his jaw. "She's his daughter?"

Rita nodded. "By his first wife. They married young, and Barbara was the firstborn. She was a rebellious kid, though, much like her dad. She got caught up in the drug scene and ran away from home at seventeen, got married and was pregnant at eighteen, had a baby at nineteen, and was divorced at twenty."

Rem tried to absorb the unexpected information and the repercussions.

"She's been married three times since," said Rita, "but, like her dad, none have stuck."

"Is that why she hates us so much?" asked Rem. "Because of her dad?"

"She's a member of the society, too," said Daniels. "She must have brought Rook to CIW as a client."

"I'm sure she did," said Rita. "Once Barbara got past the rebellious phase, she and Damien have been close."

"I still don't understand the grudge." Rem picked up another fry. "What did we do to them?"

Rita reached over and put her hand on Rem's forearm. "Barbara's child? The one she had at nineteen?" She paused. "Her name was Allison Albright."

Rem dropped his french fry.

Chapter Twenty

MIKEY TOLD HERSELF SHE was doing what she had to do to find Vera's killer. Besides, she didn't owe Rem anything. Not after last night. She knew where she stood with him.

Margaret smirked as if she'd won a free pass out of the facility. "Tell me about him."

Mikey put on her game face. "There's not much to tell. He goes to work. So do I. We come home—" she stopped when she saw Margaret's eyes flash.

"Home?" she asked. "You moved in with him?"

Mikey forced herself to breathe. "Yes. But I've moved out."

"Why?"

"Mikey," whispered Marjorie. "Don't do this."

Mikey pushed forward. "We had a fight last night, and I left."

"About what?"

"He came home drunk. We disagreed about me visiting you."

"That's not what made you leave, though, is it?"

Mikey hesitated. "We've been arguing for a while now. Ever since his cousin..." She stopped. "Well, he's been angry."

Margaret gripped a crayon. "His cousin?"

Mikey bit her lip. "His cousin Cain was murdered. By the people Rem's investigating. He's grieving and angry about it."

Margaret smiled. "That's a shame."

"Don't pretend you care," said Mikey. "Because I know you don't."

"If *you* cared so much, why did you leave?" Margaret drew circles with the blue crayon. "I know what a bleeding heart you are."

Mikey looked away.

"You don't have to say another word," said Marjorie.

Margaret stopped drawing and waited.

Mikey took another shaky breath. "Because Rem told me if I left, it would be easier. He wouldn't have to deal with Jennie's things, or mine, if I wind up dead too."

Margaret tapped the tip of her crayon on the paper. "Ah. Dear sweet Jennie. The love of his life. The one you're constantly compared to."

"Stop it," said Marjorie. "How can you say that to your sister?"

"Because I tell the truth," said Margaret with a satisfied sneer. She eyed Mikey. "I don't fill your head with platitudes and well-wishes. Rem loves Jennie and always will. You will never take her place."

Mikey fought back tears, determined not to show Margaret any weakness.

Margaret put down the blue crayon and picked up the green one. "Tell me about the cousin. How did Rem find out?"

Mikey shook her head. "No. Now it's your turn. Tell me about the man in the grove."

Margaret stared back with an amused expression. "His name is Winnie. Or at least that's what I always called him. He and Victor were friends, which is how I met him. Winnie could do things Victor wouldn't. Like removing infiltrators." She started drawing with the crayon. "I admired Winnie. He always told the truth, and would know when someone was lying, and wasn't afraid to do what had to be done."

"Where is he now?" asked Mikey.

She shrugged. "How would I know? I'm in here."

"Have you been in contact with him since arriving here?"

Margaret looked up. "Tell me about the cousin."

Mikey swallowed.

Marjorie squeezed Mikey's hand again. "Mikey, please," whispered Marjorie. "This isn't worth it."

Mikey straightened her shoulders and refocused. "Rem was devastated."

"How close was Rem to his cousin?"

"They were close when they were young, but not recently. Cain had joined this society..."

Margaret kept drawing. "What society?"

"I'm not sure, but members have bird tattoos."

Margaret briefly stilled. "Interesting. And they killed Cain?"

"Yes," said Mikey. "Rem found him."

"Really?" Margaret looked up. "How did he react?"

Mikey jutted out her chin. "Your turn. Have you been in contact with Winnie since being admitted to this facility?"

Margaret resumed her drawing. "Yes."

Mikey sucked in a breath. "When?"

"Not long ago."

"What did he say?"

She looked up. "He told me what he was up to."

"And what's that?"

"He's keeping busy. He's still good at stirring up trouble."

"What kind of trouble?" Her mind traveled back to her friend Nathan getting a phone call, telling him to expose Vera's grave. "Is he the one who called Nathan and told him to find Vera and contact the cops?"

"He is."

"So that I could be accused of murder?" asked Mikey. "Was that the plan?"

Margaret made swirls of green on her paper. "You're sitting here, so you were never convicted. What's the problem?"

Mikey's anger bubbled up. She was tired of Margaret's games. "Where is Winnie? What's his real name? How can I find him?"

Margaret glared at Mikey. "Tell me Rem's reaction when Cain died. What did he do?"

Mikey's stomach twisted. She hated this, but she was so close to learning who killed Vera. "Cain died in his arms. Rem was there at the hospital with the family when the doctor told them Cain couldn't be saved. Rem was inconsolable. He drove for a while, and then..."

"Then what?" asked Margaret.

Mikey dreaded saying the words. "He drove to Jennie's grave."

Margaret's face softened. "And not to you. How terribly predictable."

"Stop it," said Marjorie. "Mikey, this is enough. You have to stop."

Mikey sat forward and scowled at her sister. "Tell me how to find Winnie."

Margaret's eyes glimmered. "You already know him."

Mikey frowned. "What?"

"You've spoken to him, and he's been in your, I mean Rem's, house." She leaned in and spoke softly. "You're so close, Mikey, but you can't see it. You saw him at the grove. You know his face. But you're too caught up in a fantasy about a man you can't have. And that's what Rem is. A fantasy. A dream. An illusion. He'll tell you one thing and give you another. And if you don't get out, he'll destroy you." She sat back with a sigh. "Believe me. I know. How do you think I ended up in here?"

"You tried to kill both of us," said Mikey, reeling from her sister's words.

Margaret's face tightened. "You're so stupid. I wasn't trying to kill you. I was trying to save you."

Mikey gripped the edge of Margaret's small tabletop. "You're still playing with me. You know Winnie's name, don't you?"

She set her crayon down with a groan. "I'm tired. I think our game is over for today." She looked down the hall. "Bennett?"

Bennett popped his head out of a room. "Be right there."

"We're not done," said Mikey.

"Yes, we are," said Margaret. She balled up her piece of paper. "Please convey to Rem my condolences about his cousin." She paused. "And your doomed relationship."

"We should never have come here," said Marjorie.

Margaret almost appeared cheery. "But I'm thrilled you did. You've given me more than I could have asked for."

Bennett walked down the hall and into the visiting area. "All done?" He took her crayons, tucked her table back, and undid the brake.

Margaret gripped the crumpled paper in her hand. "Nice to see you, sister, and you too, Marjorie. Tell Gordon I don't miss him, but I miss his partner. I was almost past dreaming about him, but now that I've talked to Mikey, I have so much more to dream about."

Seeing her sister's satisfied expression, Mikey had to hold back from strangling her. "I'm going to find Winnie, Margaret. And when I do, that's one more nail in your coffin."

Bennett pushed the wheelchair away as Margaret tossed her paper in a nearby trashcan. "Be careful what you wish for, sister."

Frustrated, Mikey could only watch as Bennett wheeled Margaret away.

· · · ● · ● · · · ·

Daniels stared in shock. "Allison Albright is Rook's granddaughter?" He looked at Rem, who had paled considerably.

"Yes," said Rita. "They were very close, and she's the one who introduced him to D'Mato. When she died, along with her unborn child, Rook lost his great-granddaughter too." She squeezed Rem's arm. "And he blames both of you."

Daniels shook his head. "I don't believe it."

Rem pushed his plate back and fell back against the seat.

"I know this must be hard to hear." Rita paused. "I don't know all the details, but…" She softened her voice. "…I know Allison was carrying your child."

Rem stiffened, and Daniels' stomach turned. "Is that what Rook believes?" asked Daniels sharply. "Because he's misinformed. Allison was lying."

Rita's eyes widened. "Are you sure? He told me…he said…" She eyed Rem.

"That Rem manipulated her, slept with her and got her arrested for crimes she didn't commit?" Daniels tried but failed to hide his disgust. "He's wrong. Rem went undercover to learn more about D'Mato and his cult. We thought Allison was D'Mato's ex, but she was way worse. She drugged and assaulted Rem, helped D'Mato abduct him, and then murdered D'Mato." The memories pissed Daniels off all over again. "Then she damn near sacrificed Rem, and that's why she was in jail." Daniels took a second to collect himself. "Then that manipulative bitc…" he took a second. "…woman lied to Rem, telling him she was carrying his child, and tried to blackmail him into not testifying against her."

Rem sat quietly in the booth, and Rita stared in surprise. "I should have known Damien wasn't telling me the truth."

"He may not know the truth," said Rem. "The paternity test was done post-mortem."

Daniels snorted his indignation. "Rook knows. He's got his hooks into everything, so he'd be aware of the test. But what he believes is a different story."

Rita put her hand on her chest. "I knew Allison could be manipulative and ambitious, but I didn't think she would take it that far."

"She was very good at self-preservation," said Rem.

"She excelled at it." Daniels thought back. "And it wouldn't surprise me if Rook and Allison instigated D'Mato's death to get D'Mato out of the way. Allison could assume the leadership, and she and her granddad could use the followers however they saw fit."

Rita dropped her jaw. "That would make perfect sense."

Rem sat up again, and Daniels was glad to see some of the color returning to his face. "Why, though?" asked Rem. "D'Mato's followers weren't exactly running in powerful circles. They were misfits, as most cult groupies are, except some had gifts D'Mato envied. How did they benefit Rook?"

Rita stared off for a second before dropping her palm to the table with a smack. "The drugs."

Daniels furrowed his brow. "What drugs?"

"Now it all makes sense," said Rita. She leaned closer. "The deeper Damien got with D'Mato, the weirder he became. He told me he and D'Mato had come up with something big. Something that would reach beyond the cult."

"Did he tell you what that was?" asked Daniels.

"He wouldn't come out and say it, but I started asking questions about his erratic behavior and put it together with this Raven and D'Mato. It wasn't a big leap to suspect drugs. When I asked him if he was taking something, he couldn't deny it."

"What was he taking?" Rem glanced at Daniels with a look of concern, and Daniels understood. Did this have something to do with the pill they'd taken the previous night?

Rita shrugged. "I don't know. He wouldn't give specifics. But he told me it could change everything."

"Rook doesn't strike me as some sort of drug dealer," added Daniels. "It seems beneath him."

"It wasn't like that," said Rita. "He saw this as a drug for the powerful." She sighed. "Let me think." She closed her eyes. "This Raven. Damien said the Raven could access deeper parts of his psyche." She opened her eyes. "To purge the darkness in order to amplify his strengths. It made him feel invincible and unstoppable. He thought that if he could do that for the right people, that together, they could do incredible things."

"So, he and this Raven created a drug?" asked Rem. "With D'Mato's help?"

Rita nodded. "Yes, but Damien called it a supplement. Not a drug."

Daniels thought of Allison. "How much you want to bet Allison saw the bigger picture? Maybe she planned to use D'Mato's followers to sell or distribute this supplement?"

"It's certainly possible," added Rita.

"That doesn't sound like Rook," said Rem. "D'Mato's followers were beneath him."

"Maybe not," said Daniels. "If that drug was potent enough, they could see the dollar signs. Can you imagine what giving something like that to the cult could do? If it purged their darkness and made them feel invincible? Especially if they had gifts? And then you send them out to do the same to others?"

Rem made an unpleasant face. "Based on what it did to us, I don't see that as a plus."

Rita sucked in a breath. "You took the drug?"

Daniels rubbed his stomach, which still wasn't quite right. "It was part of the initiation ceremony. We had to take a pill."

Rem sighed. "And based on its effects, it didn't do us any favors."

Rita rested her elbows on the table. "Damien would have complete control over the composition of the drug." She stared off again. "Ezra Grimm..."

"You know him?" asked Daniels. "He's another member, and almost as pleasant as Barbara and Morrow."

"But do you know who he *is*?" asked Rita. "He's cousins with Ruben and Gloria Montes, whose family runs—"

"Montes Pharmaceuticals," said Rem with shock. His eyes widened. "Hell."

Daniels understood the implication. "With Grimm's help, Rook could have access to labs and researchers."

"And Rook could tell them exactly what he wanted," added Rem.

Daniels closed his eyes. "God knows what we took last night."

"Certainly not Allison's variety," replied Rem. "Something tells me her version would have included floating purple zebras and swirling square lollipops."

"No doubt." Daniels spoke to Rita. "You think Rook has been taking this stuff?"

"I know he has," said Rita. "I think it's the reason he started acting so bizarrely, and it's not getting any better. I truly think he believes himself to be indestructible. God knows what long-term exposure to this supplement does to the mind."

"Or what long-term exposure to this Raven does," said Rem. "That might scare me even more. If this Raven was part of the development of this drug, and knowing D'Mato's penchant for the paranormal..."

Daniels shot a look at his partner. "What are you saying? That this drug has some sort of paranormal connection? In what way?"

"I don't know. You know what happened to us last night. It brought out the worst in us."

"That doesn't make it some sort of paranormal power drug."

"It changed our personalities." He sucked in a breath. "What if this has something to do with how young Rook looks?"

Daniels pursed his lips. "That's a bit of a stretch."

"Is it? You said so yourself at the party that if you didn't know better, you'd put him in his sixties, which is how old he was when he got involved with D'Mato."

Rita leaned closer. "You think Damien, Victor, and this Raven figured out how to stop aging?"

"Aging suggests weakness, especially to a man like Damien." Rem rested his elbows on the table. "It's something to consider."

"Still," said Daniels, "saying the reason for Rook's good looks is paranormal is a gigantic leap. Now, maybe if you could read my mind..."

"I already do that," said Rem, "but what about reading someone else's mind, or even seeing things, or...or..." his face fell, "or establishing some sort of unseen connection to whoever takes it."

Daniels didn't buy it. "Well, can you read Rita's mind?"

Rem glanced at Rita, paused, and focused.

Rita stared back at him, and Daniels rolled his eyes.

"Well?" asked Rita after a pause.

"You're definitely unhappy with Damien," said Rem.

"Like that's hard to read," said Daniels. "What's her favorite color?"

Rem focused harder. "Blue."

Rita sighed. "Sorry. It's pink."

Rem deflated.

"Would you be serious?" asked Daniels.

"I am being serious," said Rem. "Maybe we can't read other people's minds, but what if this drug made us vulnerable to someone who can? We have to seriously consider this Raven's involvement. What does she get out of this? Rook can't be getting all the perks."

Daniels had to admit that made sense. "Until we know more, conjecture gets us nowhere. Let's just focus on what we have. Rook's got a drug he's using and giving to his society members, which makes them all think they're invincible after supposedly purging all their bad habits. How do we prove it?"

"Giving a supplement to your members who take it voluntarily isn't against the law," said Rem.

"No, it isn't, but when you add conspiracy, blackmail, murder, attempted murder, extortion, assault, and a dozen or so other charges, it doesn't look good. Plus, depending on what's in it, we might get a possession charge out of it too."

Rita clutched her elbows. "Murder? You think Damien's capable of murder?"

"Not of actually pulling the trigger himself," said Rem, "but certainly of hiring someone to do it. He blackmailed us into killing for him."

Rita dropped her jaw. "You killed someone?"

"Rook thinks we did," said Rem. "We had to make it look convincing for Rook to invite us in."

Daniels squirted some lemon into his tea from a slice in his glass. "And we think your brother's responsible for the death of Reginald Durning and two other men."

"He hired a hit woman to kill them and brand them with a star," added Rem.

Rita gaped at them. "Those murders in the news? You think *Damien* did that?"

Daniels set the lemon on his small plate. "And he's responsible for Rem's cousin's death, and my wife's miscarriage. And another man died recently. Martin Bailey. He was a member too, and we believe he got on Rook's bad side."

"And to make it even creepier," said Rem, "the vics got a weird hand-made doll with a black feather in it before they died. None of them understood what it meant, so they discarded it, but now we know it's a death sentence."

Daniels eyed the door when a couple walked in. "I'd be willing to bet a chunk of life savings that the doll comes from the Raven."

"Same with that weird circle, the smell, and the candles in the abandoned building and that room in Rook's house," said Rem.

Daniels pointed at Rem. "The cackle."

Rem cursed. "You think the cackler is the Raven?"

"I bet the Raven was watching last night. There was a camera in the corner of the room." Daniels shivered just thinking about it.

Rem ran his hand through his hair and gripped his neck. "Hell. What are we dealing with here?"

His appetite gone, Daniels pushed his plate back but noticed Rita's faraway stare. "You okay, Rita?"

"I realize we've thrown a lot at you." Rem reached for another fry. "But I assure you, we're telling the truth about Rook. He's dangerous, and the farther you stay away from him, the better."

"The last thing you need is to become his next target." Daniels waited for her response, but none came. "Rita?"

She finally looked at him. "It may be too late for that."

"What do you mean?" Rem dunked his fry in ketchup.

She reached for her purse and pushed it to the side of the booth. Beside it was a small plastic grocery bag Daniels hadn't noticed. She reached into it and pulled out a doll that looked exactly like the doll found in Martin Bailey's car. Only someone had glued the red felt patch on the chest.

Daniels' heart dropped.

Chapter Twenty-One

MANETTI KNOCKED ON THE door of Roseanna's house and waited. After a few seconds, the door opened, and an attractive Hispanic woman with braided hair greeted him. "Detective Manetti?" She eyed his badge, which he held out. "Thank you for coming on a Saturday afternoon. I'm Rosie." She opened the door wider.

"Nice to meet you." Manetti stepped inside. "And today's not a problem. If Lola is ready to talk, I'm happy to listen."

Roseanna closed the door. "Come in." She gestured toward the living area.

"Thank you." Manetti walked toward the couch.

"I'll get her. Have a seat. Can I get you something to drink?"

Manetti sat on the sofa. "I don't suppose you have beet juice?"

She pursed her lips. "How about vegetable? I get it from the local market."

Surprised, Manetti nodded. "That would be great."

"Not all of us drink soda and eat junk food. I try to get my girls to eat right. Doesn't always work, though. Be right back."

She stepped out, and Manetti pulled out his small notebook and pencil from his pocket. He'd spent the morning weeding his veggie garden, and while Annabelle had taken a nap, he'd showered and headed over to see Roseanna and Lola. He waited on the couch for a few minutes, and Roseanna returned with his juice. She set it on the coffee table in front of him and turned back toward the door. "Come on in, Lo."

Manetti looked over to see a woman with long legs, wearing short shorts and a halter top, standing to the side of the door. She wore no makeup, and her brown hair was slightly damp, like she'd just got out of the shower.

He stood. "Lola?"

She stared at him as if she expected him to snarl at her.

"I'm Detective Manetti." He pulled out his badge and showed it to her.

Her reaction was immediate. She shook her head and turned.

"Lola, stop," said Roseanna. "Don't waste this man's time. You said you would talk to him."

Lola looked back. "I can't."

Roseanna stepped toward her. "Honey, you still have nightmares about what happened to you. You can't continue to live in fear. You have to say something."

Lola's face fell, and she stared at Manetti.

Manetti put his badge away. "All I want to do is talk. You can say as much, or as little, as you want. And if you want to keep whatever you tell me between us, I can do that."

She hesitated.

"You can trust me, Lola," said Manetti. "I won't report anything you don't want me to."

"You can do this, Lo," said Roseanna. "Please. Just tell him what happened."

Lola took another second, and Manetti half-expected her to dart up the stairs, when she took a few tentative steps toward him.

"That's it. Come sit," said Roseanna. "I'll get you something to drink. You want a soda?"

Lola crossed her arms and nodded.

Roseana gestured toward a chair next to the couch. "Have a seat."

Lola cautiously walked toward the chair, keeping her eyes on Manetti the whole time. She glanced toward Roseanna. "You'll stay with me, Rosie?"

"I'll get your drink and stick right by your side." Roseanna smiled and left the room.

Lola eyed Manetti warily and sat in the chair. She crossed her arms and gripped her elbows.

Manetti sat again and picked up his vegetable juice. "You like veggie juice?" he asked, sipping the drink. It was surprisingly good.

She made a face. "I'd rather drink piss."

He chuckled. "Not a veggie fan?"

She shrugged. "I can stomach broccoli, but that's it."

"I like broccoli myself, but I love brussel sprouts. My wife, Annie, makes a mean veggie pasta."

"Veggie pasta? What's wrong with regular pasta?"

Sensing her discomfort lessening, Manetti relaxed. "We avoid processed foods."

Her brow furrowed. "That's just sad."

He chuckled again. "It's not that bad once you get used to it."

"I could never give up chocolate."

Manetti leaned in and whispered. "Don't tell my wife, but sometimes I sneak it."

She half-smiled. "Mum's the word."

"Thanks."

Roseanna returned with a can of soda and another glass of veggie juice. She gave the soda to Lola and kept the glass for herself. She sat beside Manetti, nearer to Lola. "You ready?" she asked Lola.

Lola studied Manetti. "Okay," she whispered.

Manetti held out his notebook. "I'm just going to take some notes, but I won't use them for anything if you don't want me to."

She glanced at the notebook.

Glad she was more comfortable, Manetti took his time. "Why don't you start at the beginning?"

Lola looked at Roseanna for reassurance. Roseanna reached over and squeezed Lola's wrist. "Go ahead."

Lola nibbled her lip and opened the soda. She stared at the open can but didn't drink anything. "It happened a few months ago." She eyed Roseanna again, who nodded at her. "It was a new client."

Manetti scribbled. "Did you know him, Roseanna?"

Roseanna shook her head. "Never seen him before. He said his name was Louis, but I doubt it was his real name. He came on a Friday night and showed me a wad of cash. I let him in, and he came in here." She gestured at the area they were sitting in. "The ladies were in the room, and he immediately gravitated toward Lola. They went upstairs soon after."

"Was he intoxicated?"

Roseanna nodded. "I sensed he'd had a few drinks, but nothing that indicated he could be violent. I'm usually pretty good at picking those types out." She eyed Lola with sadness. "But that night, I missed it."

Lola sipped her drink and set it on the table. "It's not your fault, Rosie," she whispered. She put her hand over Rosie's, which was still clutching her wrist.

"What happened when you got up to the room?"

Lola hesitated again but squeezed Rosie's hand. "At first, it was okay. Some guys like to talk first, and he was one of them. He took out a small bottle of liquor from his pocket. He drank from it, then took a pill from his jacket pocket and swallowed it."

"A pill?" asked Manetti. "Did he say what it was?"

Lola shook her head. "No. He just said he needed to relax. It had been a stressful week. We talked for a few minutes."

"Did he tell you anything about his personal life?"

She shrugged. "He said he had a high-pressure job, and that he worked with stupid people who didn't understand him. He said he had a girlfriend too."

Manetti took more notes.

"I asked him what she'd think about him being with me, and he just smiled. He said she wouldn't care. They had an open relationship."

"And what happened then?"

Lola tensed in her chair. "We started up...well, you know....and he went fast. But he had trouble, you know...with performing."

Manetti looked up. "I get the drift."

"It made him mad. I told him it was fine. It happened. I said we could wait a few minutes and try again. He cursed at me and said it was all my fault. That's when he got up...like to leave, you know?"

"You thought he was leaving the house?"

"I thought so, but then he said he had to use the bathroom. He stomped out in just his boxers, and I wondered if he had gone to take more drugs or something. He'd left his liquor bottle behind though, and I...well...I had a sip. I figured it might help me relax."

"And what happened next?"

"I waited and got bored." She eyed Rosie. "I know we're supposed to mind our own business and not go through customer's stuff."

"It's okay," said Rosie. "Just tell him what happened."

Lola sighed. "I flipped through his pockets, wondering if there were more drugs. I didn't plan to take anything. I just wanted to know what I was dealing with." She paused. "I heard footsteps, and I stepped back to the bed, and that's when he walked in. He closed the door and stared at me. I asked if he wanted to try again, and he…he…"

Rosie squeezed Lola's fingers.

"He what?" asked Manetti.

"He went crazy." Tears sprang into Lola's eyes. "He called me a whore and a bitch, and he started to beat me. I was so shocked I could barely respond. And then, well, he hit me hard and everything blurred, and then he was on top of me. He forced himself on me, and this time, he had no trouble. I just wanted it to be over, but when it was, he kept hitting me and calling me names." Tears streamed down her face, and her breath caught. "I thought if I were submissive, he'd leave me alone, but that only seemed to make him madder." She gripped Rosie's hand harder and sniffed. She spoke barely above a whisper. "And then he started to strangle me."

Although this wasn't Manetti's first time hearing a story like this, it never got easier. "How did you get away?"

She stammered. "Everything is fuzzy. I thought he was going to kill me, but then he stopped. He stared at me and the room like he didn't know who I was or why he was there."

Rosie pulled a tissue from her pocket and handed it to Lola. "You're doing great, Lo. Keep going."

Lola wiped her eyes with the tissue. "I rolled off the bed, trying to breathe. I wanted to run out of the room, but I was scared it would set him off again. He calmed down and sat on the edge of the bed. After a few seconds, I got the nerve up and told him he had to go."

"What did he do?"

"Nothing. He just stared." She picked at the tissue. "I've dealt with a few crazies before, but this guy? He was different. I didn't know what he was going to do next."

Manetti wrote that down. "How did you get out of there?"

"When he didn't move, I ran for it, and that made him mad. He grabbed me, threw me on the bed and started wailing on me again, saying things like, 'Nobody disobeys him,' and 'I need to be put in my place.'" More tears fell down her cheeks. "I started screaming, trying to get him off me, and that's when Rosie came into the room. She had her gun and told him to get away from me."

Manetti frowned at Rosie. "You have a gun?"

"In this business?" said Rosie. "You better believe it. Know how to use it too."

Manetti decided not to ask if she had a license for it. He could deal with that later. "What did he do?"

"He stopped," said Lola. "He saw the gun and smiled."

"I've never seen anything like it," said Rosie. "He just stared at me with this odd blank expression and then dared me to shoot him. Said he couldn't be touched, so it wouldn't matter. Then he stood, got dressed, left some extra cash, and left, like he was leaving his day job or something. He hasn't been back since."

"Can you describe him?"

"He was tall and thin, but muscular," said Lola. "He had short brown hair and hadn't shaved in a while, and he wore brown slacks with a blue shirt."

Manetti took more notes. "Anything else you can tell me about him?"

Lola bit her lip again and looked at Rosie. "It's okay," said Rosie. "Tell him."

Lola swallowed and wouldn't look at Manetti.

Manetti wondered what could possibly be worse than what she'd already mentioned.

"He, uh, he..." Lola clutched Rosie's hand like a vise.

"He what?" asked Manetti. "Did he come back?"

Lola shook her head. "No."

"She was bleeding from her head and nose, had a split lip, and her eyes and neck were already bruising," said Rosie. "She was a mess. I got her to the doctor and wanted to report it, but she refused. I kept pressing though until she finally told me why she was scared to talk to the police."

Manetti waited to hear the answer. "What was the reason?"

Lola shifted uncomfortably in her seat. "When I went through his pockets, I saw..." Rosie's fingers tightened around Lola's. "I saw..." Lola looked at Rosie for reassurance.

"Go on," said Rosie. "Say it."

Lola swallowed. "I saw a badge." She set her jaw and shifted again. "Like yours."

Manetti didn't like what he was hearing. "Are you saying this man was a police officer?"

She nodded.

"Are you sure?"

She stiffened. "I'm not lying. I know what I saw." Her confession seemed to bolster her. "It said 'Detective' on it."

Manetti stayed relaxed, but his heart was thumping. "Think carefully, Lola. This is important. You said you saw 'Detective' on the badge?" He paused. "Did you see a name, too?"

She bounced her foot.

"Lola?" asked Manetti, afraid to hear the answer.

Lola finally looked at him. "I did." She bit her bottom lip. "It said Detective Frank Monk."

Chapter Twenty-Two

DANIELS ENTERED HIS HOUSE with Rem. "Erin?" he asked, looking for his sister and son.

"Daddy!" J.P. raced in from the living room.

Daniels picked up his son and held him in his arms. "Hey, buddy. Where's your Aunt Erin?"

"Right here," said Erin, walking in from the living room. "We've been playing with his toys."

J.P.'s eyes widened when he saw Rem. "Uncle Rem!" He reached for Rem.

Rem took J.P. from Daniels and sat him on his hip. "Hey, little dude. How's it hanging?"

They walked into the kitchen.

"Is Marjorie back yet?" Daniels asked Erin. On the way back from seeing Rita, Daniels had received a text from Marjorie telling him she and Mikey had left the psychiatric facility and were on their way home.

"Not yet," said Erin. She smoothed J.P.'s wild hair. "I got J.P. some lunch and was about to put him down for his nap."

"We played twains and disaurs," said J.P. with a big smile.

"You did?" asked Rem. "Did you bite a dinosaur?" He tickled J.P.'s stomach.

J.P. laughed. "I bit a big rex." He opened his arms wide.

"You've been a tremendous help, Erin. Thank you," said Daniels.

She smiled. "It's been nice watching my nephew. I've never been able to do that."

Daniels watched J.P. play with Rem. "It's nice to have an aunt to watch him. He's never had that either."

Rem snarled. "I'm a velociraptor, and I like..." He pulled up J.P.'s shirt, "...tummies." He pretended to bite J.P.'s stomach, ran his stubbled chin over it, and then blew a big raspberry against his skin, making J.P. squeal with laughter.

"After I put him down, I'll head out," said Erin.

Daniels frowned. "Head out where?"

"Home."

Daniels shook his head. "You can't go home."

"Why not?"

"With everything going on," said Daniels, "it's too dangerous. You should stay here. At least for a few days until Rem and I sort this out."

"You think it's that risky?"

Rem put J.P. back on his feet. "Daniels is right. You should stay here at least through the weekend. We can reevaluate tomorrow night, or Monday."

J.P. grabbed Rem's hand and tried to pull him toward the living room. "Let's play twains."

"But I didn't bring clothes." Erin looked down at herself. "These are Marjorie's sweatpants and T-shirt."

Daniels picked up J.P. "Marjorie will be back soon. I'm sure she can lend you whatever you need. But if not, I'll take you to your place and you can pack a bag."

J.P. tugged on Daniels' shirt. "Play twains and disaurs, Daddy. With Uncle Wem."

"Sorry, buddy. But it's your nap time." J.P. wiggled to get down, but Daniels held on.

"No. I want to play." J.P. looked at Rem. "Pwease."

"How about this?" asked Rem. "You go with Erin and get your nap, and we'll play later. And maybe I'll bring out...," he snarled and raised his hand with curled fingers, "*the claw.*"

J.P. squealed again and tried to get away when Rem grabbed at him. "Save me, Rin." He reached for Erin. "Save me."

Erin took him and clutched him. "I got you. That claw won't get you."

Smiling, Daniels was amazed at how quickly J.P. had formed a bond with Erin.

Rem continued to snarl and reach for J.P. with his curled fingers, and Erin ran with J.P. to the stairs.

"Better take that nap, J.P.," said Daniels. "Or that claw is going to get you."

"Hurry," said Erin. "Before it finds us." She ran up the stairs as J.P. continued to squeal.

Rem smiled as Erin disappeared into J.P.'s room. "At least there's some goodness in this world."

Daniels nodded. "J.P.'s kept me and Marjorie sane through all of this."

"Me too," said Rem, coming back to the kitchen. He checked his phone with a sigh. "Not a word from Mikey."

Daniels reached for a glass in the dish drainer. "You need to give her some space. Between your argument and visiting Margaret, she's got a lot on her mind." He held up the glass. "You want some water?"

"No, thanks." Rem pulled out a chair and sat. "It's not like her, though, not to at least return my calls or texts. Even if she's mad."

"She just left her sister, so there's no telling what frame of mind she's in." Daniels added some ice to his glass and filled it with water from a dispenser in the kitchen. "She's dropping Marjorie off. You can see her in a few minutes."

Rem dropped his head into his hand. "I'm not sure what I'm worried about most. What I said to her or what happened with Margaret."

Daniels pulled out a chair beside Rem and sat. "You two will work it out."

"Yeah." Rem raised his head. "In the meantime, what do we do about Rita?"

Daniels sipped some water. "We told her to get out of town for a few days, and we've got the doll, although I don't know what good that will do. Unless Forensics finds a tag on it that says *Made by the Raven*."

"Even that won't help until we actually locate this Raven."

Daniels set his glass on the table. "Something tells me she's the key. We find her, it could tumble Rook and his entire organization."

"Easier said than done. This whole elusive voodoo mystery person is terrifying."

"You think it's some kind of voodoo?"

"Isn't that what you think when you see the dolls? In the movies, Voodoo priests or priestesses create dolls in the image of a victim, and then they stab it or curse it, and that affects the victim." He leaned in. "Have you seen *The Serpent and the Rainbow*?" He shivered. "Scariest movie ever."

Daniels huffed. "Those are movies, Rem."

"Based on reality." He pointed. "You can't discard that."

"Maybe that's the whole point. To create the idea of something terrifying, when in fact, Rook is using that fear to control others. Like the wizard in *The Wizard of Oz*."

Rem narrowed his eyes. "That's your third movie reference today." He reached to put the back of his hand on Daniels' forehead. "Do you have a fever?"

Daniels swatted Rem's hand away with an eye roll. "My point is, let's not jump the gun on this Raven and turn it into some boogeyman. It's probably someone like Rook who's having fun with us."

Rem slumped. "I hope we didn't piss the Raven off, too. I'm still struggling with Allison and Rook being related."

"That was a kick to the gut, wasn't it?"

"If Rook actually believes I killed the woman carrying my child and his great-grandchild, no wonder he hates me. Barbara too."

"Rook just doesn't want to believe the truth. The drugs have messed with his head, and he needs someone to blame."

Rem crossed his arms. "I can certainly understand." He stared off. "After Jennie died, I wanted to kill the driver who hit her. I even got his address and drove by his house." He looked back. "Did I tell you that?"

Rem's confession didn't surprise Daniels. "And you want Tex for killing Cain. I want Rhonda for hurting Marjorie, and Mikey wants the man at the grove for shooting Vera. Those are all natural responses because they're actual criminals. You're not a criminal, and neither am I. We were doing our jobs, and you certainly didn't kill Allison. If you could have prevented her death, you would have."

Rem ran his hands over his face. "You think one bad guy's gone, and another pops up in their place. When does it ever end?"

Daniels ran his finger down his water glass. "There's always Bolivia."

Rem made a snort. "If they had Taco del Fuegos and zero bad guys, I'd be on the next train."

"I'm sure they've got the tacos, but bad guys can fly to Bolivia. Ravens, too."

"Don't forget prison. We could certainly go there."

Daniels didn't want to think about that. "Don't remind me." He heard the key in the lock. The door opened, and Marjorie walked in. He stood and hurried over to her. "You okay?" He pulled her close.

She hugged him back. "I'm okay." Looking pale and tired, she dropped her purse on the front table. "But I've also been better."

Rem walked to the door. "Where's Mikey?" He looked outside.

"She left." Marjorie rubbed her neck.

"Left?" asked Rem. "She didn't want to come in? Or talk to me?"

Marjorie eyed him with concern. "She's upset, Rem."

"Is it Margaret? What did she say to Mikey? What happened?"

Marjorie put her hand on Rem's forearm. "It's a lot of things. Mikey is reeling right now. She told me about the argument between the two of you."

"What did she say? I don't remember any of it."

Marjorie frowned.

"I don't remember anything either," added Daniels, "except a brief memory of you and Erin getting me up the stairs."

"What the hell happened to you two last night?" asked Marjorie.

Agitated, Rem ran his hand through his hair. "What did Mikey tell you?"

Marjorie hesitated. "She said you two argued about Margaret. You were furious and called Mikey stupid for wanting to see her sister. Then you said it would be better if she left so you wouldn't have to clean out Jennie's closet, or Mikey's stuff either, if she wound up dead."

Rem stilled, and his face turned gray. "I said that to her?"

Daniels could imagine how Rem felt. "You didn't mean it."

"That's why she wanted to see Margaret this morning," said Marjorie. "She's angry and hurt. So when she called and told me that was her plan, I couldn't let her go alone."

Rem looked stricken. "I've got to talk to her. Did she go to Mason's?"

Marjorie nodded. "Rem, listen…"

Rem patted his pockets. "Where are my keys?"

Daniels pointed to the front table. "Over there."

Rem grabbed them.

"Rem," said Daniels. "Are you sure this is the best time?"

Marjorie stepped closer. "Rem, she's got a lot to deal with. When she saw Margaret, she…she…"

"She what?" asked Rem. "What did they talk about?"

Marjorie stared back, and Daniels could see the worry behind her eyes. After a long pause, she took Rem's arm again and squeezed his elbow. "She should be the one to tell you. You need to talk about it."

"Then that's what we're going to do." Rem headed out the door and looked back at Daniels. "I'll call you."

"Be careful," said Daniels. "Watch your back."

Rem waved and ran to his car.

· · · · ● · ● · · · ·

Croft knocked on the door of Rook's home office and opened it. He figured if Monk could get away with it, so could he. Seated behind his desk and talking on his phone, Rook swiveled toward Croft and glowered.

Croft stood and waited.

"I've got to go," said Rook. He hung up. "I don't recall saying, 'Come in.'"

Croft approached the desk. "We've got a problem."

"Problems are issues of the mind, of which I have none." Rook sat back and interlaced his fingers. "Let's call it a challenge."

Croft didn't care what Rook called it. "All right. We have a challenge. I pinged the phone I gave to Daniels and Remalla. They were at a diner over on the west side."

"I suppose they're recovering from last night with a greasy breakfast. Why do we care?"

"Because we pinged the tracker on your sister Rita's car at the same diner at the same time." He paused. "They're talking to each other."

Rook exhibited brief tension in his shoulders before relaxing again. "I suppose I shouldn't be surprised. Despite our reconciliation, Rita insists on setting me straight."

"She should not have been invited to the party."

"That was out of my hands. It was suggested I invite her, and I did."

When Rook offered no more explanation, Croft moved on. "If the detectives told her about last night..."

"Then they have broken their oath."

"Something tells me they don't care." Croft sat in one of the chairs across from Rook's desk. "And if Rita fills them in on what she knows..."

Rook shrugged. "That's not my concern. She's a minor challenge that will soon be dealt with."

Croft debated asking his next question, but felt he had to. "You mean the doll?"

"It was delivered, was it not?"

"Last night, as you requested." Croft leaned up. "But she's your sister."

"That's none of your concern or business. And, as you can see, it's necessary. She's an enemy, and threats must be removed."

Croft didn't argue. "If that's the case, then how do you want to handle Daniels and Remalla?"

Rook swiped something off his pant leg. "I've never considered their interest to be legitimate, but I was willing to play along." He reached up and touched the stone that hung from his neck. It was round, smooth, and black. Rook never took it off. "But there can be benefits to letting your enemies get close."

"They took part in the initiation ceremony," said Croft. "They took the pill and the pledge."

Rook smiled. "That was all part of the plan. Now we enact the next phase."

Curious, Croft sat back in his seat. "What's that?"

"We let them believe we're still oblivious to their deception, and give them their next assignment."

Understanding, Croft dropped his jaw. "You mean Rita?"

"Exactly, but with a few more parameters."

"They'll never do it."

"No. They won't. But it will distract them as they try to determine how to get to me before they have to kill her."

"I don't get this. Why not just kill them and get it over with? Why all the games?"

Rook's expression turned stony. "After all those two have done to me and my family, I have plans for them. Plus, I rely on the guidance and counsel of another, as does our group. I have been told they serve a purpose. Their bond is envied and can be used to make us all stronger." He rested his elbows on the armrests. "In my early days, I would have been impulsive and rid the earth of their presence without a second thought. But what I have learned after purging the darkness is patience. Like D'Mato tried and failed to do, I now use the strength of my enemies to improve my own."

Croft didn't understand any of that but suspected it had to do with the mysterious Raven. He didn't question Rook's motives but was glad he wasn't Daniels and Remalla. "You realize what this means, don't you? They lied about Jerry Lee Caruso. He's still alive."

Rook smirked at Croft. "That was known from the beginning, by eyes more gifted than my own."

"What do you want to do about it? I take it you still want to find him?"

"I do. Caruso makes us vulnerable. He saw one of our own in the act. It's a sign of weakness, and he must be dealt with."

"I don't suppose your friend has seen where they're hiding him?"

"That has not been revealed."

"Too bad. That would come in handy. What about the other assassin? Monk's lady friend?"

"She will be beneficial when needed, but right now, we will use Caruso to get what we want from the detectives. They lied, broke the pledge, and will pay the price."

"So string them along? Tell them to kill Rita and wait for them to make a move against us? What do we do in the meantime?"

Rook ran his finger over the edge of a folder on his desk. "We motivate them."

"Aren't they already motivated? We have Remalla's gun and Daniels' paid debt, plus a couple of offshore accounts in his name."

Rook swiveled in his office chair. "They must learn the consequences of their actions. They are not loyal or committed to our cause, and their only action is against us. We told them what would happen. Take Remalla's gun and demonstrate our dominance." He tilted his head. "Kill the reporter."

The order surprised Croft. "Lexie Logan? That will create a lot of publicity."

"Good. Daniels and Remalla will race to confront me and you." He smiled and rested his head back. "The Raven foretold it."

"You want to send a doll?"

"No. Let's not give them a heads-up."

"When do you want this done?"

Rook turned his head toward Croft. "Tomorrow."

"And what happens when they confront us?"

Rook chuckled. "We'll be ready." He crossed one leg over the other. "By the time we're done with them, they'll be begging to tell us Caruso's location, and the Raven..." he eyed Croft with satisfaction, "will take the rest."

Chapter Twenty-Three

DANIELS SAT MARJORIE DOWN at the dining table. Still visibly shaken, she clutched her hands together. Daniels poured her a shot of bourbon, placed it in front of her and sat beside her. "Take a sip. It'll calm your nerves."

She eyed the drink. "Oh, honey. I can't drink that."

"Just a little. It'll help."

She stared at it, then picked it up and drank some. After a pause, she set the glass down and took a deep breath. "You're right. It helps."

"Tell me what happened with Margaret."

Marjorie grimaced. "It was awful. I thought I understood what you and Rem meant when you said she was evil, but I didn't. Now I see her in a whole new light."

Worried, Daniels rested his hand over hers. "What did she say to you?" He listened in shock as Marjorie told him about her and Mikey's conversation with Margaret. He heard how Margaret had used Rem and his love for Jennie to rattle Mikey, and it had worked. Mikey had told her sister about Rem and Cain, and Cain's death. In return, Margaret had told Mikey that the man who killed Vera was Winnie, and that Winnie was someone she knew who'd been in Rem's house.

Daniels cursed. "No wonder Mikey didn't want to talk to or see Rem." He picked up the glass of bourbon. "Take another sip." Marjorie did as he asked. She shivered and set the glass down. "You think Margaret was telling the truth about the man in the grove?" he asked. "Or was she just stringing Mikey along?" He made a mental note to check the visitor logs at Margaret's facility. He doubted it would be that easy to find Winnie, but it was worth checking.

"She was telling the truth. I think she delighted in telling Mikey the person she's looking for is right under her nose."

Daniels tried to think who it could be but came up blank. "Did Margaret say whether Rem knew him too?"

Marjorie shook her head. "She ended the conversation before Mikey could get anything tangible. It was all like a big riddle, designed to mess with Mikey's head, and in return, Margaret got a chance to refuel all her fantasies about Rem. You could almost see her soaking it all in with maniacal delight. It made me sick."

Daniels hated knowing how Rem would feel once he found out. It would be a hard pill to swallow, especially since it was Mikey who betrayed him. Betrayal felt like a harsh word, but that's how it felt to Daniels. He expected Rem would feel the same. "Is Mikey going to tell Rem what she did?"

"I don't know. I tried to talk to her, but after what happened last night, she felt justified. And Margaret only deepened the wound. She sensed Mikey's sensitivity and capitalized on it."

Daniels massaged his tight neck. "This is a hell of a mess."

"I know. I wanted to say something to Rem, but I couldn't."

"He needs to know. If Mikey doesn't say something, I will."

"Mikey doesn't want to talk to him. She told me she packed a bag and got out."

Distressed, Daniels picked up Marjorie's glass and downed the remains.

"You sure you should drink that after last night?"

Daniels set the glass down. "Seemed like a good idea."

Marjorie straightened and pushed back her hair. "Now that you're caught up, how about you fill me in about yesterday? I can't wait to hear what turned you and Rem into complete opposites of yourselves."

Daniels reluctantly told her about the party, the ceremony, Rook's mention of the Raven, and taking the drug. And how he couldn't remember anything afterward.

Marjorie stared at him, wide-eyed. "Are you and Rem crazy? Why did you take that pill? Don't you watch the news? For all you knew, it could have been laced with fentanyl."

Daniels understood her anger. "It wasn't our brightest move, but it didn't seem logical that Rook would give us something that would kill us, especially during his birthday party. Plus, it's hard to add new members if they don't live past the initiation. Add to that, Rook wants us right where he's got us. Under his thumb. And taking part in the ceremony proves our allegiance to him and the society. We can't get far without that."

Marjorie gaped at him, and he knew he was in hot water.

"And before you yell at me for being stupid, we've made some progress. Rem and I met with Rook's sister this morning." He filled her in on Rita and their meeting at the diner. "So, we're getting somewhere."

"Isn't that enough to arrest Rook?" she asked. "Can't Rita's testimony end this whole thing?"

"I wish, but it's not enough. It doesn't prove Rook was behind the Star murders, or Cain's death. It doesn't give us Rhonda or Tex, and it doesn't prove my or Rem's innocence. We need more."

Marjorie held her head again. "I think I'm going to need more bourbon."

"The bottle may not be enough." He jumped when the burner phone rang from his jacket pocket. "Speak of the devil." He put his finger to his lips and answered. "Hello."

Croft responded. "Hope you and your partner have recovered after last night."

"Care to fill us in? What happened after we took that pill?"

He chuckled. "Let's just say you two know how to have fun."

Daniels chose not to ask what he meant.

"And since you're such eager recruits, you have a new assignment."

Daniels gripped the phone. "I thought we proved ourselves."

"You still have to work for the man if you expect to get paid."

"Who?"

"Rook's sister. Rita Vittorio."

Surprised, Daniels sat up. "Why her?"

"Don't ask questions. You've got seventy-two hours, and this time, it better be in the news. We want to hear all about it."

"But—"

"Call me when it's done." He hung up.

Daniels lowered the phone and cursed.

· · • • • • • • · ·

Manetti knocked on the door of Monk's apartment. After talking to Lola and assuring her story would stay with him until he figured out how to handle it, he'd left Roseanna's and driven around, debating what to do. He recalled finding Margaret's pictures in Monk's desk drawer. And how his partner had found Vera's name in a file where she'd never been listed. Did either have anything to do with what had happened with Lola? Manetti had told himself there were reasonable explanations for both but had never questioned Monk about them. Now he wondered if he'd made a mistake.

Monk had always struck Manetti as an intense man, but never violent or abusive. He spoke little about his personal life; Manetti didn't even know if he had a girlfriend or boyfriend. Manetti had never been one to push, though. He figured if Monk wanted him to know something, he'd mention it.

But after hearing Lola's story, he saw his partner in a new light. He'd visited a sex worker, taken drugs, assaulted, strangled and nearly killed her. The timeline fit, too. According to Lola, Monk's visit coincided with his suspension when he'd pushed too hard with Lozano after trying to arrest Mikey for Vera's murder. Had it upset Monk greater than Manetti realized? His partner had seemed to take the suspension in stride, but Manetti had obviously misread the signs.

After driving for an hour, he finally decided that he owed Monk a chance to explain. It's what partners did for each other. If either Daniels or Rem hit rock bottom, they would be there for one other, and Manetti wanted to do the same.

When Monk didn't answer the door, Manetti knocked again. "Monk? It's Manetti. You home?"

He heard a thump and then Monk's voice. "One sec. Be right there."

Manetti jangled the keys in his pocket, wondering how to broach this subject, and how Monk would handle it.

After a few more seconds passed, Monk opened the door. His hair was tousled, and he wore a robe. "Sorry, Manetti. I was just about to jump in the shower."

"Sorry to bug you. Do you have a second?"

"Sure." Monk opened the door wider. "Come in."

Manetti stepped inside and saw Monk's neat apartment. He'd only been there once before, and it had been just as neat then, too. "Thanks."

Monk shut the door. "What's on your mind? Aren't you supposed to be weeding your garden today?"

Manetti half-smiled. "Yeah. I suppose." Now that he was there, he didn't know what to say. "I got sidetracked."

"You want something to eat or drink? I don't have much in the way of veggies."

Manetti shook his head. "I'm good. Thanks." He turned and walked behind the couch. "You been busy?"

Monk didn't respond, and Manetti faced him.

"What's up, Manetti? I know you didn't stop by to ask me about my weekend."

Manetti slid his hands into his pockets and jangled his keys again. "No, I didn't."

"Then what's on your mind?" Monk crossed his arms and waited. "It's nothing serious, I hope. Annabelle okay? She go baby shopping?"

"She's fine. But tired. She's shopping with her mom tomorrow instead." Manetti struggled with forming the words. "I, uh, was out driving and I stopped at..."

Monk raised a brow. "Stopped where?"

Manetti's stomach lurched, and he clenched his hands. In that one second, something told him not to say a word to Monk about Lola. "Actually, that's not important." He started to sweat.

"You're not making any sense."

Manetti took a deep breath. "I have to admit something. It's been on my mind, and I feel bad about it, and when I was out this morning, I decided I should talk to you."

Monk's face fell. "What could be so serious?"

Manetti told part of the truth. "I found Margaret's drawing, the one she gave to me, in your drawer. I was looking for something, and I saw it, and it weirded me out. I had thrown it away, and you fished it out of the trash? What for? Why would you keep something like that?"

Manetti stared at him with an unreadable expression. "You went through my desk?"

"It was stupid, and I apologize. I didn't mention it because I was embarrassed. But I can't stop thinking about that drawing."

Monk was quiet. "That's why you came here? To talk about the drawing?"

Manetti thought fast. He knew his story sounded odd. "Well, there's another thing I've been meaning to ask you about. I want to take some time off when the baby comes. I talked to Crow about it. I was thinking maybe a month. But I haven't passed it by you yet. What do you think?"

Monk took a step into the room. "Take all the time you need. It doesn't bother me."

"You're sure? What about our cases?"

"I'm sure Crow will assign someone to cover for you while you're out. I'll be fine."

"Good. I was worried about what you'd think. I didn't want you to feel like I was dumping everything on you."

"You're about to be a dad. Why would I be angry about you spending time with your family?"

Manetti shrugged. "Just wanted to be sure. Partners should talk about these things." He felt Monk's perusal and stayed relaxed.

"I'm more concerned about the drawings. When did you find them?"

"When we were investigating Mikey."

"And you were looking for something?"

Manetti suspected Monk wasn't buying that explanation. So he dove in and asked the bigger question. "I was wondering about something you did. Something I couldn't figure out."

"And what was that?"

Manetti gathered his courage. "How did you find Vera's name?"

Monk paused. "You know how I found it. In the file from Research."

"You couldn't have. Because Vera's name was never in it. I looked, and it's not there. I even called Research thinking there had to be an explanation, but even they said it was never listed, because her name had been removed from Missing Persons by the original investigating officers."

Monk didn't move, and Manetti sensed his mind racing. "There has to be some mistake," said Monk. "Because that's where I found it."

"There's no mistake. I double and triple checked."

Monk waved his hand. "I'll check the file on Monday. I have it saved on my desktop. I bet it's in there. Maybe you and I got separate files."

"Why would that happen? Research sent the same file to both of us."

"Maybe they did and maybe they didn't, and it seems they didn't, because that's where I got Vera's name."

A smidge of doubt made Manetti tense. Could Research have sent separate files? Manetti hadn't considered that Monk could have been looking at different information than him. "Maybe you're right."

"We'll check Monday. I'm sure there's a reasonable explanation." Monk scoffed. "What are you thinking? That I somehow knew Vera was in that grave?"

Hearing Monk say it out loud, all of Manetti's insecurities fired at once. "I may have overreacted a little. There must have been a file mix-up."

"I'm sure of it. But what's got me worried is you searched my desk because of it."

"I didn't search your..." He sighed. "All right. I kinda did."

"And you found Margaret's drawings. Big deal. I kept mine and yours because she fascinates me. Such a bright mind darkened by psychosis. I find her intriguing, and those drawings, while morose, are examples of a troubled soul. Plus, one day, they might fetch some cash."

That surprised Manetti. "Cash? You'd sell them?"

"Hell. Why not? Have you ever heard of dark tourism? There's a market for that stuff. People visit murder sites, graves, and places where the worst has happened. How much you want to bet someone would pay good money for art created by a murdering psychopath?"

The thought made Manetti slightly ill. He'd experienced enough darkness already. "I hadn't thought of that."

"Then put your mind at ease. I don't know Margaret Redstone, nor did I know Vera was in that grave. Have you been thinking that this whole time?"

Monk was doing a good job of making Manetti feel foolish, but Manetti still had an ominous sixth sense telling him not to mention Lola. "I guess it's pretty silly, isn't it? Sorry I took it so far. I should have said something sooner."

"You should have. Just keep your mitts out of my desk. I don't need you secretly stealing my Mallomars." He chuckled.

Manetti chuckled, too. "Sorry about that."

"And don't worry about the time off. We'll figure it out."

"Great. Thanks."

They stood silently in the room while Lola's story played through Manetti's mind. How could his friendly partner do what he'd done to Lola? It still made little sense. Could Lola be elaborating on her story to make it look worse because she was accusing a cop?

"Anything else?" asked Monk.

"Actually, since I'm here, can I get the name of that keto vegan cookbook you mentioned the other day? I think I'll stop by the store on the way home and buy it for Annabelle." Manetti didn't really want it but felt the need to change the subject.

"Recipe book?" asked Monk. He pursed his lips. He pointed at the desk near Manetti. "Check the top drawer. I think I wrote it down and put it in there."

Manetti turned toward the desk. "Thanks."

"If you'd like to search it though, feel free," said Monk with a slight edge to his voice.

Manetti chuckled uncomfortably and opened the drawer. "I suppose I deserved that." He rifled through a few papers and found one with the name of a cookbook. "Here it is." He was about to close it but froze when he moved a piece of paper and saw a large black feather. His heart thumped, and he brushed it with his fingers. The doll found at Cain's had a similar black feather tucked into a slit in the front, but Martin Bailey's doll had the slit, but no feather. He recalled Monk's words in Crow's office. *Be on the lookout for a black feather.*

"You okay, Manetti?" asked Monk from behind him. "Is that the wrong cookbook?"

Manetti quickly shut the drawer. "Nope. It's the right one." He waved the paper. "Annie will love it." He walked toward the door. "I should get out of your hair."

Monk studied him. "Thanks for stopping by."

"Thanks for talking to me. Sorry about the whole desk-Vera thing." He was doing his best to act normally, but his heart rate was soaring. Monk had a black feather? He assaulted Lola? What did it all mean? Who was his partner? He needed to get out of there and think.

"Not a big deal," said Monk. "We'll sort out the Vera thing on Monday."

Manetti opened the door. "I'm sure we will. Enjoy the rest of your Saturday."

"You too, Manetti. Say 'Hi' to Annie."

"Will do." Manetti waved, opened the door and hurried away.

· · · ● ● ● ● · · ·

Monk closed his door and eyed Manetti through the peephole. His partner walked down the hall to the stairs and disappeared. "It's clear," he said out loud. "You can come out."

Rhonda, wearing a skimpy negligee, walked out of the bedroom. "What are the odds? My first time here in months, and he shows up."

Concerned, Monk turned away from the door. "He's smarter than he looks. He knows about Vera. Or thinks he does."

"Knows what?" She walked over to him.

"That I didn't find her name in the file." He snorted. "And he went through my desk."

"Sounds like your partner is growing a pair. I thought you said he wasn't a problem."

"I didn't think he was, but I underestimated him."

"Since when do you do that?"

"Because he's never lied to me...until now." Monk recalled the sensation he'd felt the minute Manetti explained why he'd stopped by. "He came to say one thing but said another." Monk eyed the desk. "And then, when he went through the drawer..." Monk stepped over to the desk and opened it. "Something got his attention." He stopped cold when he saw the black feather. "Son-of-a-bitch." He picked up the feather and held it up.

Rhonda's eyes widened. "Is that what I think it is?" She sucked in a breath. "One of those feathers from the dolls? From Rook's crazy lady?"

Monk glared at the feather. He'd wanted nothing to do with the stupid dolls and had told Rook to stop delivering them. But he'd been too caught up with his sorceress to deny her. Monk had put up with the supernatural stuff with D'Mato because it had its advantages and D'Mato understood its power, but Rook had taken it in a new direction when he'd hooked up with the Raven after D'Mato's death.

"Why the hell is that in your drawer?"

Monk put two and two together. "Croft."

Rhonda's expression shifted. "He's setting you up?"

Monk twirled the feather between his fingers. "Give the man some credit. I didn't think he had it in him."

"He's trying to get you out to take your place? With Rook?" Rhonda cursed. "Slimy asshole."

"He is, but doesn't realize who he's dealing with." He eyed Rhonda. "Looks like we're going to have to move up our timetable."

Rhonda smiled. "I'm ready when you are. Just say when." She put her arm around his waist.

Monk dropped the feather onto his desk. "You have another assignment first. One I'm disappointed about, but it was coming eventually."

Her eyes lit up. "Manetti."

"He's become a problem. He knows too much, and now with the feather, he's signed his death warrant."

"What will Rook think? Are you going to go through him?"

Monk smirked. "Between Croft and Manetti, I think I'm going solo. Once we finish with them, we'll deal with Rook."

Rhonda moaned and pulled him closer. She ran her hands over his shoulders. "Where and when with Manetti?"

He thought about it. "Soon, so I don't have to explain how I found Vera and before Manetti runs his mouth to Daniels and Remalla." He paused. "And it's better to do it at home when we're not on duty. I don't need any of this blowing back on me." He considered his options. "Tomorrow. Annabelle is spending the day with her mom to shop for the nursery." He wrapped his arms around Rhonda and pulled her against him. "How does a Sunday morning murder sound?"

She giggled when he nuzzled her neck. "Sunday funday," she laughed, running her hands down his chest and under his robe. "You want me to use the star?" she whispered against his throat.

Eager for her, he slipped the straps of her negligee off and nibbled her shoulders. "Make it look like a robbery. Get in and get out. And we'll meet at the cabin." He picked her up, and she squealed. "And celebrate." She kissed his neck hungrily as he carried her to the bedroom.

Chapter Twenty-Four

REM HURRIED INTO HIS house and shut the door behind him. "Mikey?" He tossed his keys onto the front table and went into the bedroom. "Mikey? Are you home?"

The room was empty. He jogged back to the front and looked up the stairs. "Mikey?"

No answer.

Disappointed, he went into his living room and sat on the couch, wondering what to do. After leaving Daniels' house, he'd driven to Mason's, but Mikey wasn't there. Mason had told him that Mikey had called after dropping Marjorie off. She'd said little other than that she was going to drive around for a while. He'd tried to talk to her about Margaret, but she'd refused, saying she'd fill him in later.

Rem had explained to Mason about the party, his argument with Mikey afterward, and his need to apologize. Mason, thankfully, understood, but encouraged Rem to give Mikey some time. After seeing her sister, Mikey would need to decompress, but once she returned, he would talk to her and encourage her to contact Rem. Rem had left, hoping Mikey might have returned home, but he'd been wrong. The house was quiet, and there was no sign she'd been back since leaving the previous night.

Needing to do something, Rem stood and paced, trying to think about where she might go. Sitting and waiting had never been his strong suit. What he'd said to her made his heart ache, and he desperately needed to tell her he had meant none of it and to come home, but she wouldn't give him the chance.

His phone rang, and he eagerly pulled it from his pocket, praying it was Mikey. The display read an unknown number, but thinking she could be calling from a different phone, he answered. "Mikey?"

A woman replied, "No, Rem. It's not Mikey."

The voice was familiar, and he tried to place it. "Who is this?"

The voice softened but dripped with false charm. "Don't you know? Has it been that long?"

A stabbing pain shot through his chest. It couldn't be. Not Margaret. Stunned, he couldn't respond.

"Cat got your tongue?" She laughed, and his heart thudded. "Mikey came to visit me. She didn't seem very thrilled with you."

His fingers shook, and he tightened his hold on his cell. "How did you get a phone?"

"I'm very resourceful. I may be in a cage, but the bars are made of string. All I have to do is pull the right one."

Rem found it hard to breathe. Feeling off balance, he sat on the couch. He wanted to hang up, but a small part of him told him to stay on the line. "What do you want?"

"I want to talk. I miss our conversations."

"We've never had conversations. All you ever do is threaten."

"Then maybe it's time we changed that. You've got me on the line. Anything you want to discuss?"

He forced himself to talk. "What did you say to Mikey?"

"Do we have to talk about her?" She sighed. "How dull. But if you insist. I only told her the truth. You two can never be together. It was doomed from the start."

He clenched his eyes shut.

"She knows you love Jennie. She just doesn't realize how much, and that love can never be extended to her."

Anger rippled through him. "That's horseshit. You're just angry that I want Mikey and not you. Well, let me state the obvious. I will never want you. I never did. I don't even like to look at you, much less hear your voice."

Her voice sharpened. "Is that what you said to Mikey last night when you argued?"

Shocked, Rem's skin chilled as if he'd been doused in cold water.

"Yes. She told me she'd moved out. She told me a lot of things about you."

Rem struggled to comprehend Margaret's words.

"I'm so sorry about Cain."

Hearing his cousin's name, the knot in Rem's stomach rose into his throat.

"And how you found him lying in a pool of his own blood? Such a jolt that must have been. And for him to die in your arms. I can imagine your anguish." She let out a moan. "I wish I'd been there to see it."

Rem's disbelief almost eclipsed his devastation. Mikey had told Margaret about Cain?

"It still stings, doesn't it?" she asked. "The pain of grief is almost as bad as the pain of guilt. And I know you. You blame yourself. You think you could have prevented it." She paused. "Which means you probably could have."

Rem wanted to hurl the phone across the room.

"Mikey also mentioned you were investigating the people with the bird tattoos. How's that going? Any progress?"

That revelation snapped him back to reality. He tried to put Cain out of his mind and forced himself to use this call to his advantage. Margaret knew the man who killed Vera, and she knew Victor. That likely meant she knew Rook, too. Maybe even the Raven. "Mikey told you that?"

"She was a wealth of information."

"What did you tell her in return?"

"I gave her what she needed to know. She'll fill in the rest."

"You know who killed Vera?"

"I do."

"And you knew Allison."

Her tone turned to disgust. "Never cared for her, although I know you did."

Rem ignored her insinuation. If he didn't take the offensive, he was going to end up curled up on his couch, drooling. "Her grandfather is Damien Rook, who was friends with D'Mato. Do you know Rook?"

She went quiet.

"Cat got your tongue?" he asked. "I heard Rook and someone called the Raven are close. You know anything about that?" He could hear her breathing and did his best to control his own.

"You've done your homework."

"I'm good at what I do."

"I bet you're good at a lot of things. Too bad you waste those talents on Mikey."

He didn't let her change the subject. "Tell me about the Raven. What does Rook want with her?"

"If you take one piece of advice from me, take this one. Stay away from the Raven."

"Why?"

For the first time, he heard hesitation in her voice. "Who do you think taught me how to curse the stone Victor sent to Daniels?"

An image of the creepy stone that had almost cost Daniels his sanity flashed in Rem's brain. He wished he could forget it.

"Allison and Victor got caught up in something they never understood, and it cost Victor his life. My family is gifted, but there are things even I don't mess with. Rook thinks he can control that power, but he will learn the truth, eventually."

"What truth is that?"

"The Raven is using him, and when she's done, she'll discard him."

"Using him for what?"

"For power. The more she takes, the more powerful she becomes. She'll take from you, too." She paused. "If you and Daniels are aware of her, then she's aware of you."

Rem didn't know whether or not to believe her. "Rook and his little minions need to be stopped, and Daniels and I plan to do that. That includes your little buddy who killed Vera, doesn't it?"

"He's a dangerous man who, like Rook, can take care of himself. But if he's caught up with Rook and the Raven's games, he deserves what he gets."

"Tell us who he is, and we'll stop him."

She laughed. "Winnie is good at playing his own game. You won't stop him."

"We stopped you, didn't we?"

"Is that what you think?"

He told himself to stay strong and not let her get to him.

"You think that just because I'm in here, that I can't get to you? I thought you were smarter than that, Aaron." She lowered her voice. "I easily manipulated my sister into telling me all about you. I'm calling you from the facility where I'm considered mentally deranged. I can contact whoever I want. I know where you live. I know your friends. I know your past."

Rem sucked in a wrenching breath. Her ability to get under his skin almost buckled him.

"I'm in your dreams and your nightmares, just like you're in mine. The distance between us means nothing. Do not underestimate me."

He fought back the urge to vomit but would not let this woman play with him. He sharpened his tone. "Are you done?"

She laughed with derision, and the sound transported him back to the stone where he'd been tied down. Margaret's face had loomed over his while Allison waved the knife over him, and then he flashed to Margaret standing in his living room, where he was sitting now, threatening him and Mikey with a gun. "I've had my fun for now," she said. "But know this. Everything I just said? It pales compared to the Raven. You choose to confront her, and well, I'll have to find someone else to torment."

"I'm sure you'd cry your eyes out."

"I might shed a tear."

"Isn't it time for your feeding?" He was desperate to get her off the phone but determined not to give her the satisfaction of sensing his fear.

"You tell Mikey it was a pleasure. I wish you both the worst."

"Go to hell."

"You'll get there first if you meet the Raven. If she gets her claws into you, just remember, there's no shame in screaming." She uttered another ugly laugh and hung up.

Rem slammed the phone down on the coffee table. He was so tense, it was hard to breathe. His fury growing, he clutched his chest. His heart raced faster, and on emotional overload, he stood and paced. Hearing Margaret's words in his head, he kicked out at the end table, toppling it and the lamp on top of it. Then he grabbed the edge of the coffee table and flipped it onto its side. His phone fell to the floor, and he almost stomped on it, but at the last second he aimed his heel at the table instead. Still trying to catch his breath, he couldn't grasp Mikey telling Margaret about him and Cain, Cain's grisly death, and how Margaret had used that to pierce his defenses.

No matter what he'd said to Mikey, she'd had no right to tell Margaret about his cousin. Mikey understood how her sister would feed off that knowledge, but Mikey had done it anyway. That hurt Rem the most. She'd fed him to the wolves to identify Winnie, except she hadn't succeeded. Margaret had used her sister like she used everyone. And Rem had paid the price.

The more he thought about it, the worse he felt. The room spun, and he leaned over and put his hands on his knees. His hair hung in his face, and he still couldn't get a full breath. Everything swirled, sweat popped out on his skin, and his chest throbbed. Holding his stomach, he thought he might throw up when his phone rang. Thinking Margaret was calling back, white-hot rage shot through him. He picked up his phone and answered. "Stop calling me, you bitch."

There was a moment of quiet. "Rem?" said Daniels. "Is this a bad time?"

Rem's fury abated. "Daniels?" He wheezed into the phone. "Sorry. I thought...I..." Cursing at himself when his body betrayed him, he gripped the edge of the couch. "I can't...can't...breathe."

"What's wrong? What happened? Did you talk to Mikey?"

Dizzy, he sat on the couch. "No." Stars appeared in his vision. "Marg...Margaret. Called me." He gripped his temples.

"Margaret called you? Just now?"

Rem clutched his ribs. "I think...I think..." He tried to suck in some air. "...I'm having...a heart attack."

"Take it easy. Take long, slow breaths. Listen to my voice."

Rem couldn't focus. Everything was spinning faster. "Call...911."

"You're not having a heart attack, Rem. You're having a panic attack. Slow your breathing down. You have a paper bag?"

"No."

"Talk to me. Focus on my voice. Calm down."

Rem tried to listen and slow his breathing. "Everything is moving. My chest...hurts. I can't...stop sweating."

"Are you sitting down?"

"Yes." It came out as a wheeze.

"Breathe with me. Can you do that?"

Rem heard Daniels take a slow, calm breath over the phone. Rem tried to mimic it, but wasn't successful. "I...can't."

"Yes, you can. Try again." Daniels took another long breath, and Rem attempted to do the same. He improved the second time.

"Better," Rem whispered.

"Again."

Daniels continued breathing as Rem tried to follow his tempo. After several minutes, the room stopped spinning.

"How do you feel?"

Rem pulled his shirt away from his damp skin. Sweat ran down his back, and his fingers shook. "Breathing better, but I'm losing it."

"You think you are, but you're not. You want me to come over?"

Rem finally took a normal breath, and his shoulders relaxed a little. "Nothing you can do. Stay with Marjorie and Erin."

"Who's staying with you?"

He eyed his damaged coffee table, toppled lamp and empty house. "No one."

"Tell me what happened."

Finally able to talk without fear of passing out, Rem filled his partner in on not finding Mikey and getting Margaret's phone call. "I lost it after she hung up. You called at the perfect time."

"Lucky me."

"No. Lucky me. I would have been hauled out of here in a straitjacket if you hadn't helped."

"I would have found you and bailed you out."

Exhausted from his mental overload, Rem hung his head. "At this point, a padded room might be nice."

"Don't let her get to you, Rem. I'm going to call that facility and the warden. They'll toss Margaret's room and find out who gave her that phone."

Rem's vision briefly swirled, and he blinked to clear it. "Until the next time she gets one. But that's not even the worst. Mikey told her about me. I never thought she'd do that."

Daniels went quiet. "Mikey's not in the best state of mind right now."

"It doesn't excuse it. She knows her sister loves to pull this shit with me. I thought I could handle it better, but..." he sighed with defeat. "Hell."

"Margaret used Cain to get to you. That wound is fresh. Don't let that be the judge of your mental capacity because it's a lousy gauge. And kudos to you for using Margaret to get information on Rook and the Raven. Not many could have done that, so stop selling yourself short."

Rem dug his fingers into his neck to relieve the tension. "I need an aspirin and a really big drink."

"Are you well enough to come over? I can get you both."

"I can stay here. I'm not panicking anymore."

"It wasn't a request. You shouldn't be alone, and J.P. is expecting the claw. Bring a change of clothes, and you can sleep on the couch. Besides, we need to talk. I have some updates."

Exhausted, Rem fell back against the couch cushions. "Did you win that raffle that offered a year's supply of vitamins that prevent hair loss?"

"It was vitamins for healthy hair, Rem. It had nothing to do with hair loss."

"You say tomato, I say tomahto."

Daniels sighed. "We got a call on the bat phone. Guess who our next assignment is?"

That got Rem's attention. "You're kidding? Already? Who is it?"

"Rita."

Rem's heart dropped. "Rook's sister?"

"She got that doll. Now we know why. We've got seventy-two hours, and Rook wants it public."

"We can't do that."

"I'm aware. I called Lexie too, to fill her in. She's staying with her mom, but we're meeting her tomorrow at her place to go over the list, discuss what we know, and figure out what to do next."

Rem couldn't wrap his head around it all. How were they going to stop Rook before they were expected to kill Rita? "I'll be there within the hour."

"You aren't, and I'll come looking for you."

"Don't worry. I'm sane now. Not that it matters, because if we don't crack this within seventy-two hours, I might as well put that straitjacket on."

"With any luck, we'll put it on Rook instead, and maybe the Raven, too."

Remembering Margaret's words about the Raven, Rem questioned who would wear what after seventy-two hours. It could be straightjackets, prison garb, or body bags. "I hope you're right. I'll see you soon."

"See you."

Rem hung up, and trying not to think the worst, he went to pack a bag.

Chapter Twenty-Five

MIKEY POKED AT HER eggs, thinking about her dream the previous night. She'd slept fitfully at Mason's. Tossing and turning, her mind had persistently replayed her argument with Rem and her visit with Margaret. When she'd finally fallen asleep, she'd dreamed of Vera. Vera had been watching her, and Mikey had asked her about her sister's revelations. Who had been in Rem's house? Who had Mikey missed? Vera refused to answer, but she'd softened her gaze, and said, "Relax, Moonflower. Don't try so hard." She'd put her hand on Mikey's shoulder, and Mikey had come awake. She hadn't slept since.

Trying to eat so Mason wouldn't worry, she did her best to focus on Vera's killer, and not Rem.

Mason entered the kitchen. He eyed her plate. "Not hungry?"

"I'm getting it down."

He looked around. "Where's Chester?"

"Asleep on my bed."

He pulled out the chair and sat across from her. "Have you talked to Rem?"

She shook her head. He'd left several messages but had stopped calling since the previous afternoon. "I'm not ready yet. I'm still thinking about what Margaret said."

"Mikey, maybe you should take it easy."

She put her fork down. "What do you expect me to do? This man is someone I know. How could I have missed him? I know his voice. I've seen his eyes."

"What happened to Vera traumatized you. The brain won't unlock what you're not ready to handle. And your argument with Rem isn't helping."

Mikey wondered what Rem was doing. She wished she could discuss this with him, but each time she considered it, his angry words echoed in her ears. And she didn't want to talk to him about her visit with Margaret.

Mason helped himself to the piece of toast on Mikey's plate, which she hadn't touched. "I hope you're not letting Margaret get in your head. You can't listen to her, especially when it comes to Rem." He took a bite of the toast.

"She wasn't that far off-base."

"I told you what Rem said. He'd been drugged at that party. He and Daniels were both affected."

"Daniels didn't kick Marjorie out of the house. And that drug only lowered Rem's inhibitions enough for him to say what he really thought."

"Is that what you think?"

She nodded.

"Maybe stop to consider that it did the opposite. It brought out all his fears. He lost Jennie and now Cain. And he blames himself for both. And now he fears losing you, too. What better way to allay that fear than to push you away?"

"Or maybe he was telling me the truth? He might love me, but he'll always compare me to Jennie. I can't live like that, always wondering if I measure up to a ghost."

"That's more about your insecurities. Why don't you think you measure up?"

Frustrated, Mikey stood and brought her plate to the sink. "I'm not in the mood for a shrink."

Mason set the rest of the toast on a napkin. "And I won't sugarcoat it. You don't think you're good enough. At some point, you need to figure out why."

"Maybe because I'm not. Rem made that very clear."

Mason sighed. "You two need to talk. Maybe do a little counseling. You could talk to Tarina."

Mikey recalled going with Mason to see his addiction counselor. She turned to face him. "What part of *I'm not interested in a shrink* did you miss?"

Mason stood with a sigh. "Mikey, you can spend all your time searching for Vera's killer, but what happens after you find him? Are you going to spend the rest of your life alone? Wondering 'what if'? Rem loves you, and you love him."

Mikey ran her hands through her hair. "Can we worry about the rest of my life later?" She stared off. "And sometimes, love isn't enough."

"I disagree. You two are special. Don't throw that away because of a dumb argument and your sister's stupid accusations."

Mikey crossed her arms, feeling her throat tighten.

"Just think about it, okay?" Mason rubbed her arm.

Doing her best not to get emotional, Mikey studied her feet.

"You want to change the subject?"

"God, yes."

"Okay. Trick and I need to talk to a new client this morning. I'll be gone for about an hour. You want to come?"

She looked up at him. "No. I'd rather be alone."

He hesitated. "With everything going on, I'd rather you weren't."

She pushed off the counter. "I'll be fine. I'll lock up and set the alarm."

"Mikey—"

"Mason, please. I could use the quiet. I need to meditate. I think that will help calm me and settle my thoughts. The only way to do that is to get you, Rem, and Margaret out of my head. Besides, it's only an hour. I doubt any black bird baddies are lying in wait to get me. If anyone should worry, it's Rem and Daniels."

Mason studied her. "My extra gun is in the safe if you need it. And there's the safe room."

Recalling how Mason had turned his bathroom into a safe room and how it had once saved her life. "Now who's being dramatic? I won't need your gun or the safe room."

"I'm just saying—"

"Oh my gosh, you're worse than Mom was. Just go. Nothing is going to happen." She blinked her tired eyes. "Between you, Rem, and Margaret, I'm going to need a Valium."

"I can't help you there."

Realizing what she'd said, she put her hand on her head. "I'm sorry. I shouldn't have said that."

"Mentioning it doesn't make me crave it. It wasn't my drug of choice."

"Still, it was insensitive." She took his wrist.

He smiled softly. "It's fine. You don't have to guard your words with me. I don't with you."

She smirked. "That's obvious."

He walked to the front door and grabbed his hat from the hook on the wall. "I won't be gone long. Call me if you need anything."

"I will. Maybe pick up some ice cream on the way home. I could go for some butterscotch."

He put his hat on. "You got it. Enjoy the quiet." He opened the door. "Lock it and turn on the alarm."

She rolled her eyes. "I will. See you in an hour."

"Make it an hour and a half if we're stopping for ice cream."

They said their goodbyes, and he left. She closed the door, turned the lock, and set the alarm. Listening to the quiet, she savored it and went to sit on the couch. She leaned against the cushions, crossed her legs, took a deep breath, and settling in, closed her eyes. Allowing herself to relax, she followed Lena's instructions. It took several minutes, but Rem and Margaret finally faded from her mind, and she sat in the quiet void, forcing nothing. She waited. She'd done this enough times to know that when she reached this state, whatever she needed to know would usually come to her.

Drifting in the quiet, she didn't think about the passage of time. She could have been there for three minutes or thirty when Vera stepped forward. Mikey said nothing and watched her. Vera smiled gently, and holding something in her hand, she approached Mikey.

Mikey remained calm, and Vera leaned close. "Relax, Moonflower. You already know."

Mikey did as Vera requested and relaxed even further. She sank into the pillows and rested her head back. She watched as Vera placed the object she was holding into Mikey's palm. It was the moonstone pendant in the shape of a flower that Vera had given her when they'd been members of Victor's cult. In her mind, Mikey flipped it over and read the inscription. *To my sister Moonflower, may your journey be guided by the light of the moon.*

The pendant stirred memories and emotions. Vera and the pendant faded from view, and Mikey opened her eyes. Frustrated that she'd lost her connection to Vera, Mikey bit her lip, but the mental turmoil she'd been avoiding spilled over and she burst into tears. Rem and Margaret's words and their impact hit her hard, and she dropped her head and let herself cry. Wiping her face and nose with her sleeve, she sobbed until the tears slowed, and she reflected on the pendant Vera had given her.

Mikey had originally found it in a shoebox when she'd been packing to move to Rem's. It had been the catalyst for remembering her friendship with Vera and witnessing her murder. She'd brought it to Rem's and showed it to him and then put it in a drawer. Recalling Detective Monk serving the search warrant on Rem, and the subsequent search of his home, Mikey remembered an officer finding the pendant and handing it to Monk. Her anger surfaced at the memory. Monk had been so determined to—

An image of the grove and the man standing with Margaret and smoking the cigarette flashed in her mind. She gasped. She replayed his voice in her head and recalled Detective Monk's. He'd questioned her about Vera and accused her of murder. He'd taken the pendant after the search, and it had never been returned. Her thoughts spinning, she closed her eyes. Monk's voice. His eyes. She remembered Margaret's words–she'd seen Winnie recently, and he'd been in Rem's house. Monk and Manetti had questioned her sister at the facility, and Monk had been in Rem's house during the search. She thought again of the man in the grove named Winnie. His voice. His eyes.

Her stomach lurched violently, and she forced back bile in her throat. "No. It can't be." She opened her eyes. "No. No. No."

But the more she denied it, the more she knew the truth. Detective Monk was the man in the grove. He was Winnie.

She sat for several minutes, attempting to absorb the shock, and willing her stomach and her mind to settle. Her stomach finally did, but her mind refused. She compared the two men again and again in her mind, and her gut told her she was right. Certain that Detective Monk was the man who killed

Vera, she had to tell someone, but who? She could hear Rem's voice in her head. She had no evidence. It would be her word against Monk's.

She considered calling Rem but didn't want to involve him and Daniels yet. Bringing them in would mean one more problem and distraction to handle. Plus, Rem would want to keep Mikey as far from Monk as possible. He and Daniels would take charge and relegate her to the sidelines. Mikey couldn't allow that. She'd tell them eventually, but first she'd tell someone else. He should know anyway, and then Mikey would do whatever he thought was best.

She grabbed her phone and accessed the address she needed, then jumped off the couch and ran to Mason's gun safe. She punched in the code and took the small pistol. Between her brother and Rem, she knew how to handle and shoot a gun, although she preferred to avoid them. But in her current situation, it would be safer to have it. Tucking it into the back of her pants, she threw on her jacket, grabbed her small purse, and after turning off the alarm, she raced out of the house.

· · • • • • • • · ·

Daniels drove down the street on the way to Lexie's apartment. Rem sat beside him in the passenger seat. "You should have slept in instead of going for that long run this morning," said Daniels.

Rem looked over at him with fatigued eyes. "I wasn't sleeping much, anyway."

"That couch is comfortable."

"It's not the couch. It's me. I couldn't stop thinking...about everything."

"I should have given you one of my pills my doctor prescribes for my headaches. Those things knock me out."

Rem put his elbow on the ledge of the window and held his head.

"Have you called Mikey since talking to Margaret?"

"No. I figure I've called enough. The ball's in her court now."

Daniels could hear the hurt in Rem's voice. "Maybe it's for the best. We've got a few other things on our minds."

"That's the truth."

"And you shouldn't have jogged alone this morning. Until this is done, we need to stick together."

"I figure until we renege on killing Rita, we're safe. Rook still thinks we're on the team."

"Maybe. Maybe not." He turned onto Lexie's street. "We can't trust Rook, especially since we know why he holds his grudge against us. He could—" He slowed the car as he approached Lexie's complex and saw several police cars out front. "What's going on?" He pulled into the lot and parked in the nearest space.

"Must be a robbery or something." Rem unbuckled his seatbelt.

Suddenly anxious, Daniels opened his door. "That's a big police presence for a robbery."

Rem shot him a dubious look as they left the car and walked toward the entrance. "You said Lexie was meeting us here?" asked Rem. "And she spent the night at her mom's?"

Daniels took an uneasy breath. "That's what she said."

They approached an officer as he walked out. Daniels didn't recognize him. "What happened?" Daniels pulled out his badge and showed it.

Rem pulled out his badge, too. "Somebody get robbed?"

The officer glanced at their badges. "I wish. It's a homicide."

Daniels' uneasiness turned to fear. "What floor?"

"Third."

Hearing Lexie's floor, Daniels cursed along with Rem. They darted past the officer and took the stairs. After running out of the stairwell, Daniels' heart stopped when he saw several officers milling around Lexie's front door. "No."

They ran over, but another officer stopped them. "Rem? Daniels? I didn't think you two were assigned to this."

Daniels recalled the officer's name was Appleton.

"We're not." Rem stepped around Appleton and looked into the apartment.

Daniels did the same and saw the covered inert form lying in Lexie's living area. His body turned to ice, and he froze. "What happened?"

"Looks like the vic startled an intruder. Took a shot to the head. We're waiting on the coroner."

Rem stood like a statue before he raced inside.

"Hey," said Appleton. "You're not wearing gloves."

Daniels ignored him and followed Rem. They stopped at the covered body, and Rem squatted next to it. "God, please," he said in a whisper. "Don't let it be her."

Daniels said the same silent prayer as Rem raised the covering.

Chapter Twenty-Six

MANETTI SAT IN A chair on his patio, staring at his garden, which he still hadn't finished weeding. All he could do was think about Lola, Monk, and the black feather.

Thankfully, Annie had left an hour earlier to shop with her mom, and they wouldn't be back until later. Manetti was glad they weren't there. He needed time to consider his options.

The longer he sat, though, the more confused he became, until he finally decided he was overthinking it. The only logical thing to do was to tell Captain Crow everything first thing in the morning. He debated telling Rem and Daniels first, but that only put them in the same situation as him—wondering what to do and how to handle it. Crow had been made captain for a reason, and he needed advice.

Just as quickly though, he second-guessed himself. What did he have? The drawings of a killer? Suspicions about how Monk found Vera's name? A black feather in a desk drawer? On its own, it was nothing. Crow could tell him to stop wasting time and get back to work. But when he put it together with Vera's murder, the missing feather from the doll left at Bailey's crime scene, Lola's abuse at Monk's hands, and Margaret Redstone's potential involvement, it raised some alarming red flags. Who the hell was Frank Monk?

He jumped when his doorbell rang. Checking his watch, he wondered who would stop by on a Sunday. When it rang again, he got up, entered his house, and walked up to the door. It rang again, and he looked through the peephole. "Mikey?"

He frowned and opened the door.

She walked in before he could invite her. "Hi, Manetti. I need to talk to you."

Manetti closed the door. "You all right, Mikey? Is Rem okay?"

"He's fine." She held a small purse and looked around. "Is Annie here?"

"No. She's out with her mom."

"Good." She walked into the kitchen. "Where can we talk?" She peered out the back window.

"I was sitting outside."

"Perfect. Let's go out there." She opened the back door and walked onto the patio.

Confused. Manetti followed. He sat in his chair. Mikey sat beside him and set her purse on the table.

"What's this about?" asked Manetti.

She crossed her arms. "Sorry to bug you on a Sunday, but this is big."

"It must be. Where's Rem?"

"He's with Daniels, I'm sure. But this isn't about them."

"What's it about?"

She fixed her intense gaze on him. "Your partner, Detective Monk."

Manetti didn't expect her to say that. "What about him?"

"I remembered."

Manetti furrowed his brow. "Remembered what?"

"Vera's murder? If you recall, I saw it happen. I was watching from the trees."

"You said it was a masked man who was smoking a cigarette, right?"

She nodded. "He was friends with Margaret. She calls him Winnie."

Manetti thought of Margaret's drawings and his heart rate quickened. "Okay."

"I went to see my sister yesterday. I asked her about Winnie."

Manetti didn't expect to hear that either. "You did? What did she say?"

"She said I knew him. He'd been in Rem's house. I've talked to him."

Manetti tried to keep up. "You mean recently?"

"Yes, very." She bounced her foot. "I've been racking my brain trying to figure it out. And I finally did. This morning. I did a meditation, and I saw Vera, and then I knew."

Manetti dropped his jaw. "You saw Vera?"

"She's been helping me, but that's not important. What's important is that I know who Winnie is. I heard his voice. I know his eyes. And he's been in Rem's house."

Manetti waited with anticipation. "Who?"

She set her jaw. "Your asshole partner, Frank Monk."

· · • • · • • • · ·

Rem muttered a small prayer of thanks when he eyed the body. It wasn't Lexie. Looking closer, he recognized her neighbor, Lonny. Lonny had an ugly wound in the back of his head, and blood had pooled beneath his face and neck.

"It's not her." Daniels let out a relieved breath. "Thank God."

"Not so great for Lonny." Rem lowered the covering.

Appleton came over. "You know the vic?"

Rem stood. "It's the neighbor, Lonny. Don't know a last name."

"Who found the body?" asked Daniels.

Appleton shot a thumb toward the door. "Another tenant was walking by. He saw the door was ajar, and no one was around. He knocked, but when no one answered, he pushed the door open, and saw the vic." He glanced at the body. "So who lives here?"

"Lexie Logan does," said Rem. "We're supposed to meet her."

Appleton pulled out a notebook. "Any idea where Lexie Logan is?"

Daniels pulled out his phone. "I'll call her."

Rem had another scary thought when it occurred to him that whoever killed Lonny could still be after Lexie and may have found her. He waited as Daniels dialed and paused for her to pick up.

A familiar female voice traveled from the hall. "What the hell is going on? This is my apartment."

Daniels lowered his phone as Lexie, carrying a grocery bag and her big purse, pushed past a patrolman at the door. She stopped at the threshold and eyed the covered form on the floor with wide eyes. "Oh, my God."

Happy she was alive, but dreading having to tell her about Lonny, Rem stepped away from the body and walked with Daniels to the door.

Appleton approached her. "You can't be here, ma'am. This is a crime scene."

"This is my apartment!" She looked at Rem and Daniels. "What happened?"

"This is Lexie Logan, Appleton." Daniels took her arm and tried to steer her away. "Come with us."

"We'll talk to her," said Rem to Appleton.

"I'll need her statement."

"You'll get it," said Rem. "Just give us a sec."

Appleton nodded and walked away.

Lexie resisted leaving. "What is going on?" she asked Daniels. "Who is that?"

Rem took her other arm and, with Daniels' help, they guided her back into the hall. "We just got here too." Daniels paused and looked at Lexie with somber eyes. "It's Lonny, Lex."

She gaped at him. "It's what?" She shook her head. "That can't be. Why would Lonny be in my apartment?"

"We don't know." Rem had an idea though, and he didn't like it.

Daniels tried to pull her farther away as the coroner arrived and entered the apartment.

Lexie's face lost its color, and she dropped her grocery bag to the ground. "This can't be happening. You've got to be wrong." She gripped her head. "Lonny is dead?"

"When we got here, we thought it was you," said Rem. "It scared us to death."

She couldn't stop staring at her front door. "I...I...stopped at the grocery on the way back from Mom's. I just...I..." She looked at Rem. "When did this happen?"

"We don't know," said Daniels.

Tears sprang into her eyes. "Not Lonny. Who would kill Lonny?" She made a strangled sound and held her chest. "He was my friend."

"I'm sorry, Lex," said Daniels.

Tears spilled over her eyelashes and ran down her face. "This makes no sense."

The more Rem thought about it, the more it made sense to him. "He wasn't the target."

She wiped tears from her cheeks and made a soft gasp. "What are you saying? I was?"

"In all likelihood," said Daniels, "Lonny saw someone go into your place and surprised them. And was killed because of it."

More tears slid down her cheeks. "No. No." She shut her eyes and opened them. "But who...and why?"

Daniels shot Rem a knowing look. Lexie saw it and sucked in a sharp breath when the realization hit her. Rem guessed she was thinking the same as him and Daniels. It had to be Tex, following orders from Rook and the black birds. "Oh my God." She grabbed her elbows, dropped her head, and dissolved into tears.

· · • • • • • • · ·

Mikey waited as Manetti stared at her like she'd just sprouted a second nose. She could imagine what he was thinking. "Before you tell me I'm crazy, I'm not."

He looked away. "I'm not going to tell you you're crazy."

Seeing his reaction, Mikey sat forward. "You know something, don't you?"

He paused. "I might."

"What do you know?"

"I can't tell you that."

Mikey huffed. "I can't prove anything. Can you?"

He shook his head. "No. But there's plenty of circumstantial evidence."

"Like what?" She scooted her chair closer. "We have to compare notes before we decide what to do next."

"If any of this is true, it's a police matter. There needs to be an investigation."

Mikey smacked the tabletop with her palm. "That's bullshit, Manetti. That's why I didn't want to bring this to Rem and Daniels. They'll follow procedures and go after Monk and leave me out of it. But I *saw* him kill Vera."

Manetti glanced at her. "He was wearing a mask."

"But I heard his voice. I saw his eyes. It's Monk."

"How come you didn't recognize him sooner?"

"Because I didn't even remember Vera's murder! And it almost killed me when I did." She thought of Mason's words. "The brain only unlocks what you're ready for, and I wasn't ready until now."

"A jury might find that hard to swallow."

"What are you saying? I thought you believed me."

"I do. But what I believe and what we can take to a prosecutor are two different things. Rem and Daniels would tell you the same."

"But you're Monk's *partner*. How can you possibly continue to work with him?"

"I can't. I just need to figure out how to handle this." He shifted to face her. "If Monk is Winnie, he didn't get this far by being stupid."

"I'm aware. Why do you think he came after me for Vera's murder? He knows I saw him."

"But you can't ID him."

"Yes. I can."

Manetti hardened his tone. "Miss Redstone. Did you see Detective Monk standing in that grove?"

She squared her shoulders. "Yes. I did."

"You saw his face?"

She hesitated. "No. I didn't. But I heard his voice. And saw his eyes."

"He questioned you extensively about Vera's murder. And he served a search warrant at your boyfriend's property while you were present. How come you didn't recognize his eyes and voice then?"

Mikey understood where Manetti was going. "Because I didn't. But I remember them now."

"You were angry with Detective Monk for accusing you of murder, weren't you?"

Mikey straightened. "Yes."

"Mad enough to accuse him of the murder of your friend? Who was shot by a masked man you barely saw from a distance through the trees?"

Mikey dropped her shoulders. "Fine, Manetti. I see your point."

"You need more. So do I."

"Tell me what you know. Maybe if we put two and two together, we can figure something out."

Manetti stared out over his garden. "Rem would kill me."

She smacked her hand on the table again. "Rem is not here. I am. You and I know Monk for who he truly is. We're the only ones who can do something right now." She gripped the edge of the table. "So tell me what you know."

Manetti rested his elbow on the armrest. "This is just between you and me."

Mikey eagerly leaned in.

Manetti told her about Monk keeping Margaret's drawings, how he lied about finding Vera's name, his abuse of Lola, and finding the black feather. Hearing it all, Mikey could barely believe it. "That's how he knew Vera," she said. "Because he was there."

"And he's obviously capable of violence."

"And he kept Margaret's drawings because he knows her," added Mikey.

"And that black feather suggests he's a black bird."

"Winnie's name is on the list." Mikey cursed. "Monk is definitely a member."

Manetti rubbed his face and groaned.

"What are we going to do?"

After a pause, Manetti held up two fingers. "We have two options. Take it to Crow, or Rem and Daniels."

"Crow's father is a black bird. If she talks to him…and warns Monk, we're screwed."

Manetti opened his mouth to respond when a crash traveled from inside the house.

Mikey turned toward the sound. "Is someone here?"

Manetti stood. "Must be Monsterman. We're watching my sister-in-law's cat while she's out of town. And he keeps knocking things over." He headed toward the door. "I'll check on him."

"Monsterman?"

"The name fits."

Mikey stood too and followed Manetti inside. "What if we try to set Monk up? Where a wire or something? And get him to confess?"

Manetti walked into the kitchen. "Are you crazy? You watch too many crime shows." He looked around the kitchen. "Monster. Here, kitty kitty." He left the kitchen and walked into the living room, where a lamp was lying on its side.

Mikey searched for the cat. "It might work. He's a narcissist. He'd think we're too dumb to outsmart him."

Manetti picked up the lamp and put it back on the table. "There's no way he'd—"

He turned and stopped, his eyes widening.

Seeing his expression, Mikey turned too. Her heart skipped when a woman with blonde hair and heavy makeup stepped out from behind the door. She held a gun and aimed it at them.

"Don't worry," she said. "You'll both be dead before you have to worry about Frank Monk." She swiveled the gun toward Mikey. "Sorry. Witness dies first."

Manetti took a step forward. "Don't."

Everything happened at once. Mikey went for the gun tucked into her waistband. As she grabbed the handle, Manetti flung himself in front of her as the woman's gun discharged.

Mikey screamed as Manetti fell onto her and knocked her to the floor. The woman fired again, and Mikey felt a pinch on her shoulder. She raised her gun and pulled the trigger as another bullet grazed her cheek. Knowing the woman wouldn't miss again, she straightened her aim and kept firing.

The woman yelped as a bullet hit her arm. Blood sprayed from the wound, and she darted out of the room as Mikey's shots blew small holes in the wall. She forced herself to stop before running out of bullets.

With her adrenaline soaring, she kept the gun pointed at the empty doorway, anticipating the woman's return. She was shaking so hard, she had to hold the gun with both hands. When the woman didn't return, Mikey tried to get up, but Manetti was lying over her lower legs. Warmth spread over her calves.

Terrified the woman might return, she watched the door and nudged him. "Manetti. Get up. Hurry!" Manetti didn't move. "*Manetti.*"

Reality pierced her shock. She didn't think it was possible to feel more scared, but when she moved her legs and realized the warmth was blood, fear overwhelmed her. Monitoring the door, she wiggled out from beneath Manetti and leaned over him. His eyes were closed, and blood poured from a wound in his chest. "God, no. Manetti." She shook him again, but he didn't respond.

Panicked, she jumped up and raced to find a phone.

· · • • • • • • · ·

Daniels leaned against the hood of his car. Lexie was beside him, and Rem was on the other side of her. They stared as the body bag was taken out on a stretcher and loaded into the coroner's van. After Lexie had taken some time to absorb and adjust to the news, she'd talked to Appleton, telling him only that she didn't know who would break into her apartment, and that she'd spent the night at her mom's. She gave him her mom's contact info and also told him she was a reporter who'd pissed people off over the course of her career, and yes, someone could have targeted her. She didn't mention Rook, Tex, or the black birds.

Appleton had taken her information, told her to stay in town, and said he'd be in touch.

"We'll get them for this, Lex," said Rem.

Still pale from shock, Lexie watched the coroner's van drive away. "How?"

Daniels tried to put the pieces together. "Rook jumped the gun and came after Lexie. Why?"

Rem crossed one ankle over another. "It was a message to us." He eyed Daniels. "You think he knows we're lying to him?"

"Then why not come after us?"

"He's making a point," said Rem. "Showing us who's boss."

Daniels considered another problem. "How much you want to bet Lonny was shot with your gun?"

"It crossed my mind." Rem cursed and stared up at the sky. "And guess where I was this morning."

Daniels almost answered *my place*, but then remembered. "You shouldn't have jogged alone."

Lexie widened her eyes. "They'll try to pin this on you?"

Rem nodded. "If they can, they will."

"Rook's tightening the screws," said Daniels. "Maybe he knows we're hesitating about Rita."

"How would he know that?" asked Rem.

Daniels didn't like the answer that came to mind. Noting Rem's look, he knew his partner was thinking the same thing. "He knows we met with her."

Rem shook his head. "We should have been more careful."

Lexie acted as if she barely heard them. "I should have told Appleton about Rook and Tex."

"It wouldn't do any good," said Daniels. "Tex is too smart to leave evidence behind. And Rook wasn't here."

Rem stretched his neck. "He'll just claim you're a journalist with an ax to grind, and he's just a wealthy business owner who reporters write crap about every day."

"That new development is getting plenty of bad press," added Daniels. "He'll say he's an obvious target and you're unstable."

Lexie pushed up from the car. "Damn it. He can't get away with this."

"The bigger issue is, will he try again?" asked Daniels.

"And now that we know he tried to kill Lexie, how do we respond?" asked Rem.

"I say with force," said Daniels. "Maybe it's time to let Rook know we're not amateurs."

"I'm inclined to agree." Rem made eye contact with Daniels. "Maybe it's our cue to go on the offensive."

Lexie kicked a rock on the ground. "You'll just get yourselves killed. Like Lonny."

Daniels kicked the same rock when it rolled near his foot. "Maybe, but maybe not."

"Depends on how we handle it." Rem's phone rang, and he pulled it from his pocket. He read the display and paused. "It's Mikey." He let it ring again.

Daniels noticed the indecision run across his partner's face. "Are you going to talk to her?"

It rang again, and Rem took a deep breath. "Yeah." He straightened. "Give me a sec." He answered and walked away.

Seeing Lexie pace, Daniels moved closer and put his hand on her arm. "You okay?"

She sniffed and wiped her eye. "No. I'm not."

"Can you stay with your mom again tonight?"

"I don't want to—"

Rem's alarmed voice stopped their conversation. "Slow down, Mikey." He walked back over. "What happened to Manetti?"

Daniels and Lexie turned toward Rem.

"When?" Rem widened his eyes. "My God. Are you okay?"

Daniels' heart rate quickened. Lexie's forehead furrowed.

"What hospital?" Rem turned toward the car door.

Daniels and Lexie took his cue and headed toward the driver's side.

"We're on our way." Rem opened the passenger door. "Who's with you?"

Lexie got in the back seat, and Daniels slid behind the wheel.

Rem got in and shut the door. "Stay with Annabelle. We'll be right there. Don't move." He paused. "Promise me."

Daniels started the car.

"I love you too." Rem hung up and lowered the phone. "Manetti's been shot. They just took him into emergency surgery. It's not good."

Stunned, Daniels had a million questions but put them on hold. Rem told him the name of the hospital. Daniels hit the gas and raced out of the lot.

Chapter Twenty-Seven

REM PUSHED OPEN THE doors to the waiting area. Officers were already gathering, and Rem saw a heavily pregnant Annie sitting with an older woman with salt-and-pepper hair. Mikey sat on the other side of Annabelle and looked up when Rem entered. She had a bandage on her upper arm, a graze on her cheek, and blood all over her clothes. She jumped up and ran toward him.

Seeing her ashen face, he met her and pulled her into a hug. She started to cry, and he held onto her. "It's okay."

"No. It isn't." She clutched his jacket.

Daniels and Lexie stopped beside Rem. "What happened?" asked Daniels.

Mikey gulped some air between sobs. "He...saved my life. He...he jumped in front of me." Another sob choked her.

Not understanding, Rem guided her to a chair. "Come sit down." He sat with her, but Mikey was crying so hard all he could do was hold her.

"I'm going to check on Annie," said Daniels, and he and Lexie went over to speak with Manetti's wife. Glancing over, Rem could see her red-rimmed eyes and remembered sitting in a similar waiting room while Daniels was in surgery. It was not a memory he relished.

He held Mikey close and saw Lozano enter the waiting area. He glanced at Rem with Mikey, and headed over to talk to Annie. Behind him, Mason and Trick entered as well. They jogged over. "Mikey," said Mason, pulling a chair over. "Are you okay?"

Trick sat beside Rem. "What happened?"

Mikey had her head buried in Rem's neck. "All I know is she was with Manetti," said Rem. "Somebody fired at them, and Manetti jumped in front of Mikey and took the bullet." It scared him just to say the words.

"My God," said Mason. He glanced toward Annie, who was talking to Daniels. "How's his wife?"

Mikey struggled to speak. "She's a mess. I called her as soon as the EMTs arrived."

"Mikey," said Mason. "Were you at Manetti's house?"

She nodded. Trick grabbed a tissue from a box on a nearby table and handed it to her. "Why?" he asked.

She used the tissue to wipe her nose. "I...I..."

Daniels came over with Lexie. "How's it going over here?" He grabbed a chair for Lexie to sit, and he sat on the other side of Mikey.

"Not great," said Rem. "How's Annie?"

"Not great," said Daniels. "But she's hanging in there. Lozano's talking to her now."

Rem noted the room was slowly filling with officers but didn't see Monk. "Where the hell is Monk? He should be here."

Mikey abruptly sat up. "No. Don't call him."

Rem heard the fear in her voice. "Mikey. What is going on? Why were you at Manetti's? Who shot at you?"

Mikey gripped her tissue. Trick gave her another one, and she wiped her red eyes. "I remembered."

Rem tensed. "You mean the man in the grove? You know who he is?"

More composed, Mikey nodded. "I do." She paused. "It's...it's Detective Monk."

Nobody said a word, but they all stared in shock.

"Are you sure?" asked Daniels.

"I am. It's him," said Mikey. "That's why I went to Manetti's. To tell him."

"What did he say?" asked Mason.

"He wasn't surprised," said Mikey. "He'd picked up on some things that didn't make sense until I told him what I knew."

"What did he pick up on?" asked Lexie.

Mikey told them how Monk had kept Margaret's drawings, how he'd known Vera's name despite it not being in a file, and about his assault on Lola.

Daniels spoke with disbelief. "Monk is the one who attacked Lola?"

"That's what Manetti said," replied Mikey. "He was trying to figure out what to do when I arrived."

"Who is this guy?" asked Trick.

"A sociopath, apparently," said Mason. "What happened next?"

Mikey sniffed and wiped her cheeks with the tissue. "We were trying to figure how to handle the information. Everything was circumstantial. We can't prove anything. Then there was a crash in the house. We went inside...and...and... there was a woman."

Fresh tears spilled over her lashes, and Rem ran his hand down the back of her head. "Take a breath."

Mikey took a deep one and sputtered. "She...she had a gun. She...she told us we wouldn't have to worry about Frank Monk and aimed at me. Manetti...he...he jumped in front as she fired. I fell back and pulled out my gun..."

"Gun?" asked Rem. "You had a gun?" He trembled when it became clear how close he'd come to losing her.

"I took Mason's from the safe." Her breath caught. "I started firing."

"Hell," said Mason.

"I think I hit her arm. She got my shoulder and scraped my cheek but ran off. That's when I realized Manetti had been hit."

Rem touched the wrap on her upper arm. "She shot you?"

Mikey shook her head. "It's not bad. The EMTs checked and bandaged it. Told me to go see my doctor. I'm okay."

"You're lucky to be alive," said Daniels.

"This blood...," Mason pulled at the stiff fabric of her pants. "It's Manetti's?"

She nodded. "He fell on me, and then I tried to slow the bleeding." Her face crumpled. "There was so much blood."

Careful of her shoulder, Rem pulled her closer. "Thank God you're okay."

"Any sign of this woman?" asked Trick. "Can you describe her?"

"There's no need," said Lexie. She looked at Rem and Daniels. "I don't think it requires a degree in rocket science to know who she is."

Daniels cursed. "Rhonda."

"*The* Rhonda?" asked Mason. "The assassin you two have been chasing?"

"This just got a whole lot more interesting," said Trick.

Lexie set her large purse at her feet. "And Mikey just became another witness to one of her crimes."

Realizing the implications, Rem held Mikey closer. Rhonda and Monk would stop at nothing to kill Mikey.

Lozano came over and stood beside Mason. He eyed Mikey and the rest of them and raised a brow. "What did I miss?"

Trick stood and gestured toward the seat. "Oh, Captain. Sit your butt. You're gonna love this."

·· • •• • • •· ·

Daniels helped himself to another cup of coffee from the table in the waiting room. Between his tough morning and worse afternoon, it was the most coffee he'd drunk in one day since...hell, he couldn't remember.

They'd been waiting for almost three hours, and the room was filled with officers, all waiting to hear about Manetti's condition. Elsa Crow had arrived, along with Chief Patterson. Marjorie and Erin arrived soon after. Daniels had called Marjorie on the way to the hospital to be sure she, Erin, and J.P. were okay. After hearing the news, Marjorie had insisted on coming to help Annabelle. She understood what it felt like to sit and wait to hear if your critically injured husband was alive. She'd dropped J.P. at her mom's and had brought Erin with her.

Not long after their arrival, Lozano, Trick, and Mason, along with Lexie and Erin, had gone downstairs to purchase plenty of coffee, water and snacks for everyone. Rem sat with Mikey, who was still visibly shaken after her encounter with Rhonda. Daniels had talked with Elsa Crow, who'd informed him she'd assigned Georgios and Titus to Manetti and Mikey's case.

Knowing Mikey would be questioned, Daniels and Rem had discussed with her how much she should say. Without more evidence, and without Manetti to back her up, it was Mikey's word against Monk's. Until they could prove Monk was Winnie, Mikey's life, and Manetti's, if he survived, would be in danger. They determined that for now, they would keep Monk's name out of it.

After Georgios and Titus' arrival, Mikey had told them how she'd gone to see her sister at the psychiatric facility that morning, and how Margaret had told her that the man who'd killed Vera was someone Mikey knew. Concerned, she'd gone to see Manetti because he and Monk were still assigned to Vera's case. She'd told Manetti what Margaret had said, and that's when an assailant in the home shot at them. When Georgios and Titus asked why she'd brought a gun, she'd said that after what Margaret told her, she was scared and felt safer bringing it with her.

Rem had watched her with a flat stare, but Daniels could tell his partner was as impressed as he was. Mikey had told Georgios and Titus everything without mentioning Monk's name.

Murmurs circulated through the waiting area, though, about why Monk wasn't there. Elsa Crow had asked Rem and Daniels if they'd spoken to him, but they'd told her they couldn't reach him. Daniels could already hear the whispers among the officers. Had Monk been targeted too, along with Manetti? Was he even alive?

Eating a chip from a bag Marjorie had given him, he watched his wife, who was sitting with Annie and holding her hand. Marjorie had not left her side since arriving. He made a mental note to tell his wife how amazing she was when he had the chance.

Rem came up beside him and refilled his coffee cup from a large thermos on the table. "How's Mikey?" asked Daniels. He glanced toward the chairs. Mikey sat next to Marjorie. Her body language suggested she remained as terrified as when they'd arrived.

"Still upset and scared," said Rem, adding cream and sugar to his coffee. "She won't get much better until we hear from the doctor."

"Yeah." Daniels checked his watch. "I hope we get some news soon. This waiting is torture."

"Tell me about it." Rem set his cup down and grabbed a bag of cookies. "It's like a nightmare from the past."

Daniels could imagine. His partner had endured the same miserable wait when Daniels had been injured. "Let's hope the outcome is the same."

"I keep praying it is. If we lose him…" The muscle in Rem's jaw tightened.

Daniels couldn't imagine Manetti's death. "Yeah. I know."

After a pause, Rem cleared his throat and opened the bag of cookies.

Putting his coffee cup next to Rem's, Daniels sighed. "I know the timing isn't great, but we need to make some decisions about Monk and Rook."

Rem pulled a cookie out of the bag. "I know." He popped the cookie into his mouth and chewed.

Looking around, Daniels guided Rem to a corner where they wouldn't be overheard. "Monk's out there with Rhonda," said Daniels. "They're both pushed into a corner but won't stay there for long. They'll have to deal with Mikey and Manetti. Plus, Lexie could still be a target." He quieted when someone walked by. "Time is no longer on our side, partner. If we're going to do something, it's going to have to be now."

Rem swallowed his cookie. He reached over, grabbed his coffee and set it on a table beside him. "Any ideas?"

"One option is to come clean. Tell Elsa everything. Or the FBI."

Rem wiped a crumb off his shirt. "We don't have enough. We can't clear our names or Lozano's either. And Monk could have Rhonda shoot him, come forward, and claim he's a target too. Mikey won't stay quiet long, and he'll claim her accusations are lies because she's harboring a grudge, and with Manetti incapacitated, we can't prove he's wrong."

Daniels eyed Elsa Crow, who was talking with Chief Patterson. "And can we trust Elsa Crow? Would she talk to her father?"

"And can we trust the FBI?" Rem glanced behind him. "If we come forward, *we* could end up in jail instead of Monk. And that makes Mikey a sitting duck." He shook his head. "Coming forward is too big of a risk. We need proof."

"Then how do we get it and protect Mikey, Lexie, and Manetti at the same time?"

Lozano approached, holding a half-filled water bottle. "You two are in deep conversation. Anything I can help with?"

"We're considering our options, Cap," said Daniels. "And they aren't good ones." He reached for his coffee and caught sight of Mason, who was talking with Trick and Annie's brother and mother. Figuring they should all contribute, he tipped his head at them. They disengaged from their conversation and headed over. Lexie, who'd pulled her laptop from her bag and was studying it with Erin, saw them. She closed her laptop, slid it into her big purse, and she and Erin joined them.

"You talking about how to stop these monsters?" whispered Lexie.

"The sooner, the better." Trick held his cowboy hat. "I doubt your adversaries are going to bide their time. They're like rats in a trap, which makes them even more dangerous."

"But we have to move with caution." Mason glanced toward Mikey. "I'm worried about Mikey. Detective Monk will take the offensive. He's not showing himself, so he's planning."

Rem ate another cookie. "He'll either come forward and risk exposure, or clean house and run."

"He's not a runner," said Lozano. "At least not until he cleans house. Especially if he's working with Rhonda. Neither will want loose ends."

Daniels' head started to pound. "Let's think this through."

"Go for it, sport," said Rem, "because my brain is mush."

Daniels tried to pull all the threads together. "We've got two enemies to confront. Monk and Rook."

"Don't forget Rhonda and Croft," added Lexie.

Trick drank some coffee from the cup he was holding. "You two are such overachievers."

"We take pride in our ability to piss people off," replied Rem.

"So do Red and I," said Trick. "But you two got us beat."

"Assuming we survive this," said Daniels, "we'll claim our trophy, but for now, let's assume that if Manetti lives, Mikey's story gains credibility with him to back her up. Monk and Rhonda don't want that. They'll have to deal with him and Mikey."

Lozano raised his water bottle. "But that's not so easy. If Mikey and Manetti both end up dead, that brings scrutiny Monk can't afford."

"He knows that," said Lexie. "So what will he do? Leave town with Rhonda?"

"If he's this Winnie you all keep talking about," said Erin, "that doesn't sound like a Winnie thing to do."

"No, it doesn't." Daniels tried to focus despite his headache. "We know Winnie's name is on Ackerman's list, but let's go back. Mikey witnessed Winnie, aka Monk, shoot Vera. That means Monk is friends with Margaret. And we know Rook was friends with Victor, so by association, we have to assume Monk and Rook are friends, too."

Rem cursed. "Talk about a worst-case scenario."

"So all this time, you've been working with the man who's been trying to kill you?" Mason tossed his cowboy hat on a nearby chair.

"We should have known," said Rem with frustration. "He gave off a vibe with me and Daniels. It's hard to believe he's the one who helped Margaret try to kill us, and now it seems he's helping Rook."

"Is he helping, though?" asked Daniels. "They're both narcissists. Do you see them getting along with each other?"

Lozano knitted his brow. "Are you talking about Damien Rook? The real estate mogul?"

Daniels realized they hadn't told Lozano about Rook and his involvement in the society, nor about how he was blackmailing him and Rem.

"It's a long story, Cap," replied Rem. "But Rook is the ringleader of the black birds, and Daniels and I have been working to infiltrate his society. We've identified Tex as Tyson Croft, who works for Rook."

Lozano arched his brow. "How far have you gotten with the society?"

Daniels set his coffee cup next to Rem's. "Far enough that Rook expects us to kill for him."

"We convinced him and Croft we murdered Jerry Lee Caruso," added Rem.

Lozano's brow arched higher. "You two have been busy."

Rem chewed another cookie and picked up his cup of coffee. "And we've been informed that our next assignment is Rita Vittorio, Rook's sister."

"Sister?" asked Lozano.

"That's cold," said Trick.

"Frigid," said Daniels. "We met with her, which is one reason we think Rook wants her dead. Rem and I were given seventy-two hours to complete the task, which we obviously can't do."

"This is escalating quickly," added Mason. "And based on what I'm hearing and sensing about Monk and Rhonda, they'll act now. Not later."

"That's our thought too," added Daniels.

Rem glanced at Daniels. "That means taking down Rook, Tex, and Monk now. Not later."

Trick half-smiled. "Maybe you can catch a movie and pizza while you're at it."

Rem swallowed his cookie and took a gulp of coffee. "Tempting, but Daniels hates movies. And pizza too."

Daniels made a snort. "You can see what we're up against, Cap."

"I do." Lozano pursed his lips. "You think you can play Monk and Rook against each other?"

"I don't see either of them sharing the spoils," added Rem. "Rook considers himself the leader of the society."

"I doubt Monk likes that," said Lozano.

Daniels considered another issue. "I doubt Monk likes Tex either. Especially if Tex has been horning in on Monk's action."

"And now we've got Rook bringing us in," said Rem. "I doubt Monk wanted that, either."

"Especially if he thinks you two are possibly replacing Rhonda," said Lexie. "If Monk and Rhonda are working together, then they both have conflicts with Rook."

Daniels waited while someone walked past the group. "If Monk's really planning to wrap up unfinished business, then it wouldn't surprise me if he is conspiring against Rook and plans to take over the society or some part of it."

"He'll eliminate Tex, too," said Rem.

Daniels nodded. "If Rook's actions are stirring up questions and he ordered Tex to kill Lexie today, Monk could use that as a reason to prove Rook's instability and remove him."

Mason, Trick, and Lozano widened their eyes at Lexie. "That's a new curve in a straight line," said Trick.

"Tex failed," said Lexie. "Killed my neighbor instead." She tightened the grip on her purse.

"When did this happen?" asked Mason.

"This morning," said Rem. "We think it's Rook's way of retaliating since we met with his sister Rita and he knows we're lying to him."

Lozano's water bottle crinkled when he clenched it. "You two *have* been busy."

"Wait until you hear about Rook's birthday party," said Lexie.

"The point is," said Daniels, "that Rook has targeted Lexie." He tapped his watch. "And now we have forty-eight hours left to deal with this."

"Maybe less," said Lozano, glancing toward Mikey.

Mason eyed his sister, too. "Then how do we stop them?"

Erin leaned in. "Seems obvious to me. Confront them first."

"She's right," said Trick. "We take the battle to them. Go on the offensive before they do."

"Agreed," said Mason. "They may be smart, but we're smarter."

Daniels eyed Rem. "We appreciate your offer of help," he sighed, "but Rem and I can't ask any of you to get more involved. The stakes here are too high."

"More involved?" asked Lozano. "Hell. All of us are plenty involved. They framed me, threatened Erin, almost killed Lexie, and now they're after his sister." He pointed at Mason.

"And she might as well be mine," said Trick. "And we know what they did to Cain and Marjorie." He raised his hand. "So sorry, fellas, but you've got our help whether or not you want it." He smiled at Mason. "Besides, this reminds me of our Ranger days, right, Red?"

Mason smoothed his mustache. "I don't recall battling an evil society, a corrupt detective, a cold-blooded assassin, and an evil megalomaniac all at one time, but I'm up for it."

Trick smacked Mason's arm. "It's good for the soul, partner. As my momma would say, it'll put hair on your chest."

"Hair on your chest is one thing," said Rem, "but we're talking about your lives."

"These people killed Lonny," said Lexie with a glare. "So, I'm in."

"Me too," said Lozano.

Erin, Mason and Trick all agreed as well.

Daniels' emotions bubbled up at the realization of what their friends were willing to risk. Grateful, he smiled softly. "Thank you, although saying that doesn't seem nearly enough."

"No thanks required," said Mason. "You'd do the same for us."

"We'll throw a party when this is done," said Lozano, "and we're all still alive. It'll be at my place."

"I'll bring the drinks, Captain," said Trick.

"You're on," said Lozano.

Praying they would all be able to enjoy it, Daniels took one of Rem's cookies from the bag. "Now that we know where we all stand, what's our next move?" He bit into the cookie.

"If we're going on the offensive," said Rem, "then we contact Rook. Let him know we're not thrilled about Lexie. He thinks he's invincible. Maybe we'll make him think he's not as invincible as he believes."

Daniels stopped chewing. "You mean use Monk?"

Rem shrugged. "Monk screwed up. Mikey's another loose end, just like Jerry Lee. She knows Monk killed Vera, and now she can ID Rhonda as Manetti's shooter. If Monk gets caught, it could lead straight to Rook."

"You can add in Tex, too," said Lexie. "I did some digging into Tyson Croft. He's got a warrant out for his arrest in San Francisco for aggravated assault. I wonder if Rook knows that."

Daniels pointed. "We could mention Rita too. And Barbara, and how we know about Rook's connection to Victor and the grudge he holds against us."

"Don't forget the Raven," said Rem. "He might not be too thrilled to know we've been digging into her. And there's Delaina. Based on the way she was acting with me, we might get away with claiming she's an ally." He took a step away to get more coffee.

"Who's this Raven?" asked Lozano. "And what grudge?"

Daniels answered. "The Raven is D'Mato's former spooky sorceress who now works with Rook. Rook uses her, or vice versa, to control the society, and

Rook is Allison Albright's grandfather." He paused. "He blames me and Rem for her death and the death of her unborn child."

Lozano dropped his jaw.

Trick whistled. "That's another big kink in a straight line."

Mason stilled. "I don't like the sound of this Raven." He rubbed his arm, and Daniels could see goosebumps on his skin.

Daniels glanced toward Marjorie to see her still sitting with Annabelle. "We don't like the sound of her either."

"Where did you learn this?" asked Lexie.

"Rita filled us in," said Daniels.

Rem returned with more coffee and spoke to Daniels. "So we've got enough to make Rook think he's in trouble. If we threaten him with what we know and act like we want to make a deal, we may have a way in. But once we're in, what then? Use what we have to get him to talk about his crimes?"

Daniels finished his coffee and crumpled the cup. "Getting in the door isn't enough. No matter how corrupt we pretend to be."

Rem snapped his fingers. "What if we scare him enough to think he's got a mole on the inside, feeding us intel...we'll tell him it's not Rita or Delaina, but someone from the society."

Daniels considered it. "Make Rook paranoid and use the mole as bait?" He nodded. "That could work."

"Sorry, but even if he confesses, it's still not enough," said Erin. "You need tangible evidence to bring a man like that and his buddies down. How do you get that?"

Daniels recalled his conversation with Bernie at Rook's party. "We have to get into Rook's office. Something tells me everything we need is in there."

Lexie scoffed. "He wouldn't be that stupid."

"If Rook truly believes he's untouchable, he might be," said Mason. "Men like that, who've been in power as long as he has, get cocky. His perceived control gives him a false sense of security. He'll keep his secrets where he can keep an eye on them."

"But how do you get into his office?" asked Lexie.

Rem took the last cookie and tossed his empty cookie bag in a nearby trashcan. "Rook's not going to let us look around, no matter what we offer him. What we need is a distraction. If one of us can divert Rook, the other can go for the office."

"That's a big ask," offered Daniels. "How do we get him out of the house?"

Rem held his cookie but didn't eat it. "After we inform him about his vulnerabilities and the mole and suggest we can protect him with the right amount of cash, we'll see how he responds."

Daniels imagined Rook's reaction. "He'll either hate us more, or be open to working with us."

"I predict the former," added Lozano.

Rem glanced at Daniels. "That's when I'll ask to speak with him privately." He ate the cookie.

Daniels frowned. "What are you going to say?"

Chewing, Rem stared off with an unreadable expression. "I'll give him what he wants." He swallowed his cookie. "Me."

Alarmed, Daniels raised his voice. "No way."

"Just hear me out," said Rem.

"Rem..."

"He's pissed at me..."

"He's pissed at both of us."

"But he thinks I fathered his great-grandchild. What if I play the part? I'll offer to tell him all about what happened between me and Allison. Act like the cruel person he thinks I am. Better yet, I'll tell him exactly what he wants to hear. That I planned it all and killed Allison. And while we talk, you can—"

"No." Daniels shook his head. "I don't like it."

"If he comes after me, you can call the cavalry, and then he's fair game. They'll search the office and—"

Daniels pointed at his partner. "I am not sacrificing you to get this guy."

Rem blanched. "I didn't say sacrifice. Been there, done that."

"That is my whole point." Daniels had to force himself to keep his voice down. "You've been through enough."

"If we play this right, nothing will happen to me," replied Rem. "Between the two of us, we'll figure it out. All we need is an opportunity, and I can provide that." He paused. "What other choice do we have?"

Daniels hesitated. He didn't like the answer to that question.

"He's got a point," said Mason. "If you've got leverage over Rook, you need to use it." He spoke to Rem. "But you better be careful."

"What you need is backup," said Trick. "If you don't show yourselves or call in the cavalry by a certain time, then someone else does."

"I agree," said Lozano. "I don't like you two going in alone. If something happens, we need to be able to pull you out."

Daniels tried to think of other options, but nothing came to mind.

"We can do this, partner," said Rem, "and both walk out alive."

"If anyone's going to do it, it's you two," said Lexie.

"What about Mikey?" asked Rem. "I don't want to leave her vulnerable."

"You let us deal with Mikey," said Mason. "Trick and I will keep her safe." He glanced at Lozano. "Care to join us?"

"I'd love to," said Lozano.

"What about me and Erin?" asked Lexie.

Still uncertain about Rem's plan, Daniels tossed his crumpled cup into the trash. "If this goes sideways, and Rem and I don't make it out, then you write the most damning article you can about Rook and his group. Erin can help, and so can Marjorie. Use whatever you have. Ackerman's box. The list of names. Croft. Our trip through Elmwood. Tell what happened to Cain, Marjorie, and us. Talk to everyone, including Rita. You may not get him for blackmail or murder, and his attorneys will keep him out of jail, but you sure as hell can do some damage to his reputation. You stir up enough dirt, and the members will scatter, and he'll be vulnerable. Hit him where it counts. His pocketbook."

Lexie's eyes sparkled. "With pleasure."

"In the meantime, watch your back," said Rem. "And tonight, you, Erin, J.P., and Marjorie are all staying somewhere with lots of people and cameras around. It's unlikely they'll come after you, but better to be safe."

"There's a hotel downtown that fits their needs," said Lozano. "I know a guy who can get you a room at a discount. I'll make the arrangements."

"Thanks, Cap," said Daniels. He still didn't like Rem using himself as bait, but all he could do was hope that another option presented itself. "If we're going to enact this little plan tonight, how do we get in?"

Rem held out his hand. "You got the bat phone?"

"Sure do." Daniels reached into his pocket and handed it to Rem.

Rem took it. "Be right back." He hit the number to call Tex and walked away.

"I don't even want to know what he's going to say," said Lozano.

Daniels shook his head. "Whatever it is, Cap, I know we'll be expected at Rook's tonight."

Trick ran his fingers along the brim of his hat. "Expected maybe but not welcomed."

Daniels noted a commotion across the room. His stomach flipped when he saw the surgeon outside the doors to the surgical area. "It's the doctor." He headed over along with the others and held his breath when he heard the surgeon talking to Annabelle.

"Your husband made it through," said the doctor. "It was a difficult surgery, but he's alive. He's not out of the woods yet, but we're hopeful."

Annabelle burst into tears and hugged her mom.

A whoop traveled from within the group, and a few others clapped as everyone breathed a collective sigh of relief. The doctor guided Annie, her mother and brother to another room to provide more details as those in the waiting area talked with more energy than they had all afternoon. Daniels said a small prayer of thanks that Manetti was hanging in there.

Holding the phone, Rem worked his way through the crowd and approached Daniels. "What'd I miss?"

"Manetti made it through surgery," said Lozano.

A nearby officer patted Daniels on the back as he walked by. "The doctor's guarded but hopeful," replied Daniels.

"Thank God," said Rem. He eyed Mikey, who Daniels saw sitting in her chair with her knees up and her head down. Mason had gone over to sit beside her. Rem handed the bat phone to Daniels. "I need to go talk to her."

"What happened with Tex?" asked Trick. "Are you two in?"

"They eagerly await our arrival at nine o'clock tonight." Offering no details, Rem walked away.

"And so it begins," said Trick. He spoke to Lozano. "You, Red, and I need to talk." He regarded Daniels. "I look forward to Lozano's party when this is over."

Seeing Marjorie walking toward him, all Daniels could do was nod as Trick and Lozano walked away.

Chapter Twenty-Eight

FRANK MONK SAT ON the floor beside the window of the small house down the street from Mason Redstone's home. Once he'd heard that Mikey and her brother had left the hospital, he'd driven to Redstone's neighborhood and had arrived just in time to see Mason and Mikey drive up, park in the driveway, and enter his home.

Sitting in his car, Monk had debated his options. He'd driven down the street, and seeing a house for sale nearby, he'd stopped and called the realtor. He'd told her he was in town for only a short time and asked to see the house within the hour. She'd complied, and he'd met her there. He'd stayed long enough to learn that the house was ideal for his needs. The owners didn't live there, the alarm system was not active, and it had a perfect view of the street. And since he needed to stay out of sight, it would allow him to monitor Redstone's residence without sitting in his vehicle. After a brief walkthrough, where he'd unlocked a back window, he'd told the agent it wasn't what he was looking for and left.

Thirty minutes later, after parking in an inconspicuous spot, he'd walked down the alley, accessed the backyard, and entered the home through the unlocked window. Now, from his spot at the front of the house, he used his binoculars to watch the street and Mason's home through the blinds. Satisfied his plans were coming together, he lit a cigarette and watched a car drive down the road. Since he'd arrived, Mason's house had been quiet.

Rhonda, who'd been sitting outside the waiting area at the hospital, had been keeping in touch, telling him about the activities of those who'd gathered to hear about Manetti's condition. Disguising herself, she'd worn a long black wig with bangs, glasses, and bulky clothes. No one had given her a second glance.

He'd been dismayed after she'd filled him in on what had occurred at Manetti's. After shooting him, and taking a bullet in the arm from Mikey, who'd been an unexpected but informative visitor, Rhonda's gun had jammed, preventing her from killing Mikey and forcing her to escape the house.

It had taken Monk several minutes to pull it together and think. In survival mode, he'd told her to meet him at a rundown motel on the outskirts of town. After hanging up with her, he'd grabbed his go-bag, left his cell phone behind, taken his burner cell, and had left his apartment, likely never to return. Before leaving though, he'd taken his switchblade and cut his palm. Bleeding, he'd left several drops of blood on the carpet, stuck his injured hand and switchblade in his pocket, and left, avoiding any cameras on the way out. Before going to the motel, he'd thrown on heavy-framed glasses, a hat, and an oversized coat, and stopped at a drugstore to grab supplies for his hand and Rhonda's injury. Once at the motel, he'd booked a room under a fake ID, treated his palm, and waited.

Rhonda had joined him soon after, and he'd treated and bandaged her arm, and they'd discussed their next steps. Mikey had remembered him, and along with Manetti's suspicions, it was too risky for Monk to come forward, especially with Rook looking over his shoulder. Rook didn't like messes, and right now, he and Rhonda were in a big one. And with Croft looking for any opportunity to oust Monk, he and Rhonda were going to have to make some major decisions, and fast.

Before the disaster at Manetti's, Monk had spoken to Croft and learned about Rook's plan to kill Lexie Logan. That hadn't pleased Monk. It was stupid and unnecessary. There were better ways to get at Daniels and Remalla other than taking out the reporter, but Rook hadn't asked Monk. That was another red flag. Rook was slowly squeezing Monk out, just like he'd done with Rhonda.

The way Monk saw it, if he got rid of Mikey, that would end any concerns about tying him to Vera, Rook, Margaret and the society. Plus, it would be satisfying to kill Remalla's girlfriend, knowing he would suffer yet another loss. That would be far more effective than murdering Lexie Logan.

He thought back to that night at the grove. After he'd shot Vera, Margaret had convinced Monk not to kill Nathan and Mikey. He'd been wearing a mask, Nathan had been high on drugs, and Mikey was too terrified to talk. When he'd later learned that she had no memory of the murder, he'd left it alone.

After leaving the cult, he'd worked in L.A. as a detective for a few years. It had been a lucrative time. He and his partner had used their influence and skills to their benefit. They'd protect those who paid them and bust those who didn't. It had been easy until his partner had second thoughts and wanted out. Monk made sure he got out by killing him and making it look like a suicide. After that, he'd left L.A. when Margaret had gotten back in touch and asked him to join her. Victor was dead by then, and she had set her sights on a detective who'd used Rook's granddaughter, Allison Albright, another cult member, to infiltrate and disband the cult.

With Allison incarcerated and supposedly pregnant with the detective's child, Rook had used his and Allison's considerable influence to prevent her from going to trial, but it wasn't enough. Allison ended up poisoned, and she and her unborn daughter died. Rook changed after that. His involvement with the cult's practices and ceremonies deepened, especially with the help of Victor's witch, affectionately known as the Raven. Monk had only met her once and didn't care to repeat it. Rook, however, had been entranced. She'd been the one to encourage him to start the society. She'd emboldened him with false praise and superficial promises, and he'd believed her. Following her guidance, he'd coerced powerful people to join his group, and after Margaret's capture, Monk had joined him. He was all for manipulation and control. Rook had used the members to do what most leaders couldn't. Embolden them to use their influence to remove the weak and protect the strong. Without it, Rook believed society would crumble. Using his connections with Ezra Grimm and following the Raven's supernatural guidance, Rook had created a powerful drug that he believed would flush out the darkness, purge weakness and personify strength.

Rook took the drug religiously. Monk had taken it twice. The first time, he'd woken up lying in the woods outside Rook's estate with no memory of how he'd got there. The second, he'd ended up in a whorehouse with a woman named Lola. That night was foggy too, but he recalled the feeling of invincibility. He'd felt untouchable, and empowered, like he could do anything, and no one could stop him. What he didn't enjoy was the sense afterward of someone being in his head, like his thoughts were no longer his own. That strange sensation had taken time to fade, and he hadn't taken another pill since.

After Allison's death, Rook had held a deep grudge against the detective and his partner for her and her child's deaths. He'd worked with Monk to arrange for Remalla and Daniels to die in the town of Elmwood. Monk had even hired Tyson Croft and his buddy to do it, but before they and Rhonda could finish the job, Rook had changed his mind. Angry, Monk had asked why, but Rook had only told him he had made other plans for the detectives. Monk realized then that Rook was taking his directions from the Raven. Monk didn't like it, but he'd backed off.

It wasn't long after that when Rook had told Monk of his plan to reveal Vera's grave and use it to accuse Mikey. Monk had been reluctant, but had also seen it as an opportunity. Would Mikey remember him? And if she did, how would he respond? Could he use it against her? Rook had insisted it needed to be done, and if she remembered, he would use his influence to protect Monk. Plus, Rook believed it would provide invaluable information about the detectives regarding their need to protect each other and their loved ones. Monk secretly suspected the Raven had also dictated this task. If Monk hadn't been eager for the challenge, he might have balked at the plan.

Shifting his position on the floor, Monk wished he'd gone with his gut and killed Mikey in that grove. It would have saved him from having to kill her now. He debated how to do it. He realized Remalla and her brother would do everything to protect her. Would her brother keep her with him? His mind spun with thoughts of how to get to her, even if it meant killing whoever was with her.

His phone rang, and he answered it. "I'm here."

"Are they still there?" asked Rhonda.

"They are. There's been no activity since they arrived."

"What's your plan?"

"I'm pondering that. Where are you?"

"Still at the hospital. Sadly, Manetti is still alive. Daniels and Remalla just left with Marjorie, Erin, and that reporter. You want me to follow them?"

Monk considered it. "No. They'll go back to Daniels' home to figure out what's next. I'm just surprised Remalla isn't with his precious Mikey."

"I can tell you why. Rook just called me."

Surprised, Monk sat up. Rook had never called Rhonda directly. "Do tell."

"He asked me to come to his house tonight. Says he overreacted and didn't appreciate my skills. He told me Daniels and Remalla will be there later. He has plans for them. Told me to bring the star."

Monk wondered what Rook was up to. "That's interesting."

"I plan on going."

"You should. This could be the opportunity we're looking for."

"I was thinking the same."

Motion got his attention, and he peered through the binoculars. Down the street from Mason's home, a car pulled up at a distant corner and stopped at the stop sign. He studied the occupants and, seeing who was in the vehicle, he smiled. "I'll be damned." The car turned and drove down the road in the opposite direction.

"What is it?" asked Rhonda.

Monk lowered the binoculars. "Captain Lozano just drove away with Mikey Redstone."

"I thought you said there was no activity at the house?"

"Apparently, that's what they want anyone watching to think. Lozano must have gone around back, picked up Mikey, and is taking her somewhere else."

"Shouldn't you be following?"

"No need. I know where he'll take her. That cabin of his at Secret Lake."

"You sure about that?"

"I am. That's how they think. But I'm one step ahead of them." He took a drag of his cigarette, exhaled smoke, and stubbed it out on the wall. "I think you and I are going to have a productive night."

"What do you want me to do?"

He gathered his things, put them in his bag, and stood. "Find out what Rook wants. My guess? He's circling the wagons. He's getting rid of the detectives and using you to do it." He left the window and headed to the back of the house.

"It's about time."

"But after what happened today, he'll kill you and blame you for their deaths. He could try to blame me, too. So after you finish with Daniels and Remalla, take out Rook and Croft. Bonus points if you can use Croft's gun and make it look like he did the killings and turned the gun on himself. Put his fingerprints on the star and brand Rook. Once I'm done with Mikey, I'll meet you at Rook's. We can go through that office, take what we want, and head for the mountains." He paused to appreciate his brilliance. "I think the aspens are in bloom this time of year, aren't they?"

"I think that's in the fall."

"Doesn't matter. We'll wait." He slipped through the back window and closed it.

"What about the other group members and Rook's crazy lady?"

"Don't worry about that. When the police arrive, we'll have taken what we need to reconnect with and restart the society. They all know enough to keep their mouths shut for now, and the police won't touch the old woman. I never cared for her anyway." He left out the back gate and walked down the alley.

"They'll know the office was ransacked."

"Maybe, but they won't know what was taken. If we're lucky, and this goes the way we want, they'll blame Croft."

"What about the drugs? Don't we need the old woman to make them?"

"That information will be in the office. And once we have the formula, who needs her? Rook should have gotten rid of her a long time ago, but he wouldn't listen to me."

"You sure everything's in that office?"

"I am. Rook's fanatical about it. We'll grab his computer and files and erase the security footage. Plus, there's a safe I know the code to."

"How do you know that?"

He slung his bag higher on his shoulder. Still wearing his oversized coat, glasses, and hat, he watched for any nosy neighbors. "The way I know most things. I pay attention. Rook is as predictable as everyone else."

"What about work? Everyone is looking for you."

"Let them look. I left almost everything at the apartment, including some drops of blood. They'll think whoever shot Manetti may have taken me out, too. They'll search for a while, but they won't find anything. Meanwhile, I'll switch identities just like you."

"What about Mikey's death? Will they suspect you?"

"Maybe, but it's more likely they'll think they have a gunman on the loose who may have shot Manetti, come after me, and then Mikey." He perked up when he had another idea. "If we're really lucky, before we leave Rook's, we can make Croft look like the guilty party. He could go down for arranging Manetti's shooting, and Mikey's." Monk relished the thought.

"They know it was a female who shot Manetti."

"So what? They'll search but won't find you. And with Remalla and Daniels dead, along with Damien Rook, the city will be on edge, and the story will dominate the headlines and make Elsa Crow's job a nightmare. Even if Croft doesn't get the blame, they'll hunt for an elusive killer they'll never find." He smiled. "After the heat dies down, life will go on."

"And if Manetti survives?"

Monk considered that. "So what if he does? With Mikey gone, he's got nothing. By the time he recovers, Croft will have taken the blame. And even if he convinces them I'm involved, we'll be long gone."

She giggled. "What time will you take care of her?"

"It will be late, after they're asleep. Call me when you're done and be careful. Especially with Croft."

"Oh, honey. Don't worry about Croft. Like Rook, he's predictable." She sighed into the phone. "It's going to be a satisfying night."

"Enjoy it, because after it's done, we're lying low for a while."

"I'll savor every moment."

He turned out of the alley and headed for his car on a parallel street. "I love your confidence."

"And I love yours. You be careful too."

"Always." He monitored his surroundings, but the neighborhood remained quiet. "I'll see you tonight."

"See you."

Monk hung up, and after walking a few more minutes, he got to his car. He tossed his bag onto the back seat and slid into the front. Thinking of how he would access Lozano's cabin, he drove out of the neighborhood, hit the gas, and drove onto the highway.

· · • • • • • · · ·

Daniels drove up the driveway of Rook's mansion and parked. Night had fallen, and the only illumination was the exterior lighting of the home.

Rem sat in the passenger seat and checked his watch. "Five till nine. At least he can't kill us for being late." He looked out the window.

The uneasy feeling in the pit of Daniels' stomach grew. "I don't like this."

Rem looked back. "We discussed it."

"I know we did, but I still don't agree with you offering yourself up on a platter because it might get me access to Rook's office. If he's going to kill you, he's not going to let me wander the property while he does it. Plus, if I don't fight to protect you, Rook will see right through it."

"I won't be a total asshole. Just enough of one to distract Rook."

His head still hurting, Daniels rubbed his forehead. He'd avoided taking another pill to ward off one of his headaches because they made him sleepy, but he suspected if he lived long enough, he'd pay the price tomorrow. "How do you plan to do that?"

"I've been thinking. If he's resistant to leaving the house, and I can get him worked up enough, I can mention the Raven. Maybe ask to meet her. You can pretend to be against it and ask to stay back."

"That is ridiculous."

"Why is that ridiculous? I think Rook's been itching from the start to get us in front of her, and if I piss him off enough, he might be tempted to do it."

"Again, he's not going to leave me behind."

"He will if you tell him you'd rather work for him than with me. Tell him you never agreed to Allison's death. Tell him I'm a loose cannon." He paused. "You could even offer to take out Monk."

Daniels gaped at Rem. "He's not going to believe that."

"Depends on how good of an actor you are. Me too."

Daniels imagined that scenario, but the uneasy feeling wouldn't lift.

Rem shifted to face Daniels. "Listen. I know this sucks, but what other choice is there? I'm the one he blames for Allison. If we can convince him there's some sort of wedge between you and me, he might want to add you to the team like he did Croft." He paused. "Which means if Croft's here, Rook will probably leave you with him while he deals with me."

"So I'm supposed to take out Croft, access the office, find the evidence we need, all while you're being sacrificed to the Raven?"

Rem put his hand on the dash. "You forget. We're talking about Rook and an elderly woman. If things go sideways, I think I can handle myself."

"You don't know that. What about Tiny? The human steamroller, who was with Rook and Croft when Rook recruited us? You going to handle him?"

"Either of us could end up handling him. He may not even be here. Nothing about any of this is certain."

"Rem—"

"Daniels, what do you want to do? Sit here and keep rehashing this? All we can do is play it by ear. If Rook wants us badly enough, and we can convince him he needs us, he might trust us enough to share some secrets. I may not need to distract Rook. Or Croft could take you away and leave me to deal with Rook and the office. The only thing I know for sure is that in one hour, if Marjorie doesn't hear from us, she's calling the cops. That doesn't give us a lot of time."

Anxious, Daniels ran his hand through his hair. "It doesn't feel right."

"When does what we do ever feel right?"

Daniels gripped the steering wheel. "Why invite us here at this time of night?"

"Because I told him we needed to talk. Today. I didn't like the way we were being treated, and if he wanted to keep us, he needed to show a little respect."

Daniels studied the front door of the house. "It's possible he could back off of killing Rita and Lexie."

"Even if he *says* it, do you trust him?"

Daniels understood Rem was right. It was unlikely that anything would go according to plan. Once they were inside, all they could do was trust each other and hope for the best.

"It's now or never, partner," said Rem. "Something tells me this is our only shot. We can't risk Rook pulling up stakes and leaving and taking Croft with him. And we can't risk my gun being found and both of us being accused of murder." He pointed at the house. "This asshole is responsible for Cain, and Marjorie, and your unborn child. Not to mention Durning, Beelson, and Morgans. And Martin Bailey."

"I don't want him to be responsible for you, too."

Rem's face softened. "You think I'm comfortable leaving you behind with Croft?" He sighed. "Besides, we only have an hour. How much can happen in an hour?"

Daniels huffed. "You seriously want me to answer that?"

Rem's face fell. "Not really."

Daniels resumed his stare at the house. "Okay. We go in and play it by ear. Like we always do." He aimed his finger at Rem. "But don't get cocky. If it doesn't look good, we end it, leave and call Marjorie. This is not worth losing our lives, too, all right?"

"Believe me. I don't want to die any more than you do." He eyed his phone. "Plus, I'm worried about Mikey. She wasn't great when I left her."

"She's in better hands than we are. We just need to be sure you survive this long enough to get back to her."

Rem lowered his phone. "Yeah. I suppose."

Daniels heard the concern in his partner's voice. "Once we get through this, you two will work things out." He glared and pointed again. "As long as you don't get cocky."

Rem put his phone away. "You seem to forget that you are just as capable of pissing people off." He reached for the door handle.

"Who do you think I learned it from?"

Rem smiled. "That's why you're so good at it." He opened his door. "You ready? We don't want to be late."

Daniels hesitated. "Just be careful, partner."

Rem paused. "You too."

They held a brief look that communicated all that needed to be said before they shifted their body language to prepare for what came next. Emboldened, Daniels got out of the car with Rem, and they headed toward the house.

Chapter Twenty-Nine

REM KNOCKED ON ROOK'S front door. Daniels waited beside him. Willing himself to stay relaxed, Rem shook out his hands, forced Mikey out of his mind, and as the door opened, he let the cop side take over.

Croft stood at the threshold. He looked them over and pulled the door open wider. "Come in."

They stepped inside into a much quieter house. Without the energy of the birthday party and multiple guests, the home carried a somber feeling, like going to a funeral.

Croft closed the door behind them. "You know the drill." He walked to a bureau against the wall and opened a drawer. "Phones off and put them in here. Burner cell too." He pulled out the same wand-like device he'd used before. "Arms up."

Daniels pulled out his phone and the burner and turned them off. "So much for the circle of trust."

Rem turned his phone off, too. "I guess that whole pledge thing doesn't mean much." He put his phone in the drawer along with Daniels'.

Croft waited with the wand and didn't respond.

Daniels and Rem raised their arms, and Croft waved it over them. When he was satisfied, he lowered the wand. "Have a seat in the living room. Rook will be out in a minute."

Rem walked out of the front entry, down a few steps, and entered the living area. He recognized the two large white couches that sat on either side of a glass coffee table. Rem sat on one side of a couch and Daniels sat on the other. Looking around, Rem saw a closed door across from the living area. Based on

Daniels' description, he guessed that was Rook's office. He leaned back and crossed one leg over the other.

Croft joined them.

Rem bobbed his foot. "I hope we're not keeping Rook up past his bedtime."

"You two wanted to meet today," said Croft. "Mr. Rook has a busy schedule. This was his only available time."

"Where is he?" asked Daniels, checking his watch. "I thought he appreciated punctuality."

Croft half-smiled. "He'll be here." He crossed his arms. "I'd offer you a drink, but this isn't a social visit."

"Would you offer us one if it were?" asked Rem.

"Not likely."

Daniels scoffed. "I'm starting to think that being a member of Rook's little group doesn't garner much respect."

"You'll get your respect when you've earned it," said Croft.

"That works both ways," added Rem.

Croft smirked. "Rook would agree."

Rem wondered what that meant when the door across the room opened and Rook stepped out. He eyed Daniels and Rem with an unreadable expression. "You're on time. Good." He gestured toward the room he'd left. "Come in. Let's talk."

Rem kept a flat stare and didn't look at Daniels. The last thing he'd expected was to be invited into the very room they wanted to search. He stood and walked with Daniels into Rook's large office. A substantial oak desk took up a large section of the space. Shelves lined with books covered the wall behind the desk. Oil paintings covered the rest of the walls. To the right of the desk was a small round conference table with four chairs, and two leather chairs faced Rook's desk. Opposite the desk was a long wooden cabinet of drawers, and Rem spotted a closed door near the back corner.

Rook sat behind his desk and waved his hand. "Have a seat."

Looking around, Rem's mind raced with how to get Rook out of there. He sat in one of the leather chairs, and Daniels took the other. "Nice office," he said.

"It's where I do most of my work." Rook leaned over his desk and interlaced his fingers. "I'm told that you may be unhappy with our arrangement."

"You could say that," said Daniels. "You tried to kill Lexie Logan. Why?"

"I needed to send a message." Rook sat back. "You met with Rita."

Rem remained relaxed. "We didn't realize that was against the rules."

"She's my sister," said Rook. "You met her at my party. Please don't insult my intelligence and pretend you hit it off. I know my sister."

"Is that why you expect us to kill her?" asked Daniels. "Because we met with her?"

Rook sat back. "My sister has been a thorn in my side for a while now. I held off dealing with her, but when I realized she'd contacted you two, it became clear what I had to do." He reached up and took hold of a black stone pendant around his neck.

"You don't even know what we talked about," said Daniels.

"I'm not sure *I* remember what we talked about," added Rem. "We were pretty hungover after that little pill you gave us."

"I gave you nothing," said Rook. "You took it all on your own." His expression darkened. "Plus, you took a pledge, and violating that pledge comes with consequences."

"Who says we violated the pledge?" asked Rem.

Rook frowned. "What did you talk about? The weather?"

"We had some questions," said Daniels.

"If you had questions, you should have brought them to me."

"Like you're a fountain of information." Rem took a deep breath and sat straight. "Rita told us about your grudge against us." He paused. "We know you're Allison's grandfather."

Rook's jaw tightened. "And I know what you did to her."

"Rem did nothing to her," said Daniels with a glance at Rem. "She was poisoned while she was in prison. If we could have saved her, we would have."

Rook leaned forward. "She never would have been there if it weren't for you two."

Hearing Daniels go off-script, Rem trusted his partner's instincts and went with it. "She and Victor abducted me. She killed Victor and then almost killed me. What happened to her is her fault. Not mine. And not Daniels."

"You lied about everything," said Rook, his voice rising. "You took advantage of her, used her to get to Victor, assaulted her and got her pregnant. Then threw her to the wolves. She was a victim, abused by Victor, and then by you."

Rem forced back his swirling emotions. "Allison was in control from day one, and I think you know that. You were friends with Victor. You were part of his cult. I suspect you and Allison conspired to get rid of Victor so you could control Victor's groupies yourself."

"We heard you got cozy with Victor's friend, the Raven," said Daniels. "Did she conspire with you and Allison, too?"

Rook tightened his grip on the pendant around his neck. "You know about the Raven?"

"Rita filled us in," said Rem. "And the working theory is this Raven worked with you to create that new party drug of yours. The one we took during the pledge." Rem tipped his head. "Let me take a wild guess. You and Allison planned to use the cult to distribute the drug once you had it perfected?"

Daniels nodded. "That would make sense. Get rid of Victor and keep all the proceeds for yourself. Pretty slick. Except we intervened when we investigated the cult."

"And all those plans went down the toilet," said Rem. "Is that the real reason you're so pissed off?" He narrowed one eye. "Because Allison didn't really strike me as the family type."

Rook's cheeks flared a dark red. "She died carrying your child and my grandchild. I will never forgive you for that."

Rem didn't bother to correct him and kept up the pressure. "And you created a society responsible for the deaths of good men, including my cousin," he gestured at Daniels, "and his unborn child. I will never forgive *you* for *that*."

Rook glared at Rem.

Daniels broke the silence. "Where is this Raven?"

Rook broke the connection with Rem and spoke to Daniels. "That is not your concern."

"I think it is," said Daniels. "She's the reason you started the society. I mean, the black bird tattoos? Your last name means crow, and she's the Raven? Catchy. And this drug you two created to do what? Eradicate weakness and make yourself invincible?"

"How's that working out for you?" asked Rem.

"What exactly are you planning, Rook?" asked Daniels. "To take over not just a society of evildoers, but the world?"

"Haven't you seen a Marvel movie? Here's a hint." Rem lowered his voice. "It never works out."

Rook gazed intently at them, rubbing the black stone with his fingers. "If you'd taken the pledge seriously, you might have found out."

"This is where you're confused, Rook," said Rem. "It's not about any pledge. It's about power. And Daniels and I want it. But that requires information and trust. That's why we talked to Rita. To find out what we were dealing with." He leaned back and sighed to put Rook at ease. "You want to deal drugs with this Raven? Fine. We can live with that. We can also help. You may hate us, but don't let that stop you from seizing a prime opportunity."

"Hate is a weakness," said Daniels. "Maybe that pill can help you purge it."

Rook's penetrating gaze became a glare. "What are you suggesting?"

"Use us," said Rem, going with his gut, which seemed to be working. "Doing what we do, we can work on the inside. You sell the drug, and we'll look the other way."

"And if someone obstructs your path," said Daniels, "we'll take care of it."

"Which brings us to your associate, Detective Frank Monk," said Rem. "We know he's a black bird, and we know he's connected to Rhonda. He's a liability. He's been linked to Vera Canmore's murder, which links him to you. You can't use him anymore."

"Accusing and proving are two different things," said Rook.

Daniels shot Rem a look that Rem interpreted as, *trust me*. "Not when Monk admitted to someone else that he killed Vera."

Rem didn't flinch. He realized what Daniel was doing and thought it was brilliant.

Daniels rested his ankle on his knee. "Someone we've talked to wants to file a report about how Monk assaulted her and confessed to killing Vera. Admittedly, he was flying high on your drug at the time, but it doesn't look good."

Rem's heart raced as their plan took shape. Monk had said nothing to Lola about killing Vera, but Rook didn't know that. "And now his partner, Manetti, has been shot, likely by Monk's lady friend, Rhonda." Rem waved a finger. "Those two get caught, they could do a lot of damage."

Rook let go of his pendant and gripped his armrest. "Monk will be handled."

"By who?" asked Daniels. He jerked his thumb toward the office door. "Your pretty boy Tex out there?"

"He goes against Monk, and he'll lose," said Rem. "Monk is way smarter."

"And more deadly," replied Daniels.

"Which means you're in a tight spot," said Rem. He prayed he and Daniels were making headway, and to make his point, he hit Rook where it mattered. "Even worse, you're vulnerable."

Rook's shoulders straightened, but his eyes reflected his uncertainty. Rem waited to see if he and Daniels had hit their mark.

After a long pause, Rook grabbed his pendant again. "What do you want?"

Rem bit back a sigh of relief. "I think it's time we knew everything." He glanced at Daniels and back at Rook. "I want to meet the Raven."

Rook raised a brow.

"And I want Tex out," said Daniels. "I don't trust him. You want us? He has to go."

Rem's heart thumped faster. So far, playing it by ear was paying off.

They waited for what felt like hours while Rook rubbed his pendant, stared at both of them, and swiveled in his chair. "I have to admit," he finally said, "this is not how I envisioned this evening would go."

Rem held his breath. "Daniels and I are famous for screwing up plans."

"It's one of our gifts," said Daniels with a sly smile. "One I think you'll come to appreciate."

Rook let go of his pendant. "Very well." He opened the top drawer of his desk and took out a key. "You want to meet the Raven?" He stood. "It will be my pleasure to introduce you." He eyed Daniels. "You stay here. I'll send Tex in. You can deal with him as you see fit."

Rem almost leapt out of his chair, but stayed calm and stood. He eyed Daniels. "Looks like you get all the fun jobs."

Daniels held his gaze. "Say hi to the Raven for me. I bet she's a barrel of laughs. Just don't eat any toads."

"I'll do my best." Rem waited as Rook walked around his desk and went to the door.

He stopped before opening it. "There's just one thing I require first." He opened the door, and Tex walked in, aiming a gun at Rem and Daniels. Rook smiled. "Tell me where Jerry Lee Caruso is, and then we'll see if you live long enough to exact your demands."

Rem's heart dropped.

Chapter Thirty

DANIELS EYED CROFT'S WEAPON. "What is this?" He wondered where he and Rem had failed.

"I'm calling your bluff," said Rook. "This game you're playing? You're good at it, but I'm better. I know you've been lying. You didn't kill Caruso, and you won't kill Rita."

"You're wrong," said Rem. "Caruso is dead."

"No, he isn't," said Rook. "You're hiding him."

"What makes you so sure?" asked Daniels, keeping an eye on Croft's gun. "We took the pledge, remember?"

"Which you never intended to honor. Stop playing me for a fool." He touched his pendant. "You think I'm weak, when the truth is, I've been stronger than both of you all along."

"Those pills have gone to your head," said Rem. "We're not playing any games."

Rook narrowed his eyes. "That's where you're mistaken. You've been playing, just not the game you thought you were." He glanced at Croft. "Croft."

Croft straightened his aim. "Put your guns on the desk."

Rem hesitated. "We're still cops, Croft. You can't get rid of us so easy."

Croft ignored him. "Your guns. Now." He shifted his gun toward Daniels. "Or he dies first."

Daniels stiffened and raised his hands. "Easy, Croft."

Rem raised his hands, too. "Okay." He slid his hand into his jacket and pulled out his gun. He held it by the handle, stepped back into the office, and placed it on Rook's desk.

Moving slowly, Daniels did the same.

"Step into the living room," said Rook.

Still aiming his weapon, Croft backed up. With his hands raised, Daniels took small steps and returned to the living area with Rem behind him.

Rook waited and closed the office door.

"Sit on the couch," said Croft.

Rem moved around one sofa and sat on it. Daniels sat beside him. "What's your plan, Rook?" asked Daniels. "There's already been one cop shot today. You going to shoot us too, and then go after Monk?"

"The whole damn force will be out looking for the killer," said Rem. "You really trust your society brothers to keep quiet after that? They'll think you're a maniac."

"I've considered that." Rook sat on the opposite sofa. Croft remained standing, holding his gun on them. "But I'm three steps ahead of you." His gaze darted up, and he scowled. "Go back to your room. Now."

Daniels followed Rook's gaze and saw Delaina on the second-floor landing, staring down at them. Rem looked too.

Delaina hesitated.

Rook raised his voice. "Unless you'd prefer to stay in the guest house?"

Delaina scowled back, turned, and walked down a hall until she was out of sight.

Rook returned his attention to Daniels and Rem. "You insist you killed Jerry Lee?"

"We did," said Daniels. "He's fish food at the bottom of Secret Lake."

Rook nodded. "Then I'm going to give you both the chance to prove yourselves. If you expect to be trusted members, then you will have to face your enemies and defeat them. Weakness cannot be tolerated."

"We're all ears," said Rem.

Rook stood and walked past the coffee table. "You pass this test, and I will willingly accept you into the society. You'll have the same standing as Monk and Croft. In fact, you'll take their places. You fail, and well, you die."

"Any other options?" asked Daniels.

Rook turned. "We could go with my first choice. Torture one of you until the other talks."

Daniels shared a look with Rem. "We'll go with option one," said Daniels.

"You can thank the Raven for changing my mind." Rook walked over and faced them. "Or, you can willingly tell me where you're hiding Caruso. Once we've located him, you two can take another pill and wake up in your homes as if nothing ever happened. The police will find your weapon, Remalla, and evidence of your bribes, Daniels, and you can take your chances with the courts."

"That's not an option because Caruso is dead," added Rem. "And if we end up the same, you'll have to deal with the repercussions."

Rook smirked. "Croft will dump your bodies somewhere remote and bury them. Then drive your car, which will have your guns and phones in it, and park it at the airport. When they search your homes, they'll find evidence of your crimes and assume you took off. By the time your remains are located, if they ever are, any connection to me or the society will be a distant memory."

Daniels' stomach rolled. "I think I speak for both of us when I say we'll stick with option one...with plans to win."

Rook clasped his hands behind his back. "I was hoping you'd say that. It makes it much more interesting."

Daniels couldn't imagine what Rook had planned for them. "What enemy are we facing?"

"Not *we* detective," said Rook. "You." He walked behind Croft. "You will each face your own nemesis. One you've been eager to confront."

Rem scooted forward on the couch. "What do you mean?"

Rook pointed at a closed door beyond the kitchen. Daniels recalled it led to a hallway where he'd used the restroom.

"You will go through that door, Detective Daniels," said Rook. He eyed Rem. "And you will stay here."

"What the hell are you talking about?" asked Rem.

Rook spoke to Daniels. "You will face your nemesis..." He raised a brow at Rem. "...and you will face yours." He gestured at Croft.

Daniels tried to assimilate what he was hearing. Rem would face Croft, aka Tex, who'd killed Cain. But who would Daniels face? Only one name came to mind. The woman who'd gone after Marjorie. *Rhonda.*

Croft sneered at Rem. "Care to tango, Detective?"

Rem glared back. "I thought you'd never ask."

Rook walked to the other side of Croft. "You survive, and we'll talk. You don't...then well," he chuckled, "I can't help dead people."

Daniels hated asking the next question. "What if one survives, but the other doesn't?"

"One new team member is better than none. Unless the survivor's grief prevents them from performing their duties, then they might as well join the other."

"What are you going to do?" asked Rem. "Watch like some rabid fan at the Roman Colosseum?"

Rook faced them. "I've got some packing to do. Delaina and I are headed out of town. It's better I'm gone while this mess is dealt with."

"What happens when we win?" asked Daniels. "How do we find you?"

Rook walked behind the couch where Daniels and Remalla sat and leaned between them. "If I thought that would happen, I'd stay."

"Not exactly a vote of confidence," said Rem. "But I plan on surprising you."

"Me too," said Daniels.

"Give it your best shot," said Rook. "If your victory comes soon enough, you might catch me and Delaina before we leave." He straightened and checked his watch. "But you better hurry. Time's running short."

Rem swiveled to face Croft. "I'm ready when you are."

Rook walked around the sofa, looked at Daniels, and gestured toward the closed door off the kitchen. "Detective?"

Pausing, Daniels shared a knowing gaze with Rem before he stood. "See you in a few."

Rem stood too. "We'll pop some champagne when you get back."

Daniels spoke to Rook. "I suppose you've got a decent bottle in the fridge?"

"There's a bottle worth a grand on the bottom shelf," said Rook. "But I think it will go untouched tonight."

"We'll see about that." Rem eyed Croft. "I'll toast your remains."

Croft sneered again. "I won't bother wasting good champagne."

Preparing himself, Daniels' heart thumped faster. He shared a look with Rem. "You be careful, partner."

"You too." Rem paused. "And I'll see you soon."

Daniels refused to believe otherwise. "I'll see you too." Bracing for whatever he was about to encounter, he turned and walked toward the closed door. He put his hand on the knob, took a deep breath, and without looking back, opened it and walked into the hall.

· · • • · • • · · ·

Mikey sat on the sofa in the cabin and stared at her sandwich on the paper plate. She'd taken a few bites but couldn't eat anymore.

Lozano sat beside her and took the last bite of his food. "You should eat something. Keep up your strength."

Mikey set the plate on the coffee table and dropped her head into her hands. "You really think this is going to work? Don't you think Monk or Rhonda will find me?"

"There are no guarantees." Lozano chewed his bite and swallowed. "But it's better than sitting at Mason's. That's the first place they'll look."

"Monk and Rhonda aren't stupid, Captain."

"No, they're not, but they're not invincible, either."

She raised her head. "It doesn't feel like that."

"And that's what they want. They're used to it. And like Rook, that's what makes them vulnerable."

She sighed. "What about Manetti? They'll come after him too if he lives."

"Manetti is safe for now. He's in the CCU with Annabelle, and a slew of nurses watching over him. In my experience, that's safer than any armed force standing guard."

Thinking of Manetti, Mikey's heart ached. "It won't matter if he dies."

"That's what Monk's hoping for, but don't count Manetti out."

Tears welled up in her eyes. "If he doesn't make it..." Her throat closed up.

"You have to stop blaming yourself. None of this is your fault. And if you hadn't been there, Manetti would certainly be dead. Rhonda wasn't expecting you."

"He jumped in front of me." She wiped her eyes. "He saved my life."

"And you can thank him when he wakes up." Lozano set his empty plate beside him. "That's how you have to think about it, Mikey. If you don't, it will eat you up inside."

Mikey sniffed. Lozano handed her a napkin, and she took it and dabbed her cheeks. "I'll try." She thought of Rem. "Any word from Rem or Daniels?"

"No. But it's early."

"I'm not so convinced their plan will work any better than this one."

"Working with those two as long as I have, I'm sure it won't."

Surprised, she looked up.

"But universal forces somehow align to get them out of a scrape. I have no reason to believe that won't happen again."

"This is a pretty big scrape."

"The bigger the scrape, the bigger the help."

She fiddled with her napkin. "You sure about that?"

"I have to be, or I could never do my job."

Mikey bit her lip. "Rem and I...we argued." More tears surfaced. "We didn't have time to talk."

"You will when he gets back."

"But...what if..." She stopped when she caught Lozano frowning at her. "Right," she said. "I can't think like that."

He picked up her plate and set it on top of his own. "Why don't you go lie down? Try to get some sleep. You've had a hellish day."

She almost laughed. "Sleep? You expect me to sleep?"

"You're more tired than you realize. It'll hit you when you take a second to slow down. Just close your eyes. If you sleep, great. And don't worry if you do. I'll wake you if I learn anything."

Mikey rubbed her face and had to admit that the day's events were catching up with her. "You promise? You hear from Mason, Rem, or Annie, you'll tell me?"

"I'll wake you out of a sound sleep. Cross my heart." He ran his fingers in an X pattern over his chest. He pointed toward the bedroom. "Go rest before you collapse."

Her injured arm aching and her head fuzzy, she pushed herself to her feet. "Okay."

"I'll stay out here. And remember. The curtains stay closed, and no peeking outside of them. Got it? And try not to worry."

She snorted. "That's like asking Rem not to eat a Taco del Fuego after a twelve-hour shift."

He chuckled. "I think not worrying is the easier ask."

She smiled and headed toward the main bedroom. "You're pretty tired yourself."

"I'll stay on the couch. I need to check in with my wife, and I'll wait to hear from Marjorie. When I know something, you'll know something."

Mikey nodded, and doing her best not to worry, she went into the bedroom.

· · · · ● · ● · · · ·

Monk stared through his binoculars at the cabin. The curtains were drawn, but the lights were on inside, and he could see the shadows of two people. Lozano's car was parked at the side of the cabin, tucked under the trees and away from the road. Monk had studied the area after arriving and was happy to see no activity in the neighboring cabins. It looked like Lozano's cabin was the only one occupied. That would work well for him, and he didn't expect any issues. Once enough time passed, Lozano and Mikey would let their guards down and go to sleep. Then he'd make his move.

He thought of Rhonda and wondered how it was going at Rook's. He almost wished he were there, but this assignment was equally satisfying. While Rhonda took care of Remalla and Daniels, he would take care of Mikey Redstone, and Lozano, too, if he got in the way.

He sat up when a light in the cabin went out. Now, only one light in the cabin's windows remained on. Smiling to himself, he settled back in his seat and prepared to wait.

Chapter Thirty-One

After Daniels left the room, Rem remained standing and eyed the gun in Croft's hand. "You consider this a fair fight?"

Croft flicked a glance toward Rook, who slid his hands into his pockets. "I'll leave you two to handle your grievances. Delaina and I will leave soon." He turned toward the stairs. "Just do your best not to destroy the place. Whoever remains standing will have cleanup duty." He picked up an ornate vase sitting on a pedestal near the stairs. "I'll take this with me." He walked up the stairs to the second landing and looked down. "Good luck."

"I'll be in touch soon, sir," said Croft.

"Let's hope," he smiled, left the landing, and disappeared from view.

Rem faced Croft and steadied himself. "You seem pretty certain you're going to win this."

"This will be over before Rook finishes packing. I'll probably be able to drive him to the hangar."

Rem eyed the gun. "You shoot me, and I suppose you will. If that's your plan, then it's clear you know you can't beat me in a fair fight."

Croft smiled. "Rook said the Raven foresaw us confronting each other. Only one can survive. But it must be an equal match."

"The Raven, huh? Sounds like Rook has a boss, too."

"I suppose if you live long enough, you'll find out for yourself."

Rem held out his hands. "Then what are we waiting for?"

Croft walked toward the kitchen and placed his weapon on the counter. "Before we start," he reached for something, "I'm supposed to give you this." He picked up a doll made of fabric and showed it to Rem. It had long black yarn for hair, buttons for eyes, a black feather poking up from the chest, and a patch of red over the heart.

Rem fought the urge to be sick. "Keep it. I'm not into dolls."

"Looks like the Raven foresaw your death as well."

Rem understood now why Rook had been so confident Croft would win this battle. "I put little stock in an evil witch's predictions."

"So be it." Croft tossed the doll back onto the counter. "Just know I'll bury the doll with you, so you can always be together."

"Thoughtful."

With his hands out, Croft returned to stand across from Rem. "If you've changed your mind, I can kill you quick and go find your partner."

Rem couldn't think about Daniels right now. He had to focus. "The same goes for you, only I'll hunt down whoever Daniels is facing."

"I think you might prefer me. Of the two, I think I'll inflict less damage, but the outcome will be the same."

"You sure talk a lot for someone who plans to kill me."

Croft chuckled. "I don't talk nearly as much as your cousin did. You should have heard him beg for his life."

Any semblance of self-control snapped, and Rem lunged at Croft.

· · · • · • • · · ·

Daniels walked down the quiet hall. He passed the guest bathroom he'd used during the party and kept going. Not sure what to expect, he stayed alert to any sounds but heard nothing. He passed a closed door and tried to open it, but it was locked. Pictures and paintings of people hung on the walls, but he ignored them. All his senses were attuned to anyone nearby. He did his best not to think about Rem and his battle with Croft. If he did, it would only distract him, and he couldn't afford the risk.

Moving farther down the hall, he passed a laundry room. He peeked his head in but saw only the clothes washer and dryer. He walked a few more steps and stopped at an open door. Looking in, he saw an ornate library with a large stone fireplace. The walls were built-in shelves filled with books. An old, dusty radiator sat in a far corner. In front of the fireplace was a plush oriental rug, which lay under two large high-backed upholstered chairs with a small round brass table between them. The chairs faced the fireplace. On the table sat an antique lamp and a half-filled glass of amber liquid.

He stepped inside, wondering why Rook didn't use this impressive space as his office.

A female voice broke the silence. "Hello, Detective."

He stopped cold and saw a hand with a sparkly ring on a finger pick up the glass of liquid. Whoever was there was sitting in the chair.

Holding her glass, Rhonda stood and turned to face him.

Daniels didn't move, but an icy finger of dread ran up his back.

"Come join me." She remained by the chair and sipped her drink.

Telling himself to stay cool, he stepped farther into the room. He studied the woman he and Rem had transported through the town of Elmwood, believing she was a witness for a murder trial. Gone were the baggy clothes and dark hair. She wore slim jeans and a snug T-shirt, and long blonde hair brushed her shoulders. Her right bicep sported a bandage, and he guessed that was where she'd been hit by one of Mikey's bullets. Her fingernails were bright pink, and he thought of Marjorie. Rhonda had tried to frame his sister Erin for Marjorie's accident by painting her nails a similar color to Erin's.

"Long time no see," she said.

He wasn't sure what to say. He couldn't see any weapons on her, but he remained alert. "You've had a busy day."

"And it's not over yet."

"I hear we're supposed to face each other, winner take all."

She lowered her glass. "That's the plan. It's nothing personal, though."

"Let's hope for your sake you have better luck than with your last two hits."

Her smug look fell. "Third time's the charm."

"We'll see." He debated taking the offensive and tackling her but couldn't risk it. He looked for cameras in the room; he didn't need an unknown adversary coming at him if he jumped the gun.

She set her glass down. "I have to ask. Did you and Remalla really kill Jerry Lee?"

Daniels kept up the ruse in case they were being watched and listened to. "We did."

"I didn't think you had it in you."

"You should have learned in Elmwood that Rem and I are survivors."

She walked around the chair. "I almost got to Jerry Lee."

"Almost is a lousy word for assassins." He surveyed the room to search for anything he could use as a weapon. "You killed Bertrand, though, didn't you?"

"Of course." She stopped behind the chair. "In order to redeem myself, I have to kill you. Then I get to brand you, like the others." She tipped her head toward the fireplace.

Daniels spotted the brand in the shape of a star lying on the mantel. His skin prickled, and his heart thumped harder. "I hate to tell you, but I won't go down easy."

"I wouldn't expect you to."

"Then what's your plan?"

She reached behind her and pulled out a switchblade. She flipped it open and held it in her hand.

Daniels stilled. "Where's my weapon?"

"I'm looking at it. You're a big guy, and I'm just a petite little thing. I figure we're evenly matched." She smiled and waved the knife.

Daniels took a second to appraise the situation. He had the size advantage, but she would be quick. "You sure you want to do this? Wouldn't you and Monk prefer to ride off into the sunset and leave all this behind?"

"Me and Monk?"

"We know you're both part of Rook's society. You tried to kill Manetti to protect Monk, right? You two take orders from Rook."

Her smug look fell. "Not for long."

Daniels took another step closer but stayed a reasonable distance away from her. "So, you know Rook is using you."

"I do, but he'll learn soon enough that he's the one about to be used."

He glanced at his watch and was dismayed to see it was only nine thirty. Plenty of time for him and Rem to die before help arrived. "What's your plan?

Kill me and assume Croft kills Rem. Then you kill Croft and Rook, and you and Monk ride off together?"

"Something like that."

"Good luck."

"Luck has nothing to do with it."

He doubted he could stall her long enough before reinforcements arrived. But if he could take her out sooner instead of later, he might be able to help Rem. "Before we do this, I have a question."

"I suspect you have more than one, but shoot."

"Was Monk the one who arranged to have me and Rem killed in Elmwood?"

"He did, on Rook's orders."

"And you killed and branded Morgans, Beelson, and Durning?"

"I did."

"Also on Rook's orders?"

"Yes."

"I see. And do you and Monk have tattoos, like all the rest?"

She pushed the waist of her jeans down to reveal a small tattoo of a black bird on her hip. "Monk's is in the same place."

"Of course it is."

She let go of her waistband. "Is that it?"

"Where do you and Monk plan on settling down after we're all dead?"

"Not sure yet, but someplace nice. Maybe the mountains."

"How do you plan to support yourselves?"

She grinned. "We've got plans. Someone has to pick up the slack after Rook is gone."

Daniels got the picture. "You mean the society? And Rook's drug enterprise? How industrious of you both."

"We thought so." She held the knife at waist-height. "Anything else?"

Daniels thought of Marjorie. "You're the one who caused my wife's accident, aren't you?"

She pursed her lips. "Again, it wasn't personal. We needed to send a message and throw you and Remalla off balance."

He clenched his fingers into fists. "She almost died, and we lost our child."

"I'm a killer. It's what I do."

"You ever hear that you reap what you sow?"

"I'm doing okay so far." She tightened her grip on the knife. "Any more questions?"

"I think that's it for now."

"Good." She stepped toward the chair but never took her eyes off of him. "I'm supposed to give you this." Rhonda picked up a fabric doll similar to Rita's and Martin Bailey's, only this one had yellow straw for hair, the same black feather, and a circular piece of red felt on the doll's stomach.

Unnerved, Daniels swallowed.

"I hear the Raven made it." She shook the doll. "Remalla's, too." She tossed the doll back onto the chair. "Personally, it's a little drab for me, but I hear it's not about the look. It's about the message." She regarded Daniels. "You ready?"

Daniels slid his jacket off, wrapped it around his forearm, and steeled himself. "I am."

"Good." She stepped past the chair toward him. "And don't worry. I won't brand you until you're dead. You won't feel a thing." She stopped in front of him, bent her legs, and held the knife out.

Daniels relaxed his muscles, raised his arms, and waited for her to make the first move.

Chapter Thirty-Two

REM TACKLED CROFT AT his midsection, knocking him backwards into the wall, where he hit with a heavy grunt. A hanging picture of wildflowers fell and hit the floor. Rem punched Croft in his gut, and Croft punched back, hitting Rem in the side of his ribs. Rem fought to hold Croft against the wall, but Croft shifted, lost his footing and fell to the floor.

Rem stayed on top of him, trying to maintain his leverage, but Croft was strong, and he shoved Rem to his side. Evenly matched, the two struggled for dominance; Rem went for Croft's throat and Croft deflected, punched Rem in his side again, rolled away, and got to his feet.

Rem jumped up, and breathing hard, faced Croft, who picked up a long, narrow vase from a shelf and swiped it at Rem, who leaned away just before it hit him in the face.

Before Croft could swing a second time, Rem ran at Croft, tackled him again, and knocked him into the breakfast table. They both fell on top of it. Croft attempted to hit Rem with the vase, but Rem knocked it from Croft's hand. The vase shattered on the tiled floor. Rem grabbed Croft's arm, and Croft grabbed Rem's throat with his free hand and squeezed. Rem instinctively pulled back, but the shift in weight made him lose his balance. He slid off the table, taking Croft with him. The table crashed to its side, and Rem hit the edge of a chair going down. His ribs took the brunt, and a slice of pain rocketed through him. He ignored it, though, when Croft fell on top of him.

Fighting to gain the advantage, but caught between the table, the wall, and Croft, Rem kicked the table back. He grabbed the remains of the vase, knocked Croft in the head with it, and squirmed away. Scrambling to his feet, he shoved a chair back just as Croft stood, his cheek bleeding and holding what looked like the broken leg of a chair. He swung the leg at Rem, and Rem, his ribs burning, jumped back, narrowly avoiding another hit. He retreated into the living room to get away from the fallen table and scattered chairs.

Standing near the couch, he tried to catch his breath as Croft encroached, still holding the chair leg. "Tired yet?" Sweat glistened on his forehead.

"Not yet," said Rem. He darted back as Croft swung the leg, but this time, Rem caught Croft's arm. He swiveled, kicked his foot out, and flipped Croft down to the floor.

Croft hit hard and let go of the chair leg. His ribs flaring, Rem reached for it, but Croft rolled toward him and onto Rem's legs. Unable to catch himself, Rem fell backward and hit his head on a section of the tiled floor. The impact dazed him, and before he knew it, Croft was on top of him again. He slugged Rem in the face and reared back to do it again, when Rem lifted his upper body and grabbed Croft by the throat. He squeezed, and Croft grabbed Rem's wrists. His eyes widened, and Rem squeezed harder. Croft stopped struggling, let go of Rem and punched him in the side where he'd been injured.

Searing pain made Rem gasp. His grip loosened, and Croft took advantage, punching Rem again in the midsection and twisting away. Before Croft could get to his feet, though, Rem used his legs to trip him, and Croft fell face-first into the carpet. Rem tried to keep him down, but Croft kicked at Rem. Unable to hold on, Rem let go. Croft got back to his feet, and Rem forced himself up, holding his side.

Croft wiped sweat from his eye as blood dripped down his cheek. "Looks like you're injured."

Rem ignored the pain and faced Croft. His ribs throbbed, and his eye pulsed as it swelled. "You worried about me?"

"Worry isn't my strong suit."

Rem stepped around the coffee table. Croft stepped to the other side, maintaining his distance from Rem. Rem looked for anything he could use against Croft, but nothing around him was suitable. "Anyone you want me to contact when you're gone?" Rem's gaze found Croft's gun on the kitchen counter.

"Won't be necessary." Croft glanced at the gun, too. "Can you get to it before me?"

"What happened to the fair fight?" Sweat trickled down Rem's back, and his side ached.

"We both have equal access," said Croft. "Unless you want to dance around and do this all night."

"Don't like your chances?"

"I like efficiency."

Rem watched Croft's eyes. "Me too."

They both ran for the gun. Rem got to it first, grabbed it by the handle, but Croft grabbed it too, and they struggled for control. Rem lost his grip, and the gun slipped from his grasp, fell to the other side of the counter and clattered to the tiled floor.

Croft shoved Rem against the counter and slugged Rem in the nose. Rem saw stars again, but before Croft could get in another punch, he wrapped his arms around Croft's midsection and shoved forward. Croft stumbled backward, and they both fell into the glass coffee table, Croft's back taking the brunt. The table shattered, and they hit the rug, glass crunching beneath them.

Rem straddled Croft and went for his throat, but Croft was faster, and he punched Rem again on his injured side. Rem gasped and fell back.

Gaining the upper hand, Croft swiveled, knocking Rem to his side, and then straddled him. Rem fought to get away, but Croft wrapped his hands around Rem's neck and squeezed.

With his airway cut off, Rem clutched at Croft's wrists, trying to release the pressure. The need to breathe exploded. Rem's head throbbed, and his vision swirled.

Croft's expression turned maniacal, and he leaned over Rem. "Time's up, Detective. After you pass out, I'm going to get my gun and shoot you in the heart, like I did your cousin."

Fighting panic, Rem thought of Daniels and Mikey, and something in him shifted. One clear thought punctured his fear, and he let go of Croft's wrist with one hand and ran it over the carpet, feeling the sharp shards of glass from the coffee table. Finding a bigger one, he gripped it, swung it up, and jabbed it straight into Croft's neck.

Blood instantly spurted from the wound. Croft let go of Rem and grabbed for the shard, his eyes widening. He pulled the shard from his neck, and a jet of blood shot from his wound, dousing Rem in it.

Sucking in much-needed oxygen, Rem squirmed out from under Croft, who'd fallen to his side. The glass crunched beneath him, and he pushed back to a cleaner part of the carpet. Croft gasped for air and clutched his neck, but the blood spurted out of him at a rapid rate.

Rem held his aching throat with his bleeding hand and coughed. Watching Croft's skin pale and his breathing slow, Rem whispered, "That's for Cain," before Croft's eyes went dull and his body went limp.

· · • • • • • · ·

Rhonda swung the knife, but Daniels dodged it. They circled each other, and she swung out again, but still missed.

Watching her, Daniels had the sense that she was studying him, like a lion studies its prey from the high grass, waiting for the perfect time to pounce.

Daniels studied her too, looking for the right chance to grab the knife and take her down. If he could do that, he could overpower her, and this fight would be over.

She swung again, and again, he dodged it. He kept his covered arm in front of him to protect him from the blade. With each swipe, though, she seemed to maneuver him into the corner of the room, where he'd have less of a chance to escape her swing.

On her next move, he went for the knife, but she was quick, and she swiveled away from him, swung the knife, and this time caught his jacket. It didn't get his skin, but he stepped back into the center of the room to avoid her.

She smiled. "I'm getting closer."

"Close only counts when Rem's near a hot dog stand."

She lunged and narrowly missed his side when he dodged again, but then she swiveled once more, only much faster. She caught the side of his abdomen. His shirt sliced open, and blood trickled from the wound.

The sting of the injury made Daniels gasp, but thankfully, the damage wasn't bad, though it rattled him.

"Does that count?" She smiled again.

"It's gonna take more than that to win." He watched her and the knife intently.

"I like to take my time," she said. "Enjoy the moment." She jabbed again, and he jumped back.

Feeling blood dripping down his skin, he ignored the wound and kept his full attention on her. When she jabbed at him again, he went for her wrist, hoping to catch her off balance. She surprised him though, when instead of moving away from him, she shifted her balance toward him, turned before he could get a hold of her, arced the knife and caught him in his upper arm.

Blood spurted from the wound, and he jumped back and cursed. This injury was deeper, and blood coursed down his skin. His shirtsleeve turned red, and pain flared up into his shoulder, but he couldn't afford to lose focus because she'd moved back into a defensive position, ready to swing again.

"At this rate," she said, "I'm going to cut you into pieces."

"I'm not dead yet." He moved to his left as she moved to hers.

"My next target is your gut, and then you'll be D.E.D., dead." She giggled.

Daniels continued to dodge her, but the more they sparred, the more he noted the way she moved and the look in her eyes. He sensed her goal was to tire him, so when she went for the final blow, he'd move slower and be less able to fight back. He did his best to keep his movements light and fast, and took slow, deep breaths to conserve as much energy as possible.

When he found himself in another corner, he waited and didn't try to escape. He suspected this was where she wanted him, and he anticipated her fatal move. Watching her, he noted her sudden inhale, the slight widening of her eyes, and the tightening of her grasp on the knife. She lunged and swiveled, but instead of dodging, he swiveled too. Narrowly missing being stabbed in his stomach, he deflected the knife, shoved her arm away, and using her balance against her, shoved her face first into the wall near the radiator.

She hit hard, and he grabbed her hand with the knife and, using his body weight, he pinned her into the corner. He knocked her wrist hard against the wall while she writhed beneath him, desperate to escape.

Almost losing his grip on her, he slammed her wrist harder, and she screamed and finally let go. The knife fell to the floor. She went limp, and Daniels made the mistake of lessening the pressure of his body against hers. She instantly bucked and shoved him back enough to squirm out, but he grabbed hold of her before she could escape. She flailed, using her arms, legs, feet, and hands to get away from him. He fought to hold on to her and keep her away from the knife, but she was strong and fought like hell to get away.

With one last lunge, she kicked him in the leg near his groin, and a wicked flare of pain almost buckled him. She shifted and reached for the knife. Using all his strength, he gripped her leg and dragged her back while she kicked and screamed.

She pummeled him with her hands and slapped at his face, scratching him with her fingernails. Getting a grip on her arms, he reared back and slapped her. Dazed, she fell to the floor but remained conscious. While he had the chance, he grabbed her wrists and dragged her over to the radiator. Before she could retaliate, he pulled his cuffs from his pocket and slapped one on her wrist, then slid the other cuff behind a pipe on the radiator and secured it to her other wrist.

Rhonda now contained, he fell back to the floor, exhausted from the effort. Bleeding heavily, his arm throbbed. His stomach hurt too.

She came awake then and, realizing her situation, she began to shriek and pull at her handcuffs. She cursed at him and called him some of the nastiest names he'd heard, and he'd heard a lot.

Catching his breath, he unwrapped his jacket from his arm and moved it to his upper arm, where he wrapped it tightly around his injury to slow the bleeding.

Rhonda continued to fight but was tiring with the effort. "You think this is over?" she sneered. "You're not going anywhere."

He checked his watch and was shocked to see that only ten minutes had passed since the last time he'd looked at it. Gathering his strength, he got to his knees. "Neither are you." Wincing, he slowly stood.

"Your partner's probably already dead. And you'll be next. You think Rook's just going to let you walk out of here?"

"Supposedly, I'm now part of the team." Daniels guessed Rook had no intention of bringing him or Rem on board. He thought of his partner. "But I plan to find out." He headed for the door. "You sit tight. I'll be back."

"You son-of-a-bitch," she screamed. "Let me out of these cuffs." She pulled at them, and they clanged against the radiator. "If Monk finds you, he'll kill you."

"I thought Rook was going to kill me first." He rubbed his sore right thigh where she'd kicked him.

She pulled at the pipe of the radiator. "If I get out of here, I'm going to slice you to shreds."

He thought of the knife, walked back over, and picked it up. "No. You won't." He closed the switchblade and put it in his pocket. Holding his arm and favoring his sore leg, he returned to the door. "Try and relax. It'll go easier on your wrists."

She screamed and called him another ugly name. Ignoring her, he opened the door and walked out.

· · • • • • • • · ·

Sitting on the floor and trying to gather the strength to stand, Rem leaned back against the wall. Tempted to lie down, he remained upright because he didn't trust he'd be able to get up again. His back and side ached, his head and neck throbbed, his hand and nose were bleeding, and his eye was swelling fast, but he was alive. He thought of Daniels. Who and what was he facing? That thought got him moving, and he struggled to stand when the door across the room where Daniels had disappeared opened.

For a split second, Rem braced. If it was the killer, Rem didn't have the energy to win another battle, but when he saw his partner, he let out a moan of relief and sank back against the wall.

Seeing Rem, Daniels' eyes widened. "Rem? Oh, my God." He headed over and stopped when he saw Croft's body lying beside the sofa. He paused, leaned over and pressed his fingers against Croft's neck. After a pause, he relaxed. "Thank God." He turned and went to Rem and squatted beside him. "You scared me to death. I thought you were dead."

Rem held his side. "I may look it, but I'm still here."

Eyeing Rem, Daniels' look of concern returned. "Where'd he get you? Are you shot?"

Rem shook his head. "Not my blood. It's his."

Daniels blew out a relieved breath.

Rem studied his partner and frowned. "What the hell happened to you? Did you fight a bear?"

"I might as well have." Daniels grimaced and rubbed his arm, which had his jacket wrapped around it. "Rhonda's cuffed to an old radiator in the library. If you listen, you can hear her screaming."

Rem focused and heard faint shrieks from the direction of the hall. "She is pissed, isn't she?"

"Very."

Rem noted the blood dripping from Daniels' arm. "You're bleeding. A lot."

Daniels tightened the jacket around his injury and winced. "She got me with a knife. The pressure is helping, but a doctor would be a good idea. What about you?"

Rem clutched his aching ribs. "Pretty sure I have a busted rib or two. I sliced my hand, and my head took a hit."

"Your nose doesn't look too great, either."

Rem smirked. "Have you seen your face? What'd she do? Drag her fingernails down your skin?"

Daniels touched his cheek. "Something like that." He checked Rem's bloody palm. "That's pretty deep."

"I'll live. Like you, I just need a doctor."

He grabbed Rem's arm. "Can you stand?"

Rem held his breath, grabbed onto Daniels' arm, and, cursing, got to his feet. He held on to his partner until he got his balance. "We need our guns."

Daniels nodded. "Stay here. Hang on to the wall."

"I'm all right. Now that I'm up." Rem stayed where he was while Daniels returned to Rook's office and tried to open the door, but it was locked.

"Damn it." He turned the knob again, but it didn't open.

Rem leaned his shoulder against the wall. "On the kitchen floor. Croft's gun."

Holding his arm, Daniels went into the kitchen. Pausing, he picked up the black-haired doll and held it up. "Nice resemblance."

"I don't think she captured my good side."

He dropped the doll, leaned over, and picked up the gun. He checked the clip, slid it back in, and started checking drawers.

"You hungry?" Rem gasped when his ribs pulled. "We can get a taco and a beer later."

"One sec." Daniels stopped and pulled out a cloth napkin from a drawer. He returned to Rem and held out the gun. "Here. Take this." Rem took the gun with his good hand, and Daniels tied the napkin around Rem's bleeding palm and tightened it. "That should hold you until we can call for help."

"Thanks." Rem slid the gun into his waistband. "Although maybe you should take the gun."

Daniels reached into his pocket and pulled out a switchblade. He flicked the blade open. "I've got Rhonda's weapon of choice."

Rem arched his brow. "Lucky you."

"Nobody's lucky until we get the hell out of here. I think our black bird membership has been revoked. Rhonda told me Rook won't just let us leave. And she doesn't strike me as a liar."

"So much for the champagne." Rem held onto the wall so he wouldn't fall over. "Supposedly, Rook's catching a flight out of town. He went upstairs."

"Let's hope he stays there." Daniels hooked his good arm around Rem's good side. "C'mon, partner. Let's get out of here."

Rem pulled the gun from his waistband but had to hold it with his left hand. They walked across the living area, passed Croft, and were about to enter the kitchen when a familiar odor drifted into the room. Rem grimaced. "You smell that?"

Daniels stopped. His face scrunched. "It's impossible not to."

"It's the same stench from the ceremony. Only worse."

"Let's go." Daniels helped Rem through the kitchen, but Rem didn't miss the blood still dripping from Daniels' jacket.

"Hurry." Rem's eyes watered, and he held his breath.

Daniels coughed, and together they made it out of the kitchen, walked back into the front entry and to the cabinet where Croft had put their phones. The smell was much worse up front, though, and Rem gagged. His vision swam, and he had no choice but to breathe.

Daniels fell against the wall, coughing harder.

Rem reached for the cabinet drawer, but his knees buckled, and he went to the floor. He started coughing as hard as Daniels and couldn't catch his breath. "Daniels." He could barely utter the word.

Daniels leaned against the wall, rubbing his eyes. Weaving, he slowly slid down the wall until he sat on the floor. "Rem." He sputtered. "I can't... breathe."

Rem struggled to get air, but his lungs protested. Dizzy, he fell sideways onto the floor. Pain shot through his midsection, and he curled into a fetal position. He could barely see through his burning eyes and blurry vision. Gasping, he struggled to get up and move, but another wave of dizziness overwhelmed him. His body failing, he closed his eyes and shivered when a faint cackle echoed against the walls. It was the last thing he heard before he closed his eyes and lost consciousness.

Chapter Thirty-Three

MONK SQUATTED LOW IN the trees, watching the back of the cabin. After seeing the lights go out in Lozano's windows, he'd left his vehicle, and staying in the trees, he'd walked up behind the cabins and stopped behind Lozano's. He'd waited there and watched to ensure it remained quiet, and no one got up to get a glass of water or use the bathroom.

Once enough time had passed, he crept slowly to the back door. Thankfully, the moon was up, which allowed enough light for him to see without using a flashlight. This would be the critical part–getting into the house without waking anyone. He slowly inched the screen door open, grateful it didn't squeak. Once he had it wide enough to move through it, he pulled out his tools to pick the lock. Picking locks was a skill he'd honed over the years, and he found he enjoyed the challenge. He used to test himself to see how fast he could pick a lock, and after sliding the tools into the knob with his gloved hands and manipulating the tools by feel, he smiled when the knob turned. Pleased his skills were still intact, he returned the tools to his pocket and slowly eased the door open. He stopped when it squeaked and waited again. When he still didn't hear anything, he pushed the door open wider until he could squeeze through it.

Not wanting it to squeak again, he didn't shut it. Seeing he was in the kitchen, he pulled his weapon from its holster, removed the suppressor from his pocket, and screwed it onto the muzzle of his gun. Standing in the kitchen, he took a second to get his bearings. He took a slow breath, closed his eyes and relaxed his body. Listening to the sounds of the cabin, he opened up to his surroundings. It was something Margaret had taught him, and he'd found it helped in tense situations.

Once he felt centered, he tiptoed through the kitchen and passed a small dining table with four chairs. He peered around the corner and saw the living area with a couch, TV, a loveseat, and a coffee table.

He stepped up to the couch and went still, listening again for any noise. From where he stood, he saw a door to a bathroom in between two other doors, which had to be the bedrooms. He moved closer to look. The bedroom door to his left was partially open, and moving up to it, he heard soft breathing.

Staying still, he made another effort to relax and center himself. Satisfied he was still in the clear, and no one was awake, he peered into the bedroom. It was dark, but his eyes had adjusted, and dim moonlight brightened the windows despite the closed blinds.

Seeing a person in the bed covered by a blanket and long hair splayed against a pillow, he smiled. Quietly pushing the door open, he entered the bedroom, approached the bedside, and aimed his weapon.

· · • • • • • · · ·

Sweltering heat assailed Daniels, and he tried to move, but his limbs would not comply. Everything felt heavy, especially his eyelids, and the migraine he'd been fending off bloomed. He thought he was conscious, but everything spun, and he heard and smelled strange things. In his mind, he saw Marjorie smiling and laughing and then shrieking and running from him. He chased her but couldn't catch her. Then he heard a baby wail. His gut churned, and he turned to see a baby in a pink bassinet. He approached, certain it was his daughter, but when he got closer, the bassinet began to burn. He screamed, and just before touching it, it faded and disappeared. Desperate, he searched for Marjorie, believing if he found her, he would be okay. Sweat ran into his eyes, and he couldn't see anything.

He heard Rem's voice and swiveled, eager to find his partner in the chaos, but a dense fog rolled in from nowhere, and Rem's voice and presence faded.

Confused, Daniels walked through the fog, shouting for Rem and Marjorie, but neither responded.

· · • • • • • • • · ·

Lying on the hard ground, Rem slowly became conscious. The first sign he was alive was feeling the beads of sweat trickling down his skin. Not knowing where he was, he tried to open his eyes, but they felt swollen shut. His back stung, and the memory of the glass digging into him while Croft strangled him helped revive him. He was aware enough to feel his injured palm burn and his head throb. Lying on his side, he moved his hands and felt what he thought was dirt and rocks beneath him. Confused, he tried to speak, but nothing emerged. Was he alone? Where was Daniels?

Telling himself to stay calm and not panic, his heart leapt into his throat when he felt a presence beside him. Hoping it was his partner, he reached out but felt nothing, but in his mind, a dense fog rolled in and surrounded him. A form took shape and emerged from the fog. Rem froze when he recognized his cousin, Cain.

Cain walked toward him and squatted beside Rem's head.

"Help me," croaked Rem. His throat was so dry, he could barely hear his own words.

"Sorry, cousin," said Cain, "but I can't."

"Cain..."

"You should have helped me first, but now it's too late." Cain stood. "Bye, Rem."

Rem reached for him. "Cain, wait..."

Cain ignored him and walked into the fog.

· · • • • • • • • · ·

Monk tightened his finger on the trigger when light suddenly brightened the room. Surprised, he squinted and felt something hard press against the back of his head. A male voice spoke. "Drop it."

The form in the bed turned. The covers fell back, but the hair on the pillow remained. Monk stood in shock when Mason Redstone sat up, pulled his own weapon, and aimed it at Monk. His eyes sparkled with animosity. "I'd listen if I were you."

Monk eyed the long-haired wig on the pillow and realized he'd been played. Mikey and Lozano weren't in the cabin, but Redstone, and Monk guessed Redstone's partner, Trick Monroe, were.

The pressure on the back of his head increased. "I said drop it, or I'll part your head in two."

Monk lowered his weapon, and Redstone got out of the bed.

"I think there's been a misunderstanding, gentlemen," said Monk, thinking fast.

Redstone took Monk's gun, and the man behind pulled him by his shirt and shoved him back first against the wall. Seeing the tall man with the cowboy hat and annoying smirk, Monk confirmed it was Redstone's partner. "Did you hear that, Red?" asked Trick. "Detective Monk here says we've made a mistake."

Redstone held his weapon on Monk. "You came here to kill my sister."

Monk raised his hands. "I came here to save her."

"Then we apologize." Trick turned Monk around to face the wall. "Assume the position." He pushed Monk forward. Monk placed his palms against the wall, and Trick kicked Monk's leg out.

While Mason kept his gun on Monk, Trick searched him. "He's clean." Trick grabbed one of Monk's wrists and pulled it behind him. "We're taking you to the authorities, Detective Monk."

Monk cursed. "You two have no idea what you're doing."

Trick cuffed Monk's wrists behind him. "Then enlighten us." Trick roughly turned Monk back around and shoved him back against the wall.

Redstone lowered his gun. "We're listening."

Monk straightened. "I have connections. Serious ones. They'll protect me. That's why I'm here. I was told Mikey's life was in danger. The killer, who branded those men, was coming after her. I know what happened to Manetti, and I didn't want to be next. That's why I didn't come forward." He pulled on his cuffs. "You two uncuff me, and I'll come in and explain everything." His mind raced, and he thought of Rhonda. "I even know where the killer is. Right now. I can give her to you."

Redstone walked up to him. "What do you think of that, Trick? We've got ourselves a real-life hero."

Trick snickered. "Maybe they'll give us a medal, Red, for rescuing him."

"Let's call Lozano." Redstone pulled out his phone. "See what he thinks." He hit a button.

"Lozano's okay?" asked Monk. "What a relief."

Redstone stared with a flat expression and put it on speaker. It rang, and a man answered.

"Captain Lozano?" said Mason. "We got him. You two okay?"

"Mikey and I are fine," said Lozano with an edge to his voice. "Don't let that snake slither away."

"He's not slithering anywhere," said Trick.

"We'll be right there." Lozano hung up.

Monk guessed what had happened. Lozano and Mikey had arrived at the cabin, closed all the blinds, and turned on the lights. Then they'd snuck out the back and gone to another nearby cabin, which they'd kept dark. Unbeknownst to Monk, Monroe and Redstone had snuck in and taken their places, pretending to be Mikey and Lozano. "Pretty smart," said Monk. "Doing the switcheroo."

"Men like you get arrogant," Trick adjusted his hat, "and easy to fool."

"What comes up must come down," said Redstone. "And we were ready to catch you."

"Move." Trick grabbed Monk by the shoulder and shoved him into the living area.

"You'll find out soon enough that you have the wrong man," said Monk. "You've got nothing."

Redstone walked up to him. "That might work with one of your lackey detectives, but we're former Texas Rangers. We smell shit from a mile away."

"I smelled you the minute you walked into the woods." Trick shoved him toward the front door. "Move your ass."

Redstone opened the door and Trick, holding Monk's shoulder, pushed him outside onto the porch.

Lozano walked out of the trees, and Mikey ran up to Mason and hugged him. "Are you okay?" she asked.

"We're fine." Redstone held Mikey and spoke to Lozano. "Care to bring him in, Captain?"

"Love to." Lozano grabbed Monk by the arm. "Right this way, Detective." He pulled Monk down the steps and toward his car.

"Mind if I join you, Captain?" asked Trick. "I love when a corrupt officer is about to face the consequences of his actions. Gives me a thrill."

Lozano tossed Trick his car keys. "You can drive."

Monk's confidence faltered. "I told you. You're making a mistake."

Mikey stomped toward him. "I know what you did. You killed Vera. I saw it. Manetti knows it too. He spoke to Lola, the woman you assaulted. She can identify you. We know you're Winnie, Margaret's accomplice. You tried to kill Rem and Daniels."

Monk broke free from Lozano's grasp. "Prove it," he yelled.

Mikey yelled back. "I saw Rhonda. I can identify her. She shot Manetti, and when we find her, you'll never smell freedom again."

Trick and Lozano grabbed him, but Monk's control snapped. "Not unless she kills you first, you bitch."

Redstone walked up to him and slugged him in his face.

Monk's head rocked back, and blood spewed from his nose.

"Get him out of here," yelled Redstone.

Trick roughly yanked Monk toward Lozano's car. "You should learn to stop when you're ahead, Monk."

Monk spat blood from his mouth and looked back. "You want to know where Rhonda is?" he shouted. "I'll tell you. She's killing your precious Daniels and Remalla."

Mikey's eyes widened.

"You may have me, but you'll never have them." He grunted as Trick shoved him hard into the side of the car. "And if the Raven gets a hold of them, dead or alive…" Lozano opened the door. "You'll never have them again." He sneered with satisfaction as Lozano told him to shut up and pushed him into the back seat.

Chapter Thirty-Four

REM MOVED HIS HEAD, feeling the grit of whatever he was lying on against his cheek. Everything still swirled, and he didn't know where he was. He sensed he wasn't alone, though, but opening his eyes required more strength than he could muster. His visions of Cain in the fog continued, only now Jennie and Mikey would occasionally join him. Each time, he begged for their help, but they would blame him for what he'd done to them and leave.

He thought of Daniels but didn't know where to find his partner. He'd called for him several times, convinced he had to be in the fog, but had not received an answer. After a brief surge of hope when he'd heard a moan, he'd tried to move, but the pain in his ribs felt like a knife in his side, and he'd given up from exhaustion. Emotionally spent and fighting to stay focused, he forced himself to stay aware. This had to be temporary. Wherever he was, it couldn't last forever.

Time passed—he didn't know how much—when the fog lifted. His head, which still hurt, cleared too, and his senses became more acute. He could hear footsteps, the sound of something boiling, and faint chanting. Coming awake, he felt immense relief when he realized his visions of Cain, Jennie and Mikey had only been dreams. The heat, though, had not been a dream. He was either burning up with fever or he'd been taken to a tropical jungle and left in the sun. His throat was so dry it felt like he'd swallowed dust.

His limbs feeling like oak trees, he cracked his eyelids open to slits. It was dark, but there were sparkling lights. His vision blurred, and his head pounded, so he closed them again.

Telling himself to stay calm, he guessed he'd been drugged because his body felt like dead weight, and he couldn't focus on one thing. All he could remember was that he'd killed Croft, Daniels had showed, and it was a blank after that. Had they made it out of Rook's house? Had the police been called? And where was Daniels?

That last thought scared him. His partner had been injured and bleeding. Was he still alive?

That question roused him enough to make a slight moan. Still lying on his side, he attempted again to move and slightly raised his head.

Footsteps made him still, though, and he went limp. Despite the heat, his blood ran cold when he sensed a presence looming over him. He heard his name whispered in a raspy voice, and someone touched his head.

He did his best to lie still as what felt like a hand slid down his hair. It lifted and stroked his head again. He didn't move when he felt a tug on his head, then the rustle of clothes as if the presence walked away. The chanting grew louder.

The activity motivated him, and he cracked his eyelids and kept them open, determined to find Daniels and get to safety. Waiting for his vision to clear, he blinked several times, and finally the blurring stopped, and his vision sharpened. A dark room came into view. The sparkling lights became lit candles. They were everywhere and provided the only illumination except for a brighter light in front of him. He blinked again and realized it was a small fire. *No wonder I'm hot*, he thought to himself. Above the fire, on a small stand, was a pot. Steam rose from it.

He moved again. A sharp lance of pain rocketed through his chest, and he tried not to gasp. He didn't want to attract the attention of whoever had touched him.

Trying to be quiet, he moved his hand over the floor and saw a fine white dust swirl in the air. Some of it was gritty, and he could feel sharp shards under his skin. Where the hell was he?

He heard a moan and almost lifted his head when the familiar shuffling returned. Staying still, he kept his eyes cracked and saw movement. A figure blocked out some of the light from the candles. It stopped and squatted. He heard a whisper and opened his eyes wider. Focusing, he saw Daniels lying on the opposite side of the fire. A woman crouched beside him. Rem forced himself not to react when he saw her, but he couldn't look away. She was old, but how old was hard to tell. Her skin was pale and wrinkled, with almost a translucent quality. Her eyes were piercing black, and she had long, silver-white hair woven in intricate braids, interlaced with dark feathers and what looked like small bones.

She wore a flowing black robe adorned with strange symbols. Around her neck hung a pendant with a large, black gemstone that seemed to absorb light rather than reflect it. Long fingernails extended from her bony fingers, which were laden with rings of tarnished silver and blackened gold, each one bearing symbols like the ones on her robe. Her presence exuded an aura of power and dread.

She leaned close to Daniels, whispered into his ear, and ran her gnarled hand down the back of his head.

Daniels moved his head and moaned again.

Rem fought the urge to yell at his partner to stay still. The woman ran her hand down his partner's hair again and stopped. She took a piece of his hair in her hand and snipped it off. Rem lowered his lids to slits but continued to watch her as she stepped past Daniels, and added the snippet of hair into the pot of boiling liquid. Then she stepped away from both of them.

Rem's memories flooded back. He recalled the vile stench that had over-whelmed him and Daniels before leaving Rook's house. Looking around, his fear ramped up when he realized he and Daniels were no longer at Rook's. They were at the guest house. He and Daniels were with the Raven.

· · · · · · · · · ·

Daniels was sure his head had been split in two. His visions of Marjorie, J.P., his unborn child, Rem, and his sister Erin had made him sick to his stomach. They'd yell for his help, but he'd failed to save them each time, and he'd watched in horror as they screamed his name and disappeared into the fog.

As the fog slowly faded, though, his awareness improved, and he sensed his surroundings. Relief flooded through him when he understood his visions were just that—visions, and nothing more. Trying to rouse himself, he faltered when everything hurt. His head felt like it was about to explode, and his arm throbbed. His alertness improving, he felt the wetness of his shirt. He wondered how much blood he'd lost and how much longer he could hold out. All he could manage was a moan, but that encouraged him. If he could moan, he could breathe, and that was a start.

Rem popped into his head, and he caught his breath. Thinking of his partner got his brain back on the job. Where was Rem? He felt the hard ground beneath him, but he wasn't at Rook's. The smells, sounds, and feel of his surroundings were different. He heard footsteps, heard his name whispered, and felt someone stroke his head. Even though he was hot, icy chills ran through him. Whoever was with him made his heart pound and skin prickle.

His instincts told him to stay still, and he didn't move. He wanted to open his eyes, but his head hurt so badly, he was almost frightened to do it. But when he sensed the presence behind him move away, he took the risk and opened them slightly. Thankfully, it was dark, and the minimal light didn't blind him. It took him a second to get his bearings, but when he did, it shocked him to see that he was lying in front of a fire in a candlelit room, and Rem was lying on the other side of the fire. His eyes were closed, or at least they appeared to be.

He heard movement and closed his eyes again. A woman started to chant, and he felt her presence again. He took another risk, peeked again, and saw her standing over a steaming pot above the fire, adding something to it and stirring it. He could see only her profile, but that was enough. Her mere presence terrified him, and he grasped that he and Rem were in the guest house with the Raven.

Staying still, he waited until she stepped away again, and it went quiet. After several seconds passed, he widened his eyes and looked across at his partner. He saw Rem staring back with glassy eyes through the fire. He looked just as confused and scared as Daniels felt.

Daniels' mind raced with what to do. They were both injured, likely drugged, and being held by a petrifying woman who practiced bizarre and apparently occult rituals. What was their next move? How did they get out of there?

Before he could think the next thought, he heard a loud bang and a shout. Someone yelled, and a flashlight pierced the darkness. The light made him wince, and he felt a hand on his shoulder. Someone pulled him roughly up, and he gasped in pain. He saw Rem grabbed too, and yanked up into a sitting position, and then they were both hauled out of wherever they were. Before leaving, he saw a large circle drawn on the floor. The fire was in the center, and white dust and rocks covered the ground. He and Rem had been lying inside the circle before being abruptly yanked away from it.

They were dragged outside, down a wooden porch, and roughly dumped on the ground. Rem fell to his knees, groaned and held his chest, and Daniels tried not to throw up when his migraine flared and his arm pulsed with pain. Trying to catch his breath and figure out what was going on, he grimaced and found the strength to look up.

Shock rippled through him when he recognized Sammy Caruso.

· · • • • • • • · ·

Clutching his ribs, Rem looked to see who had pulled him and Daniels out of the house. It was dark, but the moon was up, and he saw two men holding flashlights. Between them stood Sammy Caruso.

If he'd had the strength, he would have sat up, but he could barely draw a breath without wanting to curse in pain.

Daniels gaped at Caruso, but his face looked pale, and his eyes were dull. He dropped his head and held it, and Rem recognized the signs. His partner was in the middle of a doozy, what Rem called one of Daniels' bad migraines. Between that and his partner's wounded arm, Rem knew Daniels needed a hospital. He summoned the energy to speak. "What are you doing here?" he croaked. He wished he could get a drink of water.

Caruso loomed over him. "Apparently, I'm saving your ass, but don't get your hopes up. If you didn't have something I want, I'd leave your asses right where I found them."

Daniels lifted his head and opened his eyes. "How'd you locate us?"

Caruso snorted. "I did my homework. You think I'm going to leave the safety of my grandkid to you two clowns? You guys have been pulling my chain since day one, and I am officially done."

Rem cleared his throat. "Caruso, listen—"

One of Caruso's goons kicked Rem in his side. "Shut up."

Blinded with pain, Rem partially succeeded in biting back a scream and fell to his side. He curled up to protect his aching ribs.

"No," said Caruso. "You listen, asshole. I figured out who your little friend is that you two met in that crappy bar. He led me to Damien Rook. I did a little digging on Rook and learned he's almost as dirty as I am. But I know how to deal with people like that. I got myself a little mole. His girlfriend, Delaina. I offered her a pretty penny to keep me informed, and if anything important happened, especially if it pertained to Jerry Lee, she needed to call me, which she did."

Caruso stepped over to Daniels. "According to sweet Delaina, Rook seems to think Jerry Lee is alive and you know where he is, although you insisted you'd killed him." He grabbed Daniels' injured arm, and Daniels sucked in a breath. Caruso leaned over and got in Daniels' face. "You better pray it's the former."

He let go of Daniels' arm, and Daniels doubled over with another gasp.

Rem forced himself to uncurl and tried to get up as another man, holding a flashlight, ran out of the woods toward the group.

"Boss," he said, running up. "There are flashlights up at the house. They're searching for these two. It won't be long before they head this way."

Caruso scoffed. "This place?" He looked around. "This is like a tick on a sheepdog's ass. No one's finding it anytime soon." He stuck out a thumb. "Get back there and keep watching."

The man nodded and ran back into the woods.

Caruso returned his attention to Rem and Daniels. "Now, which one of you is going to tell me where my grandson is?" He nodded at one of his men.

The man came over to Rem, grabbed him by his hair, and yanked him up. Rem yelped and tried to protect his ribs. He stilled when he felt the muzzle of a gun against his head.

"How about a fun game of Russian roulette?" said Caruso.

Rem didn't move.

"Patricia," said Daniels quickly. "He's with Patricia."

Caruso grabbed Daniels by his hair and pulled his head back. "My daughter?" sneered Caruso. "Don't lie to me, Detective. Or Melly over there is going to pull the trigger."

Daniels winced. "I'm not lying. We pretended to kill Jerry Lee to protect him from Rook. We hid him with his mother. He's been staying with her."

"How stupid do you think I am?" yelled Caruso. "My daughter hasn't told me shit."

"Are you surprised?" Rem tried not to think about the gun aimed at him. "We told her not to tell anyone and continue acting as a distraught mom worried about her missing kid. Because of the press, she was already keeping the blinds closed. Jerry stays inside, and no one knows he's there."

"It's called hiding in plain sight," said Daniels. "And it worked."

Caruso stared at Daniels with narrowed eyes. "Hardy." He held out his hand. "Give me my phone."

The second goon pulled a cell from his jacket and handed it to Caruso. Caruso let go of Daniels' hair and dialed a number. "You better pray she answers." He put the phone to his ear and walked away.

Rem made eye contact with Daniels and, not knowing if they'd survive this, they held the look until they could hear Caruso talking. Rem tried to breathe and bit back a groan when his ribs pulled, but he was more worried about Daniels. He'd seen the blood dripping from his partner's arm and assumed he'd lost a lot. Knowing there were people searching at the main house, he wondered if he could yell loud enough to get their attention. Considering he couldn't take a breath, he doubted it.

Caruso raised his voice, and Rem caught enough bits of his conversation to realize he was talking to his daughter. He eyed Daniels again, willing him to hang in there. Daniels' eyelids drooped, though, and Rem's worry ratcheted up a notch. They had to get out of there.

Caruso hung up with a curse and walked back over. He eyed Melly and waved a finger. Melly lowered his weapon and stepped back from Rem.

Rem released a relieved exhale and winced in pain.

Caruso regarded them. "You two have more lives than ten cats."

Rem tried to stay upright. "We get them at a discount." His voice shook. "We know a guy."

Caruso chuckled. "Good thing, because you almost ran out of all of them tonight." He squatted beside them. "But you protected my Jerry Lee." He pointed. "And I won't forget that."

Rem wondered how mobsters could go from preparing to kill you to thanking you. "How about getting us some help?"

The third man, who'd been keeping watch, ran out of the woods again. "Those flashlights, boss. They're getting closer."

Caruso stood. "Looks like your help is coming." He eyed his men. "Hardy. Go get the car."

Hardy nodded and ran into the woods.

Daniels opened his eyes and looked at Caruso. "Rook will still come after Jerry Lee if he knows he's alive."

Caruso grinned. "Don't you know by now, Detective?" He chuckled. "I know how to handle problems, and Rook won't be bothering you, or my Jerry, anymore."

Rem widened his eyes. "What did you do?"

Caruso gave his phone to Melly. "The less you know, the better." He eyed his men. "Let's get out of here."

"Wait," said Daniels, breathless. "What about the woman?"

Caruso paused and regarded Melly, who shrugged. "What woman?" asked Caruso.

"The one in the house," said Rem. "She was with us when you busted in."

"No one was in there except you two," said Melly.

"She was old," said Rem. "Had long silver hair in braids."

"I think you were seeing things, Detective. Good drugs will do that." Caruso turned away. "Have a nice night. And no hard feelings, right, fellas?" He chuckled again and walked into the woods with his men.

Grateful to be alive, Rem scooted carefully over to Daniels, who'd hunched over and was holding his head. "Hey. You okay?"

"My head." Daniels clenched his eyes shut.

"I know. How's your arm?" Rem eyed the blood dripping from his partner's injury.

"Hurts less than my head." Daniels groaned and rolled to his good side.

Rem guided Daniels' head to rest on his leg. "Help's coming, buddy. Just hold on." He eyed the woods, hoping to see flashlights.

Daniels curled up. "You okay?"

Rem would have laughed, but it hurt too much. "Considering we had to fight for our lives, got drugged and left with the Raven, and were almost murdered by Sammy Caruso, I'd say I'm fine." He listened for anyone yelling his or Daniels' name. "Our night definitely did not go according to plan."

Daniels clutched his temples. "I gave us a fifty-fifty chance. At best." He whispered. "Just didn't want to tell you."

Rem eyed his bleeding, dirty palm. The napkin was gone, and his hand was covered in white dust. "Like Han Solo says, 'never tell me the odds.'" His vision briefly swam again, and he blinked until it righted itself. "I'll be honest, though. I thought our odds were slim, too." He put his hand on Daniels' shoulder, careful not to touch his injury. "Looks like we beat 'em, though. Again."

"Yeah." Daniels grimaced and moaned again.

"Stay with me." He rubbed Daniels' shoulder.

Daniels uttered another whisper. "Not going anywhere. You can't survive without me."

Rem was relieved his partner's humor was still intact. "And vice versa."

Daniels paused. "Yeah."

Rem heard a shout and saw a flashlight bobbing in the trees. "Over here," he tried to yell. He gritted his teeth and held his side. "They see us."

"Hang in there, partner." Daniels winced. "I got you."

Rem smiled. "I know you do." He managed another meager yell when the voices became louder, the light grew larger, and two officers ran out of the woods.

"Over here," one of them yelled. "We found them."

Rem almost collapsed in relief. "We made it, buddy. They're here."

Daniels, his face pinched and his skin paler than before, clutched Rem's leg. "Knew it all along."

Even though it hurt, Rem chuckled.

Chapter Thirty-Five

"AND WE'RE BACK," SAID the orderly.

Sitting in a wheelchair, Daniels opened his weary eyes and saw the door to his hospital room. The orderly opened it and pushed Daniels inside.

Propped up on some pillows, Rem was lying in the bed across the room. He opened his eyes at Daniels' return. "There you are. I wondered if you'd made your escape to Bolivia."

The orderly wheeled Daniels to the other bed and stopped the wheelchair beside it. "All the flights were booked." Daniels groaned as he stood from the wheelchair and got into bed. His arm was in a sling and his head still throbbed, but not with the intensity of the previous night. The orderly adjusted the pillows and covers and left with the wheelchair.

"Still got all your brains?" asked Rem.

Daniels settled back into the pillows with a sigh. "Nobody seemed alarmed while they did the test, so I think so."

"How's your head?"

"Better. Whatever they gave me helped."

"Good."

Daniels thought back over their long night. Following their discovery, an ambulance sped them to the hospital while police searched Rook's house. Marjorie, Mikey, Erin, Lexie, and Mason were all waiting for them at the ER. Lozano and Trick were at the police station, handing Monk over to the authorities. Daniels and Rem had been relieved to hear that the plan to capture Monk had worked, and Mikey was safe.

He couldn't remember much after that, other than Marjorie joining him in the ER, and a vague recollection of his arm being cleaned and stitched. The doctors had done tests, and despite knowing he'd been drugged, the doctor eventually gave Daniels something for his migraine, and he'd been out of it since. He'd woken up briefly to see Marjorie at his side, who told him he was sharing a room with Rem, who had three broken ribs, a mild concussion, a stitched palm, and, like Daniels, numerous cuts and bruises. Doctors had kept them both overnight for observation.

Daniels had fallen back to sleep after insisting Marjorie go home and didn't wake again until the orderly had arrived to take him for his test.

Daniels looked for a clock. "What time is it?"

"Almost ten o'clock," said Rem. "You get some sleep?"

"I did. You?"

Rem shifted in his bed and grimaced. "Not as much as I would have liked."

Daniels could imagine. He'd suffered through a few rib injuries, and they were miserable. "Only hurts when you breathe?"

"It's way worse than when I broke my ribs in Merrimac."

"You were in plenty of pain." Daniels recalled their eventful trip to Merrimac, where Rem's Aunt Genevieve lived. "And you only broke two ribs back then, not three."

"Lucky me." Rem rested his head back. "I think they plan to spring us today, assuming that test of yours is negative."

"I can't wait to get back in my own bed."

"Yeah."

Daniels heard the subdued tone in Rem's voice. "Did you see Mikey?" He couldn't recall if she'd joined Rem in the ER. When they'd arrived, Rem had been sent in one direction, and Daniels in the other.

"I saw her. She was there when they brought me back and waited while they did my tests. She and Marjorie were keeping everyone apprised of our conditions."

"How long did she stay?"

"Until they got me up here and settled. I was exhausted and in pain, though. Whatever they gave me didn't help much. Apparently, you're the one who got the good stuff."

"That's because I cried. Next time, turn on the waterworks."

"Good tip."

"Did you two have time to talk?"

"No. I told her to go home, meaning our home, but she said she'd be at Mason's and would be back to pick me up when they discharged me."

"That's understandable. After what she went through, I doubt she'd want to be alone."

"I get that," said Rem. "But it was more about the tone she used."

"I wouldn't read too much into it. It was a long night for all of us."

Rem sighed. "Maybe."

Daniels shifted his head to look at his partner. "Have you heard anything about Monk? Or Rook? Or anything that happened after they found us?" Now that he was feeling better, he needed an update.

"I only know what Mikey told me. She said Manetti was hanging in there, and that Mason's plan worked, and he and Trick caught Monk in the act. He was arrested last night." He moved in the bed and grimaced again. "I gave a statement to Mel and Garcia and told them what I could, but that's all I know."

Protecting his arm, Daniels pushed himself up on his pillow. "You told them everything?"

"As far as my muddled brain can remember, yes. I didn't see the point in hiding anymore. Plus, I was too tired to care. If Rook escaped and managed to take all his society secrets with him, there's nothing we can do. And I was tired of lying."

Daniels recalled fighting Rhonda and seeing Croft's dead body. "You mentioned Croft?"

"I did. Told them what happened. They'd likely already found his body, and it won't be hard to link his death to me. I told them about Rhonda too."

"Did they find her?"

Rem shrugged. "I have no idea. I'm not sure how much Mel and Garcia knew at that point. They were tight-lipped."

Daniels' concern grew. Had Rhonda been captured? Or had she escaped? Was Rook alive and accusing Rem and Daniels of breaking into his home and murdering Croft? Where was Sammy Caruso? "Hell," he said. "Maybe I shouldn't get too excited about going home. We could be arrested."

"I've been trying not to think about that."

There was a soft knock. The door opened, and Lozano poked his head in. "You two up for a visitor?"

"Hey, Cap," said Rem.

"C'mon in," said Daniels.

Lozano entered. "Glad to see you're both okay. You gave us a scare last night." He pulled a chair over to sit between them. "When we didn't hear from you...well, I feared the worst." He sat on the chair. "As usual, though, you made it through."

Daniels had a sudden vision of the Raven and shivered.

"Our luck is still holding," said Rem. "How's Manetti?"

"Still in CCU," said Lozano. "He's critical but stable. Doctors are guarded but optimistic."

"Thank God," said Daniels.

"That's great news," said Rem. "I don't suppose you have any updates about us? Daniels and I are hoping we don't spend tonight in jail."

Daniels held his breath and waited.

Lozano raised the side of his lip. "I wouldn't worry about that. You two are likely to be commended."

Rem held his side. "What do you mean?"

"Mel and Garcia have been up all night. They just told me the latest. Officers have been combing through Rook's house and office. It's a treasure trove of evidence. Rhonda's in custody, along with Monk, and they're both turning on each other. They found the brand with the star, the gun that killed Cain and Bertrand, which also appears to be the weapon that killed Lexie Logan's neighbor, and evidence of me being set up. Croft's body was taken from the scene, but they've already identified him as a former detective with a dubious history wanted for assault." He pulled his jacket off.

Daniels raised his head. "Rook. Where's Rook?"

Lozano's face fell. "Dead. They found his body in his private airplane hangar with a bullet in his head. Delaina, his girlfriend, was found locked in a bathroom."

Rem's mouth fell open. "Rook's dead?"

Lozano nodded. "Delaina told police two masked men came in, locked her up, and she heard a shot."

"I don't believe it." Daniels recalled Caruso telling them about Delaina's involvement and assuring them that Rook would be dealt with.

"Not only that," said Lozano, "but they've found documentation of Rook's black bird society, and Lexie provided the contents of a box presumably owned by Marvin Ackerman, who was a member of the society, and who, as I recall, blew himself up." He frowned at them. "Did you two know about this box?"

Daniels hesitated. "Maybe."

Lozano grunted. "Logan also provided a list of member names that came with the box. Did you two know about that?"

Rem fiddled with the edge of a bedsheet. "Maybe."

"They also found documentation of your debts being paid, Daniels. And the gun they found at Rook's? That was used to kill Cain and Arnold Bertrand? It was registered in your deceased father's name, Remalla." Lozano's voice turned gruff. "Did you know about *that*?"

Rem shrugged. "Kinda, sorta."

Daniels pursed his lips.

"Let me guess," said Lozano. "Rook was framing you two?"

Daniels shared a look with Rem. "He was, Cap," said Daniels. "But we couldn't say anything. Considering the names on that list, we didn't know who to trust."

Lozano tossed his jacket over his legs. "You took a hell of a risk."

"We didn't have a choice," said Rem. "We had to clear your name, and ours, plus take down Rook's society."

"Speaking of that," said Lozano. "Based on what we're finding, you two have cracked a major conspiracy reaching into the upper echelons of our city and even state. The people on that list are scattering as we speak."

"I bet they are." Daniels sighed with immense relief that he'd be going home tonight.

"Plus, Jerry Lee Caruso has been found safe and credits you two for saving him. He'll do a lineup soon to see if he can ID Rhonda as Durning's killer.

Needless to say, the press is all over this," said Lozano. "Lexie had the major scoop, and her reporting is going national. Don't be surprised if the press calls."

"We'll start practicing our 'No comment,'" said Rem.

"Good," said Lozano, "but don't get your hopes too high. We won't be able to catch all the members. That list proves nothing. It's going to take months to go through all of Rook's files and connect anything nefarious to various followers. Some will fall, and others will only lose their reputations."

"All that matters is that the society is toppled and Rook's gone," said Rem.

Lozano pointed. "You two may be heroes now, but to members of the group you've taken down, you'll be enemies. Don't forget that."

"We'll add them to the list," said Daniels, "which just seems to get longer."

"Maybe we should frame it," said Rem. "Hang it on the wall and admire it."

Lozano arched his brow. "You do you, Remalla."

"Anything about Sammy Caruso?" asked Rem. "I told Mel and Garcia about how he found and threatened us."

"You sure about that?" asked Lozano. "Mel and Garcia informed me that, according to Caruso's business manager and his personal assistant, Caruso's been in Chicago. Hasn't left the city in months."

Rem made a snort. "They're all lying. Caruso's responsible for Rook's death."

"Are you surprised, though?" asked Daniels. "Caruso knows how to cover his ass." He thought of the threat Lozano hadn't mentioned. "What about the Raven?"

Rem straightened, sucked in a breath, and held his ribs. "Did you find her?"

Lozano shook his head. "There's no sign of this woman you call the Raven."

Daniels frowned. "What about the guest house where we were taken?"

"They searched it. It's creepy as hell. It's all rotted wood, broken windows, and peeling paint. I doubt anyone was living there. But the main room had a circle drawn on the floor, lots of used candles, and white dust and bones scattered around the room."

Daniels' skin crawled. "Did you say bones?"

"That's what was all over you two when they brought you in. Bone dust."

Rem rubbed his belly. "Hell."

"But there was no sign of any woman." Lozano eyed Rem. "Your elderly, silver-haired witch with black eyes and a dark robe doesn't seem to exist. And, so far, there's no mention of her in any of Rook's files."

"She exists," said Rem. "I saw her."

"Me too," said Daniels.

Lozano paused. "You two were drugged. Any chance you were hallucinating? About her and even Caruso?"

"No way," said Rem. "Caruso was there, and the Raven is as real and about as fun as one of Daniels' headaches."

"Worse." Daniels still felt the fear in the pit of his stomach when he'd woken up in the guest house. "She may have left, but she's not gone."

"Well," said Lozano. "They'll keep looking. Based on your description, Remalla, she shouldn't be hard to identify."

Rem ran his hand through his hair and pulled on a strand. He stared off as if remembering. "You won't find her."

"She may have some relation to Victor D'Mato," said Daniels. "Tell them to start there."

"I'll pass it on," said Lozano.

Hearing that, Daniels had to ask the obvious. "Are you back? What's happening with Elsa Crow?"

Lozano shifted in his chair. "I spoke to Chief Patterson on the way here. Based on what they've found at Rook's, Elsa Crow is out. That her father's name is on the list is enough to cast a cloud over her, whether or not it's deserved. Patterson says it will take a few days and some paperwork, but I'll likely be reinstated by the end of the week, if not sooner."

"That's great, Cap," said Rem with a smile. "I bet you can't wait to get back and especially to work with us again."

Lozano glared. "Based on what I'm hearing, you two went out on your own without communication with or consent from your superior. Plus, you kept critical information to yourselves, even when I was there." He pointed. "You pull that crap again, and you'll wish Elsa Crow was back."

Daniels sighed. "We hear you. And for what it's worth, we found no connection between Elsa and the black birds. As far as we know, she's clean."

"An internal investigation will have to decide that," said Lozano. "But Chogan Crow has a lot of explaining to do, especially when it comes to the permits he pushed through for that new development going in, which Rook Enterprises benefits from enormously."

"I sense a few lawsuits coming," said Rem.

"More than a few," said Lozano. "Rook would have been up a raging river without a life jacket if he'd lived."

Daniels rested his head against the pillow. "So what's next for us? I assume Mel and Garcia want to talk to me?"

"As soon as you're ready. In the meantime, both of you rest up. Has anyone mentioned you look like hell?"

Daniels had caught his reflection while waiting for his test. He'd seen his puffy face, and the red scratches on his face and neck. Rem had two black eyes, one of which was swollen, and a bruised neck and nose.

"It's not all bad," said Rem. "I told the nurse I battled a bad guy and won. She was impressed."

Daniels smirked. "Did you tell her about how brave you were with the Raven?"

Rem's face fell. "I left that part out."

"Probably wise."

Lozano stood. "Seems like you two are feeling better." He returned the chair to the corner. "I can't wait to listen to this again every day."

Rem pulled up his covers. "Admit it, Cap. You missed us."

"We certainly missed you," said Daniels.

Lozano went to the door. "Like I said, I can't wait to listen to you two again every day." He paused. "And I meant it."

Daniels smiled. "Welcome back, Cap."

"I'll get you a Taco del Fuego on the first day we're all together," said Rem. "We'll celebrate."

Lozano scowled. "You know I don't eat that crap, Remalla. Besides, I have a party to plan. You can bring all the tacos you want then."

Rem chuckled and winced. "I'll bring one, anyway. And one for Daniels, too. I'll eat what you two don't want."

Daniels rolled his eyes. "Of course you will."

Lozano smiled softly. "Take it easy. I'll get in touch after you're discharged."

"Okay, Cap. And thanks," said Daniels, feeling better than he had in days.

"You're welcome." Eyeing them both with a warm expression, Lozano opened the door and left.

Chapter Thirty-Six

REM FOLLOWED MIKEY INTO his house after she opened the door. Moving carefully, he dropped his bag from the hospital onto the floor, and stepped into his living room, hoping to sit on the couch provided he could do it without hurting his ribs.

After Lozano had left him and Daniels earlier at the hospital, Mel and Garcia had stopped by to take Daniels' statement. After they'd left, the doctor showed up and given his okay to discharge them, provided they made appointments to see their own doctors and got plenty of rest. Mikey and Marjorie arrived afterward to take them home.

While in the car with Mikey on the way back to his house, Rem had kept the conversation light. Mikey had been subdued, but had answered his questions and asked a few of her own, but had also kept it casual.

Walking into his living room, Rem debated what to say to start the heavier discussion when he saw a new recliner next to his couch. "What's that?"

Mikey tossed her keys onto the front table. "It's for you. I had it delivered just before you were discharged."

Not understanding, Rem frowned. "Is it my birthday?" He rubbed his temple. "How hard did I hit my head?"

Mikey smiled. "No. It's just that with your broken ribs, it's going to be hell getting in and out of bed. I thought this might help." She walked over to the chair and pushed a lever on the side. The chair reclined. She pulled the lever, and it rose almost to a vertical position.

Rem gaped. "That's perfect." He wondered if this was a peace offering from her but didn't ask. He went over to the chair and slid carefully into it. "You didn't have to do this. It must have been expensive." He hit the lever with his good hand, and the chair slowly lowered until he was sitting comfortably and leaning slightly back. He sighed when his ribs didn't pull.

"It wasn't too bad," said Mikey. "Trick knows a guy who knows a guy who sells recliners. This is an older floor model, so I got it at a discount."

Rem played with the lever until he found the perfect angle. "Thank you."

"You're welcome." She set her purse on the couch. "Can I get you something? You thirsty?"

Rem eyed her. "Not right now. Why don't you sit?"

She fiddled with her hands. "Rem, I—"

Sensing her discomfort, Rem raised the chair slightly. "Sit. We need to talk."

She stilled but then nodded and sat.

He debated where to start. "Everything's been going ninety miles an hour since I went to that damn birthday party at Rook's."

She rubbed the bandage on her arm but stayed quiet.

"I heard about how I behaved and what I said to you when I got home, and I'm so, so sorry."

She studied the floor.

"When Daniels and I were at the party, we took something. A pill. Whatever the hell it was, it messed with both of us. We'd been drinking too, so that didn't help. All I can remember after taking it is waking up in the bathtub upstairs and wondering how I got there and where you were."

She wouldn't look at him.

"Marjorie told me I'd kicked you out and said something terrible about you and Jennie and the upstairs closet."

She looked up with steely eyes. "You told me it would be better if I left so you wouldn't have to deal with the closet since you'd never wanted to clean it out in the first place."

Rem dropped his jaw. He hadn't heard that part. "Mikey, I never meant—"

"What kind of pill?"

He paused. "What?"

"What kind of pill did you take? What do you think it did to you?"

Unsure of how to answer, Rem sputtered. "I'm not sure. Daniels and I believe Rook concocted it with the Raven. We think it had something to do with purging your darkness in order to embrace your strengths, or something like that. Rook said something about us confronting our fears."

Her gaze hardened. "So, basically, it made you face what you couldn't face without it?"

He understood what she was thinking. "If you believe I was venting about what's been on my mind since you moved in, you're wrong."

"Am I? Because you seemed pretty certain that it would be a relief if I left."

Rem tried to think of a way to explain. "That's not what I was confronting."

"Then what was it?" she asked with an edge.

He kept his voice calm and spoke softly. "Mikey, that anger you saw had nothing to do with you. I may have used you to express it, but that's because you were there. If it had been Daniels, I would have been just as cruel. I was lashing out and hitting all the buttons I knew would hurt you the most. That pill exacerbated all my fury about Cain and how he died, what I went through with Margaret and Allison, and losing Jennie. It all came at me at once. With Daniels, that pill made him confront his guilt. For me, it was anger." He sighed with regret. "And unfortunately, you were the target."

She went back to staring at the floor.

"And I apologize for all of it. Please believe me when I say that none of it is true. I love you, and I want you to stay." He reached out to touch her hand, but she pulled away. Rem took a deep breath. "Mikey—"

She stood abruptly. "What am I supposed to do? Pretend I didn't see the hate in your eyes? That I can't recall your anger? And how you spoke to me?"

Rem fought to find the words that might console her. "Mikey, you know me better than anyone, next to Daniels. Do you honestly believe I meant any of that?"

She hesitated. "That's just it. I never thought it would be possible for you to ever treat me like that, but I saw it, and now I can't forget it."

"I know it's bad. And I know I have a lot of work to do to redeem myself. But I'll do whatever it takes. Just give me a chance to do that. Come home."

She shook her head and rubbed her arms. "I can't."

That surprised him. "Why not?"

Mikey stepped away. "Too much has happened."

Rem thought of what had occurred with her and Manetti. "Manetti isn't your fault. You know that, don't you?"

She tensed. "He took a bullet for me. He saved my life."

"He's a cop. It's what he's supposed to do. And when he recovers, you can thank him."

"If he recovers."

Rem sighed. "The doctors are optimistic. Manetti's a tough guy with a baby on the way. He's not going anywhere if he can help it."

She shook her head. "I should have taken that bullet. Not him."

Rem trembled at the thought. "Then you'd both be dead." He tried to sit up, but his ribs flared. He wished he could stand and take her in his arms. "You can't keep blaming yourself. It'll just fester until you need a shrink, a drink, or a pill."

Her face tightened. "Is that some sort of dig at Mason?"

"No, it wasn't, but he knows what I'm talking about. I'm sure he would tell you the same."

Her cheeks turned red, and she put her hands on her hips. "Are you telling me I need a shrink?"

"Between Manetti, Monk, your sister, and me, you've been through a lot." He hated including himself in that sentence. "It wouldn't be a bad idea. You know I've been to a couple. We could go together if you want."

"Why? So you can yell at me again?"

He shook his head, determined not to get impatient. "No. I will never do that to you again."

"Unless, of course, you take another pill."

"That won't happen. The case is over. Rook is dead, and his society is crumbling as we speak."

"Until the next case comes along."

That made him pause. "What are you saying?"

"I'm saying there's always another case. And another threat. And another reason for you to be mad."

"Mikey, I'm a cop. You know what I do, and my sordid history. And let's not forget, you've gotten into some serious scrapes yourself. You take plenty of risks." He raised his hand. "Hell. You went to see Margaret to get her to talk about Vera's killer." He'd meant to bring Margaret up when he and Mikey could comfortably discuss her sister, but that time had passed.

Her eyes widened. "You're damn right I did. It was important."

Recalling Margaret's phone call, Rem gripped the armrest. "And what exactly did she tell you, and what did you have to tell her to get it?"

Mikey hesitated. "I got the information I needed from her."

"Did you? Did she give you Monk's name?"

Mikey crossed her arms, but didn't answer.

"Did she give you anything other than riddles?" he asked, his voice rising.

Mikey spoke with a clip. "She told me what I needed to know."

"At what cost?" Rem waited to see if she'd tell him the truth.

She looked away. "I did what I had to do."

Rem's frustration bloomed. "You told her about me and Cain." He saw her stiffen. "You told her how I watched Cain die in my arms, and she reveled in it, didn't she?"

For a moment, her posture softened. "I answered her questions."

"You gave her exactly what I told you she'd want. A way to manipulate me."

Mikey shifted to face him. "She's in a hospital, Rem—"

"She called me," he yelled. Holding his side, he cursed himself and lowered his voice. "And told me all about your visit, and what you'd told her about me. She loved every sick thrill of it, especially the part about Cain."

Mikey's eyes rounded. "What? She called you? How?"

Rem couldn't help himself and jabbed out his hand. "Because she's Margaret, that's how." He grunted when another lance of pain shot through him. "That's why I didn't want you to see her. Because she would use you to get to me. I bet she filled your head with all sorts of lies about the two of us, didn't she? About how I couldn't possibly love you the way I loved Jennie?"

Mikey froze, and her cheeks colored. "I know how she is. I'm not stupid."

"I didn't say you were, but she still gets in your head."

"So you're telling me I was wrong to see her?"

"I didn't want you anywhere near her. But no matter what anyone says, when it comes to your sister and your damned stubbornness, sometimes you make rash decisions."

"Says the man who took a strange pill at a madman's birthday party."

Sighing, he couldn't argue with that. "Point taken."

Mikey dropped her head, and they had a moment of quiet.

Rem watched her and wished he could find the words to make her feel better, but there were none. "So here we are. I got angry and said horrible things to you, and you betrayed me to Margaret."

Her head shot up. "I didn't betray you."

"What would you call it?"

Her eyes watered. "I did what I thought was best. I didn't mean to hurt you."

"And I didn't mean to hurt you, either." He carefully sat back with a wince. "So, where does that leave us?"

She dabbed at her eye with a finger. "I don't know."

He asked the question he dreaded. "Do you want to move back in?"

Her red cheeks turned redder, and she shook her head. "I think it's better if we take some time."

Her answer hurt Rem worse than his ribs, but he didn't argue.

"I know you're injured, though. I can stay upstairs and help you out until you get back on your feet."

Rem's heart fell when the reason for the chair became obvious. It wasn't a peace offering. It was a way to appease him. He tried to keep the emotion out of his voice. "No. You go." He paused. "I don't want a nurse. I want my girlfriend."

Her tears glistened and spilled over her lashes. "I put my key on the table." Her breath caught, but she pushed through it. "I stocked your fridge, too."

Seeing her cry, Rem fought back his own tears. "Thanks. You didn't have to do that."

"I'll call and check in on you." She sniffed, went to the sofa, and grabbed her purse. "You want anything before I go?"

Somber, he shook his head. "I'll manage."

"You sure?"

"This ain't my first rodeo. I'll be okay." He wished he could get up, walk her to the door, and give her a kiss, but it hurt too much, physically and emotionally.

She hesitated. After a pause, she slid her purse strap over her shoulder. "You can call if you need something."

"Same to you. If you want to talk, or anything."

"Yeah...ok." She wiped a tear from her cheek and swallowed. After a pause, she turned and headed toward the door. She stopped and looked back. "I'm sorry, Rem."

Rem held it together. "Me too."

More tears surfaced, and she opened the door and left.

Rem sat in his chair for several minutes, just staring at the door, hoping she might walk back through it, but she didn't. Finally, the quiet of the house unnerved him. He hit the lever to raise himself high enough where he could stand with less pain. Emotionally spent, he wanted to cry to relieve the pressure in his chest, but the tears wouldn't come. Trying not to think about what had just occurred, he opened the fridge, wanting a beer, but because of the pain meds he was on, he couldn't have any. He grabbed a soda instead, closed the fridge, and popped open the can.

Desperate for a shower and moving on autopilot, he grabbed his bag of belongings and headed into his bedroom, trying not to think about how empty the house felt. He slowly pulled off his jacket when his phone rang. Being protective of his bandaged hand, he took his cell from his pocket and saw it was Daniels.

Carefully tossing his jacket onto the bed, he answered. "Hey."

"Hey," said Daniels. "How's it going?"

"I've been better."

"Ribs hurt?"

"Like hell. How's your head?"

"Still attached, but the headache's bearable. I figure after another pill tonight and a good night's sleep, I'll knock it out."

"I wish my ribs would heal that fast."

"Sorry about that, but maybe some pizza will help."

Rem entered the bathroom and studied his bruised face in the mirror. "Pizza?" His long hair needed to be brushed, and he ran his fingers through it.

"Erin called and offered to bring us all pizza for dinner. I know you and Mikey haven't been home long, but if you're up for it, you can join us. Erin's bringing your favorite. Pepperoni and sausage."

A shorter piece of hair stuck out, and Rem pulled on it. "Sounds great, but I think I'll pass." A memory of the Raven squatting next to Daniels and cutting a snippet of his hair surfaced.

"Hurts too much?"

"No." Rem hated saying the words. "Mikey and I just broke up." Pulling on his shorter tendril, Rem realized the Raven had cut his hair as well.

There was a pause. "Excuse me? You what?"

Rem lowered his arm, wondering why the Raven had wanted their hair. He thought about what else she might have taken. "Mikey just left. She's not coming back." He took a second. "Says we need time."

Daniels took a second. "She just left?"

"Yeah. She gave me a recliner, though. That was nice." It hit him that he and Daniels had both been bleeding, so the Raven could have taken their blood too. He shivered at the thought.

"A recliner?"

"For my ribs. I guess I can sleep on that tonight. Getting into bed might kill me right now. I can flip on the TV and pretend I'm in Bolivia, which is sounding really nice right now."

"Rem, I'm sorry. I thought after you talked..."

"Me too." Rem let out a strained breath and steadied himself. Between Mikey and memories of the Raven, he wasn't feeling too great. "Guess I'm not as alluring as I thought."

"Mikey will figure it out. She'll remember how alluring you are. She's just dealing with a lot."

"The Manetti situation is definitely messing with her, plus what I said to her, and what happened with Margaret. I guess I can't blame her."

"Be patient. She'll work through it and come to her senses."

He pictured Mikey's tear-stained face in his mind. "I'm not too sure about that."

"You okay?"

"I'm moving one step at a time." Rem reached to turn on the shower and gasped when he moved too fast.

"What's wrong?"

He cursed. "It's my damn ribs."

"You shouldn't be alone right now. I'm calling Erin and telling her to stop by your place after she picks up the pizza. Pack a bag for a couple of nights. You'll stay here, and we'll keep an eye on you."

Rem clutched his side. "It's okay. I'll manage. I've dealt with injuries on my own before."

"Not three broken ribs. You keep moving around, you'll be crying instead of sleeping in your recliner tonight."

Rem rested his hand on the bathroom counter. "I'm close to that right now." He thought again of Mikey leaving, and a swell of emotion hit him. "And not just because of my ribs."

"I wish Mikey had stayed at least to help you."

"She offered. I declined." He heard Daniels inhale sharply. "How are you?"

Daniels cursed softly. "I'm trying to change my shirt, and my arm isn't making it easy."

"We're quite the pair."

"Tell me about it. You sure you don't want to come over? I know Mikey's dealing with a lot, but so are you."

Rem debated and almost said yes. "Nah. You have dinner with your family. Call me tomorrow."

"They're your family too."

A lump formed in his throat. "I know. I just feel like all the strength's run out of me. I'm going to take a shower and eat something. Then take another pain pill and crash."

"You can do that here. We can set you up in the guest bedroom. We'll pile up the pillows and make you comfortable. We'll tell J.P. that the claw is on injured reserve."

Rem half-smiled.

"Rem, really. I think you should—"

Daniels went quiet, and Rem waited to hear what Daniels thought he should do. "You there?"

Daniels whispered. "Oh my God."

Hearing Daniels' tone, Rem furrowed his brow. "What's wrong?"

"Where are you? In your bathroom?"

Rem questioned whether Daniels' doozy was returning. "Yes. Why?"

"Open the drawers."

"What are you talking about?"

"You have a drawer, don't you? By the sink? Open it."

Rem eyed his drawer, where he kept his toothpaste and floss, and other toiletries. He opened it. "Okay. Why—?" He froze in mid-sentence. A large black feather was lying next to his comb. His heart rate sped up, and with trembling fingers, he picked it up.

"Did you get a black feather?"

Rem gaped at it and thought of the Raven. "Yes."

"I got one too," said Daniels. "In my drawer, by the sink."

"How...?"

"I don't know."

The Raven's face with the translucent skin popped again into Rem's mind, and the thought of her being in his house made him want to race out of it. "What do you think it means?"

"Nothing good," said Daniels. "Maybe it's her way of saying she hasn't forgotten us."

Rem swallowed. "She took samples of our hair."

"She did?" asked Daniels, sounding alarmed. "All I can remember is her standing over that boiling pot."

Rem had another flashback. "She put our hair in that pot. And God knows what else." He recalled her pendant. "And she wore a black stone around her neck. Like Rook did. You think that meant something?"

"Probably, but don't ask me what."

Rem could still hear the Raven's chanting in his head. "We weren't in the guest house for our health. She wanted something from us."

"Yeah." Daniels went quiet, but Rem could hear him breathing. "Something tells me, Rem, that we haven't seen the last of her."

Rem closed his eyes, not wanting to think about that.

"You sure you still want to be alone tonight?"

Rem dropped the feather onto the bathroom counter and wiped his fingers on his shirt. Looking at it, his skin broke out in goosebumps. "You say Erin can pick me up?"

"I'll call her right now."

Wondering what had happened to them in that guest house, Rem looked back at his ashen face in the mirror. "I'll bring my pillow."

What Happens Next?

Daniels and Rem are taking a brief hiatus, but no worries. They will be back soon! Until then, enjoy the premiere of a new series by J.T. Bishop, featuring a spin-off character from Daniels and Remalla.

In *The Forgotten Night*, book one in Lexie Logan's investigative thriller series, a presumed whistleblower is murdered right before meeting with Lexie. When Lexie wakes up in a hospital after an assumed overdose with no memory of the meeting, she must dig deep to find out the truth behind the murder and a massive conspiracy. But uncovering dangerous secrets risks exposing her own, and the price may be too high to pay.

Enjoy an excerpt below.

Want more from J.T. Bishop?

Subscribe at jtbishopauthor.com to get the Daniels and Remalla prequel novellas, *The Girl and the Gunshot*, and *The Magic of Murder*, plus future books, for free, in addition to extra content.

Did you know there's a Daniels and Remalla Prequel Novel, and an Omnibus?

Discover *Murder Unveiled*, the prequel novel to *Haunted River*, book one in the series. A prominent art dealer is found murdered after the unveiling of a famous, but cursed, painting. When Daniels and Rem are assigned to investigate, they'll learn that a curse may prove more deadly than a killer, and they could be the next targets.

Or catch up on the series with *Shadows and Secrets*, the *Detectives Daniels and Remalla* omnibus, which includes the first three books in the series – *Haunted River*, *Of Breath and Blood,* and *Of Body and Bone.*

How did it all begin with Daniels and Remalla?

Check out the *Family or Foe* Saga, where the detectives first appear. This four-book series focuses on a murderer with a mysterious background and powerful abilities who's out for revenge against the family he believes wronged him. Can Daniels and Remalla stop him before he seeks his vengeance?

And did you know the Redstones have their own series?

Mason and Mikey Redstone, introduced in *Of Breath and Blood*, book two of *Detectives Daniels and Remalla*, were so engaging and fun to write, they got their own series.

Mason Redstone, a former Texas Ranger turned medium and paranormal investigator, along with his sister Mikey and partner Trick, take the cases others won't and risk their lives in the process. If you like a little more paranormal thrown into your mystery thrillers, then this series is for you. Plus, there's the added bonus of appearances by Daniels and Remalla.

Note: Because the Daniels and Remalla books and The Redstone Chronicles are a spinoff and crossover series, they share an overarching story, and the characters from each are mentioned or appear in all the books, so reading both is ideal. The books published alternate between the two series. A list of books in chronological order follows below.

Fan of Paranormal Romance, Urban Fantasy, and Light Sci-Fi?

Discover Bishop's first series, *The Red-Line Trilogy*. Yanked from her predictable world, Sarah Randolph learns she's the key to unlocking a secret that will ensure the existence of a hidden community. One man, assigned to protect her from a dangerous adversary, will risk everything to keep her alive, but when he falls for her, will their destiny be enough to save them both?

In *The Fletcher Family Saga*, the four-book sister series to *The Red-Line Trilogy*, a distant but deadly threat risks the lives of three unique siblings, but life can't stop because of who they are. They'll endure love, loss and a dangerous enemy determined to destroy them all.

Either series can be read first. Take your pick. Boxed sets are available too!

A Note From J.T.

Black Bird was a challenging book, but well worth it. After *Dominion, Illusions,* and *Vendetta*, I had a lot of threads to tie off. It was difficult to keep track of them all. When I started the book, I had an idea of where I wanted to go but wasn't entirely sure of how to get there.

Monk, Rhonda, Rook, and Croft all had to be dealt with, but how to stop all of them in a way that made sense wasn't clear. Plus, I'd already had the idea of the Raven in my mind, and I wanted to introduce her because, let's be honest, she's a powerful character. She's mystical, mysterious, and terrifying. Who is she, and what does she want? That remains to be seen, but she will return, and of course, wreak havoc on Daniels and Rem.

When it clicked that I could spread the wealth and have Rem confront Tex (AKA Croft), Daniels confront Rhonda, and Mikey, along with her brother, Mason, and Trick (who were fun to include, especially if you read *The Redstone Chronicles*) handle Monk, it all came together. I enjoyed bringing Lozano into the action too, since we typically only see him behind a desk. Sammy Caruso was the perfect person to take out Rook, and Delaina became the conduit for Rook's demise and ultimately Rem and Daniels' rescue when Caruso comes looking for them.

And I had plenty of side characters to remember. I killed off Jerry Lee while keeping him safe at the same time. Manetti was crucial because I needed him to suspect Monk, which ultimately led to Manetti's shooting and Monk and Rhonda's downfall. Mikey's role is also pivotal, especially as she deals with her guilt regarding Vera's death and determination to find Vera's killer, which leads to her confrontation with Margaret. That causes her disagreements with Rem, who's facing his own guilt and anger, which were only exacerbated by his actions while undercover. Mikey and Rem's conflicting views allowed me to examine their relationship in more detail, and I loved revealing their flaws.

Their breakup at the end was the next logical step between two headstrong characters who are both struggling with their inner demons. Will they get back together? We'll have to see, but you can be sure it won't be easy with those two.

And last but certainly not least, there's the enduring partnership between Rem and Daniels. I love to throw in a few tender moments between those two, which reveal the depth of their friendship. I wanted some action in this book, and enjoyed pitting them against their adversaries, and having them both face the Raven and Sammy Caruso together at the end. This time around, instead of one partner rescuing another, they both had to rescue each other.

But there's always more to come. With the secret society disbanded, you can be sure that it's not gone forever. As Lozano says at the end, Rem and Daniels have made new enemies. Who will return to cause problems? Not sure, but whoever it is, I can promise it's going to be entertaining.

But before we get there, I'm going to dive into a new series and focus on a character I've grown to love. I've been considering this for a while, but I've finally immersed myself in the world of Lexie Logan. As an investigative journalist, she provides all sorts of imaginative opportunities. I've already started book one, called *The Forgotten Night*, and I'm churning out the pages. She's got a lot of dramatic backstory, there will be a love interest, and of course, Daniels and Remalla will make an appearance (or two). She's a rich character who is full of complexity and the perfect choice to center a series on. I hope you end up loving her and her series as much as I do.

Black Bird was a thrill to write, and I'm so pleased to share it with you. I'd love to know what you, the reader, thought. Reviews are crucial to the success of a book, and I'm eager to hear your opinion of *Black Bird*. I welcome your comments too.

Now, on to the next book!

Books in Chronological Order

Although recommended but not required, in case you prefer to read in order...

Red-Line: Prelude to The Shift, a short story (subscribers only)

Red-Line: The Shift

Red-Line: Mirrors

Red-Line: Trust Destiny

Curse Breaker

High Child

Spark

Forged Lines

**

The Girl and the Gunshot, a novella (subscribers only)

A Hamburger Christmas, a novella

The Magic of Murder, a novella (subscribers only)

First Cut

Second Slice

Third Blow

Fourth Strike

Murder Unveiled

Haunted River

Of Breath and Blood

Lost Souls

Of Body and Bone

Acknowledgements

Another book is complete, and again, I have many to thank. This doesn't happen alone, and I am indebted to family and friends for their help, support and encouragement. It is truly appreciated.

I also want to thank my Beta and ARC teams. You guys keep me on my toes, ensure I write a great story, and help with early reviews. Thank you for being honest and offering your guidance.

I love writing about the bonds between loving family, deep friendships and the ties that hold them together. Plus, my fascination with the unknown thrown into the mix makes for a satisfying story and hopefully, adds a little more thrill for my readers.

I especially want to thank my fans. Hearing from you and knowing that you're enjoying my books makes all the hard work worthwhile. None of this would matter without your tremendous support. If I can help you escape from this crazy world for a short period each day, then I've done my job.

Here's to more stories, more fun, and more time for yourself. If you can have a little of that each day, you're on the right track.

About the Author

AWARD-WINNING AUTHOR, J.T. BISHOP, is a writer of mystery thrillers with a paranormal edge. Growing up, she read Stephen King, Mary Higgins Clark, and Dean Koontz, devoured every episode of the X-files and watched plenty of TV shows with great partnerships that leave you wanting more. She loves tangled relationships, unexpected twists and turns, heart-stopping love stories and the complications that come with all the above. Throw in a little supernatural fun and she's hooked. Her evil plan is to hook you, too.

She's the author of The Red-Line Trilogy and its sister series, The Fletcher Family Saga, which features touches of urban fantasy, light sci-fi, and paranormal romance. She's also happily writing mystery thrillers featuring two charismatic detectives who may occasionally encounter a supernatural villain or two, and a crossover series which follows the exploits of a gifted, but troubled, paranormal P.I. and his spunky sister.

All the above keeps her busy, but in her spare time, she loves good movies, tasty food, an unfortunate sugar addiction, and traveling.

Enjoy an excerpt from The Forgotten Night, Book One in the Lexie Logan Series

"WHAT DO YOU MEAN you can't tell me anything? That is absurd. What kind of hospital is this?"

Lexie registered the words but barely made sense of them.

"And what kind of doctor are you? Look at you. You can't be over forty."

Lexie's mind cleared enough to recognize her mother's voice.

"Mrs. Logan, I understand your concerns, but until she wakes up, I can't tell you much more."

Lexie heard the male voice but couldn't discern what he and her mother were talking about.

Her mother's voice returned. "But you've done all those tests."

"I've already told you, Mrs. Logan. The tests don't tell us everything. We need your daughter to tell us the rest."

Lexie clenched her eyes. Were her mother and the man talking about her? Where was she?

"Doctor McCabe." Her mother's voice took on the impatient tone Lexie recognized well. "Please don't take this the wrong way, but I think I'd like someone with more experience. I want another opinion."

Did her mother say doctor? Stirring, Lexie fought to get her brain to engage. She wanted to speak, but her mouth wouldn't comply.

The doctor's voice sounded equally impatient. "That is your right, Mrs. Logan, but another doctor will only tell you the same thing. Your daughter will come around. Just give her some time. Considering her state when she was brought in, she's lucky to even be alive."

Hearing that, Lexie fought harder. Becoming more aware, she could tell she was lying in bed. The soft sounds of beeping and the feel of the sheets under her fingers made her heart thump. Was she in a hospital? She tried to open her eyes.

"I'm aware of how lucky she is. The staff around here never cease to remind me."

"Your daughter needs time to regain consciousness. She had a substantial amount of alcohol and drugs in her system."

Lexie's mind couldn't keep up. Alcohol? Drugs?

Her mother paused. "I understand." Her impatient tone had softened.

Inside her head, Lexie struggled to respond. I'm awake. I'm right here. She heard soft footsteps and felt a presence near her. Someone touched her forehead.

"Just try to be patient, Mrs. Logan."

Her mother scoffed. "Patience is not my strong suit, Dr. McCabe."

Lexie felt warm breath on her cheek and her mother's whisper in her ear.

"You listen to me, Lexie Rose Logan. This is your mother speaking. You need to wake up. Right now. I've got an inane doctor telling me you need more time, and I'm missing my trip to the Appalachian Trail. Gary isn't thrilled, but he can wait. I told him how tough you are and that you will be up in no time. So don't make me a liar."

Lexie felt fingers stroke her cheek.

"So, if you can hear me, sweetheart, open your eyes. Right now."

Lexie tried.

Her mother sucked in some air. "Her eyelids fluttered."

The doctor spoke and sounded close. "Keep talking to her."

Her mother spoke louder. "Can you hear me, Lexie? Open your eyes."

Her mother took Lexie's hand, and Lexie gripped her fingers.

"She squeezed my hand," said her mother, clutching her fingers around Lexie's. "You can hear me, can't you, honey?"

Lexie tried again to open her eyes, but they felt cemented shut. A hand jostled her shoulder.

"C'mon, Lexie. You can do it." The hand jostled her some more. "Open your eyes."

"Mrs. Logan. Don't rush it. Give her time."

Her mother's voice turned harsh. "Don't tell me how to talk to my daughter. I'm the only one around here who seems interested in rousing her." Her voice relaxed. "Lexie, honey, open your eyes."

Lexie tried again. She felt like she was blinking, but her eyes didn't actually open.

Her mother's voice got louder in her ear. "Lexie Rose. Open your eyes, or I will contact your brother, sister and your father and tell them all that you're in the hospital, fighting for your life, from a drug overdose."

Lexie tightened her grip on her mother's fingers.

"Ouch," said her mother.

Lexie opened her eyes. The light blinded her, and she shut them again.

"I knew it." Her mother's tone turned impatient again. "See, doctor. I told you."

Lexie heard him sigh, and she opened her eyes again. Everything was blurry, and she blinked several times. She adjusted to the light, and her vision slowly cleared.

"Honey. Can you see me?"

Lexie's mother's face sharpened into focus, and Lexie tried to speak. "Mom?" it came out more as a croak.

Her mother reached for something, and Lexie saw a cup with a straw. "Here. Take a sip." She helped Lexie raise her head.

Lexie sucked on the straw. Blessedly cool water hit her tongue, and she swallowed.

The doctor leaned over the bed. "Take small sips."

Lexie swallowed some more and lay back. "That's better," she whispered. Her voice sounded stronger.

Her mother returned the cup to the table. "How do you feel?"

Lexie had no idea how to answer. "Where am I?" It seemed like the better response.

"You're in the hospital, dear." Her mother looked behind her. "This is Dr. McCabe. He's been supposedly treating you."

Lexie didn't miss the slight tightening of the doctor's shoulders before he slipped back into professional mode. "Hello, Miss Logan." He stepped closer and held up three fingers. "How many fingers am I holding up?"

Her mother grumbled. "You're kidding? That's what you want to ask her?"

"Three," said Lexie.

"Good." He eyed her mother. "If you don't mind, Mrs. Logan. I'd like to examine your daughter. Would you mind waiting outside?"

Her mother's mouth fell open. "I will not."

Her focus improving, Lexie could almost read the doctor's mind. His fuse was growing shorter by the second. It was a common trait among most who spent time with Leona Logan. "It's okay, Mom."

Her mother stared at her, and then at the doctor. "Fine." She straightened and smoothed her pink silk shirt. Even in a hospital, her mother still dressed to impress. "I'll be right outside."

"It won't take long." The doctor gestured toward the door.

Her mother scowled. "Nothing happens fast at this hospital. It's unbelievable the amount of time wasted around here. Someone should talk to your supervisor."

"I'd be happy to give you the hospital administrator's name." He stared without a hint of empathy.

Her mother huffed, found her purse, and walked out of the room.

Lexie blinked again and focused on the doctor. Her mother had been correct. Lexie put him at around forty. He had short brown manicured hair, a firm jaw and thick eyebrows. He wore glasses that emphasized his brown eyes and wore the typical long white doctor's coat with Dr. William McCabe embroidered on the pocket. He asked her several questions that she answered, studied the machines in her room, and made notes on a tablet he held in his hand.

While he focused on the tablet, Lexie, feeling more alert, raised the bed and sipped water from the cup he'd handed her.

He lowered the tablet. "Good news. I think you're going to make a full recovery." He slid the tablet into his pocket. "Any questions?"

Now that she'd had a few minutes to assimilate where she was and felt stronger, she had plenty. "What happened to me? Why am I here?"

He crossed his arms. "You were brought into the ER early yesterday morning unconscious. Your blood alcohol level was twice the legal limit, and your blood tox came back positive for cocaine and fentanyl. You're lucky someone found you when they did, or you wouldn't be here right now."

Lexie's head swam. She couldn't understand any of that. "There's got to be a mistake. I don't drink. And I don't do drugs." He studied her, and her cheeks reddened at his appraisal. "I'm telling you the truth."

"Miss Logan. What happened to you is not for me to judge, and it's none of my business who you associate with, but as your doctor, I would be remiss not to suggest addiction counseling." He glanced toward the door. "I'm sure your mother would agree."

Lexie felt her face burning. The slight headache that had been threatening bloomed. She wondered what her mother had told Dr. McCabe. She thought back to her last few days, but they were a blank.

"What do you remember?" he asked.

Lexie rubbed her forehead and closed her eyes. The last thing she recalled was sitting and eating dinner at her place. She opened her eyes. "Nothing about taking any drugs or drinking."

"That's not unusual for an overdose. Your memories will come back with time. I suggest lots of water and rest. Healthy food, and..." he eyed her solemnly, "no more substance abuse."

Lexie shook her head and regretted the action. Her head hurt, and she suddenly felt sick to her stomach. "Doctor. I don't know what happened. I haven't had a drink in years. I have no reason to do this."

He tipped his head at her. "Have you been stressed lately? Under a lot of pressure? What do you do for a living?"

"I'm an investigative journalist." She thought back on her previous few months. It had been a whirlwind of activity. After breaking the Damien Rook case and exposing his secret society and their multitude of crimes, she'd been on a nonstop press junket. Her reporting had gone national, and she'd been in demand with several news organizations. She'd even started her own podcast to expose all she knew about Rook and his members' extensive and nefarious activities. Her mother, who worried about her attracting the wrong attention from those who'd been exposed, had warned against it, but to Lexie, it seemed like the next logical step in her career.

"Your mother implied you'd been under considerable strain recently."

Lexie rolled her eyes. "She worries too much."

McCabe slid his hands into the pockets of his coat. "She does have her opinions."

"She's a former advice columnist. It comes with the territory."

He paused and knitted his brow. "She's not Leona Logan, is she? From *Ask Leona?*"

"The one and the same."

"Now I understand the alcohol and drugs."

Lexie frowned at him.

"Sorry. That was unprofessional."

"Doctor, I didn't take drugs or drink."

"Your toxicology report says otherwise."

Hating that he didn't believe her and knowing his reaction would be exactly what she could expect from everyone else, Lexie's emotions stirred. "I'm telling the truth."

"If that's true, then how did this happen? Were you forced to do this? And how so? Do you have any recollection of an assault? Or do you know someone who would want to hurt you?"

A tear threatened to spill over her lashes, and Lexie wiped it away. Her mother's warnings echoed in her mind. Had someone from Rook's society decided to pay her back for revealing their crimes? She had to consider it. "Maybe. I've made some enemies."

"Then I suggest you talk to the police. If something happened to you, they would need to take it from here." He stepped away from the bed. "I'd like to keep you another night for observation. Assuming there are no complications, I'll approve your discharge tomorrow."

She toyed with the edge of the sheet, still trying to recall what had happened to her. "Thanks, doctor."

"You're welcome." He reached for the door handle. "And my advice? Reduce your stress and keep a reasonable distance from your mother."

"Easier said than done."

"I'll be back tomorrow. Get some rest." He pulled the door open just as her mother pushed it from the other side.

Lexie moaned but tensed when she saw two people walk in behind her mother.

"Are you done?" asked Leona with a withering stare at Dr. McCabe.

"We are. She's all yours, but don't overdo it." The doctor walked around her and left the room.

Leona walked past him with a glare, and the two people, one a younger woman around Lexie's age and an older man who looked to be in his sixties, entered the room. They wore slacks, collared shirts, and jackets, and looked serious.

"Lexie," said her mother. "These two are detectives from the SDPD. They want to talk to you."

The man and the woman flashed their badges. The woman spoke first. "I'm Detective Samantha Carlson, and this is my partner, Detective Phil Justini. You're Lexie Logan?" Carlson was an attractive woman with dark brown shoulder-length hair and a slim but sturdy physique.

"Yes." Lexie wondered what was happening now. Was she in trouble? Were they going to arrest her?

Justini stepped closer. He had salt and pepper hair and a mustache, and the intense gaze of a man who'd seen a lot of awful things and wished he could forget them. "We'd like to ask you about two nights ago."

Her mother walked up to the side of the bed. "You don't have to say a word, Lex." She pulled out her cell. "I'm calling Gary."

"Appalachian guy?" asked Lexie.

"Yes." She held the phone to her ear. "He's an attorney, and a prominent one." She shot laser beams with her eyes at Carlson and Justini.

"That's your right, ma'am," said Carlson. "But we just have a few questions for your daughter."

"Questions now. An arrest later." She cursed at the phone. "Damn it, Gary. Pick up."

"It's okay, Mom. I'll talk to them. Just give us a second."

Her mother scowled. "I am not going anywhere."

Lexie rubbed her forehead again. Her headache was growing by the second. "What are your questions?"

"We understand you were brought in early yesterday after an overdose," Justini tucked his badge into his jacket pocket. "Is that correct?"

Lexie debated how to answer. "I suppose that's the way it looks."

Carlson frowned. "What does that mean?"

"It means I almost died from too much alcohol and drugs, but I didn't take them." Lexie anticipated their response and wasn't disappointed.

Justini half smiled. "So who did? Your alter ego?" He paused. "You have a mental disorder?"

"Certainly not," added Leona. "Don't be vulgar, Detective."

Justini shrugged. "I call them as I see them."

Lexie wanted to cry, but she forced back her tears. "I have no memory of what happened to me. The last thing I recall was eating dinner at home. After that...it's a blank."

Justini's smile grew. "It must have been one hell of a party."

Lexie clenched her jaw. She knew how it sounded.

Detective Carlson stepped closer. "Do you have any knowledge of how you ended up in an alley outside an abandoned warehouse?"

Lexie stiffened. "Alley? What alley? I assumed I was found at my apartment." She looked at her mother.

Her mother lowered her phone. "No dear. Someone found you and called an ambulance. You should stop talking now." Leona put the phone back to her ear. "I'm trying Gary again."

Lexie spoke to the detectives. "Who found me?"

"We don't know." Carlson pulled a notebook from her pocket. "Does the name Dr. Mira Patel ring a bell?"

Lexie opened her mouth to say "no" when an image flashed in her brain. She'd been eating dinner. Her phone had rung, and she'd answered.

"Miss Logan?" asked Carlson.

Lexie held her stomach, which was churning. "She called me."

Leona lowered her phone again.

"Dr. Patel called you?" asked Justini. "When?"

Lexie clenched her eyes shut as the images flashed again. "She did. She asked if I was Lexie Logan, the journalist. I said yes. She said she wanted to meet but wouldn't say why. Only that it was important and it had to be right then. She gave me an address."

"You typically meet with strangers in alleys at night?" asked Justini, looking dubious.

Lexie fought to recall everything Dr. Patel had told her. "I think she said she had information about her employer."

Carlson found a pencil and scribbled in her notepad. "Did she give any details?"

Lexie shook her head. "No."

"How'd you get there?" asked Justini. "We didn't find your car."

Lexie thought back. After talking to Patel, she'd hung up, grabbed her purse, and headed out the door. "I took a rideshare. My neighbor, Lynn, borrowed my car to go on a date. Her car's in the shop."

Carlson took more notes.

Lexie sat up. "This must have something to do with what happened to me. Have you talked to Dr. Patel?" Lexie had to wonder if Mira Patel had some connection to Rook's fallen black bird society. "I'm a journalist. I broke a big story recently that exposed a lot of people and their crimes. This must be some sort of payback." Feeling like some pieces were falling into place, she hoped the detectives would have more reason to believe her. "She must have lured me out to give someone access to me."

Carlson and Justini glanced at each other.

"My daughter wouldn't lie." Leona faced the detectives like she was their superior. "This Dr. Patel must know what happened. My daughter's reporting took down powerful people. Someone tried to kill her. I demand that you figure out who. This doctor needs to be questioned immediately."

Carlson didn't act the least bit fazed by Leona. She eyed Lexie. "Miss Logan, Dr. Patel was murdered two nights ago. Her body was found in the warehouse next to the alley where you were located." She paused. "And we'd like to know why."

Justini crossed his arms. "Care to explain, Miss Logan?"

Leona's composure slipped. "Don't say one word, Lexie."

Suddenly terrified, Lexie felt the blood drain from her face.

www.ingramcontent.com/pod-product-compliance
Lightning Source LLC
Chambersburg PA
CBHW070834260626
47170CB00007B/2373